PENGUIN BOOKS

THURSDAY AFTERNOONS

Monica Dickens, great-granddaughter of Charles Dickens, has written over thirty novels, autobiographical books and children's books, and her works are beginning to be adapted for television and film. Her first book, *One Pair of Hands,* which arose out of her experiences as a cook-general – the only work for which her upper-class education had fitted her – made her a best seller at twenty-two, and is still in great demand.

Although her books arise out of the varied experiences of her life, she has not taken jobs in order to write about them: working in an aircraft factory and a hospital was her war work, not research. When she joined the Samaritans, it was the work of befriending distressed fellow human beings which she found compelling, although her novel *The Listeners* came from that experience.

She set up the first American branch of the Samaritans in Boston, Massachusetts, and lives nearby on Cape Cod with her husband Commander Roy Stratton, who has retired from the U.S. Navy, and her horses, cats and dogs. She has two daughters.

D1513188

MONICA DICKENS

Thursday Afternoons

PENGUIN BOOKS
IN ASSOCIATION WITH MICHAEL JOSEPH

Penguin Books Ltd, Harmondsworth, Middlesex, England
Penguin Books, 625 Madison Avenue, New York, New York 10022, U.S.A.
Penguin Books Australia Ltd, Ringwood, Victoria, Australia
Penguin Books Canada Ltd, 2801 John Street, Markham, Ontario, Canada L3R 1B4
Penguin Books (N.Z.) Ltd, 182–190 Wairau Road, Auckland 10, New Zealand

—

First published by Michael Joseph 1945
Published in Penguin Books 1949
Reprinted 1951, 1953, 1954, 1956, 1958, 1960, 1962, 1965, 1967, 1969, 1972, 1977

—

Made and printed in Great Britain
by Hazell Watson & Viney Ltd,
Aylesbury, Bucks
Set in Monotype Baskerville

To
NICKY

'PLEASE HAND THE DOCTOR YOUR CASE BOOK ONLY, NOT YOUR OUTPATIENT REGISTRATION CARD.'

The notice on the clinic door was very large and plain, and hung directly opposite the benches on which the patients sat. Perhaps it was because they had to wait so long with nothing to look at but the green door with its dusty fanlight, and the 'Next, please!' appearances of the nurse, long-skirted and stiff-waisted, like a figure in a weather house, that the very familiarity of the notice had made it meaningless. For patient after patient, perching on the chair at the right of the doctor's big desk and handing over the green case history folder, unfailingly laid the registration card on top of it.

Steven Sheppard wondered if this would ever cease to annoy him. Sometimes he handed back the card and said patiently: 'I don't want this.' Sometimes he said: 'You'd better hang on to this; you can't get in next time without it.' Sometimes he passed it over without a word, or left it lying on the desk, where it distracted his eye during the consultation, until he gave it back with the medicine card which the patient took to the dispensary. Sometimes he ignored it, and it fell to the floor when he opened the folder, and the nurse would have to come round the desk and pick it up. If she was busy at the sink, or in one of the examination rooms, the patient might go off without it, and she would have to chase after him down the Outpatients' hall, holding her cap on with one hand.

It did not matter which of these things happened; the card

5

still appeared faithfully at the next visit. If not actually on the desk, it was held like a talisman in the hand, or popped in and out of a vast handbag, or even offered hopefully in reply to some stumping question such as: 'When did you last see the dentist?'

The nurse wished the patients would not be so dense about their cards, whose only function was to get them past Miss Meiklejohn, in the registration office. The nurse's mission on Thursday afternoons was to save Dr Sheppard as much trouble as possible. To this end, she opened doors, handed towels and rubber gloves, addressed envelopes and, while he was writing, stood over him with blotting paper poised to pounce on ink already dry. There was not much to do in a medical clinic. No dressings or fomentations, or anæsthetics, as in the surgical and orthopædic clinics and in Dentals. In between ushering the finished cases out at one door and the next ones in at another, the nurses usually subsided against the wall behind the doctor and watched the clock for teatime.

But Dr Sheppard's nurse, whose name was Audrey Lake, always found plenty to do to keep herself in evidence. She would hover at his elbow with the alert expression of a conscientious crowd actor, her hand ready to dart forward and anticipate the form he wanted from the paper rack. Sometimes he would fool her deliberately by saying to the patient: 'I wonder if we ought to get that leg X-rayed again,' and when she triumphantly placed the green paper before him with all the details filled in and needing only his signature, he would say: 'No, Nurse. Massage form, please.'

It was convenient to be handed things like ear mops and kidney dishes without having to snap your fingers, as you did to get some of the nurses out of their coma, but she was always handing him things he did not need. He had only to mention a throat to become aware, out of the corner of his eye, of a spatula mutely waiting, and the merest hint of noises in the head was enough to call forth auriscopes and speculæ and angle forceps. If he deliberated for a moment

6

over the medicine card, Nurse Lake would weigh in with the date. During a long interrogation, when even her ingenuity could find nothing to do for him, she would stand with her listening expression until she felt she had been out of the picture long enough, when she would take a turn or two to the sink and back.

Once he had looked round crossly and said: 'Nurse, I wish you'd get a pair of shoes that don't squeak.' She had stopped dead in her tracks, staring at him like a wounded animal, and for the rest of the clinic had moved about on elaborate tiptoe. All her off-duty that evening had been spent vainly rubbing liquid paraffin into the seam between the soles and uppers. The next day she had bought a bottle of black shoe dye and converted quite a new pair of brown Oxfords into uniform shoes, which meant that she only had brogues or an over-run pair of court shoes to wear with her coat and skirt.

He had said the same thing once to the nurse who had taken his clinic when Nurse Lake was on holiday. She had replied pertly: 'I will if you'll give me the money to buy them, sir,' and laughed with him, and gone on cheerfully squeaking about the clinic.

On the days when Steven Sheppard woke with a clear head and a lurking suspicion of great and lasting happiness almost within reach; when he was convinced of the essential lovableness of humanity, the importance of his work and the humour of almost any situation; when he went out of his way to make little chatty contacts – with the girl in the tobacconist's, with waiters and with complete strangers in Regent's Park; when he always took his dog out before breakfast; when he could take throat swabs from spoiled children without a murmur, and persuade obstinate men with duodenal ulcers to forswear tobacco for ever – if such a day were a Thursday, Nurse Lake's neck would be consistently flushed with gratification, from the moment when he breezed in with an: 'Afternoon, Nurse! How's Nurse?' to the moment when he chucked his white coat at her with a: 'Well, we got

7

through that lot pretty quick, didn't we?' and went whistling up to the wards, leaving her dreamy-eyed, clutching the
coat amid the litter of towels and folders and screwed up
bits of paper.

On the Thursdays when he was tired and had to be particularly polite to his patients in order not to snap at them;
when he did not care if the whole country died of smallpox
if only he could chuck up medicine and have some time to
himself; when the back view of Nurse Lake was as maddening as her front view, and her very presence in the room
made him want to loosen his collar, he sometimes seriously
considered asking the Outpatients' Sister to give him another
nurse. But he hardly liked to, as he had already complained
in the past about not having the same nurse in his clinic
each week, and Sister Lillie had snorted and given him
Nurse Lake.

Sister Lillie was short and square and possessive, with inadequate legs and tiny feet in buckled shoes. She wore her
cap very high on the top of her head, and seemed to have
come to some arrangement with the laundry to put more
starch in her aprons than in anyone else's. She behaved as if,
instead of the department being run for their benefit, the
doctors and patients were there on sufferance. The nurses
under her were 'My nurses', and could do no wrong. She
fought the Matron for extra off-duty for them, and bought
buns for their tea, although, once they had done their three
months and left the department, she would scarcely say
'Good morning' to them on the stairs. She liked to plant herself in the middle of a surgical clinic as if she were on a revolving stand, directing the traffic of patients scuttling in
and out of examination rooms and nurses slapping on fomentations and winding Elastoplast round varicose veins, and
glaring at the surgeon if he dirtied too many towels. A com-
bination of catarrh and disapproval, both chronic, had earned
her the nickname of 'Snorting Lil'. She had been on Outpatients for ten years, and nobody minded her. Long ago,
when she was a ward sister, she had married a pernicious

8

anæmia, nursed him fiercely until he died, and then come back to work at the hospital. She lived with her mother-in-law in half a house on the outskirts of Dynsford, from which she cycled to the hospital every morning, with a great display of directoire knickers.

As well as, or perhaps because of, being the only married sister at St. Margaret's, Snorting Lil was the only one who seemed impervious to Dr Sheppard. He had a way of speaking almost without moving his lips, slow, low, which made him impossible to hear through a mask in theatre, but which moved gauleiters like Sister Grainger of the women's medical ward to give him tea in her sitting-room when he had done his round. He didn't want her tea; he didn't want anything usually, after his Thursday clinic, but to get into his car and get his private visits done and get home. Tea was all right, but he would rather stop somewhere for it on the way back to London and have it as he liked, with a lot of water and very little milk, and Gentleman's Relish on hot buttered toast, and the evening paper, instead of strong and milky at a rocky bamboo table, with horrid little cinnamon cakes shaped like shells, and an instalment of the unending serial of Sister Grainger's experiences at the St. Birgit Hospital, Stockholm, a Utopian establishment, apparently, differing in every detail from St. Margaret's, and staffed by doctors whose technique was years in advance of the English. 'That *was* nursing, sir. That *was* medicine.'

Steven thought that one day he would say: 'If it was so bloody marvellous, why the hell don't you go back there?' kick over the bamboo table and go. He had almost said it once, one day when he had suddenly seen himself objectively in that stuffy room in which only women belonged yet which was so unfeminine, sitting there in expensive pinstripe trousers, spoiling his appetite for dinner with cakes that clung round his teeth and being charming. He had stood up on an impulse and actually begun: 'I honestly wonder, Sister –' when luckily a probationer had looked round the door to ask if she might go off duty, and been blasted out of the room to fold the laundry before she even thought of such a thing. So Dr Sheppard, his impulse evaporated, had escaped in her back draught, still being charming.

Being charming. Being diplomatic. Being polite. Being interested in people who would not lift a finger for you if you were dying, but who thought that you had done five years in medical school and two as a resident for the sole purpose of curing palpitations caused by overeating. Rubbing your hands and Well-welling at hot-house bedsides. Having a duty to people for whom you cared nothing, because you had the knowledge they lacked.

To be a doctor had seemed such a simple, obvious thing. To Steven it had come like a call; unmistakable, clear, it had cut across his muddled speculations about the future, and shown him what he was going to do. He had been in his last term at school. In the autumn he would be going to Cambridge to study Law, as his father had done. This had been an accepted thing ever since he could remember, and he had never been able to think of a convincing argument against it. Other vague alternatives had captured his brain from time to time : to be a miner and fight for the oppressed, to go into the Foreign Office, to work his passage round the world in a cargo boat, to be a priest, a schoolmaster – but after the first enthusiasm, these had not seemed quite right either. He could never see his future going ahead in a bee-line towards something he wanted more than anything else to do.

Until that hot Saturday afternoon, when the heap of cut grass behind the bowling screen smelt of summer picnics, when the players waiting to go in had shimmered in the haze before the pavilion, and a lark had transfixed itself miles up, bursting its heart with joy at the blueness of the sky.

He had been umpiring a lower form match. He could see that spidery small boy now – Cartwright Minor his name was, James Cartwright – taking his long, earnest strides back to measure the length of his run. Steven, at the wicket, with a piece of grass in his mouth, had watched him indolently from under the peak of his cap, which had Cartwright Minor's perched on top of it. It was too hot even to be bored by this kid's game, too hot to do more than just control the thing in a fatherly way, and be thankful you were umpiring instead of playing. With every one of the bowler's strides, each spindly leg teetered as it took his slight body weight. He was like a toy made out of pipe cleaners, wambling, un-co-ordinated. He reached the end of his run, manfully dug in a heel, spun round as if he were going to fall down and launched himself back at the wicket in a bodiless whirl of arms and legs.

He bowled a wide. That was not unusual. What was unusual was that delivery of the ball had landed him in a sitting position halfway down the pitch, screaming like a trapped rabbit. Steven pushed through the swarm of small boys which had collected round young Cartwright like flies round a sore, even before he could get there. He thought at first Cartwright had broken his right shoulder. The whole thing sloped away from his neck at the most uncanny angle, and his skinny arm, in its manly, rolled-up sleeve, hung right forward from a knob below his collar bone which stuck through his shirt. It was the sight of this knob that made young Cartwright stop screaming for just long enough to be sick.

Steven suddenly knelt down, took the boy's elbow in one hand and his forearm in the other and pushed it up and across. He didn't know why he did it, but it seemed the natural movement once he had got hold of the arm. There was a slight jar and Cartwright Minor was the right shape again. He was sick once more before Steven led him off the field, cuffing at the excited fry who piped and I sayed and Gollyed round his legs.

It was after this that Steven knew he was going to be a doctor. That moment when the arm which had felt so wrong clicked back and felt so right had given him the deepest satis-faction he had ever known. A tenderness, comparable only to mother-love, flowed from him out to the figure trotting at his side. He loved Cartwright very dearly for being cured. Fascinated, he dogged him until the end of term, constantly asking how he was, warm with pride when he saw the boy bowling wides again, feeling the arm after a game and moving it in its socket, so that Cartwright Minor, whose father had warned him in a bluff, embarrassed way about these things, avoided Steven as much as possible. He did not understand what his father meant, but this looked like it, whatever it was.

It had seemed so simple, then, that he was going to be a doctor. His father, to whom the Law had never been more than a moderately lucrative way of being your own master, had raised no more than routine objections, which Steven had been able to refute with all the ease of a clear intention. The examinations had not been simple, but the fact that you had to work like a black for six years and had to pass even if you lost touch with the rest of the world for ever, that was plain enough, and turned out to be possible. And then you were going to be a doctor and run your own life and thrive on the exquisite satisfaction of people getting well because you willed it.

But then, even with his first House Physician's appointment, the being charming began. The listening, the dissembling, the persuading, the being at people's beck and call, when really, since you were obliging them, they should be at yours.

Steven was attractive. He had dark, thoughtful eyes, in which people read things that were not there at all. His black hair, which even as a small boy had never shot straight forward from a point in the middle of his head, grew now in a widow's peak, sloping right back to the corners of his broad forehead. His movements were supple and graceful, and clothes hung as naturally on him as if Adam had been created in a jacket and trousers, and there was that wide, amused upper lip, scarcely moving with the low, blurred, friendly voice. People were drawn to him, people whom he did not want. They told him things he didn't want to know.

They battened on his charm, sunning themselves in the chemical whatever it was which radiated from him. They forced him into the limelight, expecting too much of him, settling on him the obligation to which the attractive person is doomed.

It was not his skill and keenness alone which had made such a success of the practice he bought in Dynsford. He was 'ever so kind', 'a damn sensible chap', 'so understanding, my dear, and so *interested*' according to the type of patient. Delicate ladies said he was *sympathique*. He had plenty of friends – more than he had time for – and the ones he liked best were the independent people, who never seemed to have any time either. The ones he did not like particularly, although they seemed to have become his friends, never could stay away from the charm he could not help. When he was driven to discourage them, they either did not notice or were delighted to forbear with him, and to excuse rudeness or sarcasm by telling him they knew how tired he must be.

People were always trying to get him mixed up in their lives by offering him confidences he did not invite. They would ask his advice and, if he did not dodge quickly enough, throw their troubles magnanimously on to his shoulders, where they fell none the less heavily for the small amount of interest he took in them.

Someone was always wanting something of you; that was what it came to. That was what being a doctor meant. And as you got older and more successful, and your practice expanded and your experience piled up inside you like a bank balance on which anyone could draw, the smaller grew your chances of escape.

Steven was thinking this as he drove through the outskirts of Dynsford on the last Thursday in May. He often thought like this when he had been with someone like George Marshall, with whom he had lunched today. The lunch had been late, because Steven had had an extra big clinic at his London hospital, the East Central, and it had ended early because he had to get down to his Dynsford clinic, and be back in town in time to finish his private visits. He had gone off without his coffee, leaving George to settle with himself the interesting problem of whether to have a large port or a small one.

George never seemed to have a more urgent reason for going back to his office in the afternoon than to be in time for his cup of tea and the shortbread biscuits which he had sent down from Edinburgh every week. George was the same age as Steven, and made as much money – more, when South African mines did the things they should. George had a flat in Chelsea, to which he could always return early enough to give cocktail parties, and a house in Berkshire, in which he could spend as many week-ends as he wanted. He could play in golf matches and watch cricket. He could get to the theatre on time, which was fortunate, because he was not the right shape to squeeze past people's knees. George could always keep appointments. He just had to know ahead, that was all, so that he could write it down in his book, or on the shagreen-bound pad on his desk.

Steven had a pad on his desk, too, and it was an expensive-looking one, with a supple morocco back, because patients liked you to have these things when you were in Wimpole Street. It had a fresh page for every day, and every page was always filled, but never with items like 'Sandown 3 o'clock', or 'Gents and Players. Lunch Wilf'. Sometimes it had 'Cocktails, Mr and Mrs Collyer', or 'Sherry, Sir H. H. Claridges', slipped in hopefully at the bottom by Miss Minden, who wore a white overall, and, since she had seen the Dr Kildare films, white stockings and canvas shoes.

But if Steven ever got to 'Cocktails, Mr and Mrs Collyer', or 'Sherry, Sir H. H. Claridges', it was not until the air was hazed to the ceiling with standing swirls of smoke, and the host and hostess were beginning to wonder about their dinner engagement, and there was nothing left of the decorative trays of snacks but an expanse of smeared white napkin scattered with a few sandwiches curling up to show how the anchovy paste was already forming a crust. To-day, at lunch, George had said: 'Why don't you and Ruth come down to "Four Winds" this week-end? Annette and Stewart are coming, and we've got people coming over on Saturday for tennis. Marion'll probably nip down for the day. She doesn't like leaving the kid for too long.'

'I'd love that. I haven't played tennis for weeks. I can't promise yet, though. I'll have to see what turns up.'

'What turns up!' George leaned back in his chair and laughed at him. 'Honestly, Stevie, to hear you talk, anyone would think you were a struggling young man who'd just put up his brass plate in a semi-detached house in Kidderminster instead of a disgustingly successful West End consultant with old ladies trampling each other to death on your doorstep.'

Steven laughed. 'Why Kidderminster?'

'Well – any of those places where no one ever makes any money. Let's get hold of that chap with the Stilton. Come down with me to-morrow afternoon and you won't have to drive yourself. Waiter!' George's large, innocent face took on the anxious expression which it always wore until food was safely ordered. He slewed round in his chair.

'Can't possibly,' said Steven to the back of George's head, which ran into his collar in a bulge instead of a nape. 'I've got a million things on to-morrow – and Saturday morning.'

'And celery,' said George to the waiter. He turned round and breathed out. 'Put 'em off then, for once. What's the good of getting where you have if you never get any time to yourself? You want to make yourself a bit scarcer. You've no idea how it raises your value. I tell you what, you know. Probably, if you went and hid somewhere, you wouldn't have to do any work at all. People would simply pay for the privilege of speaking to Minnie on the telephone and being told they couldn't see you.'

'Well, I might get down on Saturday afternoon,' said Steven. 'I'll let you know. I daresay Ruth could come, in any case. I don't believe she's doing anything.'

George was scooping out Stilton with the little silver

spade. He didn't say anything. People never seemed to want Steven's wife without Steven. They did not really want her with him either, only she was like a saucer that went with the cup; you couldn't have one without the other, because she never seemed to have any arrangements of her own.

When Steven got up to go, George had started off again about Dynsford. 'Why you want to keep on with that unsophisticated hospital on top of all your London work, beats me. Traipsing down there every week to see a few degenerating colonels' wives and varicosed panel patients, when you can make people pay three guineas for the privilege of saying "Ah" to you in London.'

This was one of George's favourite remarks, so familiar that Steven had long ago ceased to laugh at it, or to bother to explain why he still kept his dozen beds and his Thursday afternoon clinic at St Margaret's Hospital.

Dynsford had been his first really good practice. Before that he had been at Chester as an assistant, soon after he was qualified, then in partnership in Wales and, after a year in London to get his degree, on his own for three years in the Isle of Wight. But these had been in the nature of trying his wings. He had gained a lot of experience from them, and from his hospital work, and the Isle of Wight had brought him Ruth, but Dynsford had been important. That was where his success, which had deposited him at the age of thirty-nine as a consultant physician in Wimpole Street, had really begun.

Residential Dynsford had plenty of money. It cared about things like furniture and cars and expensive cuts of meat and vegetables out of season. It was eclectic about its commodities, so that a doctor who was at the same time so clever and so attractive was right up its street.

Steven's private practice prospered, and his panel practice was large and interesting, as St Margaret's was the only big hospital within a twenty-mile radius. When he sold his private practice, many of his Dynsford patients followed him to London. He was worth a trip to town and if you were a relic of his G.P. days, his fee was only two guineas. You could always combine it with shopping, anyway.

His panel patients could not follow him, but as at the time he did not want to lose sight of interesting cases, he retained his appointment as Honorary Physician, with a dozen beds in the medical wards, and when these particular cases were replaced by others, and others after them, and his honorary appointment at a big London hospital overshadowed anything that Dynsford had to offer, he still kept to the arrangement, and regretted it only when he was tired, and traffic or fog made getting there a penance. It was useful to have somewhere to send a case whom he thought would do better out of London, and he liked his Dynsford patients.

He liked his Thursday clinics on the whole, in spite of Nurse Lake, although each time he saw her leaping, scarlet, to her feet as he opened the door, he wished that her time in the department was up.

The nurses were not allowed to sit in the doctors' swivel chairs, but on Thursday afternoons Snorting Lil was safely on point duty in the fracture clinic, so Nurse Lake sat in Steven's chair, and read up her medical notes while she waited for him. When he came in to-day, her hand flew to her hair as she jumped up, because she was trying a new style, rolled up over a ribbon all round. It was straight, slippery hair, so that while it looked all right in front – as she had confirmed in a pocket mirror just before he came in – some wisps were escaping at the back, and one strand, which she had cut when she was trying a curl on top, was sticking straight out behind her right ear. Her white cap was anchored inside the roll. The turned-up brim was meant to be a haloing frame, but she had so confined it with thick black pins that what with the narrowness of her face below, the general impression was that she had been crushed in a door. What it lacked in width, her face made up for in length, and her chin went on for ever, and then turned forward like a hockey stick. Strictly speaking, she was not bad-looking: she had an inoffensive nose and mouth and nice mild eyes under squarish, unplucked eyebrows, but there was something lacking. It was not colour, because the blush that came and went on her neck frequently spread up to her eyes and sometimes as far as her hairline. You could actually see it creeping up that long expanse, as the sun spreads over a field when the wind is chasing the clouds. But there was no warmth in her face, no vitality, no changing expression. Steven hardly moved his lips when he talked, and yet his face was so alive that you could not take your eyes off it. Women who dined out with him recognized with surprise, on the way out, acquaintances at whom they would normally have been waving and nodding all through dinner.

But when Nurse Lake talked to you, although she moved her lips and even, when she laughed, showed her teeth to the gums, there was nothing in her face to hold your attention, and as there was usually nothing much in her conversation either, people did not often listen to what she said. She was unaware of this, because she was listening so hard herself. She was intensely conscious of herself and, instead of just doing things and saying them, she saw herself doing them and heard herself saying them, as if she were watching a figure in a film.

Her role this afternoon, as she saw it, was the Great Man's Indispensable. How the clinic had ever run without her or how it would carry on when she left the department did not bear thinking about. The caption for the scene was: Dr Sheppard would be lost without Nurse Lake. How, for instance would he have got into his white coat if she had not held it for him, settling the collar against the back of his neck, where the thick black hair that was scattered with threads of silver, like expensive overcoat cloth, grew to a slight point?

'Thanks, Nurse.' Steven put his case on the desk, knocking over her erection of pens leaning against black and red ink-wells, which he never used. He thrust his stethoscope into a side pocket and hung his head mirror over the end of the paper rack, whence, as it was bending down the corners of

18

the 'Fitness to Resume Work' forms, Nurse Lake transferred it to the desk, arranging its strap as carefully as a sailor coiling rope. Steven was rummaging in his case for some notes he wanted, and the nurse saw a packet of cigarettes and a novel with a library label, intimate glimpses, she thought, of the real man behind the professional.

'Have I got many to-day? I don't want to be late.'

'Thirty-one, sir. Seven of them are repeat medicines and injections, and there are nine new patients,' answered Nurse Lake briskly, visualizing the orderly sections which she had already marshalled on the benches outside.

'Right. I'll have the repeats and injections first, then the new patients, then the rest of the old stagers. Quick as you like.'

Steven sat down on the swivel chair and unscrewed the cap of his fountain pen, Nurse Lake crossed to the door, wondering whether her hair looked all right from the back, called: 'Come along, Mrs Pithers, *please*, Doctor's waiting,' and a small brown figure in rimless oval spectacles arrived at the trot, thrusting her green folder and registration card at Steven like a relay racer handing over the baton.

'It's me sweetbreads,' announced Mrs Munn sociably. 'That's me trouble.' The young woman sitting next to her on the last of the three benches opposite the green door turned her head, saw that Mrs Munn was addressing her and smiled briefly. She was thin and flat-chested, with a long, stooping back, and she wore brown stockinette trousers, high-heeled shoes and a loose fawn coat, hunched round her by hands clenched in the pockets. Although her head was tied up in a green scarf, you could guess at her red hair by her smooth, freckled skin and pale eyes, defenceless under the insignificant brows and lashes. You could guess, too, that she was a new patient, because she did not know Mrs Munn.

Mrs Hannah Munn, of 73 Station Walk, Redwood, *O.P. No.* CA/101, age 69, *diagnosis:* Diabetes Mellitus, had been attending Dr Sheppard's clinic for as long as most of the staff at St Margaret's could remember. She came every month for a routine check-up; more often, unless she was prevented. She also came twice a day to Casualty for her injection of insulin.

'Poor old Mother Munn,' people said, 'fancy having to trek up here every day of her life.' But without her visits to the hospital, Mrs Munn would have had no aim in life at all.

She lived alone in a kind of enclosed passage with a window at one end and a door at the other, aptly called a bed-sitting-room, for there was no room to sit anywhere but on the bed. She had no friends, and her nearest relation was married to a market gardener in New Zealand, but contact with the outside world was maintained day and night by the shunting of trucks outside her window and the gurgling of a cistern outside her door whenever anybody turned on a tap in the kitchen. Her months revolved round her visits to the clinic as other people's revolve round pay day, and her days revolved round her injections as other people's revolve round meals, for she ate very little, in blissful disregard of her prescribed diet. She was supposed to have her meals downstairs with her landlady's family, but it was a subtle way of scoring a point off Mrs Larter and her fleshy husband and daughter to be able to say that she couldn't fancy whatever it was they were so audibly enjoying, and to pucker her drawstring lips over an aloof cup of tea. Besides, it was one thing to assure those kind dears up at the hospital that she would weigh out every mouthful according to the unintelligible chart which they had taken so much trouble to explain, but it would have been quite another to go waving it at Mrs Larter and ordering her to provide: lean beef 2 oz., bread 2-3 oz., butter ½ oz., raspberries 6 oz., junket, cream 2 oz., tea, coffee, soda-water or Oxo.

Fortunately her diabetes was only mild, for she existed almost entirely on buns and rolls, which she bought at a shop under the railway bridge, and ate in bed by a persevering technique of toothless sucking and mashing. She had her pension, and she did a little dilettante charring, but the hospital was her life. She had been attending for ten years, ever since that day when everything had come over black in Woolworth's, and she had woken up in a strange bed in a flannel nightgown with a frill round the neck, and been told some rigmarole about not eating sweets. Periodically, everything came over black again in other inconvenient places, and she was brought in for a few days to have her insulin adjusted.

She had also been wearing the same pair of hats for ten years; a mock-astrakhan teacosy in winter and a black-straw soup plate in summer, which she washed every year and dried flat with a leg of the bed on one side of the brim and her Bible on the other, before sewing on new flowers. Purple and white, they were this year – pansies, the girl in Woolworth's had said, without bothering to look at them, but Mrs Munn knew they were ammynones.

The smile which the girl in the green-scarf turban gave her was only a fleeting one; it was gone from her face in a second. She sat hunched up in her coat, with her mind on herself and her eyes on the dirty bit of plaster over the carbuncle on the neck of the man in front. Mrs Munn tried again. She knew what it was with new patients. It was all very well for her, who was more at home here than anywhere else on earth, but the hospital atmosphere often made strangers feel nervous, especially what with not knowing what they'd got.

'What's your trouble then?' she asked invitingly.

The other looked at her suspiciously, and said, as if to close the subject: 'I'm afraid it's rather difficult to explain.'

'I expect you think it's cancer,' said Mrs Munn cheerfully. 'The new ones often do. And then the doctor tells them it isn't – he's ever so clever – and there they've had all that worry for nothing.'

The young woman did not seem to be listening. She was looking over her shoulder now, beckoning and mouthing at someone. A leggy little boy in blue knickers came slowly up, taking nibbles all round the edges of a Chelsea bun. He had straight, coppery hair, cut square across his forehead, a grown-up little nose and a baby's mouth, and the only colour in his face was in the violet-grey smudges under his eyes.

'Wherever did you get that bun, dear?' His mother drew him towards her, plucking at his jersey.

'The lady over there give it me.' He pointed to the canteen where voluntary Good Women in cretonne overalls succoured with cups of tea and buns those who weakened in the endurance test of waiting their turn at the clinics.

'But, dear, you had your dinner before we came.' Leaning over the back seat, she kept touching him, pulling down his jersey, straightening his tie, unnecessarily, for the boy was quite neat.

He moved a step away, still harvesting all round the bun. 'I know, Mum, but we've been here such a long time.' He had a high, sing-song voice, not whining, although it came from the back of his nose; an unexcited, resigned little voice.

'That your kiddie?' asked Mrs Munn, all gaping smile and nodding ammynones.

'Yes, this is Tom. It's about him I've come, really, but he will keep running off, and I'm so afraid it'll come our turn and he not be there.'

'But,' said Mrs Munn, at home in her own subject, 'Dr Sheppard don't see children. It's Dr Burrows you'd ought to have bring him to, Mondays and Fridays, at the children's clinic.'

Tom's mother looked blank. She let go of Tom, who drifted away. 'But I was told specially Dr Sheppard. He must see me. Dr Munroe sent me – from the surgical clinic, you know.'

'*Mr* Munroe,' corrected Mrs Munn.

'That's right. He took my appendix out, five years ago, so of course, when I come back to this district, I went to him again. That was Tuesday – well, that meant two buses, and of course Tom was sick, and then the same again to-day –

well, I don't want it all over again to-morrow. And it's the question of time, you see. I can't wait.'

'Bad as that, is it?' asked Mrs Munn, dying to know, but the girl was looking round again, not hearing her.

'I'm sure Dr Sheppard'll see me. He must. I've got a letter for him from Dr Munroe.' She brought an envelope out of the bag that lay on top of her green folder on the bench beside her.

'Oh, well, if you've got a letter, that's another thing.' They both examined the talisman, back and front, and as if to demonstrate its powers, the door of the clinic opened and Nurse Lake appeared, looking anxious. Dr Sheppard had just said: 'My hat, look at the time!' and run his fingers through his hair, which never seemed to ruffle it.

'Any more new patients?' called Nurse Lake. A woman in a shovel hat on the front bench stood up and made uncertain, darting movements forward. The nurse grabbed her and hustled her inside, as if Dr Sheppard were a flame that would go out if he were not fed that instant with a patient. Having got him safely rekindled, Nurse Lake came out again, holding the door to behind her. She regarded them sternly, heavy with responsibility.

Tom's mother was leaning over the back of the bench again, hissing at him. Mrs Munn dug her in the ribs. 'Go on,' she said. 'Tell Nurse you're a new patient. The new ones have to go in first. You'd ought to 'ave been sitting up in front anyway. Why didn't you tell her before?'

'But I'm *not*. I've been to this hospital ever so often.'

'But you're new for Dr Sheppard.'

'Yes, but that doesn't make me a new patient. I mustn't go out of my turn. They wouldn't like it.'

'But you are. You must tell her. It's not right, you know, to fly against the rules.' It was useless to argue with Mrs Munn on her own ground, but she still shook her head and whispered, pulling her coat round her: 'No, I can't. I wouldn't like to do what isn't right. I do hope it won't be long, though,' she said, slewing round again to look at the

23

electric clock which jerked the minutes away on the wall behind the canteen.

'*I'll* tell her then, if you won't.' Mrs Munn stood on tiptoe to see over the other patients and called: 'Nurse!' confidently, but while they had been arguing Nurse Lake had warned the first old patient to get on her mark, and was disappearing into the clinic. She heard Mrs Munn, but shut the door without looking outside again. Probably some patient wanting to be let in out of turn. They were always trying it on, with some story about a last bus, and you simply had to be firm. As she said to Nurse Green: it just wasn't fair. If you did it for one, you'd have to do it for them all, and then where would you be? But patients could be so difficult. That time when Dr Sheppard had come late and the patients had grumbled, and when he did come, they had tried to rush the door, and she had had to flatten herself before it like – who was it? – that girl who held her arm through the bolt and got it broken.

'Can't you understand what a busy man Dr Sheppard is?' she had asked them. 'This isn't his only hospital, you know.' She could hear herself saying it now, identifying herself with that mysterious, enthralling London world, which only released him to her for three hours every week.

'Take this patient in to undress, Nurse,' said Dr Sheppard without looking up as she re-entered, 'and I'll have the next one in right away. Quick as you like.'

Nurse Lake spun round briskly, hauled in a stout old Blood Pressure and retired into the examination room to lay out the woman in the shovel hat as if the couch were the sacrificial slab at Stonehenge.

'That's not right,' said a man in bus driver's uniform, as the green door shut behind the Blood Pressure. 'I come here before that lady, and I'd ought to go in before.'

'Excuse me,' said Miss Smythe, who wore a coffee lace modesty vest and smelt of lavender water. 'I've been here since twelve o'clock, and you were not here then.'

'That's right,' said her neighbour, who had a nodding affliction of the head which now became accentuated. 'Second one here, this lady was, and I come third. You've got to take your turn, same as the others.'

'Ah, but I got a letter,' argued the bus driver. 'Got a letter from the garridge to say I'm a public convenience and got to be seen first. It's not right that I shouldn't go in next.'

The man with the carbuncle leaned forward from the bench behind. 'Why didn't you tell the nurse then? If you've got a letter, you have to show it to the nurse and she puts you through straight away.'

'That's right, that's quite right.'

'Why didn't you tell the nurse?'

'Can't expect the girl to know by instinct.'

'Some people –'

The crowd on the benches began to murmur at the bus driver, telling each other how soft he was.

'Well, she never asked for it, did she?' The bus driver was aggrieved. 'She'd ought to have said : "Anyone to go in first?" she'd ought to have said. "Yes," I'd have said. "Me," I'd have said.' He was a big, clumsy man, with hands that hung helplessly, as if they missed the steering wheel. He went and stood by the door, lowering at the benches.

'Well, I'm going in next,' he announced. 'I got a right to go in next. Got a double-decker to take over to Barnet, I have, at four o'clock. There'll be trouble now about the time I been 'ere.'

'Well, of course you're going in next,' said Miss Smythe, getting her knitting out again from its quilted cretonne bag.

When it was Miss Smythe's turn to go in, she stepped up to the desk sedately on her narrow, buckled feet, smoothed the pleated stockinette over her knees, moistened her lips, cleared her throat in a high key and waited for the doctor to finish washing his hands.

25

He came over to her, drying them. 'Well, Miss Smythe,' he said, in the engaging, confidential tone which he could not have avoided now if he had tried. 'And how's Miss Smythe?' Silly ass, he thought to himself. Why don't you say: 'How are you?' or d'you think you can cure the poor old dear by being coy? He threw the towel vaguely in the direction of the basin. Nurse Lake picked it up, folded it and placed it on top of the sterilizer to dry.

'That silly head of mine's no better, Doctor,' said Miss Smythe uncomplainingly. 'I've had two of my goes this month – quite nasty they were. My sister wanted to send for Dr Sedgewick, but I said no, I'd sooner wait and see you.' Miss Smythe had been having goes of various kinds for nearly twenty years. Swollen legs, sciatica, acute indigestion, palpitations, indefinable abdominal pains – she had long ago forgotten what it was like to feel completely well. The dentist had extracted all her teeth, showing them to Snorting Lil for a split second with a 'There, I told you these were the trouble!' before casting the apparently normal set of fangs into the dirty dressing bin. A surgeon had whipped out her appendix, holding it aloft in the forceps with the same remark while those present in the theatre squinted over their masks at what seemed to be a very healthy bit of tissue.

At the moment, Miss Smythe's goes were attacks of blinding migraine. Steven had been working on them unavailingly for two years, trying to relieve the symptoms instead of tackling the cause. One could not cure a neurosis without revealing to the patient the original thought or desire which, repressed into the subconscious long ago, had emerged as a symbolical symptom. The symptoms might vary, but they would never disappear until the patient faced up to their psychological cause, and how was one going to make Miss Smythe, who wouldn't look at a bull in a field, face up to the fact that all she needed was a man?

In any case, how could one treat psychologically people whom one saw for ten minutes once a fortnight? Private patients could afford to have neuroses, and be cured of them,

26

given hours and hours of the physician's time, but a hospital patient must only have tangible troubles, which could be cured by a snap diagnosis, a scribbled prescription and a long wait in line outside the dispensary hatch.

And yet one could have done so much for these people if only one had the time.

He looked at his watch as Miss Smythe went out of the door by the basins. 'Ever read Freud, Nurse?' he asked, blotting Miss Smythe's notes.

'Oh – yes, sir.' Nurse Lake stepped up to the desk and put her hands behind her back. She had never read a line of Freud, but she had once read an article about him in a Sunday paper, which was just as good.

'Well, there you are.' Steven waved a hand towards the chair in which Miss Smythe had sat. 'Frustration incarnate.' Nurse Lake put on her intelligent expression, and Steven, glancing at her, saw the flush creeping up her neck. In a moment of curiosity, he saw her for the first time as a girl, instead of a pair of thin arms and a head and a pair of black legs coming out of an armour-like uniform. Had any man – would any man ever –? Perhaps he should not have mentioned Freud to this embryo Miss Smythe, but she would not connect it with herself. They never did. Perhaps it was just as well.

After waiting to see whether he had more pearls of wisdom for her, Nurse Lake said: 'Mrs Darby is ready in the examination room, sir. Blood pressure a hundred and ninety over a hundred and ten. Pulse sixty-six.'

'O.K.' He got up and she followed him in her squeaking shoes.

'Your stethoscope, sir.' Damn the woman. But why damn her? He needed his stethoscope. She was a good nurse, probably. But that was the hard part for women. Being good at their job was not enough.

It was a slow, irritating clinic this week. Because Steven was in a hurry, the afternoon seemed to be full of setbacks: a patient's X-rays were mislaid, another had lost her registration card, and sooner than face Miss Meiklejohn without it, had come in without her notes, and had to be sent to wait outside again while Nurse Lake cast about between the registration office and the Lady Almoner, and was not in the clinic when Steven wanted her to do a fomentation. Twice he was called to the telephone by his secretary, to agree to something that she had probably arranged herself already. The patients seemed determined to tell him their life histories as well as that of their cousin's wife who had been taken just the same way at Brighton last year. Answers to simple, pertinent questions could only be reached by way of an interminable narrative, and cutting them short or hustling them threw them out of their stride, so that they withheld the most important information until the consultation was over. When Steven had shut the folder and slung it on to the slowly growing pile on the window-sill, they would proffer deprecatingly, as if it were a wilting bunch of flowers, the very thing for which he had been angling.

It was hot in the clinic, in spite of the wide open windows behind him through which came the whine of traffic ascending the hill. A bird kept chirping aimlessly, and a man shovelled coke from a huge pile in the yard and wheeled it away in an iron barrow, whistling *O Sole Mio*. He was still whistling it when he came back with the barrow empty. Mrs Delacroix wondered why Steven kept looking over his shoulder out of the window. He was looking to see whether the patch of sky between the coke pile and the angle of the mortuary roof was still blue. The clouded day had begun to clear on the way down after lunch, and by the time he reached Dynsford had become the sort of afternoon which makes you think about lying on the side of a hill with your hands behind your head and the sun hot on your eyelids. He wanted it to stay like this, to wait for him until he had got through this business so that he could drive back with the roof down and the dropping sun drawing streaks of golden cloud to it on his right. He had three or four private calls to make in London, and he wanted to get them done and get home early because Ruth was going out to-night and he had promised himself dinner with a book and then some writing. This afternoon his time belonged to his patients, but each five minutes wasted was five minutes stolen from the other end, from the time that was his own.

But here was Mrs Delacroix, in her tweed dress and jacket and pseudo-Austrian hat, putting on her private patient act, which was intended to show that she was more accustomed to visiting doctors in their consulting-rooms than in clinics. She was the widow of a bankrupt solicitor, and lived with her hulking, adolescent daughter in a bungalow which smelt of bread and butter and damp tea-cloths. She could not afford to be a private patient, but was not going to let Dr Sheppard or anyone else forget that she had once been one. She went through the necessary formalities at the registration office and the Lady Almoner's with a remote, disinterested air, receiving her folder in her finger-tips with a slight laugh to show how *absurd* all this was. On the benches, she and her daughter sat immersed in books from the twopenny library, in which they kept the celluloid markers from the days when they had belonged to Boots'.

Breezing into the clinic, she felt how nice it must be for Dr Sheppard to see someone of his own kind in the middle of all the dreary folk, so when she sat down, she crossed her legs very high and made herself quite at ease to show she was his own kind. Kathleen stood beside her, ponderous and adenoidal, with her stomach stuck out and her calves bulging below the skimpy gym tunic of a futile little private school that cost hardly anything and taught her even less. She had a straight mane of lion-coloured hair cut in a long fringe, from under which she frowned her antagonism to the world in general and her mother in particular.

'Isn't it *ghastly*!' Mrs Delacroix was saying, waggling the toe of her crossed leg at Steven. 'Kathy's come out in the most awful spots. I mean, spots, of all things! Look at the child. Did you ever see anything more frightful in your life?' Nurse Lake tilted the light without being asked, and Steven got up and turned Kathleen's face from side to side with his hand under her chin.

'How long has this been coming up?' he asked. Kathleen opened her mouth to answer and Mrs Delacroix said: 'Oh, good gracious now, let's see, it seems like ages and ages, but it can't be long, because I've brought her up to you as soon as I could. I know you always like to see us at once when anything goes wrong. It makes it so much easier for you, doesn't it? I mean, these people who wait and wait until they get too bad for the doctor to do anything, and then expect him to cure them – well, I know how doctors feel about that!'

'Does it itch, Kathleen?' Steven asked.

'Itch?' laughed Mrs Delacroix. 'Like billy-o!' Steven went to wash his hands. Nurse Lake handed him the towel, and said something to him in a low voice, anything, to show Mrs Delacroix that she and he were in league against Mrs Delacroix, instead of he and Mrs Delacroix being in league against the rest of the inferior world.

'I'm pretty sure it's impetigo,' said Steven, sitting down and beginning to write on Kathleen's case sheet.

Mrs Delacroix gave a refined squawk. 'Oh, no! Oh, Dr Sheppard, it couldn't possibly be. I mean, I've always understood that's a thing you get from dirt, isn't it? And it's not as if Kathy's ever mixed with anything like that – I wouldn't dream. Oh, Kathy!' She squinted up at her scowling daughter in mock revulsion: 'Aren't you dreadful! Isn't she dreadful, Dr Sheppard?' Steven looked out of the window. The sky was still blue. 'It's quite common,' he said. 'They get it from towels and things. It's very contagious.'

'Oh, but Kathy doesn't go to the sort of school where the children would have it. I mean, I've always been so careful. I know some people don't understand how important these things are and that's one of the things that makes a doctor's job such hell, isn't it? But ever since Mr Delacroix had blood poisoning ... Of course, we didn't know you then. That was when we lived in town.'

'This isn't anything like blood poisoning,' said Steven,

pulling out the medicine card. 'It's just a simple skin infection.'

'Oh, I know, I know, of *course* – I was simply –'

'Look, Kathleen,' Steven said to the figure towering above him like Epstein's Genesis, 'I'll give you a powder to help dry it up, and I'd like you to have some rays on it.' Out of the corner of his eye he saw Nurse Lake draw a green X-ray form out of the rack.

'But, of course!' said Mrs Delacroix. 'Anything you say. What will it cost?' she said nonchalantly, knowing full well that Kathleen would get it for nothing under the Hospital Scheme. Nurse Lake had filled in the particulars on the form and passed it across to Steven for him to initial with the tall upright S.B.S., a dot under each letter and a bold line underneath. She could have forged it in her sleep. Mrs Delacroix was taking out an engagement book. 'Now then, when shall I bring her for these famous rays? I say, she won't get *burns* or anything, will she? A man we knew in town –'

'You'll fix all that with the X-ray Sister,' said Steven. 'She'll fit you in when she can. And, Kathleen, you must be very particular about using your own towels and sponges and flannels. Anything that touches your skin mustn't touch anyone else's. See?' He looked up at her with one eyebrow raised. Kathleen hated him. Mrs Delacroix said mentally what she often said vocally to her friends. 'My dear, my doctor's *so* attractive. He's a London man, you know. Comes down here specially once a week.' She now uncrossed her legs and leaned away from Kathleen in horror. 'A pariah!' she said, rhyming it with barrier. 'A pariah!' rhyming it with Uriah, to make sure. 'Now you hear what he says, infant. No spreading your leprosy about the house. I'm sure I don't want the wretched thing.' She pulled at her Austrian hat, gathering her lips.

'Oh, Mum-*ee*!' It was the first word Kathleen had spoken. Steven got up and held out his hand. It was the only way of getting rid of the woman. She sprang up. 'Oh,' she laughed. 'You want us to go, of course. I was forgetting. I suppose you've got loads and loads more tiresome people to see, you poor man. Aren't we dreadful bothering you with our beastly little troubles?' As she gathered up her gloves a thought crossed her mind. If only she could have said: 'Do come in for a drink any time you're passing our place.' She raised her head and drew down her nostrils. Well, there had been a time when she could have said that, hadn't there? She hoped Dr Sheppard thought that she could have asked him, but didn't think it was worth while when he was in Dynsford so little.

Steven bent slightly from the waist and looked into her eyes as he shook her hand. He was thinking about Ugly waiting on the front seat of the car, making the window slimy with his nose.

'He really is a charming man, isn't he, Kath?' said Mrs Delacroix, as Nurse Lake shut them into the passage that led back to the Outpatients' hall. Kathleen grunted and began to pick one of the scabs off her face.

The minute hand of the electric clock jumped on to the figure twelve and, simultaneously, the steeple of St Mary's, whose vicar always kept his clock set by the wireless, began its feeble imitation of Big Ben. Steven took his stethoscope off Mrs Milligan's chest and waited patiently for the four unresonant bongs. St Mary's always struck when he was trying to listen for a murmur. He thought he had caught Mrs Milligan's heart at it last week, but to-day he was not so sure. St Mary's unconvincing statement finished, and Steven bent forward again and listened intently, his eyes focused somewhere through and beyond Mrs Milligan, while she held open the V neck of her green jersey as if baring her breast for the arrow.

Steven was in a tunnel, bounded by muffling earth and filled from floor to roof by a giant dynamo which drove everything else out of his head. And now, from far down the tunnel, where the sea roared if you moved the stethoscope a fraction on the skin, he caught for a moment the infinitesi-

mal thickening and lengthening of the thr-r-ill of the opening valves. Or was it? Had he imagined it because it was
what he was listening for? No – there it was – no ... The
door of the clinic opened with a noise like a thunderclap
and Steven looked up irritably at the plump, smiling nurse
who had come in. Nurse Lake made frantic damping-down
movements at her, so she stayed where she was and pointed
at the clock and then at her mouth and then at Nurse Lake,
who shook her head impatiently. The plump nurse went
through the motions of lifting a cup, complete with crooked
finger. Nurse Lake's mouth framed an oblong 'No!' and the
other nurse stabbed at the clock again and framed a word
that drew her mouth back to her ears.

Steven left them to get on with this mad miming and went
back into his tunnel. The plump nurse, who had been long
enough in hospital to know that if you were sent to deliver a
message, you delivered it, even if the recipient was dead,
tiptoed exaggeratedly across the room with her eyes on
Steven's back.

'Sister says you're to go to tea,' she whispered.

'I don't want any.'

'Oh, but –' Nurse Lake was the plump nurse's senior, and
so could not be argued with, but then, Sister was senior to
Nurse Lake. 'Oh, but Sister said –'

'I never go to tea on Thursdays.'

'But, please, Nurse, Sister said you were to.' Visions rose
before her of going back to the fracture clinic, of Sister saying: 'What are you doing here? I told you to relieve Nurse
Lake,' of being sent back into Dr Sheppard's clinic, of being
sent away again by Nurse Lake, of shuttling back and forth,
perhaps in the end not getting any tea herself.

'Well, tell Sister I don't want any,' whispered Nurse Lake,
watching Steven in case he stretched out a hand for anything.

'But supposing she says –' In Steven's stethoscope, their
whispering roared and reverberated like the sea on the
shingly floor of a cave.

He swung round. 'For God's sake, can't you women do your gossiping somewhere else? I would like half-a-minute's peace to listen to this heart,' Nurse Lake blushed. The plump nurse stopped a giggle with her hand. Mrs Milligan looked at them righteously.

Seeing that the other nurse meant to hold her ground, Nurse Lake shrugged the sharp ridge of her shoulders, said: 'Excuse me please, sir,' and went over to the window sill for her cuffs. She did not want to leave the clinic. Anything might happen while she was away. Who knew what Dr Sheppard might not want, and Nurse Phillimore didn't know his ways. She didn't want Nurse Phillimore to get a chance to learn his ways either. She walked to the door slowly, to give Steven time to say: 'Don't go away, Nurse,' but he was listening again, waiting for the tortured animal that was the squeaking of her shoes to finish walking down his tunnel.

There were still five or six people on the benches outside. She would have to be quick, or Dr Sheppard would be finished and gone before she got back. Oh dear, Mrs Dovey and Mr Cann; neither of them would hold him up for long. Mrs Munn – she might only be in there long enough to have her specimen tested. And would Nurse Phillimore do that all right? She almost went back to remind her that Dr Sheppard liked Fehling's used and not Benedict's. Who was that in the green scarf? Nurse Lake did not remember having seen her before. A disturbing thought came to her.

'You're not a new patient, are you?' she asked sharply.

'Yes, she is, Nurse,' said Mrs Munn triumphantly, and Tom's mother said: 'Oh, but I'm not, Nurse. I've been to Dr Munroe ever so often.'

'Haven't you seen Dr Sheppard before?'

'No, Nurse.'

'Well, then, of *course* you're a new patient. Why didn't you say so before? You should have gone in ages ago. Dr Sheppard always likes to see the new patients first. Oh dear –' her

34

face was criss-crossed with anxiety. 'Why ever didn't you tell me when I asked?'

'But I thought –'

'I told you, didn't I?' crowed Mrs Munn. 'I told 'er, Nurse, but she wouldn't 'ave it. I tried to tell you too, dear, but you was busy. I knew she was wrong. "You're a new patient," I said. "No matter 'oom you've seen before, you're new for Dr Sheppard," I said.'

'Well, you'd better go in next, anyway,' said Nurse Lake. 'Dr Sheppard will be very annoyed, but it can't be helped. And if he won't see you now, you'll have to come again next week, that's all.'

'Oh, but I can't –' Tom's mother got to her feet. 'I must see him today.' She might have known something like this would happen. And now she had annoyed the doctor and he might not even see her, and she dared not stay another week near Dynsford. Even if he did see her, the picture of him that Nurse Lake had conjured up did not sound like the sort of man who Dr Munroe had said would be sure to help her. She didn't want to go in there now; she'd manage somehow. She looked round for Tom, drawing her coat round her and tucking her handbag under her arm.

The plump nurse came out of the clinic. 'Next patient please!'

'This patient will have to go in next, Nurse,' said Nurse Lake. 'She should have gone in ages ago. She's a new patient, only she never said so.'

'Dr Sheppard will be furious,' said Nurse Phillimore happily. It wasn't her fault. 'He always gets mad if you don't send in the new patients first, doesn't he?'

Nurse Lake looked at her sharply. How did she know? Oh, yes, she had taken the clinic that time when she had been off sick, of course. That time when she had got into such trouble for getting up against orders on a Thursday and appearing on duty with legs like cotton wool and a head that went round and round, and finally spun her flat on the floor of the sterilizing room.

35

Tom's mother looked from one to the other of them as they haggled over her. 'I don't want to make trouble,' she said. 'Perhaps I'd better not go in.'

'Don't be silly,' said Nurse Lake. 'You're to come in now, at once. Hurry up, please. Doctor's waiting.' She caught hold of her arm.

'Oh, but my little boy. It's about him I've come. He's somewhere about – he was here a minute ago. There he is by the canteen. I'll just go and fetch him.'

'No, you come in now,' said Nurse Lake. 'Go and fetch the child, Nurse. I'll explain to Dr Sheppard.'

'What on earth are you nurses playing at?' asked Steven, as she propelled Tom's mother into the chair by the desk. 'I haven't got all day for this clinic, you know.'

'I'm ever so sorry, sir.' Nurse Lake placed the green folder before him, exactly parallel with the edge of the desk. 'I'm afraid there's one more new patient. I know you don't like seeing them at the end, but she never said she was new, you see. I did ask them all, but she never said. That's what makes it so difficult.' She saw herself and Steven as allies, battling together against the stupidity of the patients.

Steven opened the folder and slit the envelope addressed to him in Mr Munroe's writing. It was true; he did like to get over the lengthy history-taking and examination of new patients at the beginning, but he said: 'Well, never mind, Nurse. Don't make such heavy weather about it,' and Nurse Lake blushed and went out as the plump nurse came back with Tom.

When he had read the letter and glanced at the surgical notes, Steven hitched his chair forward and smiled at the couple before him, the child so much more at home than the mother, leaning against her knee and playing with the beading on the edge of the desk.

'Well, Mrs Garrard, Mr Munroe has asked me if I can help you. Perhaps you'd tell me what the trouble is.'

'Well, it's about Tom I've come, Doctor. Oh, I know I'd ought to really have come to the children's clinic, but I couldn't wait, you see. I mustn't stay any longer in Dyns-ford. I went to see Dr Munroe last week – he took my appendix out five years ago, you know, and was ever so kind – and he said to come to you, so I waited another week, but I mustn't stay any longer.' She had a slow voice, all on one level. A defeated voice, that expected nothing from life.

Steven looked at the letter again: '*Can you do anything for this woman? She has a very hard story, and it seems more in your line than mine, though it's practical rather than medical help she wants.*' That was just typical of Munroe. Anything that didn't call for the knife he palmed off on to somebody else, usually Steven.

'Well, suppose you tell me about it,' he said with a swift glance at the clock.

'Mum,' said the little boy, in his queer, chanting voice, 'when are we going home?'

'Ssh.' His mother shook him, shocked.

'Look here, old chap,' said Steven, 'supposing you go with Nurse and play something for a bit while your mother and I have a chat, hm?' He looked round, and woke Nurse Phillimore from her daydream by the window. She beamed all over Tom, and he went happily enough with her into one of the side rooms, although he pulled away the hand she tried to hold.

Mrs Garrard shrugged her shoulders. 'It wouldn't really matter, Doctor. He's heard and seen so much that he shouldn't already. He's like a little old man, my mother says, more like a little old man than a child, poor little soul. That's why I want to get him away, you see.'

'Yes?' murmured Steven encouragingly.

'I'll tell you straight, Doctor.' Her smooth face accepted condemnation if he wished to give it. 'I've run away from my husband, you see, that's where it is.' There, she had said it. She had been wondering what she was going to say, but although he didn't say much, this Dr Sheppard was so easy to talk to that she had come out with it almost without thinking. She watched him to see how he would take it, but

37

he simply nodded at her with his head slightly on one side, gravely, which was his encouraging way of receiving information from patients.

'I've stood it as long as I could, sir, and if it had been just for myself, I daresay I'd have gone on with it, in spite of everything, but it was the kiddie, you see, that was where it was. Everything else I could have stood, but it was the thought that Tom wasn't getting his fair chance, that was where it was, Doctor, if you can understand.'

Steven listened and waited. At the moment he did not see where his part in the situation lay, or even what the situation was at all, but it was no use prompting. She must be allowed to come out with it in her own way.

Her unemphatic face wore a blankly secretive air, as if to neutralize her spoken confidences. Her long hands lay loosely in her lap. Her trousered legs were crossed at the ankle with the feet tucked under the chair. Even her voice was lifeless and anæmic and Steven wondered that she had ever achieved the vitality to take the step about which she was telling him.

'I left him, Doctor – three weeks ago, that was – and brought Tom to Reddage near here to my mother. I lived here as a girl, that was how I come to be under Dr Munroe, you see. Well, my husband hasn't come after me yet – too busy in other quarters' – her lips stretched in a slight smile. 'But when he does it's here he'll look for us. He knows I've nowhere else to go. So you see, I must get away before then. I was ever so upset when they said you didn't see children Thursdays, with the thought that I might have to keep Tom here, and Arthur be upon us any minute.'

'Your husband ill-treated the boy, is that it?' asked Steven.

'No, Doctor, not what you might call that, in fact quite the oppo-syte. He's just silly about the kiddie, but then in the wrong way, you see; not knowing what was good for him, if you can understand.'

'Has he made the child ill?' Where did Steven come into

this? Had Munroe recommended him purely as a father confessor?

'Not exactly what you might call *made*, Doctor. The kiddie's been ill – pneumonia it was, and how he got over the crisis we never knew – but they said at the Great Ormond Street Hospital that it was nobody's fault. No, but it was afterwards, you see. The doctor there told me I was to get the child into the country. Well, I told my husband this, and he wouldn't have it. Carried on that I was trying to get Tom away from him.'

She paused for a moment, withdrawn far from the clinic, back to that scene in the Gray's Inn Road kitchen when Arthur had shouted so, and she had known that Mrs Goldie on the other side of the wall could hear. And Tom sitting on the floor all the time with his train, taking in every word.

'So I didn't like to do it. After all, what he said was true; it was as much his child as mine. The hospital would have got Tom into a country home, or I could have sent him here to my mother, but he wouldn't have it, so Tom stayed on, never picking up, you see, just playing with his food – like a bird, his appetite is – and then, when my husband had a row at the factory and chucked up his job, well, I couldn't afford to get Tom the things he should have.'

'So you made up your mind to run away.'

'Not all at once. I was afraid to at first. I was afraid of him following us, and then all the talk there'd be, well, that wouldn't have been good for any of us, would it? No, it was not till this last time – this new, this – well, I mean, he'd been off with other women before, but this was the longest he'd ever been away, and with someone from the flats, too! I just couldn't stay there and face people.' She lowered her lids, with the inadequate lashes, and raised them again to see how Steven was taking it. Framed in that scarf and with the features all so still, her face looked remote and madonna-like. But a stone madonna, a self-righteous one, infuriating in her remoteness, uncharitable in her chastity. Steven, imagining Arthur as a lusty man in shirt sleeves with a loud voice and a red face that was darkened by beard an hour after shaving, could understand why he had gone off with other women.

From the examination room, the child chanted something unintelligible, and Nurse Phillimore gave a bubbling laugh. Through the window came the smell of hot macadam, and the man with the barrow was back again, whistling.

'So what is it, exactly, you want me to do?' asked Steven.

'Well, it's like this, Doctor. I'm not going back to Arthur, not now. I've taken the step and I'm not going back on it.' Mrs Garrard waited for criticism, and not getting any, went on: 'I'll have to find work. I can't stop on at home; my Dad doesn't earn all that much money, and my mother suffers with her legs. In any case, Arthur will look for me there when he gets over this fancy. He never goes away for good; just for a bit, and then comes back home, expecting to find everything as he left it. Well, this time he won't.' The pleasurable thought moved her lips again to their brief smile. 'That's why I can't leave Tom here neither, as I told Dr Munroe, so what he said was, come to you and you would examine the child and certify him to be sent to a country home where you get your convalescent children into. Arthur won't find him then, and I'll get a place somewhere where he won't find me, and then perhaps when the little chap's picked up a bit I might find a place where they wouldn't mind a kiddie.'

Steven leaned back in the chair with his legs stretched out and his fingers clasped. He looked at Mrs Garrard and considered, and she looked at him, not pleading, not proudly, simply offering her fate into his hands. If he did what she wanted, it would be almost conniving to rob a man of his property, and could one do that without hearing the other side of the story? He would like to do it. He was sorry for Mrs Garrard. No, it was not really sympathy that she aroused, it was more a rather stifling feeling of obligation. That monotonous, unargumentative voice had tired him, and by its listlessness had sapped his own vitality, so that he could not make a quick decision.

He drew his legs under him and stood up. 'Well, I'll examine the boy,' he said, 'and see what I can do for you.'

Mrs Garrard stood up, too. 'Thank you ever so much for listening, Doctor,' she said, 'you've been ever so kind.' He put his stethoscope into his pocket and made for the side room, stopping her when she would have come with him. She sat down again obediently, drew her coat round her and tucked her feet round the chair leg again.

'Hullo,' said someone, when Nurse Lake went into the dining-room, 'I thought you never came to tea on Thursdays. Stevie's clinic finished then?'

'No,' she said off-handedly, 'Phillimore's relieving me.' She kept up the pretence that nobody knew how she felt about Dr Sheppard, although it was a thing that everybody had known about for so long that they had quite ceased to talk about it. It was just a thing that belonged to poor old Lake, part and parcel of her, and arousing no more comment than her handwriting or the shape of her face.

She looked without expectation in the 'L' pigeon-hole of the letter rack. Her letter from home always came on Mondays. She poured out her tea at the side table and took it to her place at the bottom of the staff nurses' table. She had not yet passed the examination which would give her the right to wear a bow under her chin, fastened by a tape round her head, but, as Acting Staff Nurse of Outpatients, she had to sit at the exalted table to impress her authority over her juniors.

Three or four staff nurses were eating bread and jam at the table in the window. At the lesser tables there was more chatter and more mess made with the bread.

'What's for tea?' she asked

'Well, there *was* jam,' said a nurse who had what looked like half a pot of it on her plate, 'but you're a bit late for that sort of luxury.' She indicated the empty dish.

Nurse Bracken, who was two days junior to Nurse Lake, jumped up. 'I'll get you some more from the kitchen, if you like,' she said, picking up the jam dish.

'No, please.' Nurse Lake frowned. "All I want is a cup of tea, really, then I must dash back before Phillimore gets into a muddle. You can't go trotting about into the kitchen anyway. That's the maids' job.'

'But I always do. The maids don't come in here at tea-time, they're much too busy.'

'That's all right for the juniors to do, perhaps, but honestly, Nurse, it doesn't look awfully well for a senior to do it. I'm sure Matron wouldn't like it.'

'Oh, b—— Matron,' said Nurse Bracken unthinkingly, and looked round hastily to see if anyone had heard. It was a strain having to sit at the staff nurses' table after the carefree days among the herd. When you were a junior, you longed for the day when you would wear bows, do rounds with the doctors and be in charge of the ward on Sister's day off. That was what you worked for, passed exams for, endured insults for. That was why you spent your time off in summer in the garden with a surgery book and in winter went to bed with gynæcology and woke at three in the morning to find the light on and a cigarette burn in the sheet and gynæcology upside down on the floor.

When you had achieved your ambition, however, you frequently wished yourself an irresponsible junior again. The responsibility was exciting, but it aged you about ten years when the staff nurse was on holiday and Sister went off for the week-end with: 'If that man dies while I'm away, I shall hold you entirely responsible.' You were supposed to train the junior nurses, some of whom seemed to know more than you did yourself. If you were too strict with them, they hated you, and you heard them discussing you in the sluice while you were in the sterilizing room. If you were too easygoing and friendly, some of them took advantage of it, and went their own lawless way. Everything that went wrong in the ward was your fault, even if it happened on your day off.

At twenty-two, Nurse Bracken looked like eighteen and said she felt thirty. Her mother nearly died with pride whenever she thought about her, and said: 'My daughter's an acting staff nurse, you know', at every possible opportunity. Nurse Bracken was proud of herself, too, and when she could remember, tried to behave in the way that people like Nurse Lake seemed to think she ought.

'Anything exciting this afternoon?' she asked as she sat down again.

'Nothing much,' said Nurse Lake. 'Big clinic, though; we've been very busy.' She said that even when they had been slack. 'We had quite a decent jaundice. Dr Sheppard admitted it.'

'You're telling me he admitted it,' said a nurse from the other end of the table, with her mouth full. 'It came up in the middle of teas, and its been vomiting all over the place ever since. That fool of a junior pro put it in a bed without a mac. Heaven knows what Sister'll say when she comes on. When's Stevie coming to do his round? Has he nearly finished?'

'Won't be long,' said Nurse Lake. 'I'm going back now. I wish this tea wasn't so hot.'

'Pour it in your saucer.'

'Oh, I *can't*.'

'Well, I'm going to. I've got to get back before he comes up, but I'm not going to miss my tea, even for him.' The thought that Steven might be finished before she got back made Nurse Lake's stomach unreceptive to any more food or drink, so she left her cup half full, excused herself and hurried out.

'Love,' said Nurse Horrocks, cramming her last bit of bread and jam into her mouth, 'is a very beautiful thing.'

When Nurse Lake got back to the clinic, she thought at first that Steven had gone. Nurse Phillimore was in there alone, testing something at the table by the sink, with the flame of the spirit lamp much too high. But there was no white coat flung untidily over the back of the chair. Had he gone up to the wards in it, as he had once before, casting it somewhere by the wayside, to the fury of Snorting Lil when she checked the laundry at the end of the week? It would be just like Nurse Phillimore not to notice. She would not understand the absentmindedness of a man who was preoccupied with important things. And it would not be her fault if the coat got lost. Nurse Lake had suffered once, gladly enough, for Steven's sake, but the next time Sister might send her to Matron, and what with her State Finals next year and Sisters' posts perhaps going at the hospital after that, the less she was sent to Matron the better.

'Dr Sheppard gone then, Nurse?' she asked, and then, coming forward and seeing his case still on the desk, she relaxed. 'If he's examining a patient,' she said sharply, 'why aren't you in with him?'

'Because,' said Nurse Phillimore without turning round, 'he's gone to see Mr Munroe. Crumbs!' The blue fluid which she was boiling in a test tube suddenly sizzled and spat out on to the white tiles behind the shelf of bottles.

'Nurse!' The other crossed to her quickly. 'Whatever are you doing? That flame's much too high. And if you'd move the tube up and down, it – and why aren't you using the holder? No wonder you nurses are always getting burns and septic fingers. And you must cork up the bottles. Surely you've been taught – Benedict's!' She pounced. 'Surely you know that Dr Sheppard will only have Fehling's used? Here, I'll carry on with this. You can go now.' She blew out the flame and fussed about, tidying up the litter of torn litmus paper and spent matches.

'Oh,' wailed Nurse Phillimore. 'Why did you blow it out? That was the last match. And the stock cupboard's locked and Sister's gone to tea with the keys.'

'Who laid up this clinic, Nurse?' asked Nurse Lake, unscrewing the top of the lamp and pulling down the wick.

'I did.'

'Well, you know you're supposed to check the matchbox.

Honestly, I don't know. You're told so often about these things, but none of you seems to care. It's terribly worrying: I try and run this department properly, but you others simply don't pull your weight. In any case, a nurse should always have matches in her pocket.' She produced a box from her own and re-lit the lamp, which burnt now more docilely. One of the things you were taught in the lecture room was that a nurse's pockets should contain: scissors, fountain pen, matches, nursing dictionary, clean handkerchief, pins, and not two boiled sweets in a torn paper bag, powder and lipstick and a crumpled letter from a boy friend. The inventory of Nurse Lake's pockets, checked each week when she changed into a clean dress, was always correct. When in mufti, she transferred her scissors to her handbag, ready to be wrapped in a handkerchief and thrust between the teeth of anyone throwing an epileptic fit.

Nurse Phillimore rolled down her sleeves and put on her cuffs. 'Sorry,' she grinned. 'Can I go now, please? Anything nice for tea?'

'This is Mrs Munn's, I suppose,' said Nurse Lake, bending at the knees to get on eye level with the bobbing urinometer.

'Yes, she's in the side room. Can I –?'

'Yes, you can go, Nurse. Oh – and Nurse!' Nurse Phillimore poked her face of a happy apple round the door again. 'When you clear this clinic tonight be sure you clean all these tubes with spirit swabs and forceps. They're absolutely disgusting. I don't know what the doctors would think.'

When Steven came back from confirming Mrs Garrard's story with Mr Munroe, Nurse Lake placed a beautifully written slip on the desk in front of him. He laughed. 'That crazy woman! She's absolutely loaded with sugar again. Look here, Nurse, for the Lord's sake give her another of these things.' He reached towards the paper rack, but she was before him and pulled out a diabetic diet sheet while he was still fumbling among the admission forms. 'She simply must learn to treat herself. I haven't enough beds to keep

45

admitting her. Go through this with her in words of one syllable and try to make her understand it. I simply haven't got time.' He looked at the clock. 'I'm late as it is. That woman with the kid held me up. Sad case, rather, wasn't it? Oh, you weren't here, were you? Pity. I'd like you to have listened to that boy's chest. He's got an unmistakeable patch on the left lobe.'

The tea which Nurse Lake had drunk, the cause of her missing this treat, rose into her throat in a lump of disappointment. 'Did you admit him, sir?' she asked. She would be able to keep in touch with him through Nurse Green, who was on the children's ward, so that if Dr Sheppard mentioned him next week she could proffer intelligent information.

'No, I'm going to get him into that Home up in Cheshire. Best place for him, I think. All right, Nurse. Don't bother about me.' She was standing behind him, waiting to help him off with his white coat. 'You get along and see what you can do with Mother Munn. I'm sure you want to get off to your tea.' He said this kindly, but to Nurse Lake it only showed that he had not noticed that she had gone to tea half an hour ago.

'Good afternoon, then, sir,' she said proudly, picked up the diet sheet and squeaked into the side room, feeling on her back his eyes, which were actually busy looking in his case for the notes he needed for the wards.

He saw a packet of cigarettes and lit one, throwing the match on the floor. If Sister Grainger saw him coming along the corridor to her ward smoking, she would dart into her sitting-room for one of her beaten brass ashtrays and stand holding it out at him before she would open the swing doors into the ward. Steven went to the window, ducked his head to look out and up, and saw that the sky was still blue, and although the yard was in shadow there was sun on the mortuary roof. Would have been a good evening for golf, if he had thought of it before. He could have cut across to Wentworth and put off his private calls until he got back.

But it was a bit late to get hold of anyone now, and to beat round alone was good practice but uninspiring. Anyway, Ruth had ordered dinner for him, and if he didn't turn up for it she would worry about Mrs Hankey being offended.

He drew in his head, and heard someone knock at the clinic door. None of his business. His clinic was finished. The knock was repeated, and he saw the door-handle turn doubtfully. Another knock, and as he picked up his case and made for the door by the basins, the other door opened and Mrs Garrard came in. 'Oh, there you are, Doctor, I thought perhaps you'd gone.'

'Just going. Get fixed up with the Lady Almoner all right?'

'Yes. She was ever so kind. She's arranged it all about Tom; he's to go there directly. I'm sure it sounds very nice, and I'm ever so grateful to you, Doctor, for what you've done. You've been ever so kind,' she said flatly, and stood still, fixing him with her static gaze, her mouth half-open as if she had not finished speaking. She obviously wanted something else but hadn't he done enough for her? He opened his door and said breezily: 'Well, that's splendid. I'll keep an eye on him, and you'd better keep in touch with me. Let me know your address as soon as you're settled.' He shut the door again resignedly, as she came forward and rested her handbag on the desk, saying: 'That's what I just wanted to ask you about, if it wouldn't be too much trouble.'

'Well, what?' he asked patiently, disliking the utter dependence of her, the humble way in which she was waiting, for his permission to speak.

'It's about finding a place, sir. You've been so kind, I wondered if you knew of anybody – You see, if I go to the agency it all takes such a time, and I must get away from here as soon as possible, if you can understand.'

What on earth did the woman think he was? An employment bureau? That was the worst of helping people. It never stopped. You lent a person five pounds to settle a bill and before you knew it you were educating their children. He felt annoyed.

'I'm awfully sorry, Mrs Garrard,' he said, looking at the clock and opening the door again, 'but I'm in a great hurry. The Lady Almoner's the person to ask, anyway, not me.'

'I didn't like to. She seemed so busy.'

'Well, so am I,' he said, so nastily that he immediately had to shut the door again and say: 'What sort of work do you want?' to compensate, not to her, but to himself for the unkindness which might otherwise spoil his peace of mind.

'It would be domestic work, sir. I'm a trained house-parlour-maid. That would be the only thing I could do,' she said defeatedly. 'I thought perhaps you might know some-one who wanted – You see, I don't know anyone.' As before, she was throwing herself on his hands, piling on to him the obligation of settling her fate. It would be funny if that horse-faced nurse came in. How shocked she would be to find the great Wimpole Street practitioner, before whom she seemed to think one should strew palms and cover one's head with sackcloth, being treated like a one-man domestic agency in the King's Road. Ruth ought to be here. She wouldn't see anything funny in it. Servants to her were a problem as serious as tuberculosis. She flung herself heart and soul into finding kitchen-maids for perfect strangers with whom she got into conversation in tea-shops. She loved it. She – That was an idea.

'Look here,' he said, grabbing desperately at the chance to free himself from this woman whose helplessness was so compelling. 'You ought to go and see my wife. She might be able to help you.' The woman's face did not even light up. She absorbed his suggestion as unemotionally as a sea anemone, and waited for more. He put down his case, fished in his waistcoat pocket for a card and thrust it at her.

'Here,' he said. 'Go and see her. Tell her I sent you in case I forget,' and escaped.

By the time Steven had seen his patients in the two

medical wards and had a cup of tea and a cinnamon cake and a dissertation on the Swedish technique of subcutaneous salines from Sister Grainger, it was nearly six o'clock. He collected his hat and case from the Honorary's Room, with its leather arm-chairs which were never sat in, its grate which never held a fire, its ashtrays which it seemed nobody's job to empty, and walked across the gravel space before the hospital to the railings where his car stood between an ambulance and the Pathologist's little biscuit tin on wheels.

The sun, balancing on the roofs of the houses across the road, gave the square, grey hospital its most becoming aspect of the day. Washed with an almost Alpine glow, every window answering the sun like a heliograph, it had a certain splendour, set as it was on the crest of the town, like an Italian hill chapel built as near as possible to Heaven. But with the sun fallen from its perch and slipping away behind the roofs, with the bricks of the hospital grown cold and grey again and every window gone out, it was once more a brooding prison, set up there to remind the town tumbling away all round that disease was a crime.

Young Potter, Steven's house-physician, walked to the car with him, conscious of being part of the impressive spectacle of two medical men in consultation. He was a fat boy from Cornwall, with a face like pink plasticine and grey flannel trousers that were too short and too tight in the thigh. Nurse Cope, watching them from the window of a ward kitchen where she was making Benger's, was amused at the way he copied Steven's walk: hands in pockets, making the trousers even tighter, head lowered thoughtfully, with a quick jerk sideways and up to acknowledge a remark. He would be keeping his squashy lips almost closed when he talked, as he remembered to do except when he was excited. After working for Steven for six months, he had acquired a cartoon of his bedside manner. Taking a case history in the ward, for instance, he would approach the bed unhurriedly: Steven never rushed, however busy he was, because as he was always busy, it took more than that to jerk him out of his stride. Young Potter would have his stethoscope round his neck, white coat hanging open, with hands in the pockets and head slightly bent. Steven was tall, and so used to listening to people that this slight inclination of his neck had become habitual. To young Potter, who was shorter than most people, it was inconvenient, and necessitated looking up from under his yellow brows with a trustful air.

It was sometimes quite difficult to catch the attention of a nurse, but it didn't do to get your own screens.

'Oh – Nurse!' he would call to a flying figure, 'could you bring the odd screen, and the sphyg, please, and – you know – all the trappings?' The nurse delegated the job to someone else, who probably passed it on to someone still more junior, who could be heard to say, as she wheeled up a screen over his foot: 'Oh, dash, must I stay with him? I'm in the middle of bathing Granny.'

Steven, of course, would have been surrounded by over-eager women with their cuffs on. For his house physician, an eighteen-year-old girl with rolled-up sleeves and a splashed apron would poke her head round the screens and say: 'Will you shout when you've taken the history, and I'll come and chaperone you while you examine.' Young Potter would incline his head courteously, sit down with his knees together, lean forward and say: 'Now, madam, or young lady, or sir, or old chap,' according to the patient, 'let's hear all about it.' He had all Steven's tricks, such as listening gravely to trifles and finding a joke in more frightening things, except that his jokes were so ponderous that the patient often took them seriously and digested with horror the information that young Potter was going to amputate her leg at the thigh with a rusty penknife.

When they reached the car, Nurse Cope saw Steven pause with one foot on the running board, jingling his money in his pocket. Young Potter drew patterns in the gravel with a splay-toed shoe, looking up from under his forehead.

'I'll bring the radium down next week,' Steven was saying, 'so get that woman in in good time because she's a bit nervous. Ran a terrific blood pressure when I had her in before for observation.'

'Ah, suggested hysteria,' mumbled Potter, who liked to have everything safely labelled.

'I expect so,' Steven smiled. 'Well, I think that's everything. Don't forget I want that old man to have some blood tonight, and you can give him another pint in a few days' time if there's no further hæmatemesis. But watch him.'

'Right, sir. Oh, I say, sir, by the way –' Young Potter took a step forward, his ears crimson against his yellow hair. 'I wonder if you could do something for me?'

Steven shut the door of the car again resignedly. He supposed he would get away some time.

'It's like this, sir. I've only got another three months here, you know, and I've got a faint chance of getting into the London General. I'd be under Sir George Levinson, and I wondered if you could possibly put in a word for me. I thought you'd probably know him.'

Steven did know Sir George. Knew, too, how the fierce old man with the Rabbi beard and sarcastic eyes made pulp of all but the brightest and best of young men. He would not thank Steven for young Potter, and young Potter probably would not thank Steven for the pounding his doughy intellect would receive at the London General. However, he shut the door of the car again and took out his diary to make a note.

'I'll do what I can for you, of course, but I can't guarantee that he'll take you. And if he does, you'll have to work like a black to made the grade with him. You realize that?'

'Oh, of course, sir. I will. It's tremendously good of you, sir. I knew you would. I'm awfully keen to get the job – I mean – I hope you didn't mind my asking, but I knew you'd help me if you could.' Young Potter bubbled, forgetting to keep his lips together.

That was just it; people took it for granted that you would help them. That was why they were always asking you, getting you involved in things like fitting this very round peg into the square hole of being old Levinson's houseman, and as often as not holding you responsible if it didn't work. He would write a diplomatic letter to the old man, and he could take the boy or leave him as he saw fit. And as for young Potter – he'd give him his chance, and after that, the boy would have to make his own way. Steven was not going to get involved in his doubtful career. So he told himself, seeing, however, quite clearly the visits and letters, the requests for advice and help, the haunting of his doorstep by young Potter as by so many others before him in the past and undoubtedly in the future. It seemed that you could not travel through life without accumulating dependents, like stones in your shoes.

'All right, old boy. I'll see what I can do.' He opened the door and got in, folding at the waist and drawing his long legs after him. Young Potter sketched a cheerful salute as he drove off, and turned to go back across the gravel. Nurse Cope, who would wave at anything in trousers, leaned out of the window, disappearing suddenly as Sister came into the kitchen to enquire whether the gastrics were ever going to get their feeds.

Ugly had been folded up on the back seat, coiled bonelessly round himself like a Chelsea bun. As soon as Steven got in, he jumped into the front beside him in two moves, first his front half and then his long black legs, scrambling and slipping down the back of the seat.

'Ugly, for the Lord's sake –' Steven held his arm over his face, but the dog dodged it, dabbing wetly and slobbering, his ears pinned back and his eyes bulging. Steven fought him off enough to get the engine started and the gears engaged and drove out of the hospital gates with Ugly pressing hard against his left arm as if determined to leave as many white hairs as possible on his black coat.

Ugly was the satisfactory result of a mixture of most of the larger breeds of dog, His broad, snaky head was pure bull terrier as far as the ears, which were collie. He had a strong, deep-chested Alsatian body, a lurcher's back legs, and there was foxhound about in his stubby, turned-in front paws, the banner carriage of his tail and the pattern of his black-and-white coat. He would sometimes stiffen at things like a pointer, and faint memories of sheepdog ancestry were inconveniently stirred by things like the grubby flock in Hyde Park. He was as sentimental as a spaniel, as fey as a pedigree borzoi and as self-conscious as a young girl at her first dance. Steven had acquired him four years ago on a holiday in Cornwall. He and Carol had found him in a farmyard during one of the walks on which Ruth would never come because of the wind. The dog was chained up in a kind of dugout under a rainwater tank, and the condition of his white neck was evidence that he had been chained up all his life.

Carol and Ugly had fallen for each other instantly. It was just one of those things. They had to buy him. The farmer, who up till now had grudged Ugly even his meagre keep, suddenly discovered how useful he was for herding the cows. Skilled labour, and priced accordingly.

Ruth did not like Ugly. She had wanted Steven to leave him in the Isle of Wight after that holiday three years ago. One of her stock phrases for months had been: 'Every time I look at that dog, it reminds me ...'

'Well, why shouldn't it?' Steven would say in a voice made curt by misery. 'I don't intend to forget Carol.'

As soon as they were clear of the town, Steven stopped to let down the roof of the coupé. He had not done it earlier because, once before, young Potter's help had made of this quite simple operation a complicated and lop-sided affair, which had resulted in the car having to go to a garage before the roof could be got up again.

Steven let Ugly out, and he disappeared into a field with an impossible standing leap over a gate. When Steven was ready to go, he sat in the car and whistled, and pipped the horn until the dog appeared on the other side of the gate, apparently quite unable to jump back.

'Oh, come on, Ugly,' said Steven, leaning over to open the left-hand door. 'If you got over, you can get back. Come on! Over! Over, boy!' He raised his voice in exhortation, slapping the seat beside him, but Ugly, who seemed to have forgotten how to work his back legs, went into a frenzy and tried to squeeze through the space under the gate that might possibly have admitted a terrier. Having got his flat, snaky head through he was stuck there, with front legs prone and hind-quarters sticking up in the air with madly waving tail. His agonized eyes bulged like a hyperthyroid as Steven, cursing mildly, got out and came round to the gate. He pushed back the dog's head and patted the top bar, making high, encouraging noises and sweeps of his arm. Ugly backed and bent his hocks for the spring, his forelegs trampling like a horse. Steven found that his knees were bent too, in the effort to will the dog over the gate, but nothing came of it. Ugly simply went on trampling, making no effort to jump, his whole being yelling out: 'I can't, I can't!'

'Blast you!' said Steven, and applied himself to untying the wire that fastened the gate.

Sucking a torn finger, he started off again for London, with Ugly balanced in a half-sitting position, peering ahead for new joys, until a sudden stop bumped his nose on the windscreen and he retired into his Chelsea-bun position and was instantly asleep.

In that summer of 1939, driving in a hurry up the Great West Road was like trying to do the old-fashioned waltz on a crowded floor. It was enough to make a misanthrope of the most benevolent motorist.

Nobody's journey could possibly be as urgent as yours. Everyone else was a criminal driver, a menace to the public. Lorries with fat behinds were in league to straddle the road in front of you. Traffic lights conspired to turn red at your approach. All these silly-looking people being borne through space in a sitting posture – these flat-headed youths, girls with faces all mouth, like a gashed turnip tied up in a gaudy scarf, the seemly bowler-hatted, beetling along as if on tracks, the opulent, so used to being driven that the backs of their chauffeurs' necks were as familiar as their own faces in the mirror, the middle-aged woman anxiously semaphoring her automatic signals, the coach driver, aware that he would come off best in a collision – all these had taken to the road for the sole purpose of balking you.

There were two techniques to deal with the problem of getting in or out of London between six and seven on a summer evening. One was to trickle gently along, keeping a uniform distance from the man in front, stopping when he stopped and starting when he started instead of at the amber light, keeping your finger off the horn and your eye off the clock, worrying not, because if you were late, you were late and, short of fitting a gyrocopter device to your car and lifting it out of the ruck, there was nothing you could do about it. The other way was to rush up as close as possible to the car in front and then jam on your brakes, changing down immediately and keeping the clutch almost engaged, quivering under your foot like an eager horse, so that you could shoot forward as soon as the other man, stung by your horn, moved ponderously on. Steven favoured the latter method. At least it gave the illusion of speed.

As he crawled and stopped and started and darted into momentary gaps, Steven found himself planning his evening over and over again, making a mental timetable of his visits, judging how soon he could be home. Ten minutes for putting the car away: dinner, with the evening paper and that article of Blanchard's on burns which he had been meaning to read for the last three days; cigarette, listen to the news, then into his consulting-room and get out the typewriter and the big crammed blotter with the picture of what looked like the Duke of Windsor in a top hat, jumping a six-barred gate on a yellow horse.

If he was lucky with the traffic lights, he could be at Mrs Casson's by seven. A quarter of an hour with her – that would get him to the Marshall kid on the other side of the Park by half-past. Another quarter of an hour there – more like thirty minutes if Marion Marshall were at home. That would get him to Mrs Dudley soon after eight at the latest. He would leave that piece at the nursing home until last as it was only a minute from his house. Better, perhaps, to put the car away first and walk round. Blast this crawling bunch of prams in front! if he didn't get past them Heaven knew when he would get to town. Say twenty minutes with Mrs Casson, if the husband was in and offered him a drink, which was unlikely. He could take the short cut through Lisson Grove ...

Several times he caught himself at this fruitless worrying and planning. It was a habit which had grown on him recently, particularly when he was tired or busy. The trouble about mapping things out and anticipating your spare time was that you were childishly disappointed when things did not turn out to schedule.

Waiting for the lights at Heston Road, he was already in spirit letting himself in through his front door with the semi-circular fanlight. The hall clock would be showing half-past eight, and Ugly would dash for the kitchen stairs, his nails rattling on the linoleum as he skidded down to his enamel pie dish. Ten minutes from Mrs Dudley to the nursing home, another fifteen there – ten, if he could manage it without being rude – Stop it, Steven.

'Compulsion neurosis,' he said aloud. 'I'll be counting buttons next, Ugly,' and put out a hand to jam the dog's face into his neck in the kind of crude caress he liked. Ugly woke, half rose, and crashed into the windscreen as the baby Ford in front with the girls in white rabbit capes and artificial flowers swerved to avoid a doubled-up cyclist in a black alpaca coat who suddenly decided to make a dash for Richmond.

Mrs Eularia Casson was tiresome, but profitable. She suffered from chronic sciatica, which became acute whenever her husband neglected her for his business or her son for the sleek and screaming social set into which Casson's jams had bought him. She lived halfway up Fitzjohn's Avenue in a house which sprouted balconies and red spires in unnecessary places. Before it, a rock garden at which nobody ever looked was cultivated expensively. On the gravel space between that and the house stood a dark blue Packard complete with chauffeur, and Master Casson's green Jaguar, complete with automobile club badges and chromium girl poised nude on the radiator cap.

The chauffeur, who was rubbing up bits of the Packard with a chamois leather, paused to give Steven's grey Buick the glance of a racehorse's groom who can afford to admire a good-looking hunter, and made a lazy movement as if to open the door for him. But Steven was out of the car and up the front steps before he got there. A manservant opened one half of the double doors.

In the hall Mr Casson was being helped into his overcoat by an acid-looking maid.

'Ah, there you are, Sheppard,' he said, 'My wife's been expecting you since teatime. She's had a very bad day.'

'So sorry,' said Steven. 'I can never get here before this on Thursdays.'

'Ah yes, busy – who isn't?' said Mr Casson, a pear-shaped fruit-farmer's son from New Zealand who modelled himself on Hollywood's idea of a business executive, even, as Steven knew, down to the dyspepsia. 'Just off to a conference myself – at this time of night. These damn' war scares.'

'D'you think anything'll happen just yet?' asked Steven, thinking of something that often came into his mind.

'Might do,' said Mr Casson, nodding wisely and trying to make a grim line of his fleshy lips. 'Shouldn't be surprised if we weren't all in khaki before the year's out.' He braced his plump shoulders gallantly and adjusted before the mirror the black homburg which the manservant handed him.

'I would try and get into the Navy,' said Steven, voicing his thought.

'Oh, don't worry. They won't take you,' said Mr Casson, holding out a short arm and waggling a finger for his stick and gloves. 'They wouldn't take an eminent consultant.'

They wouldn't take you either with those flat feet and that pot-belly, you silly old porpoise, thought Steven, waiting, like a man come about the plumbing, for the maid to finish brushing off Mr Casson, and show him upstairs.

Mrs Casson was one of those vast, unbendable people who never look comfortable, even in bed. And this was a wonderful bed like a spreadeagled cloud, with apricot silk drapings on the wall at its head to match the shimmering counterpane. The part of Mrs Casson which was under the bedclothes looked like a bolster stuffed in by a truant schoolboy to deceive the dormitory prefect, and the part above toppled sideways off the pillows, in a straining nightdress cut low. She wore very white powder and orange lips whose pointed bow went up to her nostrils. Flat black curls were pulled out from under a chiffon turban. An electric fire burned in the grate, and the curtains of the west window were drawn against the evening sun. At the other window, the branch of a may-tree in the garden tapped vainly at the glass. The room smelt of Mrs Casson, and of Mrs Casson's friend in monkey fur, who sat in the arm-chair with a cocktail. Mrs Casson always tried to have somebody there when Steven came. She was proud of him.

The acid maid opened the door, looked down her blade of nose and said: 'Dr Sheppard, madam.'

Enter Steven suavely, saying: 'Well, well, well. I'm sorry to see you laid low again, Mrs Casson.' Then catching sight of the friend in a hat like one of the Dolomites tied up with cyclamen ribbon: 'Oh, excuse me. Am I interrupting something?'

'No, no, of course not,' said Mrs Casson, holding out her hand to him, palm down, as if she expected him to kiss it. 'Loretta will excuse us. This is Dr Sheppard, darling – Mrs Schumacher.'

'How do you do?' said Steven. 'So sorry to disturb you,

but we shan't keep you away long.' Loretta would have liked to stay and listen, and Mrs Casson would not have minded her staying either, to hear what a deep interest Steven took in her symptoms, but he stepped back and held the door open, so that Loretta had to rise and go out, appraising him swiftly as she did so, and considering consulting him about her catarrh.

When he had had just about all he could stand of Mrs Casson, Steven made taking her pulse an excuse to look at his watch. He had been here nearly a quarter of an hour. Time to go if he was ever going to get home tonight. All he had to do now was to cut short tactfully the martyred narrative which she had resumed immediately he stopped counting her pulse. He made one or two false starts which she brushed aside like flies, until he managed to catch on to a phrase and stop her.

'Can't sleep at night, h'm?' he murmured with concern. 'That won't do at all. I'll give you something for that. I believe there's a chemist at Swiss Cottage who doesn't shut till eight. If you could send someone out for it, you'll be sure of getting a good night tonight.'

He took his gold pencil and prescription pad out of his breast pocket and scribbled. While he was writing, Mrs Casson started to talk again, her eyes taking on the glaze of people who talk at length about themselves, but Steven rose determinedly. He carried himself away on a wave of heartiness, was aware that the acid maid thought him too breezy, and found that he had let himself in for giving Loretta a lift down to Swiss Cottage to get the sleeping draught.

On the way down the hill she told him about her catarrh, fishing for free advice, like people did at cocktail parties. Well, she wasn't going to get it. Nor, as he made quite clear by shaking hands with her on the pavement outside the chemist, was she going to get driven back up the hill.

As she turned to go into the shop, he saw without chagrin Ugly had bequeathed her some of his white hairs from the front seat of the car.

Two years as a London doctor had taught him all the short cuts. He knew which ways were best at certain times of day, which traffic lights could be trusted to turn green for you when you crossed the rubber bar, and which were interminable, like those at the Charlotte and Goodge Street crossroads. He was soon in the Park, heading for Chelsea. They had finished those trenches at last. Funny how, after the first shock, one hardly noticed them. The Czechoslovakian business last year had prepared one for the idea of war. Everyone talked about it quite glibly now, almost eagerly, even the people who had fought in the last war and, according to C. E. Montague and Hemingway and Remarque, should have been embittered. Steven himself had been at school for most of it. War to him had meant not getting enough to eat, and seeing chaps, with whom a few months ago he had been playing cricket, come back to address the school in the glory of a uniform that had been in the Flanders trenches and seeing the names of other chaps go up on the lengthening roll of honour. As soon as he could, he joined the Navy, renouncing dramatically to himself his medical ambitions. After three months' training, and three uneventful ones cruising up and down the East Coast in an armed trawler, he realized with a sense of frustrated heroism that the war was over, and he could, after all, start learning to be a doctor at a reasonable age.

Although people talked big about crusading, and fighting for freedom and to rid the world of Fascism, everyone's private ideas about war were coloured by how it would affect them personally. Many young people secretly looked forward to it as a new sensation, and there were people like himself to whom it offered a possible solution of personal problems.

Or was it because nobody believed, even then, that it would really happen, that most of us awaited it with such equanimity? Trenches were being dug in the Park, certainly, but – fighting in the Park – it was unthinkable, London could never be bombed. One had heard stories of air raids in the last war, of people trekking to the Underground, or welcoming a wet and stormy night, of the Zepp coming down at Cuffley, one had even been shown where the bomb had fallen so close – only half a mile away! – but it all had the quality of a fairy tale.

Marion Marshall was at home. She opened the front door to him herself: 'Stee – ven!' and raised herself out of her glossy little court shoes to give him a feathery kiss. The relationship between Steven and the Marshalls had gone beyond doctor and patient a long time ago. Marion had been one of his first patients when he bought the Dynsford practice. She and George Marshall had a week-end cottage nearby, and she had adopted Steven when he came to London.

Her story was that it was she who had persuaded him into Wimpole Street and, once there, had practically made him. She was one of those big-hearted people who bestowed her discoveries like largesse. It was always: 'If you're going to Paris, you must stop at the Bretonne – it's the *only* place,' or, 'You must try my hairdresser for your new perm,' or 'My little tailor'll make your suit: I'll give you a letter,' or, 'My dear, you must go to my doctor. He's the only man!' She offered Steven for everything, from ear, nose and throat to psycho-analysis.

Periodically she discovered some new universal healer – an osteopath or a dietician, or a man who could cure everything by stroking the back of your neck. Her latest was a man who called himself a Logical Naturopath and who argued that, since man was fundamentally an ape, his salvation lay in getting back to nuts. She had only called Steven in to a daughter with scarlet fever when coconut milk and concentrated cashew pills had failed to exorcise the rash.

'Heaven knows how many people she's given it to by now,' Steven had said, grimly giving his orders about isolation and carbolic-soaked sheets to the old retainer who had been Marion's Nanny, and had since preserved sanity in that household for a number of years.

Marion took Steven upstairs. 'It's just like a hospital,' she said delightedly, sniffing the disinfected air outside her daughter's room. 'I think it's too wonderful the way you've fixed it so Gilly could stay here. I dreaded her having to go to a fever hospital; they always come back with something else. They do, you know. Cross infection.' She stared up at Steven solemnly from under her bubble of sand-coloured curls. 'Nancy Jordon's boy came out of one door after scarlet, and went in at another with diphtheria. I read in a book once that it was safer to have a baby in the filthiest tenement, with no doctor or midwife, than in the most modern hospital.'

Steven laughed. 'How is Gilly, anyway?' he asked.

'Well, I think she's distinctly better. Nanny won't have it, of course, but she always hopes for the worst.'

Steven held aside the carbolic-soaked sheet and opened the door for her, and they went into the room which had been Gillian's night nursery, bare now of carpet and pictures and furniture. The fourteen-year-old girl, her square-cut, tawny hair falling over her flushed face, was sitting up in bed in one of her mother's Angora bedjackets, a tray full of small china animals on her lap.

'Hullo, Steven,' she said without looking up. 'How's Ugly?'

'Oh, he's fine, thanks. Sent you a wet lick.' Steven put on one of the white gowns which hung inside the door and tied a gauze mask over his nose and mouth. Marion copied him, wiggling her nose like a rabbit under the mask, her wide open eyes amused.

'I feel just as if I was going to perform a major operation,' she said, as they approached the bed. Looking up from her complicated game with the animals, her daughter exploded into giggles, which passed from snorts to a fit of coughing.

'What's so funny?' asked Marion with dignity.

'You are,' gasped her daughter. 'Oh, dash, you've started my eyes running now. Where's my hankie?' She scrabbled among the pillows, spilling the animals on to the eiderdown.

'I suppose you don't bother to dress up when I'm not here,'

said Steven, mumbling more than ever behind the mask. 'Now look, Marry, I told you. If you won't stick to the rules I'll have to move her to a fever hospital.'

'But I do!' Her vehemence damped the gauze over her mouth. 'I spend my day soaking linen and boiling things up. I've broken most of the old nursery cups already.'

'Hm.' Steven put his hand over the child's wrist. 'How are you, Gilly?'

'Oh, she's much better today,' said Marion, pushing up her mask so that she could talk better. 'I gave her some walnut tea last night. It's worked wonders.'

'Look here,' said Steven, getting out his stethoscope, 'I wish you wouldn't do these things. Who's supposed to be treating the child, you or me?'

'Oh, you, of course, my dear, in your funny old-fashioned way.' Marion gave a trill of laughter. 'You'll have to move with the times if you want to keep your customers. M and B! That went out with the Spanish War.'

'Oh, really?' said Steven. 'I didn't know. Quiet a minute, will you, while I listen for any rattles.' Marion could not keep quiet for long. Gillian's chest glowed like a boiled lobster and she took the opportunity of her pyjamas being open to have a scratch. Steven pushed her hand away and slapped it lightly. 'Good sign, though, the itch,' he said. 'Any peeling yet?' Gillian did not bother to answer, as she knew her mother would do it for her. 'Any earache? Pains in the back? Ever feel weepy?' Gillian pulled the tray up again and began retrieving the china animals.

'Don't bother,' said Marion. 'I know all the complications. I'll tell you if any start.'

The door opened to admit Nanny in a sagging brown woollen dress, her pepper-and-salt hair screwed into a kind of biscuit on top of her head. She came up to the bed with a jug of lemonade and began to thump the pillows.

'Nanny,' said Marion sternly. 'How many times have I told you you *must* put on an overall?'

'Tchah,' said Nanny. 'I haven't time for fancy dress. And

that's the first time I've seen you in one, come to that.'

Steven, putting away his stethoscope and pencil torch, sighed. 'I'll have to have a talk with George,' he said. 'Perhaps he can make you see reason.'

'Oh, Nanny's maundering,' said Marion. 'Anyway, Steven, I read in a magazine the other day that all these precautions are absolutely out. Infection's an entirely mental thing, this man said. If you're afraid of a disease, you catch it. If you're not, you don't. Look at Ehrlich. He never caught syph.'

'Look at Macfaddyen,' retorted Steven, taking off his gown and going to the basin. 'He died of typhoid.'

'He'd had it once, anyway. That was why he studied it. Didn't you know? Come on down, and I'll give you a drink.'

'I won't stop, Marion, thanks awfully,' said Steven, as they went downstairs. 'I've got some more cases to see, and I'm late already.'

'Oh, Stee-ven, you must. I've mixed you one.'

'Honestly, Marion, I'd rather get on. And it doesn't look well to go breathing gin all over patients.'

'Oh, come on.' Marion pushed him into the drawing-room. 'Don't be so unfriendly. I never see you, and when I do, you're curt. I don't like you so much since you became a fashionable consultant. You never used to be so smug in the old Dynsford days. You ought to relax. It's all a question of breathing. I'll show you one day ... Anyway, George wants to see you, don't you darling?'

'Don't I what?' a voice came over the back of a high arm-chair.

'Want to see Steven.'

'I saw him at lunch. He's promised to come down to the cottage this week-end.'

'Well. If that isn't typical,' said Marion. 'You keep away from us for months and months, and then when you know I'm safely stuck in town with Gilly, you and George go galli-vanting off to the cottage together. I know what you'll be like, too. You'll get so silly. George will open the 1865 brandy

64

and you'll still be sitting in the dining-room at two o'clock in the morning thinking you're awfully witty. And next time I go down I shall find an atmosphere in the kitchen.'

'Ruth's coming, too,' said George, blotting out this vision, 'and you know you asked Annette and Stewart.'

'Oh yes, of course. Ruth. Well, that's nice, though I don't think she enjoyed herself much last time.'

'In any case,' Steven said, 'I don't know definitely yet that I can make it. I'll have to wait and see how work goes.'

'Oh, you're impossible.' Marion refilled her glass from the shaker and then said all the things to Steven that George had said at lunch. 'Incidentally,' she concluded, 'if you can find time to get down to that dreary hospital once a week, you can find time to come to us. It's exactly five miles farther on. I'm going to abandon the child on Sunday and come down for the day, and if I find you not there, I'll – well, I'll get another doctor.'

'Suits me,' said Steven. 'You never pay my bills, anyway.'

Presently, he saw that he was ten minutes later than he had planned, and started to leave. Pity. He liked George and Marion. It would have been nice to have stayed chatting and drinking with them, and then had dinner and bridge. It would be nice to be the sort of person who could do that.

Marion took him down. On the stairs, she said: 'You know, I've been thinking: you ought to go in for psycho-analysis. You'd be good at it. You've got compelling eyes.'

Steven laughed. 'But I do, up to a point. How could I practise medicine without it? I see almost as many neuroses as organic troubles, only the victims don't know it.'

'I've discovered the most marvellous man,' said Marion handing him one of George's hats. 'I'm going to be done. He draws things out of you, they say, the way Yogis draw out their small intestines. Steven, take me to the ballet to-night. I've got two tickets, and George won't come. He wants to listen to a boxing match.'

'Oh, Marry, I can't possibly.' He had found his own hat and was opening the door. 'I've got masses to do. I told you.'

'Oh, do. We could have dinner afterwards. As a patient, Steven, take me. My ego needs to sit next to you and watch *L'Aprés-Midi.*'

'Take your psycho-analyst, then,' said Steven, going down the steps.

'When'll you come again?' Marion swung in the doorway like a schoolgirl.

'Oh – couple of days. She'll be all right.'

'Come tomorrow. I'd feel happier,' said Marion, her face suddenly serious.

Doctors do not notice very much what nurses look like. Fortunately, nurses don't realize this, or they might give up trying.

Steven always noticed Nurse Morrison, however. She was worth looking at, and had legs that even black stockings could not hush. He had got to know her when she was a staff nurse at St Margaret's, and now that she had finished experimenting with midwifery, industrial nursing and the psychological care of the mentally defective and settled down as a private nurse, he often called her in to his cases. She was tall and supple, with a beautifully made-up olive skin, and every hair of her black pageboy bob in place. Even amid the storm of ward life she had remained *soignée*, and now that she was in calmer waters she was as impeccable as a modern dairy.

Steven found her feeding Mrs Dudley's new-born baby, a neat papoose in a snowy shawl. Babies never cried or got the wind or were sick when Nurse Morrison fed them. Mrs Dudley, a little chicken of a woman in bed in the next room, looked more contented than ever before in her life. She was doing her nails while her husband read the paper to her. He was a man of no opinions, least of all of himself, and sought refuge behind thick black-rimmed spectacles. For the satisfaction of getting the best for his wife, he was paying Steven a lot of money which he could not afford, yet he jumped up guiltily when Steven came in and fell over his feet on the way out.

Mrs Dudley had nearly died having her baby, could not feed it now, would never be able to have another, and would probably cause her husband great anxiety all her life. They both looked on Steven as a god, drinking in his pronouncements and performing with unquestioning reverence his slightest instruction. Mr Dudley would have shifted the whole house round on its foundations if he had mentioned that it faced the wrong way. Steven, who had been called in a week after the baby was born, had not told them that he could never cure Mrs Dudley's anæmia. He knew that this was the kind of thing that people who had read *The Citadel* called hanging on to a lucrative case. And was it? Or was it because he knew that Mrs Dudley's faith in him would keep her going as no treatment could? He hardly knew himself. He never had time to analyse his motives. Decisions had to be made instinctively.

In the adjoining room Nurse Morrison had tucked the weedy baby down into the position it liked best. She reported to Steven no more and no less than he wanted to know. He grunted and looked at her charts, which were works of art.

'Like this job all right?' he asked.

'Oh yes, sir, it's grand. Mrs Dudley's very easy. *He's* more trouble, really. Gets so embarrassed making conversation to me at meals. I'm sure I give him indigestion.'

'Shouldn't wonder,' said Steven. Her dress was short and her black stockings as sheer as a Parisian widow's. When he had his own nursing home he was going to have Nurse Morrison as Matron. 'Are you free after this job?' he asked.

'I've got three weeks to spare, sir, between this and another maternity case. But I'd rather thought of standing myself a little holiday.'

'Well, think again,' said Steven. 'I want you to take on an arterio-sclerotic newspaper proprietor. If anyone can keep him from having a stroke you can. His present nurse is knocking off just in time to avoid having one herself.'

'Well, sir, I had promised myself that holiday,' said Nurse

Morrison, who had enough attractive men of her own to be unimpressed by any charm Steven might use on her.

'Of course, if you think you can't tackle it,' he murmured, picking up his case.

'Of course not, sir. Naturally, I'll do it if you really want me.' Nurse Morrison decided that perhaps she needed the money more than the holiday, and Steven left, telling himself how well he knew how to handle women.

By the average mean time of the various clocks along Oxford Street, it was eight o'clock. Passing a restaurant window dressed with cold chickens and tomatoes and a pyramid of polished apples, Steve felt hungry. Lunch with George seemed a long time ago, and no stomach could recognize Sister Grainger's cinnamon cakes as tea. Only one more call to make now, and that was going to be as quick as was compatible with giving that tiresome woman her money's worth of Sheppard. He could be home by half-past at the latest; that still left plenty of evening. Ruth would probably not be back before eleven. She usually stayed fairly late when she went out to dinner alone, because without Steven to make faces at her, she never could find her way out.

From the profusion of flowers and tropical fruit in Mrs Maclaren's room at the nursing home, you would think she had had far more than her appendix removed. Framed in an odorous bower, banked by woolly animals with bows, boxes of chocolate, all the latest novels and glossy magazines, baskets of peaches and pineapple, and an exorbitant melon that would go bad before she thought to give it away, she pouted at Steven in a white nightdress, which, with its high frilled neck and long sleeves, would have been decorously Victorian if it had not been completely transparent.

He wished she would not call him 'Sheppy' in front of the nurses. A svelte girl in a white army square, with the frustrated surely-it-was-not-for-this-that-I-endured-my-training expression of nurses in luxury nursing homes, was arranging a vase of carnations on the dressing-table, which Mrs Maclaren had had shifted so that she could see herself in it at all hours without bothering to pick up a hand mirror.

Steven well-welled and how-jollied about among the flowers for a bit while Mrs Maclaren lay back and waited for him to approach. His exaggerated heartiness was an attempt to ward off the note of husky intimacy which Mrs Maclaren always manœuvred to strike. The nurse, who should have been off duty at eight, hovered meaningly by the door, but when Steven said: 'Don't bother to wait, Nurse. I shan't need you,' Mrs Maclaren remembered her orange juice cooling in the refrigerator. Could Vickey possibly be a pet, if it wouldn't make her too late for her date? Wasn't this charming, this gay intimacy with the nurse? her eyes asked Steven. Nurse Vickers responded graciously and refrained from slamming the door behind her, thinking: She'd better come across with a pretty good present when she goes, that's all.

'Well, now,' said Steven. 'Sister tells me you had your stitches out yesterday.'

'Thank goodness it's over.' She closed her eyes for a moment. 'Sir Bruce came and took them out himself.' He would, thought Steven. Fergie was one of those surgeons who always came along with pomp and circumstance to do little things that the nurses could have done on their heads. He had once come every day to give liver extract injections into a Cabinet Minister's buttock – at a guinea a time.

'He's a charmer, isn't he?' purred Mrs Maclaren. So this was to be her line to-day: she was to make him insanely jealous by keeping on about another man. Last time her scheme had been to snuggle and pet a toy panda, and the time before, to lie back in an abandonment of wan appeal. Quite interesting, really, to study her technique, if it had not been such a waste of time.

'I thought you'd be coming this morning,' said Mrs Maclaren, who had been doing her face at intervals since nine o'clock, and had forgone her afternoon sleep for fear of disarranging her burnished copper hair.

'No,' said Steven gallantly. 'I've been working hard all day. Left my pleasant tasks till the end. Keeping the good wine, you know.'

Mrs Maclaren bridled like a short-necked pony. Amazing how women like this fell for such elementary stuff. By such easy efforts was a fashionable popularity maintained. She would probably never be ill again, yet Steven knew that she would continue to consult him at intervals. Well, it was her money; let her waste it if she wanted to. Steven could do with it, although he grudged the time which should have been spent on real cases. Life would be so simple if one did not have to make money.

Mrs Maclaren was glad the nurse had gone out. So was Steven, but for a different reason. It was more difficult to do his act if there were someone sensible in the audience. Mrs Maclaren seemed quite satisfied with the act, and continued with hers, enlarging on the charm and skill of the surgeon, who was probably unaware of what any part of her except her abdomen looked like, and finishing up: 'You shouldn't recommend attractive surgeons, you know, Sheppy. You don't want people poaching on your ground. Have a drinkie? There's some gin in that drawer and a spot of French somewhere. I usually have a nip about this time to ease my sufferings.'

'Sir Bruce know about this?'

'You bet!' She unleashed a trilling laugh. 'He had one too, last time. He's quite a gay bird. Won't you? Oh, you are a stooge.' She flopped back, snuggling her chin into the white chiffon frill, and made a pathetic grimace. 'Ow – me operation. It don't 'alf tweak.' Like all faintly common people, she couldn't speak Cockney. 'D'you think I'll have much of a scar?'

'D'you mind very much?'

She looked at him sideways. 'What do *you* think?'

'Here,' he said. 'I'm going before I commit myself.'

70

In the mews where Steven kept his car, the bandy little man from the garage next door was brushing out the wire-haired floor of his taxi.

'Evening,' said Steven, locking the double doors. 'Nice evening, Uncle.' This was not as familiar as it sounded, for the man's name was Mr Uncle, ironically, as his only nephew or niece was an abortive effort of his wife's sister's, with a deformed palate and a lolling head.

The childless Mrs Uncle, who dwelt above the garage in a rubber apron and curlers, suffered from the fact that all her husband's passions were centred in his taxi. It was a shining marvel, the round-bodied kind like a tram, with doors that slid open at the front, and whitewashed tyres. As a fanatical housewife will rush out with a hearthstone after a dirty-booted caller, so Uncle, ignoring all hails, would rush home with his flag down two or three times a day in puddly weather to clean off his wheels.

' 'Ning, sir.' He gave Steven the monosyllable which did for both ends of the day and went on hissing at the mat like an ostler.

'Looks a treat,' said Steven pausing to admire the taxi, whose plum-coloured buttock reflected him convexly, like a mirror in a fun fair. The spring evening was perfect now, pale blue above the slates and chimneys. A delicate breeze carried a hint of road tar and almond blossom. He had been looking forward to getting home, but now it seemed a pity to be going indoors, and there would be no evening left unless he did. It would be nice to be someone who did not have to piece their day together like a jigsaw puzzle, who could waste ten minutes or so chatting to picturesque characters in a mews, or could take an unpremeditated hour in the Park without feeling that because that hour was gone for ever the jigsaw would never come out. When he retired, he would live in a narrow Shropshire village in the lee of the Long Mynd and spend all day, if necessary, getting from one end of it to the other, in unprofitable rumination with the natives. And other days would go by without seeing a

71

soul, not even himself, because he would never bother to look in a mirror.

He whistled Ugly away from the garbage bins, turned right out of the mews and right again into Wimpole Street and then right again up his four black and white chequered steps to the front door, with its two brass plates over two bells on the right and on the left, its green hand-pull which said 'Servants', and long ago had made bells spring on coiled wires over the kitchen door.

Steven owned the lease of the tall Regency house, and sublet a ground-floor room to a dentist. They shared the waiting-room and the subscriptions to magazines, over the top of which patients would eye one another antagonistically, wondering who was for whom, and how long they would have to wait. He let himself into the polished, impersonal hall, and sorted out his own letters from the pile which must have come after Miss Minden had gone home. There was one for Ruth with a Malta postmark. Her sister Ursula. He left it there for her to see when she came in. Ugly had already disappeared round the hairpin bend to the kitchen stairs, up which came the smell of cutlets and cauliflower – good old Mrs Hankey. Steven hung up his hat and went upstairs, making for the cocktail cabinet in the drawing-room. Halfway up, at the turn of the stairs, an alcove overlooked the slit of paved garden at the back of the house. It had a cretonne window seat, and must have been an ideal sitting-out place in the days when the house entertained lavishly for taffetaed daughters with puffed-out hair and romantic fancies.

The noises of maids and hired footmen preparing supper would come up from the dining-room, and the innocent strains of a quartette would come down from the drawing-room, and, where they met, young men in narrow trousers would fiddle with the buttons on their gloves and wonder what on earth to say to flower-like, unapproachable girls who were also frantically searching their brains for the answer to the same question.

But nobody sat there now, except Ruth's mother, whose heart required a short rest on its laboured way up to the drawing-room. On one side of the window a tall mahogany stand held a vase of lupins, and on the other an inlaid grand-mother clock said half-past eight.

He would have dinner quickly, and then get down to work. Ruth had left the wireless on again. She wouldn't do that if she had to pay the electricity bill. But as he opened the drawing-room door he smelt eau-de-Cologne, and there she was in a chair by the grate filled with painted bullrushes, not reading or sewing or apparently listening to Eric Coates, just sitting waiting for Steven in the glazed chintz housecoat that buttoned up to the neck and made her bust look too big.

As a girl, she had been well-rounded and bright-com-plexioned, with a lot of chestnut hair which was her mother's pride. She had never cut it, and wore it now parted in the middle and flowing back to the loose coil on her neck in waves which she pinched in every night with combs. At thirty-five, she still had a very lovely skin, and there were women who felt it unjust that Ruth should achieve with only a limited technique the effect for which they suffered in beauty parlours and spent hours at their dressing-tables. Because she did not smoke and seldom drank, her skin was even good in the early morning. She had one of those narrow noses which never shine, and her hazel eyes, set too close together, were always clear, with the cornea so white as to be almost blue. She did not pluck her eyebrows, and al-though they were naturally a good shape, their heaviness made the space between them and her hairline even narrower. She had a weak chin, and had developed a habit of biting her lips and making little nervous grimaces with her mouth, so that you never saw now the soft, pretty shape of it which Steven had first known in the safe Isle of Wight days when nothing had been expected of her that she could not tackle, and her mother stood behind her like a solid wall.

When Steven married her, her figure had been self-supporting. Very pleasing she had looked in her wedding dress, which made the best of her full, firm young bosom and the creamy neck and shoulders on which her mother's pearls looked twice as good as on their owner's turtle throat. The photograph on the drawing-room piano showed her outside the church, her veil lifting in the Solent breeze, her head, on which the heavy hair was dressed too low, held high with pride at being safely anchored to the tall young man who stood easily beside her, his long fingers twined in hers, his stomach very flat and his legs very long in the perfectly-cut morning clothes, his hair as dark and glossy as his top hat.

But after the birth of their baby Ruth had never regained her figure. It was not fat she put on so much as weight, which had to be buoyed up and held in, and she lost the suppleness of her youth without losing its gaucheness of movement. At thirty she was already matronly, but neither poised nor graceful. She ran awkwardly, and walked heavily, and was clumsy with her hands. Mrs Hankey had forbidden her to wash up the glass or china, which Ruth did not mind, because domestic activities had no appeal for her. The only thing she could cook was sweets, which she sometimes made on Mrs Hankey's half-day, burning her fingers and spoiling her dinner by eating large quantities of toffee before it had time to set.

She had a box of chocolates on the table beside her now. She had just put one into her mouth when Steven came and she turned towards him chewing gently and dabbing at her lips with one of the chiffon handkerchiefs which she liked to wear twisted through her belt.

Steven knew that his voice should have risen when he said: 'Hullo, Ruth!' but before he could check himself it had dropped out on a note of disappointment.

'I thought you'd gone out to dinner, dear.' He crossed to the window, where the rosewood cocktail cabinet stood open with the light on inside.

Ruth twisted round and watched him over the arm of her chair, resting her chin on her hand. 'I couldn't be bothered.

I got as far as going up to have a bath, and then I suddenly thought of those awful peppery savouries that Betty always has, and I realized I didn't want to go at all. I don't know why I said I would, really, only she asked me over the phone and I couldn't think of an excuse in time.'

'I should have thought it was easier to think of an excuse over the telephone than to a person's face,' muttered Steven with his back to her.

'I'm afraid I've never been a good liar. I wish I was, really.' She watched him, smiling, 'I sometimes think that if I were ever unfaithful to you, you'd find out at once.'

'And have you been?' asked Steven, raising an empty bottle to the light. 'I say, what's happened to all the French?'

'Darling, *no*. How silly. Of course not.' Ruth giggled. 'Oh, look, I made you a drink. Don't mix one. It's there on the mantelpiece.' When Steven picked up the glass it left a wet ring on the paint.

'Wasn't Betty annoyed when you put her off at the last minute? She'd probably got two tables for bridge.'

'I didn't speak to her. I got Welsh to ring up and say I wasn't well. I haven't felt too bright all day anyway. It really was a relief not to have to go out. So I thought I'd stay in and keep you company. I want to talk to you about something, too. I'm very worried. What's the matter – don't you like that drink?'

'I see, now, where all the French has got to, that's all,' said Steven, looking at his glass with a wry face. 'Thanks all the same, old girl.' He went to the cocktail cabinet again.

'Well, you know I never could mix cocktails,' said Ruth complacently.

'Then why try to do it?' muttered Steven to the gin bottle. 'There's no ice, Ruth. Ring for that female.'

'Oh, I'd better not.' Ruth sat up. 'She'll just be bringing up the dinner now. I don't want to upset her again after this morning.'

'What about this morning?'

'That's what I want to talk to you about. But I won't tell

you now. Finish your drink, or bring it in with you, and go and wash and then I'll tell you all about it at dinner. I got some prawns.'

*

The original dining-room of the house, with its high ceiling, dark red dado and sepulchral fireplace had been on the ground floor, to the right of the front door. It was now the waiting-room, spiritually as well as materially transformed. It was not only that the massive, claw-footed table, which had seated twelve without a squeeze, had been replaced by a smaller, square piece of good mahogany, with a brass bowl of flowers and periodicals piled at the four points of the compass as if someone were going to play cards with them; it was not that the set of twelve high-backed chairs, two with arms for Mama and Papa, had given place to a more comfortable assortment; it was not that sailing pictures and Peter Scott geese now covered the faded patches made by darkling ancestral portraits, nor that the cavernous sideboard was gone – wheedled through the door Heaven knows how – but the whole atmosphere of the room was disinterested, transitory as a corridor. Once it had been a room where an incredible number of courses could be digested easily by the enzyme of conviviality. No one could have digested a poached egg in it now. Steven had taken over the furnishings of the professional part of the house from the doctor who had leased it before him, keeping his own furniture for the upstairs rooms where he and Ruth lived. Their dining-room was on the first floor, balancing the L of the drawing-room. There was both a service lift and a back staircase from the basement, so that there was no chance of patients meeting a lunch tray or a Hoover going upstairs, or a bundle of dirty laundry coming down. Few of them knew that Steven lived, as it were, over the shop.

Ugly was in the dining-room when he and Ruth went in, swaying in front of the electric fire with his eyes closed, the picture of a dog toasting himself – except that the fire was not on. Presently he yawned, stretched himself with his

76

hind legs flat on the floor like a greyhound and came to sit by Steven's chair. Steven gave him a potato, which he swallowed whole, with bulging eyes.

'I do wish you wouldn't feed him at the table,' said Ruth. 'It's terribly bad training.'

'Darling, Ugly got beyond training years ago. He makes his own rules. Luckily they're quite sensible ones.'

'He's much too big for London, anyway. He ought never to have been taken from the country. Why don't you send him to a kennels for a bit? There's a very good one where Marion takes her cairn to be plucked.'

'That reminds me, Ruth,' Steven said, ignoring her suggestion, 'George and Marion want us to go to "Four Winds" this week-end. We ought to, you know. We haven't been for ages.'

Ruth said quickly, with a fussy little frown: 'Oh, Steven, I can't. My grey flannel's at the cleaner's and it's not hot enough for my new linen suit.'

'Wear something else, then.' Steven had finished his food and was looking through his letters while Ruth scraped diligently at the bone of her cutlet.

'You've got loads of clothes upstairs,' he said, with his eyes and most of his mind on a letter from someone wanting a second opinion on a mitral stenosis.

'But they're none of them just right for the *country*.' Ruth had a very emphatic way of speaking, a strenuous plugging of the key words of a sentence which made her speech unrestful. She never tossed off vague, airy remarks that floated away unheeded. Even her light conversation was always pinned down as firmly as a captive balloon. 'And Marion always looks so *right*,' she went on. 'Of course, it's easy for her. She can wear slacks and those schoolgirl dresses, but she always makes me feel – too towny. That's silly, really, isn't it, when I was brought up in the country? But mother was always so careful not to let us be slapdash just because of that. She'd have a fit if she could see Marion and Gillian in those

77

gingham rompers. They look more like sisters than mother and daughter.'

'What's it matter what you wear?' asked Steven looking up. 'Good Lord, at "Four Winds" everyone wears just anything. Look at George in those awful blue football shorts and that check shirt.'

'I think he looks dreadful,' said Ruth. 'I don't know what the local people must think. Of course, I *could* wear that tan dress with the big pockets. But then I haven't any shoes to go with it.'

'But you're always buying shoes,' said Steven. 'It's one of your obsessions. You've got thousands of pairs in your cupboard. I looked in there the other day when I was trying to find my slippers.'

'I never seem to have any to match the things I want to wear.'

'Well, look,' said Steven, slitting another envelope. 'What I want to know is, can you go or can't you? Have you got anything on?'

'No, dear. I can go if you can. You know that.'

'I'm not sure yet how busy I'll be. I thought you might go down tomorrow afternoon, and I'll follow in the evening if I can get away, and if not, I'll try and get down on Saturday.'

'Oh, no.' Ruth laid down her knife and fork. 'I'm not going without you. I'll wait and drive down with you on Saturday.'

'But don't be silly, darling. I might not be able to get away at all, and then you'll have missed a week-end in the country in this heavenly weather. There's sure to be some good tennis, too. You'll like that.'

Ruth shook her head again, glancing at the back of the maid, who waited tapping her foot by the service lift. 'I'm not going without you. They wouldn't want me to, anyway. I know they only ask me because I'm your wife.'

'Ruth, honestly!' Sometimes she made him so angry that he could have hit her. 'God help you if you're going to start thinking things like that. Of all the introverted –'

'Oh, Steven, it isn't that. But you know I'm shy, I always have been.'

'Shy my foot. You're morbidly introspective. It's ridiculous for a woman of your age to pretend that she can't stand on her own two feet. What's going to happen to you when I die?'

Ruth put both hands on the table and leaned slightly forward. She was going to be intense. 'I pray sometimes that I shall die first.'

Steven could not look at her when she said things like that. 'Well, you won't,' he said abruptly, and laughed, 'if I keep on working at this pace without a holiday.' He heard her take in a breath to say her usual piece about why don't we go away, just the two of us together, like a second honeymoon, but Welsh came between then with fried bananas and cream. They were very sweet and syrupy, but Ruth asked for some sugar to be put on the table. Afterwards, Steven had cheese and biscuits, and Ruth picked over the chocolates in a glass dish.

'Well, what about the week-end?' asked Steven, dropping cheese rind into Ugly's alligator jaws and pushing back his chair. 'You'd better ring up Marion now. George said he could pick you up after lunch to-morrow and drive you down.'

'Oh, Steven, I can't. Last time they had paper games. You ring them up and say I'm coming with you.'

'Haven't time. I've got masses to do. Look, it's just on nine now. Let's have coffee in the drawing-room, then we can hear the news.'

'What are you going to do to-night then? You're not going out again?'

'No, I've done enough work for the public for one day. I'm going to do a little for myself now.'

'You going to write?'

'I am.' Steven got up and brushed off his black pin-stripe trousers.

'Oh.'

'By the way,' he said, as he held the door open for her, 'what was it you were going to tell me that was so important?'

Ruth pinched his arm and glanced over his shoulder to where Welsh was listlessly putting plates into the service lift. 'Not now,' she whispered. 'I'll tell you in a sec.'

The narration of Ruth's domestic troubles accompanied the more important items on the news, was interrupted by the appearance of Welsh with coffee, and was resumed while Steven was trying to listen to the latest comments on the alliance between Italy and Germany.

Downstairs in the kitchen, Welsh, having supper with Mrs. Hankey and the housemaid, said: 'She was telling 'im what I said to 'er.' She was an anæmic, stringy girl, with dull eyes and drooping wrists, not smart enough, in spite of her expensive maroon and organdie uniform, to open the door to a Wimpole Street *clientèle*. Ruth, who was the kind of woman who believed what advertisements said, had hired her because she had good references and was called by her surname. She sat now with her right elbow on the table, picking at her food with a fork, her left hand hanging down to pick at the heel of her shoe.

'What was it again you said, Phyll?' asked the housemaid, who had been so well brought up that she admired anybody who dared to be rude.

'I told you once. Do I have to wear me jaw to the bone because you can't take things in first time?' said Welsh, who would have repeated her conversation with Ruth anyway, unasked. 'I said to her: "Look here, Mrs Sheppard," I said, "*if* Dr Sheppard and Mr Nosgood have been complaining that I don't answer the front door quick enough, I think it only right that they should do so directly to me personally." "Well, Welsh," she says, a bit uncertain now of where she stands, "I'm only repeating what they said to me. Some of their patients have complained about being kept waiting on the doorstep." "Well, it's the first I've heard of it," I said, And then I told her: "Upstairs, madam, I take my orders from you. Downstairs, I take my orders from the professional gentleman." '

Mrs Hankey shook her broad, purple face slowly. 'It wasn't right of you, Phyll. You didn't ought to take advantage of her.'

'She gets me down,' said Welsh. 'She's got no more idea how to run this house than my Aunt Fanny, yet she thinks she can dictate to me.'

'Nevertheless,' said Mrs Hankey solemnly, loading raspberry jam on thickly buttered bread, 'we are in her employ. You can't fly against that. A lady's got a right to speak out before those to 'oom she pays wages. Don't pick at your shoes, dear.'

'Well, she needn't think I want her wages,' said Welsh, stabbing a potato and looking at it without enthusiasm before she put it into her mouth. ''*E*'*s* all right. I don't mind working for '*im*. Wouldn't mind a bit of play, either,' she added, winking at the scandalized housemaid. 'Oh, yes and then she says: "Aren't you well, Welsh? Would you like Doctor to have a look at you again? Perhaps you need a tonic." Huh, not if it's anything like the tonic he tried to give me last time – sticking a needle into me thigh, indeed – saucy beggar.'

'They say he's ever such a clever doctor, though. What about that time he had his name in the paper for attending that actress – what was her name – that was taken queer on the stage?'

'Oh yes, he's clever with the women all right,' said Welsh, sitting up straight enough to pass her cup for more tea before subsiding again. 'Don't think I haven't got eyes in my head not to notice that he has many more women patients than men. You wouldn't catch me marrying a doctor; I've worked with too many of 'em. Up to all sorts of tricks, they are, and their wives none the wiser. There you are – there's the phone again now. Not a minute's peace to even take your meals. Now we'll just see if Mrs S'll answer it. Lazy bitch.' She leaned back in her chair and listened, with her head on one side.

The telephone ran on. 'Aren't you going to answer it, Phyll?' asked Mrs Hankey reproachfully.

'She's only got to walk across the drawing-room. I've got to go upstairs to the 'all.' A door on the ground floor opened and Steven's voice shouted: 'For God's sake, why doesn't someone answer that telephone? Welsh! If it's for me, I'm out.'

Ruth and Welsh both picked up their receivers at the same time, and conducted a three-sided conversation with the worried voice at the other end, before Ruth realized what was happening and said: 'All right, Welsh, thank you. I'll take the call. Oh, excuse me,' to the voice which was now confused as well as worried, 'I was just talking to the maid.'

Outside the consulting-room, Ruth paused and listened to the spasmodic sounds of typing: a burst of clacking, then a long pause, which meant that Steven was thinking, then another furious burst, as if he were trying to pin his thoughts down before they escaped. To knock or not to knock? It was absurd, really, and undignified, thought Ruth, standing in the hall holding up the long skirt of her housecoat, to knock at your husband's door like a servant, but Steven so hated to be disturbed.

It made no difference, anyway, because he did not answer her knock, so she opened the door. Steven looked irritably over his shoulder.

'It's Mrs Crosbie on the phone,' said Ruth. 'Will you speak to her?'

'I told you I was *out*,' said Steven, and turned back to his desk.

'I'm so sorry, dear, only last time she rang you were annoyed because I let her go, and you wanted to speak to her.'

'Well, this time I *don't*,' said Steven, still typing. Ruth waited for a moment to see whether he was going to say anything else, and then went out. She saw her letter on the hall table and sat down at once to read it on the oak chest where people left their hats.

Ursula wrote just as she spoke. How amusing she was, thought Ruth, picturing the small, alert, blonde figure being the life and soul of Malta, just as she had been at Seaview, and at Fareham and Weymouth and Gibraltar – wherever she and Sandy had lived, collecting round them a whole firmament of naval officers and their wives. The family joke was that it was a mercy that she was not yet grown up when Ruth met Steven. Ruth, being safely married to him, was supposed not to mind the pleasure which he and Ursula took in each other's company, and the private jokes, whose point Ruth always pretended to see. Sandy never pretended. He basked in his reputation for being unable to appreciate anything more subtle than Crazy Week at the Palladium.

A desire to establish friendly contact with Steven before she went upstairs again made Ruth open the consulting-room door and say: 'I've just had a letter from Ursie. I must tell you what she says about when they had the C.-in-C. to dinner.' Unlike her wiser sister, Ruth was given to talking of Sandy's fellow officers as 'No. 1' and 'the Chief' and 'the Sub', just as she copied Steven in talking about streps and staphs, and describing her bilious attacks as 'D and V'. She read out Ursula's story, blundering over the key word and having to go back a page to make sense.

'Ha, ha,' said Steven, and went on typing.

When she had gone he stopped typing, whipped the paper out of the machine, crumpled it up and slung it into the waste-paper basket with the immemorial author's gesture. He had been writing nonsense while Ruth was in the room because he knew that to go on typing was the quickest way to get rid of her. Before the interruption he had been feeling his way, trying to clear out of his mind the clutter of thoughts left there by the events of the day. After half-an-hour's slogging, he was not yet within sight of that miraculous state when imagined things become real enough to enter the mind of their own accord instead of being dragged there, protesting, in stiff, unnatural attitudes. Only once or twice in his life had he ever been able to spend long enough alone with his typewriter to work himself into that trance in which the imagined world is the only world, the body is all brain and feels neither heat, cold nor hunger, when the writer might be in a hermit's cave or in the middle of Piccadilly Circus. without knowing that he was anywhere but on the paper on which the words, the right, the only words are jumping up and making him bounce on his chair and cry: 'This is it!'

For years, Steven had been one of those people who say: 'Of course, I could write a novel if only I had the time.' Then Mark Stainer had brought his gastric ulcer to him. It was small wonder that Mark Stainer's stomach was pitted like a beach after rain. He was the activating force of his own publishing business, putting in a five-and-a-half-day week in his office, contacting many people and warding more off, diplomatically lunching and dining authors, reading books and manuscripts into the small hours, and finding time somehow to write at least one novel a year himself. Steven, saying one day as he took his leave: 'Of course, I should like to do a bit of writing if I wasn't so busy,' suddenly realized the hollowness of his remark, and wished it unsaid. If this wrung out, dyspeptic little fellow with the dome-like forehead could find the time, why couldn't he? Evidently it was not necessary to rusticate with the telephone wires cut and all friends alienated to write a good book. He had had a story in his mind for some time, the story of a doctor, based on his own life, but with the consecutive, shapely plot which one's own life lacks.

So he had bought a typewriter and started during a fishing holiday in the Wye Valley. Mark Stainer had promised to publish it for him – had promised to read it, anyway. Ruth had told her friends: 'Steven is writing a book.'

At first, his sessions with the typewriter were treated with reverence. A holy hush was laid on the house. People rushed to silence the telephone and the door bell, meals were held back for his convenience. Sometimes Ruth would creep into the hall and stand outside the consulting-room door, smiling when the typewriter went like a machine-gun, frowning sympathetically when the clacking was spasmodic. She did not know that the machine-gun usually meant that Steven was copying out something he had already written, and that during the long pauses, in which she pictured her husband head in hand in stupendous thought, he was probably wandering round the room, or looking out of the window, or washing his hands in the laboratory, or even reverting to a patient's notes – anything to relieve the physical agony of trying to write a book that would not be written.

For the novel was not going well. Its title, *The Swift Stream*, was the only flowing thing about it. After a time Ruth got tired of asking in a hushed voice: 'How's IT going?' and being answered with a grunt or a change of subject. She had imagined Steven reading chapters to her, asking for admiration or advice, and getting both. He would dedicate it 'To My Wife', or 'To R. Without whom this book, etc. etc.' He had not read any of it to her yet. She had read some of it furtively once, when he was called out to a patient and had left the horse's head blotter on the desk, and was disappointed to find that it seemed quite ordinary. It was just like anyone else's book. But Steven was not just like anyone else; his book should have been different in some way which Ruth, whose literary experience was confined to the choice of the girl at the library, could not specify. It was wonderful of Steven, of course, to be able to write at all, but then Steven could do anything he put his hand to.

She soon lost interest in the novel. It was a bore now which made him late for meals and made him cross and usurped her right to be with him. She seldom enquired after it, and often dared to interrupt him when he was writing.

After she had gone out this time, Steven sat with his hands idle on the keys, listening to her heavy tread going upstairs and crossing the floor above, trying to think himself back into the operating theatre, where he had left his young hero doing his first Cæsarean. This part, as he had planned it, was to convey to the public the drama and beauty of a big operation; the perfectly staged centripetal scene whose hub is the floodlit area of pulsing tissue, round which the feature-less white figures crowd close as maggots. Beyond, the instruments catch the outer rays of the great flat light, beyond those, the humbler satellites spin, half in shadow, and beyond them the motionless watchers, climbing away towards the darkness of the high theatre roof. The concentration of all eyes, ears, thoughts, hopes and plans intensifies skill and blunders alike, and tautens nerves to irascibility so that sometimes the tiniest joke, snapping the tension, may sweep like a gust of real humour through the team. And then the exaltation, the unrealized endurance and its resultant languor, the sense of achievement, shared even by the probationer toiling over the stained towels in the sluice.

But none of this was getting on to the paper. It was ridiculous to be unable to describe things which one knew so intimately that their impact on the mind was sensual rather than visual. If it were coal miners now, or the Foreign Legion or the underworld of Chicago, he could understand it, but this – this should have flowed from him like speech.

He had once lamented this to Mark Stainer, who had replied: 'But, my dear Dr Sheppard, why worry? You are a brilliant and successful doctor. Why do you, who can do all these things, try to write about them? That is for us who, unable to do them, seek to compensate for our inferiority.' That was how Mark Stainer talked, in pedantic, polished phrases that trapped people into thinking they meant something.

'Unless the urge to write is stronger in you than anything else,' went on Stainer, 'stick to your doctoring, and praise God that you are able to live your life at first instead of second hand.' He levelled his velvet gaze at Steven from under the loom of his brow. 'You do good directly, we only indirectly, if at all.'

'But I do want to write, most tremendously,' Steven had said. This was supposed to be a medical consultation, but the

86

roles were temporarily reversed. While they were on Mark Stainer's subject, he was the oracle and Steven the eager disciple. 'I know that I could write,' he went on, 'if only I had the time.'

'Ah, time!' sighed Mark, in his faint, bodiless voice, raising his hands and letting them fall to his knees. 'Time is a commodity which people like us must seek as resolutely as the Holy Grail. If you really want to write, you will find the time.'

'I do want to,' repeated Steven. 'God knows why, but I know I want to.'

The psychologist seldom practises on himself. Steven, adept at analysing his patients' motives, did not see his literary aspirations as what he would have called, impressively, in consultation, 'Escape Symbols'. He would probably never finish *The Swift Stream* any more than he had persevered with his tennis coaching or his evening squash lessons, or revisited that isolated fishing inn or gone on the lone hike with Ugly which he was always planning. These things served their purpose for a time, but they were only the means to an unattainable end – escape from people who expected more of him the more he gave them.

Writing was a thing that took you away on your own; therefore, he wanted to write.

Beginning with examinations and games at school, he had all his life been successful at whatever he tackled. So there was no reason why he should not make something of this book, if he could get it written.

If he could get it written ... His cigarette case was empty, and he got up to get the packet from his bag. Where the devil was the bag? It was not in the consulting-room, nor on the table under the coat rack where he usually flung it when he came in.

'Ruth!' he shouted up the stairs. She had the drawing-room door shut and the wireless playing. He went up and found her writing letters at her desk with a variety programme tuned in unnecessarily loud.

'Finished already?' She looked round, pleased.

'No. Where the hell did I put my bag?' He toned down the wireless as he passed it, searching the room.

'Dear, *I* don't know. Where did you put it when you came in?'

'If I knew that I wouldn't be looking for it,' he muttered. Normally methodical, this losing his bag was one of his few lapses from efficiency. He rarely left it in the same place twice, and Miss Minden, who liked to think that she knew him better than he knew himself, was the only person who could nose it out in a hurry. Ruth made a great business of looking for it, but seldom found it, even when it was in her bedroom.

She got up now and started moving about the room, looking twice in the same places and following Steven out of the door.

'It's all right,' he said. 'I'll find it. I only wanted a cigarette, anyway.'

'Why didn't you say so? There's heaps up here.'

'I said a cigarette, not those foul round things you buy. It doesn't matter, though. I didn't want one all that much.'

'How are you getting on?' She stood at the top of the stairs while he went down, but he pretended not to hear, and banged himself into his room again.

He read through what he had written. He had got his patient on to the operating table and his surgeon gowned and masked and gloved. It was very dull. If it bored him, what would it do to the reader? He stared in front of him at the letter rack, following its curved top with his eye, rearranged without touching them Miss Minden's flowers on the corner of the desk, tilted his head to try to remove the reflection from the glass of Turner's 'Venice' on the opposite wall. He got up and moved to where he could see it. There, he had seen it. He could not look out of the window, because the muslin curtains were too discreet. He looked at himself in the mirror over the mantelpiece, bent closer and wondered whether he looked his age. He had said to Ruth

88

the other day: 'I can remember getting my first grey hair. It was just here in the parting. Carol pulled it out.' She had looked at him sideways, warning him off the taboo subject. He brushed up the side of his hair into quiffs and palmed them flat again. If only he could have a cigarette, that might get him going. He walked, balancing, along the fender, thinking of what he would write next. He went into the little examination room and weighed himself. Perhaps he ought to look again for his bag. That blood pressure woman's notes were in it. Perhaps he should ring up Mrs Crosbie in case she really wanted him. Anything, anything to postpone legitimately the physical effort of getting down to work. Poets, after all, had to wait for inspirations, so why shouldn't he? But he had done enough writing to know that an author's Muse does not drop from the blue, but only hobbles towards him with one hand on her back when her path has been beaten down by his struggles.

The telephone rang and he stood looking at it. After it had stopped he picked it up and heard Ruth say: 'I'm afraid Dr Sheppard is not in. Can I take a message for him?'

'Oh, dear,' said a girl's voice. 'Well, I suppose I ought not to bother him really, but I wanted to ask him what to do. It's my baby, you know. She's under him for her heart. She's just woken up and –' the words came in a rush '– I don't like the look of her at all.'

'Dr Sheppard speaking,' cut in Steven.

'Oh, but I thought –' said Ruth resentfully.

'Oh, they told me you were out, Doctor,' said Mrs Crosbie.

'Just got in,' said Steven crisply. 'What's worrying you about the baby, hm? ... Yes ... yes ... Can't she? Right, I'll come straight round. Keep her warm.' He rang through to the Oxygen company and gave them the address, looked round again for his bag and remembered that he had left it in the car. Ugly, whose sixth sense was of foreseeing goings-out, was already waiting in the hall, and bounded down the chequered steps with his tail circling. Hurrying round to the garage, Steven, thinking without regret of the unfinished

Cæsarean on the roller of his typewriter, said to himself: 'It's impossible to combine the two. No wonder I can't get that book written.' Yet he did not feel annoyed with Mrs Crosbie, but quite grateful to her for giving him a genuine excuse to stop struggling. His brain was already clear of *The Swift Stream* and busy with what he might be going to hear through his stethoscope, and what he was going to do about it.

Chapter 2

—

THE Marshalls' place in Berkshire was really a small house, but it was called the Cottage in the same way that their forty-foot yacht at Beaulieu was called a tub, champagne and oysters before the theatre was a glass of beer and a sandwich, and a morning drink at the Savoy, which was next door to George's office, was nipping round to the local.

The Cottage was in that pseudo-country of heath and rhododendrons and golf courses, and let for enormous sums at Ascot Week. A rustic board on the mown bank beside the gate said 'Four Winds', and if there had been another board saying: 'George W. Marshall' and a little kennel-shaped letter box on a stand, it might have been one of those properties just outside New York which bridge the gap between suburbs and genuine country without being one or the other.

Steven arrived early on Saturday afternoon and turned up the drive between the flowering shrubs and conifers. The gabled red-brick house, on which the ivy and creepers had not yet gained the first floor, got its name from the fact that it stood on a slight rise, exposed to the mild breezes blowing across the fifth fairway of the golf course.

When they stopped, Ugly bounded straight over the side of the open car and through the hall door. George prided himself on his 'Ever Open Door', but Ugly had forgotten another of his maxims: No Dogs in the House. George's own dogs, all very well-bred, lived in fine kennels by the garage, and were taken out on manœuvres of coming to heel and retrieving things and dropping to earth at the command of the referee's whistle which George wore round his neck.

Steven was still getting his bag out of the car when Ugly shot out again with his tail glued underneath him, followed by George in his broad-beamed blue shorts and striped fisherman's jersey. He was wearing rope-soled sandals, and there was a lurking threat about him that he might at any moment put on a beret.

'Glad to see you, Stevie!' he hailed. 'But I didn't tell you to bring that exuberant mongrel job.' George had recently been doing business with some aircraft firms.

'No one to leave him with at home,' said Steven shortly.

'Well, he'll be all right in the kennels, won't he?' asked George, hitching his shorts halfway up his frontal bulk. 'As a matter of fact, dogs much prefer that sort of life. It's not natural for them to live indoors.' So Ugly spent the week-end curled up in the back of the car except when he was out with Steven, and then he disgraced himself by chasing a rabbit on to the golf course, and across a green where a mulberry-faced brigadier was just saying: 'This for a half.'

'Where's Ruth?' asked Steven as they went indoors.

'Watching the tennis, I think,' said George, leading him straight through the hall to the garden door. 'We're going to swim when we've digested our lunch. First time I've had the pool filled this year. By the way, have you had any lunch?'

'Not yet,' said Steven. 'I didn't stop, as I was so late getting off.'

'My dear chap!' George turned to him a face of horror. 'I'll fix you up with something straight away. There's some not uneatable cold salmon and a Brie that'll run right off the plate if it isn't finished soon. Come out and meet the folk first, though. Annette and Stewart are here, and young Charles, and the Berrys are over for the day. You met them last time, didn't you? Funny, could have sworn you did.

He's in aircraft; got a topping house just the other side of Camberley. We're all going there tomorrow for drinks.'

Steven suddenly wished that it was bedtime. He felt very tired as he followed George across the sloping lawn to where a group of people sat in deck-chairs outside the thatched summer-house by the tennis court where two young men were playing a single. As soon as she saw him, Ruth got up and almost ran over the grass, clutching his arm and making a clumsy attempt to kiss him while he was still walking. She was wearing a sleeveless white piqué frock, too short for an ordinary dress, yet too long for a tennis dress, with a wide, shiny red belt. Over her back hair was the hair-net which Steven had forbidden her to wear.

'Darling!' she cried, as if he had been away for months. 'I'm so glad you've come.' In a young bride, such eagerness could have been touching.

'Having a good time?' asked Steven, but before she could answer, they were among the group of people, and exclamations and introductions were occurring.

Marion's younger sister Annette, clutching bare brown knees in a deck-chair, was tiny and delicate, and pretty enough to disguise the fact that her intellect was out of all proportion to her physique. She had been the most brilliant woman of her year at Lady Margaret Hall, had staggered audiences all over the States during a tour of lectures on economics, and was saved in the nick of time from accepting the chair of Economic History at Mount Holyoke by running into a Professor of Mathematics, also lecturing, whom she had known slightly at Oxford. He had clung to her as a rock in the battering torrent of American culture, out of which he pulled himself to marry her and take her home. He had a short, curry-coloured moustache, a rectangular head, a long back, and legs that looked terrible in a swimming suit. He read books with titles like *Advanced Propositions on the Higher Aspects of the Differential Calculus*, chuckling over them as other men read Wodehouse. He and Annette were perfectly happy.

The two tennis players came over to the wire netting and hung on it, chattering at Steven like monkeys in a cage. One of them was George's son Rupert, a precocious adolescent, with his mother's great eyes: but while her lashes were short and her eyebrows surprised, his lashes had an endless, indolent swoop, and his dark brows tilted faun-like at the corners. When he forgot to drawl, his voice was young and eager and resonant. He was going to Oxford next term, and his ambition in life was to produce and act in the sort of plays which nobody wanted to see in theatres which nobody could be bothered to get to.

The other youth was his stocky cousin Charles, an amiable piece of furniture in George's office, whom women found useful for carrying luggage.

The Berrys were an unexciting, prosperous-looking pair, who would sooner not go anywhere than travel third class, and never did anything, even eating, on impulse.

Steven greeted them all, exchanged a couple of insults with Rupert, slapped Stewart on his curved back, and said: 'Lordosis, my boy. If you were my patient I'd put you in a plaster cast for six months,' and still felt that he would like to go to bed. The drive from London had been too short for him to shake off the morning's preoccupations. That diabetic's sugar curve was still worrying at the back of his mind. Why was it still up? Could he trust that Sister about the diet? Dared he increase the insulin? These people here had done their week's work and were relaxed. He was not relaxed; not yet, if ever. He felt conscious of his town clothes, and of an unnatural, professional suavity still clinging round his conversation.

'I think I'll go and change, George,' he said. 'These clothes ...' He shot his cuffs and looked at his expensive black shoes.

'I'll come and unpack for you,' said Ruth, and Annette said: 'Now, Ruth, for God's sake don't be so *maternal*. The maids will have done it hours ago. They only forget things when Marion's here to upset them.'

'But, my dear,' Mrs Berry said to her as they watched Steve go indoors, flanked by the more cumbersome figures of George and Ruth, 'he *is* attractive. I'd always heard he was. My cousin went to him, you know – Mrs Drexel. She married a brother of the M.P. I must speak to Dr Sheppard about her.

'I'm sure he'll be *tremendously* interested,' murmured Annette, leaning back with her hands behind her head, watching Rupert's extravagant leaps through a pair of enormous dark glasses with white rims. Stewart lay on the grass reading the paper. Mr Berry, in the squatting position which people assume when they sit on the edge of a deck-chair, was whistling through his teeth, and plucking at the strings of his racket, hoping that his tennis was going to be good enough. Mrs Berry, to whom no silence was ever comfortable, turned to him brightly.

'And when are *you* going to have a game, Arnold?' she asked, in the polite tones which they used to one another in public. Arnold, who had not yet been asked to play, mumbled something, and Annette said: 'Stewart and I are going to take on your husband and Ruth as soon as these children have finished.'

'Don't let me take anyone's place,' said Mr Berry hastily. 'I don't mind sitting out at all ...'

'Don't be silly. You came over to play, didn't you?' said Annette, who had been exasperated by his humbleness ever since he had refused a second helping at lunch which he quite obviously wanted.

'Well, I only hope I shall be good enough to give you a game ...'

'But, Arnold, you play very nicely,' said Mrs Berry, and Annette said: 'Oh, you'll be all right with Ruth. She is surprisingly good still considering the only exercise she takes is paddling down Welbeck Street to the Book Club.'

'I thought you said *Wimpole* Street, Mrs Connor,' said Mrs Berry, who loved Facts and cut bits out of the newspapers which told her how far the red blood cells of the human body would reach if placed end to end.

'Same thing.' Annette was bored. She poked Stewart with her foot and smiled at him to reassure herself that all life on earth was not extinct.

*

'Oh, Steven, I *am* glad you managed to get down,' Ruth was repeating as she sat watching Steven eat his lunch. 'It was awful last night. We played bridge, and I'm not nearly good enough for them.'

'I don't see that matters,' said Steven, helping himself to more mayonnaise. 'Bridge with George is always a bit of a joke.'

'Well, it's one I can't see, I'm afraid,' said Ruth and sighed. 'I lost eight-and-six, darling. I'm awfully sorry.'

'It's your money,' said Steven, irritated, as always by her masochistic refusal ever to forget that she was dependent on him for every penny she had.

Ruth picked a radish out of the salad bowl and ate it with her front teeth. 'Why did you bring Ugly?' she asked. 'George was saying last night he hoped you wouldn't.'

'Well, I did.'

'Where is he?'

'In the car.'

'In the garage? Oh, Steven, he'll stifle. Carbon monoxide you know.'

'I left the doors open.'

'Oh!' Ruth picked out another radish and nibbled it crisply. 'What sort of a drive down did you have?' she asked.

'Oh, all right.'

'George and I made nearly record time,' she said, 'for that time of day. We didn't start till after three, and we were down here before they'd started tea.' Ruth often felt it incumbent on her to entertain Steven with light conversation, as if she were a dinner party acquaintance instead of his wife.

95

'The Berrys are nice, aren't they?' she said. 'I had a long talk with her in my bedroom before lunch. She's got the loveliest handbag, Steven. Real pigskin, all fitted with little compartments for everything – even for an aspirin bottle. She was telling me about her little girl. She's had a gland come up on her neck, and it didn't go down even after she had her tonsils out. They can't be sure whether it's strep or T.B. What should you think it was?'

'Look, Ruth,' said Steven, laying down his knife and fork, 'I don't often take a week-end off, and when I do I just want to forget medicine for a bit, see? It's bad enough to have almost everyone you meet thinking you're interested in nothing else, and angling for a bit of free advice. Don't you start.'

'I'm awfully sorry, Steven. Of course I oughtn't to have bothered you. It was just that I told her I'd ask –'

'Well, don't.' He stretched behind him to put his plate on the dresser and thumped down again to reach for a rich-looking creation in a glass dish. 'What's this muck?'

'Ssh.' Ruth glanced round. 'Someone might hear you. It's trifle. It's marvellous, too. We had it at lunch. Aren't you going to have any? That cheese isn't nearly so nice. It's too strong.' She scooped up a bit of the creamy, almost liquid Brie and licked her finger with a screwed-up face. While Steven was eating his cheese, her eye kept straying regretfully to the trifle. At last she said: 'I might as well finish off that trifle if you're not going to. I don't see why we should leave it for the servants.' She scraped the dish out on to the plate left for Steven, and just as she pulled it towards her and plunged in a spoon the door opened and Bacon, George's manservant, came in to clear away. With a clumsy movement, Ruth pushed the plate away from her, cleared her throat on a high note, blushed crimson and knocked over a glass of water.

'Oh, I'm terribly sorry, Bacon.' She jumped up, mopping at the spreading pool with a napkin, which Bacon took from her politely. 'Quite all right, madam. Allow me,' he said.

'Oh, thank you. I'm so sorry.' Ruth went and stood in the open french window, looking out at the garden. As soon as she heard the door close behind Bacon, she swung round to Steven with a face of tragedy. 'Oh, wasn't it *awful*! What must he have thought?'

'What d'you mean? Anyone can knock over a glass of water. Though I must say you do it rather more frequently than most.'

'Oh, I don't mean *that*,' she said impatiently. 'I mean my eating the trifle. D'you think he noticed? You see, I'd had two helpings already at lunch. I thought he looked at me a bit funnily then, because no one else did, but he'd handed it to me first, so I didn't know they weren't going to. He would come in just then. Oh, Steven, wasn't it awful?'

'I expect when the Revolution comes, he'll scythe your head off with a ham knife,' said Steven, getting up. 'I'm going to change for tennis. We in the usual room?'

'Oh, you can laugh,' said Ruth. 'You never seem to mind what servants think, but that sort of thing always makes me feel awful, I don't know why.' She gave a little laugh. 'I must be extra sensitive, I suppose.'

She followed Steven upstairs. 'You didn't do much work last night, did you?' she said, watching him rearrange the things which Marion's maid had put where she thought he ought to keep them. 'I hardly heard the typewriter at all. And then that woman ringing *twice*. I was sorry she got you; I tried to keep her off. By the way, I wish you'd wake me another time when you come in. I like to see you last thing. Was the baby all right?'

'No, it died,' said Steven, and stood in the middle of the room dangling a pair of white socks and reliving the scene in Mrs Crosbie's night nursery. He could see the tableau in his mind: himself, straightening up from the cot, his hand that drew the blanket up feeling big and clumsy, Mrs Crosbie backing against her husband, unbelieving, and the man from the Oxygen company arriving in the doorway with the unwanted little tent, his face revealing only for a split second what he felt about being called out for nothing.

*

Marion drove down on Sunday morning, bringing with her a Czechoslovakian refugee with hunted eyes. 'Be nice to him, George – Steven,' she said, cornering them in the study, where they were arguing whether to telephone now and book caddies or wait and see what the weather was going to do.

'I found him at Sybil's last night,' she said. 'He's being touted round London like an exhibit, and he's tired. He took me out to dinner – at least I took him, and he nearly went to sleep on the table. I think the waiter thought he was tight.'

'I thought you stayed at home to be with Gilly,' said George.

'Yes, but she was so well, and Nanny kept coming at me with stories about my childhood. I simply had to go out. You haven't asked me how she is, anyway, Steven. Never mind, I'll tell you: She's better. I'm going to get her up next week.'

'You'll do nothing of the sort until I say so.'

'Isn't he sweet? He rises. Hullo!' She snatched eagerly at the telephone, almost before it had time to ring. 'Dr Sheppard? Yes, he's here.' She made a face at Steven's frantic head shakings. 'I'll take a message to him if you like ... Oh, I say, how dreadful ... Oh, dear. Has he had a blood transfusion? Oh, he has. What's his pulse like? Well, you know, if I were you – No, wait a minute, Steven.' He had snatched the receiver out of her hand.

'Dr Sheppard speaking. Who is it, please?' The confusion into which Marion had thrown young Potter became even worse at this sudden switch over to the great man himself.

'T-t-t-t-erribly sorry to bother you, sir. I rang your

London number and they gave me this one. I thought I'd better tell you about old J' – long, gulping pause – 'arvis. I didn't want you to get here next week and find he'd p-p-pegged out.'

'What d'you mean?' asked Steven crisply. 'That duodenal? He was nowhere near pegging when I saw him last Thursday. Another hæmatemesis? The old devil.' Marion was listening, goggle-eyed, enthralled. 'How much blood's he had? ... You stopped it, of course. Well, I'm not far away. I'll be with you in about half an hour. Give him a shot of morphia in the meantime, and get the bed well up ... Oh, you have? Good boy.'

'Now look here, Steven, you're not –' said Marion as he rang off.

'What about our golf?' asked George, making the mouth of a disappointed child.

'Sorry, old boy, I simply must go. He's a pet case of mine. You can pick up a fourth at the club, can't you?'

As Steven was getting the car out of the garage, with Ugly shouting directions from the back seat, Marion came running out from the house with her Czech in tow. He wore a brown suit that did not fit him very well and co-respondent shoes. His thick chestnut hair was rather long, and ungreased. He did not look more than twenty-two or -three.

'Steven, do be a darling and take Laszlo, just for the ride. He simply adores motoring and, honestly, I don't quite know what to do with him now I've got him here. I thought I could put him to sleep somewhere, but he won't settle. It's all right, he doesn't understand English. He speaks French though,' she added, as Steven manœuvred the young man into the car by gestures.

Steven's French was good enough. Although he had had little opportunity to practise it, and had scarcely been abroad since he was grown up, his mother had taught him to speak it from the moment he could talk. She had been half-French, a cosmopolitan wanderer, who had been snared during her migration from resort to resort by the dark and silent barrister, Gregory Sheppard, taking a conscientious holiday among the churches and galleries of Venice.

Steven gave Laszlo a cigarette, and they exchanged a few generalities about the country and the weather. Steven felt guilty. It embarrassed him to have this haggard, beaten-looking young man who had seen Heaven knew what horrors sitting there as if in silent condemnation of a country still at peace. He wanted to tell Laszlo about what we were going to do if the Germans invaded Poland, and what he, Steven, had in mind to do even before that. But the boy had probably been surfeited with that sort of talk since he came to England. He probably would not want to talk about his escape either, nor what he had been through. He would have had enough of being brought out on that subject by people like Sybil.

Conversation flagged. Steven hummed, and thought a bit about old Jarvis. They drove up a winding hill through an aquarium-like tunnel of beechwood and at the top they came suddenly out of the trees into the dazzling sunshine, and the valley lay below them, neatly mapped in fields and farms, with the river glinting here and there at the foot of the wooded slope in shadow beyond.

'*C'est beau*,' said Laszlo, and sighed.

'You're seeing it at its best, of course,' Steven told him in his careless, erratic French. 'We don't get many days like this in England. The clouds usually come low into this valley, and everything is grey and damp.'

'*Chez moi*,' said the boy suddenly. '*Chez moi, dans les Tartras* ... ' He looked quickly at Steven to see if he was going to be bored. 'You sit in the clouds for weeks. The dampness envelops everything like cobwebs. You do not know whether the mist is rising from the ground or falling from above. Your hair is never dry, and the eyelashes of everyone carry little beads.'

'Where is your home?'

'Stary Smokovecj. It lies on the side of the mountain and looks out over the plain of Slovakia. You can see as far as the frontier of Hungary – but not, of course, when the clouds are down.'

He pronounced it Starry Smockovecks, and it sounded beautiful in his tongue. He brought Steven a picture of one of the spired villages he had seen on newsreels. The streets were cobbled, and went steeply up and down the mountain from the main street. It was evening, and as the clouds were rolling away over the roofs and through the dripping pine forests above them, one star stood out in the greenish sky over the plain far below, and everywhere you looked your eye called forth another star, until it was night, and there was nothing before you but the black, star-hung curtain falling straight into the depths whose emptiness was belied by the tiny moving fire of a train snaking towards the still deeper shadow that was the mountains of Hungary.

*

Nurse Lake, coming up from Outpatients on her way to first dinner, met Steven on the stairs, and nearly fainted from shock. She had only known him before in his black town clothes, and the sight of him in grey flannel trousers and a tweed jacket was altogether too much. As she flattened herself against the staircase wall to let him go by, he glanced at her, glanced again with recognition, and said: 'Oh! Good morning, Nurse.'

She watched his tweed back and young Potter's broad white one disappear round the bend of the stairs, and then raced up, two at a time, on her thin, black legs to get to the corridor window in time to see him get into his car. She saw Ugly on the back seat – there was a dog-lover for you, if you like – and saw Laszlo slumped in the front with a cigarette. How rude of him, whoever he was, not to open the car door for Dr Sheppard. For one mad moment she imagined herself in Laszlo's place, in a summery dress, a bright scarf, perhaps, about her hair, and her elephant hair bracelet on, driving out into the country on a Sunday morning like this with a picnic basket in the back.

'You're late, Nurse,' said Sister Housekeeper, who was doling out overcooked cold beef at the side table in the dining-room.

'Excuse me, please, Sister,' said Nurse Lake, her blush not yet subsided. You had to excuse yourself whenever you went in or out of a room in which there was a Sister or a senior nurse, as if there was something rude about your presence. She took her plate over to the staff nurses' table and helped herself automatically to beetroot and chilly potatoes. The staff nurse of the men's medical ward, who had the morning off, was there in mufti. You were not allowed to miss a meal even when you were off duty, as you were considered foolish enough to starve yourself if given the chance.

'I saw Dr Sheppard coming out of your ward just now,' Nurse Lake told her. 'What's he doing there on a Sunday morning?'

'Old Jarvis, I expect. Fancy getting the poor swine down from London, though. I bet Sister put Tubby Potter up to that. Thank God I was off this morning. She must have been up the walls. I shan't find a thing done when I go on.'

'What is Jarvis?' somebody asked.

'Hæmatemesis. He's had no bleeding for a couple of weeks, so Steven tells Pottsy to pump some blood into him – you wouldn't believe the time he took cutting down – and woosh! Up it all comes at three o'clock this morning.'

'Will he do?'

'Lord, no. I'm surprised he's held on like he has, especially with that ass Carter on night duty. I suppose she kept him going to save having to lay him out herself.'

Nurse Lake wanted to say: 'If anybody can save him, Dr Sheppard can,' but fortunately she contented herself with thinking it.

'How is the ill man?' Laszlo asked Steven, as they drove

out of the big iron gates and dropped down the hill towards the river.

Steven made a Gallic gesture with his left hand, indicating *comme ci, comme ça*.

'I thought once of studying medicine,' said Laszlo in his harsh, mid-European French, 'but my father wanted me to follow him in timber.'

'Well, you didn't miss much,' said Steven flippantly. 'It's a dog's life.'

Laszlo turned to him seriously. 'You don't like your work.'

'Oh, I love the work. Too well, in fact,' Steven added, half to himself, 'for my peace of mind. No, the work's all right. It's the circumstances under which one practises it that sometimes give me – the *cafard*,' he said, for want of a less extreme word.

'The hospitals are not good, then?' Laszlo furrowed his brows. He had thought St Margaret's dingy and archaic compared with places like the huge white sanatorium which curved round a sweep of the mountainside near his home. But England was like that. The things which should be new and modern, like hospitals and schools and factories, were grubby and old-fashioned, whereas things which should be old were new, like the Empire wine he had experienced at a party given by the West Kensington Aid to Czechoslovakia Society.

'No,' said Steven, putting his foot down as they reached the end of the thirty-mile limit, 'the hospitals are all right – as all right as they ever will be under the present regime, anyway. It's just that – oh, I don't know – one never seems to get any time to oneself, however far one gets in the profession. And then one gets so involved – people, committees, *les politesses diplomatiques* ... I tell you, if we go to war– and we shall, you know,' he said, to arrest the other's slight gesture of scepticism, 'I shall try and get into the Navy. I might get what I want there: the work without all the – the sociability, the – impedimenta.' He said it in

English. 'What's the word – *impedimente*, I don't know. Anyway, the impedimenta.'

'Ah, impedeemen-tah,' answered the Czech, politely uncomprehending, and they fell silent.

*

George was still out when Steven got back to 'Four Winds'. He and Stewart and Charles arrived in tearing spirits in the middle of lunch, and everything had to be reorganized because Marion had thought they would be lunching at the club. She kept jumping up from the table to help the efficient Bacon, who was obviously longing to tell her to sit down and let him get on with it by himself.

'Pity you weren't with us, Steven,' George kept saying through his cold game pie. 'We had a terrific round. Weather just right, greens like billiard tables – we were all in tremendous form. Young Charles here was driving like a god, weren't you, my boy?'

'Well, I was rather, as a matter of fact,' admitted Charles, smiling reminiscently into his beer.

'We picked up old Murchison for a fourth,' said George. 'You know old Murchison – fellow who does that trick with the half-crown and the wine glass – damned amusing bloke, in the Sappers. Wish you'd been with us.' So did Steven. He enjoyed the silly, healthy masculine world of golf. Two-and-a-half hours in the open air, just the right amount of exercise, and then relaxing afterwards in the bar and feeling for the moment that you were all jolly good fellows. It was just such a pleasant, uncomplicated way of spending a morning as he could have done with today. He had not been able to get away for golf for ages.

'By the way,' George remembered to say, when he had pacified his first cravings on pie and could contemplate cheese with more delicate appreciation, 'what about your old josser? Did you pull him through?'

'Oh, I think he'll do,' said Steven shortly, wishing people

would not stop speaking and listen to see whether he were going to talk medicine. Strange new trait, this fascination that medical details had for the lay mind.

*

After lunch they played tennis until the haze drifted from the sky and it was hot enough to swim. The water in the pool was coloured a deep blue by a chemical specially procured for George by a man at I.C.I. Nobody else in England had such blue water in his pool. George wore a pair of inadequate bathing trunks which made him look like an acorn out-growing its cup. He and Marion had been to the Riviera for Easter, and he was very brown from conscientious sunbathing and oiling. Marion had brought a white rubber swimming suit back from France, which emphasized her unmaternal figure. Steven tapped his knuckles disapprovingly on the knobs where her ribs met her breast-bone and said: 'You're getting a real rickety rosary, Marry. It's disgusting. Why don't you do something about it?'

'I do,' she laughed, with the light-heartedness of the woman who can eat what she likes without getting fat. 'I eat like a horse. Carbohydrates, Steven,' she added in the serious tone she reserved for anything even faintly scientific. Her eyes were huge circles in a face made tinier by the tight white cap.

'You're lucky,' sighed Ruth, who was sitting fully clad in a deck-chair near the edge. 'I have to be terribly careful. I almost never have coffee and cakes in the middle of the morning now.'

'But, my dear!' shrieked Marion, 'didn't you know? It's not what you eat, it's whether you drink with your meals that counts. Half an hour before and an hour afterwards, you have to drink a glass of water, but nothing while you're eating. What's the good of having a doctor for a husband if he doesn't tell you elementary things like that?'

'Steven doesn't approve of women trying to get thin,' said Ruth smugly, trotting out the thought with which she consoled herself when her skirts had to be let out. 'Do you, darling?'

He was floating now in the pool, wishing he were fitter, so that his body did not start to die from the extremities inwards before he had been long in the water.

'Lot of harm done by Banting,' he mumbled lazily. 'Women shrivel up their insides and then wonder why they can't have children.'

'Oh rot, Steven,' said Marion. 'You're appallingly behind the times. You're awfully silly, you know; you could make a lot of money if you'd do obesity cures. Nearly all the rich women are fat, or is it the other way round?'

'Steven manages to make a good income without having to be a quack,' Ruth started to say, but Marion had slipped into the water, and George had dived in from the spring-board with a deafening belly-flop, so no one heard.

Afterwards they had a late tea on the lawn outside the dining-room windows, and nobody wanted to get up and go to the Berrys' for drinks.

'Some of you must, at least,' said George. 'It was all fixed up yesterday.'

'Well, ring up and unfix it,' said Rupert, surprised that his father should have overlooked so obvious a solution.

'Darling,' said Marion, 'when you're a bit older you'll realize that life isn't quite so simple as that.'

'Oh, *Ma*,' said Rupert crossly, 'don't start educating me, for God's sake. You're quite the last person to talk, anyway.' He got up as gracefully as a cat, and went into the house. He often flared up for no reason at all, and Marion became worried, and went and looked up Adolescence in her *Handbook of Psychology*.

'Well, you'll have to go, George,' she said now, 'and Steven must go, because he's good socially.' Steven groaned. 'Will you go, Ruth?' Yes, Ruth would go, if Steven were going.

In the end, after a lot of discussion, they all went, except Stewart, who could not be found.

*

In his dressing-room at 'Firlands,' on the other side of Camberley, Mr Berry, getting into a tie after a somnolent afternoon in the garden, called fretfully: 'I rather wish we hadn't asked anybody, now, don't you, dear?'

'Yes,' admitted his wife from the bedroom where she was struggling into her Charnaux belt. 'But after all, we were at the Marshalls' all day yesterday, and we do owe several people round here. Anyway, it was your idea. That's the trouble with you, you get carried away when you've had a cocktail or two.'

*

In George's car, speeding towards 'Firlands' someone said gloomily: 'Well, it is a free drink, anyway.'

'Let's stop on the way somewhere and have one to give us courage.'

'Oh, no, let's get on there and get it over,' said Marion, 'so that we can be back for dinner in reasonable time.'

'What is for dinner?' asked George over his shoulder.

'Chicken crêpes, I believe. That is, if I remembered to tell Ma Bacon to do that with the chicken instead of mayonnaise. Yes, I must have, because I remember telling her no garlic. Chicken crêpes, and chocolate ice.'

'Oh, God,' groaned George. 'It'll spoil.'

*

'Well, if they're coming, I wish they'd come and get it over with.' Mr Berry fussed round the drawing-room, opening cigarette boxes and giving the shakers, already professionally agitated by his parlour-maid, extra, feeble little jiggles.

'I hope nobody stays on and expects to be asked to dinner, that's all,' said his wife, pinching her mauve-tinted waves in front of a mirror. 'There's only enough for the two of us. Stop eating those cheese straws, Arnold; they're for the guests. There! There's the bell. Wipe your mouth quickly. Why can you never eat without making crumbs?'

*

When Mrs Berry had said: 'Do, *all* of you, come over for drinks tomorrow,' she had not quite meant that. She reeled a little when seven of them turned up together – Rupert, driving Steven's car, had been tailing his father to annoy him – recovered swiftly and sailed forward in a cloud of pungent white powder.

'We're like a blooming school treat,' said Rupert to Charles in the hall. He hung about for a bit, and then made a beautiful blasé entrance, unnoticed, but satisfying to the self-respect.

A blonde girl in a linen suit and her husband, a tall, hollow-cheeked cavalry major with a skin like a weathered saddle, drinking cocktails by the hydrangea-filled fireplace, looked round startled as George's party poured in. Mrs Berry insisted on introducing everybody to everybody meticulously, which took some time and effectively killed conversation, while Mr Berry ran round outside the circle with a tray of drinks, as if he were playing 'I sent a letter to my love'.

Other guests arrived: a poor relation of Mrs Berry's, who had at last nerved herself to come downstairs, two more married couples, a girl in sailcloth trousers who had a reputation among the Army, and a square, curly-haired young man who only needed horns to be a Herefordshire bull.

Steven had two cocktails quickly, and went to talk to the blonde major's wife, leaving Ruth stranded in the middle of the room, gyrating slowly on her own axis in the hope of finding someone to talk to.

Mrs Berry came up to her. 'But you haven't a drink, Mrs Sheppard! Arnold, what are you thinking about? Beatrice! Get Mrs Sheppard a drink.'

'Oh, please don't bother,' said Ruth. 'I don't drink, you know. At least, hardly ever. Only at weddings and birthdays, and occasions like that, just so as not to be a wet blanket. I suppose I'm funny, but I don't really like the *taste*.'

Mrs Berry said: 'Well then, you must have something soft. What will you have?'

Ruth would have liked to ask: What have you got? but with Mrs Berry importuning her on one side and an elegant parlour-maid on the other saying: 'What will you take, madam?' she asked for the first thing she could think of. She saw Mrs Berry telling the maid to go and open some tomato juice, and began to say: 'Oh, please don't bother. I don't mind what I have. Anything – I don't really want –' but Mrs Berry overrode her, insisting that of course she must have tomato juice, and even following the maid to remind her to put some ice in it. The whole thing became quite an issue. In the end, Ruth never got the tomato juice, because the maid had to go and answer the door, after which she forgot, and Ruth was discovered, some half an hour later, still without a drink. Mrs Berry was volubly apologetic, and rebuked the maid, who eventually brought the tomato juice so full of cayenne that Ruth could not drink it, and had to hide it behind a photograph of Mrs Berry's son, suet-faced, on an occasional table, where she imagined it shrieking like a mandrake whenever anyone approached. What would they think of her when they discovered it afterwards? She wished Steven would not always abandon her at parties.

The rest of the company was settling down. Rupert was holding forth about T. S. Eliot to a gaunt woman in amber beads; his cousin Charles was talking golf with the Hereford-shire bull; Annette had retreated to the window seat with a drink, a cigarette, a dish of salted almonds and a magazine; George was ubiquitous, helping to make the party go, and might at any minute tell One of his Stories. Laszlo had been cornered on a sofa by a glittering woman in a purple dress who was talking at him in what he did not realize was French. He was sweating lightly, and casting agonized glances to-wards Marion, who had discovered the cavalry major.

What nearly always happened sooner or later to Steven had happened: someone, in this case Mrs Berry, was angling for a bit of free advice. He listened courteously, with his ears but not with his brain, and Mrs Berry, who had been a little frightened of him at first, remarked later to a friend, how easy it was to interest these people by talking on their own subject. 'Such a charming man; we had the most illuminating conversation. I believe I made quite a conquest.' Steven managed to convey this impression by murmuring agreeably at the right moments.

It was nearly eight o'clock before George remembered the chicken crêpes. He had been telling Mr Berry how to lay out his rock garden. His host, nodding like a hen, had not liked to let on that he had not got a rock garden and if he had would not have dreamed of interfering with his gardener.

Marion was already refurnishing Mrs Berry's drawing-room for her, and Charles, to whom these things always happened too late, was just beginning to make headway with the girl in sailcloth trousers.

*

After dinner, Ruth's fears were realized. Someone said: 'Let's play paper games!' After a short delay caused by finding enough pencils and seeing that everyone had something to drink, they began to play a game called anagrams, which George had adopted as a 'Four Winds' speciality, and enbellished with all kinds of by-laws and traditions which you were shrieked at if you broke. Laszlo was allowed to go to bed, and everyone else seemed to be either brilliant at it, like Stewart and Annette and Rupert and Steven, or witty, like George and Marion, and even Charles, who was allowed to cheat by having a dictionary, and producing improbable words of which no one had ever heard. Ruth tried to cheat by sitting next to Steven and looking over his shoulder. She was shouted at, because the idea was to choose words beginning and ending with a certain letter and then describe them abstrusely for the others to guess.

Ruth chose words like CAT and described them as 'Domestic animals', and could not understand why everyone said: 'Oh, *Ruth*!' Nor could she understand why there was such a fuss when she described 'GIFT' as 'To present'. They wasted a lot of time trying to explain to her the difference between a noun and a verb. She stuck to her point, insisting that she could not see that it *mattered*, but when she got back to London she bought a sixpenny book called *Everybody's Grammar*, and tried to work it out.

Eventually, Rupert said, 'Oh, let's play something else,' and Steven, stretched out comfortably in an arm-chair with his long legs on a footstool, said: 'Well, make it snappy, because I'm going to bed soon. I've got to make an early start to-morrow. By the way, Marry, would I be an awful nuisance if I had a cup of coffee about eight?'

'But darling, of course. You must have *breakfast*. That reminds me, I haven't said anything ...' She jumped up and went to the kitchen to leave cryptic notes on the back of the grocer's invoice for Mrs Bacon, who had gone to bed.

Rupert had made the horrid suggestion: 'Let's play Truths. So good for the ego, don't you think, Steven?' He mocked him with an eyebrow.

'Don't you laugh at your Uncle Steven,' said Marion, coming back into the room. 'He's the best psychologist in London.'

'Thank you, darling.' Steven stretched out a hand and Marion bent down and kissed him on the forehead. Ruth frowned and began to swing her shoe. When they asked her the silly question which was going round the married couples: 'Why did you marry Steven?' she reddened and blurted out: 'Because I loved him,' and then wished she had not. It was a dull answer, anyway; the others had all said something amusing.

Steven patted her hand. 'Thanks, Ruth.'

Presently, he levered himself out of his chair and said he was going to give Ugly a run before he went to bed. It was dark and silent outside. There was no moon, and the night smelt of fir trees. Having nearly knocked him over, Ugly bolted into some bushes, where he crashed about making what he thought were hunting noises. Steven strolled up and down, liking the sound of the gravel under his feet.

When they asked him: 'Why did you marry Ruth?' he

had laughed and said airily: 'Oh, for her money of course.'

Ruth, with her forty pounds a year allowance and her dresses passed on from London cousins ... The very thing over which they had first met was symbol of her girlhood's way of life. Steven remembered it clearly: a wicker travelling basket, such as governesses in books used to be saddled with. Ruth's had an old leather strap round it, and the wicker-work was coming apart here and there like the seat of a worn-out chair. It had introduced her to Steven by tripping him up on the deck of one of the paddle steamers which chugged between Portsmouth and the Isle of Wight. Steven, who had then been qualified for nearly five years, had his own practice in Ryde, which the money which came to him at his father's death had helped to buy. Although he had at last uprooted his mother from her lonely Shropshire house to which she still clung, the square yellow house, sideways on to the Solent and halfway up the hill which tilts the foundations of every building in Ryde, was still much too big. His predecessor's dilapidated tribe of children had filled it, but Steven shut up many of the rooms and was still able to extend the surgery and dispensary in expectation of the increased practice of which he was confident. Having just delivered two of Ryde's wealthiest inhabitants, Steven was returning from London, where he had been buying some equipment.

Ruth's wicket basket, which she had, of course, placed awkwardly, half into the gangway, had caught Steven on his way to see that his little crate was still where the porter had put it. He tripped, stumbled and nearly wrenched off his ankle in the effort to preserve the precious electric auriscope in its black case which he was carrying.

He swore under his breath, and turned back to move the basket out of his way, ostentatiously, so that whoever had left it there should feel bad.

'Oh, I *do* beg your pardon,' said a distraught voice, and Ruth left her seat at the seaward end of the bench and came towards him, blushing and biting her lips, strands of her thick chestnut hair escaping from under her hat and blowing about her face.

'It was silly of me to leave it there,' she said, not looking directly at him, 'but it's so heavy. I got it so far, and couldn't get it any farther, and with these other things ...' She also had a scratched green leather hatbox, a badly-trained spaniel on a chain, an umbrella and a large rubbed suède handbag.

She was twenty-four then, six years younger than Steven, and her indeterminate air and complete ineptitude for travelling alone were quite appealing. She had a lovely slightly freckled skin, and eyes which, although too close together, were a clear and candid hazel. Being unsoignée, she looked her best in the open air, where she could enjoy the sun and wind without anxiety.

Steven, who could probably have had any girl in the Isle of Wight if he chose, had hardly had time to look twice at any of them. He had half-an-hour's enforced leisure now, and was quite content to spend it with Ruth. He thought her rather sweet, and she listened enthralled to whatever he chose to talk about. When they bumped alongside Ryde Pier he helped her with her luggage after he had looked after his equipment, and took her to tea at a café on the front.

Ruth lived at Seaview, a mile along the coast, and the next time Steven drove out there to a patient he saw her being dragged along the street by the spaniel. She wore the preoccupied expression which the cares of shopping always gave her, and when he blew his horn and slid his Morris up to the pavement, it was gratifying to see her face light up. She dropped the chain, and the spaniel careered off unnoticed. Steven gave her a lift home, and it was only after he had gone that she realized about the dog, and her mother, who credited it with more sense than she credited Ruth, made her go out again after it.

Whenever Ruth came into Ryde she hung about in the neighbourhood of Steven's house, and sometimes she saw him and sometimes she didn't. At last, what she had longed for happened. She got a septic insect bite, their old doctor was away, and Ruth managed to persuade her mother to let her take it to Steven. She was his last patient that afternoon. He was just going to have tea, and he took Ruth into the domestic part of the house to meet his mother.

Ruth, who had been brought up to be solicitous of mothers, was a great success with Mrs Sheppard. After that, it was easy. She could always come and call on Steven's mother, and, as before, sometimes she saw him and sometimes she didn't.

Steven got quite used to her. She was no more trouble about the house than a bit of furniture. if not as useful. She was handy for listening when Steven wanted to talk about something to get it clear in his own head. Often, when he came in in the evening, his mother would say: 'Ruth looked in this morning to change my library book for me,' or 'Ruth came to tea. She brought me some plums'. It meant hardly more to him than the visits of the laundry or the dustman, which his mother also liked to report, but it kept her in his mind. He had once promised to take her out in his small sailing dinghy. She had bought herself a blue-and-white jersey whose horizontal stripes accentuated a bust which did not need it, and was waiting for him to suggest it again.

About this time, Steven became involved in a violent affair with a girl called Phoebe Threepmann, who was on holiday at Bembridge. She was small and fair, and looked like a primrose, and he made up his mind to marry her. After she went home he spent a lot of money and neglected his work to go up to London to take her out. They became unofficially engaged, and he brought her back to the island to spend Christmas at Ryde. His mother did not like her very much, and said she could not understand a word she said. Phoebe was bored, and grudged the time he gave to his work. She would go in the car with him on his rounds, and once, when he had been longer with a patient than he expected, he came out to find she had driven the car away and left him to get home by bus.

They had managed to make quite a joke of breaking off

their engagement: 'Darling, do you *see* me as a doctor's wife, now do you?' and had parted good friends, but Steven was terribly hurt to discover that she did not care for him enough to adapt herself.

Ruth, of course, had been in the offing all this time, continuing to change his mother's library books and coming to tea with her when Phoebe, of whom she was mortally afraid, was out of the way. She had caught Steven on the rebound through no guile of her own, simply by being there. She had certain advantages over Phoebe. She needed no living up to when he was tired, and she would never do things like driving his car away. To start with, she did not know how to drive.

There were quite a few disappointed mothers in and around Ryde when Ruth's engagement to Steven was announced. Her mother teaed out on it triumphantly for weeks.

It was when Steven's mother died that the first hint of Ruth's uselessness to him became apparent. Until now, he had quite liked her being dependent on him for everything. She was as undemanding as a dog and in her adoration as flattering. But one needs someone to lean on in grief, someone to take the initiative and make the decisions for a while. Ruth was not lacking in sympathy: it was simply that she had not the mental equipment to be of any help. Her condolences were sincere and spontaneous, but they were usually proffered at the wrong time. 'Poor darling,' she would murmur, when she found Steven brooding somewhere over a difficult diagnosis. 'You're thinking of Her. I know, I know.' Succeeding only in making Steven feel that he ought to have been thinking of his mother.

When he was smitten with the usual futile remorse: 'I could have been nicer to her; I could have done more for her,' Ruth was quite good at assuring him that a better son could not have lived but, as she thought Steven perfect whatever he did, this did not carry much weight.

In any case, she had herself to be sorry for as well now, because she was expecting a baby.

She sailed through her pregnancy with the ease of the healthy, large-built girl, and her delivery by Steven was, as he told her unbelieving mother, 'a piece of cake'. Ruth was very dramatic all during this time, and although she probably would not have let anyone but Steven touch her, he gathered that she would have liked him to have been the sort of husband who could not face the tremendous issue of delivering his wife himself. But he would have died sooner than let anyone else interfere with his baby. He was quite surprised to find that during the birth Ruth was no more to him than any gravid body. It was only after he had been away and washed and had a drink and come back to find Ruth woken from her sleep and already cow-eyed with maternal solicitude that he thought of her as his wife as well as his patient.

They stayed in Ryde until the baby girl, Carol, was three years old.

The practice which Steven bought in Dynsford was on a larger scale than even his Ryde one had grown to be, and he was able to inherit his predecessor's honorary appointment at St Margaret's Hospital. Dynsford was a sophisticated town, far enough from London not to be suburban, yet near enough for its larger houses to be inhabited by people who worked in town during the day. St Margaret's had a large and quite expensive private wing which was nearly always full. It was at Dynsford that Steven first began to make real money, and to complete his development from an intelligent and confident but still volatile young man into a perpetually charming, tactful and assured popular physician.

But Ruth did not keep pace with him. Although their way of life expanded through contacts and sociability and a growing income, Ruth scarcely progressed from the demeanour which had just borne her through the unexacting narrows of the Seaview life. Shyness is only becoming to the very young, and Ruth's utter dependence on Steven in everything had long ago ceased to be gratifying. The tremendous sorrow of their child's death, which should have brought them closer together, pushed them farther apart; Steven, self-contained and quite antagonistic in his terror of giving Ruth an opportunity to say the wrong thing, and poor Ruth, so utterly incapable of coping with a fundamental emotion like tragedy that she shut the thing away and dared not face or speak of it.

Two years in Wimpole Street with a position to uphold and the money with which to do it had matured and polished Ruth slightly. She was not incongruous in her setting as the wife of a successful West End consultant – merely unnoticeable.

*

The front door of the house opened and the rectangle of light from the hall silhouetted Marion's scanty figure in the clinging black dinner dress.

'Stee-ven!' she called, and whistled for him as if he were a dog. He drew on his cigarette so that it glowed for her. 'I'm here,' he said. 'Come and walk a bit.'

'Oh, there you are ... where? ... Heavens, it's dark. Steven, where are you? Oh, that was my nose!' Stumbling and laughing, she groped for him until she ran her face into his arm. She tucked hers through it, dragging a little because she was so much shorter, and they strolled down the drive towards the little thicket of larches by the gate, where they could hear Ugly crashing about.

'It has been nice having you,' Marion said. 'I wish you'd come more often.'

'I've loved being here.'

'Oh, no, you haven't. It's been a silly week-end – what I've seen of it. We all seem to have done the sort of things we could just as well have done in town. I often wish we had a place in the real country, but George loves it here. I like him to have what he likes, and he's so easily pleased ... it doesn't take much.'

'Pretty good wife, aren't you?' said Steven gloomily. He felt depressed by these conjugal tendernesses.

'Well, you know,' Marion said eagerly, 'I discovered quite early on the recipe for a happy marriage. You let your husband have his way in all the odd little things that don't matter so very much in the long run, then if something tremendous crops up that you really feel strongly about, you can have it your way without him feeling hen-pecked. Where's that dog of yours? I don't want him all over my daffodils.'

Steven called Ugly, who suddenly materialized icy-nosed, from surprisingly near, and they turned and walked back to the house.

'Ridiculous game, wasn't it?' Marion said suddenly. 'Who suggested playing Truths, anyway?'

'Not me,' said Steven. 'I get enough of it from my patients. Some of these women simply wallow in the most embarrassing sort of spiritual strip-tease.'

'Why *did* you marry Ruth?' demanded Marion impulsively. 'I've often wanted to ask you, but even I haven't liked to. But now that it's so dark, I dare.'

He could sense that her face was turned up to his, alive with curiosity, wondering how he would take it. 'Oh –' He tried to pass it off. 'I told you – for her money.'

'No, don't fool, Steven. I'm serious.'

'Well, all right,' he said, defiantly. 'Because I loved her.'

'That's what I thought,' sighed Marion, unconvinced.

'If it comes to that,' said Steven. 'Why did you marry George?'

'I wouldn't have, if I'd known there was anything like you about. But by the time I met you we were both heavily married, weren't we?'

'Yes ... Marion, d'you remember that dance we went to at Dynsford, at the house where they had artificial moons hung in the trees?'

She laughed. 'The Bickersleys. They never had anything real. Even their soap was made like apples and pears.'

'They had a box hedge cut to look like a cemetery wall with urns on it.'

'And you kissed me behind it, only you were so scared for your blessed professional reputation that you went indoors quickly before you could forget yourself.' It was part of Marion's policy to take things out and look at them, and, if necessary, laugh – even things that hurt. It saved a lot of moping.

'I wish –' began Steven. 'No I don't.' He thrust away a sudden, gay and charming picture of what life would have been like with Marion. It wouldn't. It would have been maddening.

*

Ruth was brushing her hair when he went into their bed-room. 'I thought you were never coming in,' she said, 'so I didn't wait. Steven, we needn't come again for a long time now we've been, need we?'

He sat on the edge of the bed and took off his shoes. 'Why not?' he said, leaning forward with his hands dangling between his knees. 'I like it here. If only I could spare more week-ends ...'

'Oh, darling, you *don't*.' She parted the front of her hanging hair so that she could look at him in the glass. 'I never feel happy here, anyway. And d'you know what?' She swivelled round on the stool to face him, shook back her hair and put on her intense voice. 'I believe Marion's a bit keen on you. I think it's disgusting, a woman of her age. She must be forty.'

'Well, I'm forty-one. Would it be disgusting if I were "keen on" someone, as you put it?'

'Oh, well, it's different for men.' Ruth suddenly sat upright, holding her hair-brush like a weapon. 'Yes, it would be disgusting.'

Chapter 3

—

EVERY six months, one of the Honorary Physicians at St Margaret's had to take his turn giving lectures to a class of senior nurses. Steven had been giving his this spring, fitting in an hour somehow before his Thursday clinics. The syllabus never varied, and he could use the original notes which he had compiled in the optimistic days when he still expected more than twenty per cent. of the nurses to benefit from them.

By now, he was fully aware that some of them, especially those on night duty, slumbered in the back row throughout the performance, that others sat tense and petrified lest he should ask them a question, when they would stare at him in dumb agony until he passed on, and that a few, carrying on the traditional warfare between the medical and nursing staff, called him Stinking Steven, mimicked his way of talking, and were ostentatiously determined to be impressed neither by the man nor his information. However, there were always some in the front rows who took a really intelligent interest, and he concentrated on these, knowing that the others would scrape through the examination by swotting it up from text-books and the notes of those who had gone before.

His stock of anecdotes and illustrations from actual cases were known as 'Steven's stories', familiar to the nurses from hearsay long before the first lecture, but giggled at politely nevertheless by the eager souls in the front rows.

This year, Nurse Lake was one of these, sitting well forward, in clean cuffs and apron, with fountain pen poised and head tilted to catch his least syllable. Her notes were masterpieces in handwriting, the same shape as herself, thin and upright, with no curves. Hoping against hope that Steven would one day ask to see her book, she laboured for

hours in her bedroom over diagrams in different-
inks, with a chair under the door-handle, because yo
forbidden to use ink for fear of the counterpane.

This last lecture, on a Thursday in June, was to be dev
ted to clearing up misunderstandings and answering questions on the course he had given them. Since the week-end,
the weather had broken, and Nurse Lake, standing up with
the others as Steven came in, noticed spots of rain on the
shoulders of his black coat. He must have come straight to
them from his car. She imagined him running for it across
the gravel, and making straight for the lecture-room, with
his long strides, which would leave Sister Tutor, who always
met him at the main door, fluttering after him like a de-
spairing hen.

He came in in a hurry, his masculinity disturbing the
feminine schoolroom atmosphere of the room with its desks
and blackboard. He had no time to waste. His 'Afternoon,
Nurses,' as he stepped on to the platform, was followed in the
same breath by: 'What are the two fundamental classes of
anæmia? You at the end.' He never could remember all
their names.

'Me, sir?' asked an affronted blonde, playing for time.

'Yes, you.' Steven slammed his case on to the high desk,
and rummaged in it for his dog-eared file of notes.

The blonde fiddled with the pile of curls behind which her
cap looked as if it would fly off the back of her head. 'Well,
sir, it all depends –'

'It doesn't depend at all.' He shut the lid of the case. 'I
said the two main classes of anæmia. They don't change
with the weather, you know.' She withered his attempt at
humour by lowering her lids, which she knew emphasized
the length of her lashes.

'Anyone else?' Steven caught the eye of Nurse Lake, sitting with pursed lips and an arm raised stiffly in the air,
quivering with knowledge. He gave her a slight smile of
recognition, which she tucked away in the bottom drawer
of her heart. 'Well, Nurse?' She stood up.

'Look,' he said wearily, 'I told you at the first lecture that I do *not* want you to stand up when you answer, and, if I remember rightly, I've been telling you at every lecture since. Could you, perhaps, manage not to do it, just this last time?'

Crimson, Nurse Lake sat down, and said in a subdued voice: 'The two main classes of anæmia are primary and secondary.'

'Mm. Subdivide the primary.'

She began to reel off: 'Pernicious, aplastic, splenic, chlorosis – er, ideopathic, hypochromic . . .'

She had learned most of her medical lectures like a parrot, and much of them in Steven's own words. Relying blindly on him, she hardly ever pursued the subject in text-books or tried to puzzle things out for herself. Consequently, as he could not possibly cover the whole syllabus in twelve lectures, she alternated between chasms of ignorance and heights of pure knowledge. Dr Sheppard had devoted two whole lectures to the anæmias, one of his pet subjects, but had barely skimmed the headlines of the pneumonias. Therefore, argued Nurse Lake's brain, anæmia must be known like the Lord's Prayer, but one need lose no sleep over pneumonia, which had been left to Sister Tutor to teach them.

As this was the last lecture, Steven felt obliged to ask a few questions all round, even if it meant waking up the backbenchers. To encourage them, he asked them the breeding ground of typhoid fever, which inspired the whole class to sit up and chant: 'Food, flies and fæces,' and subside, giggling. Nurse Bracken then tied herself in knots over the pituitary gland, and Nurse Gibbons, red-haired and spectacled, stared at him marble-eyed as if the word 'allergy' did not mean a thing to her.

Steven found himself marvelling for the hundredth time at the difference between the nurses in the lecture-room and on the wards. After each week's struggle in here, he used to do his rounds prepared for all his patients to be dead, instead of, as he found them, progressing as favourably as expert nursing could ensure.

The wise old Matron of his London hospital, who had been training nurses since the long-skirted days of leeches and cupping, had once said to him: 'My best nurses are not the ones who come top in examinations. Nurses can't hope to remember all they're told, and it's the girl who knows what to remember and what to forget – that's the one who makes the good nurse. After all, it's no use her being able to give you a minute description of the structure of the heart if she doesn't know the signs by which the organ intimates that it intends to stop beating.'

Steven looked at his watch, and told the girls to ask him questions on anything they did not understand. One or two in the front row raised quibbling points with which he dealt briefly, and there was a short argument with an Irish girl who had maintained all along that women could contract as well as transmit hæmophilia, because her godmother had died of it, and was not going to lose this last opportunity of saying so again.

Steven looked at his watch once more. Amazing how sixty minutes could drag or gallop arbitrarily. He wanted to get down to Outpatients; he had met Snorting Lil in the corridor, and she had told him he had a big clinic this week. He had two private calls to make in Dynsford, besides several in London, and Ruth's mother was coming to dinner, which would mean an atmosphere if he was late.

'Well – what else?' he asked. Each face looked as though he could not possibly be addressing her. One or two of the nurses raked their minds desperately for an intelligent question; most of them felt that they knew so little about everything that it was not worth, in the last quarter of an hour, disturbing the jelly-like mass of their ignorance. After a short silence, in which you could hear the electric clock humming, Steven said, disliking himself for his ponderous sarcasm: 'I'm to take it, then, that you all know everything about everything I have spoken of in this lecture-room? Of all the pearls of wisdom I have cast before you there's not one that has rolled through your fingers.' Discomfited giggles, and shuffling of blue cotton behinds on hard chairs.

Nurse Lake spoke up desperately, interesting shades of red spreading upwards from her stiff white collar: 'Please, sir, could you run through again the difference between a diabetic and an insulin coma?' She just remembered in time not to stand up.

'But I've *told* you ... Surely you don't want me to waste these last few minutes on something you can look up in any text-book?'

'Well, I thought perhaps, sir –' She had simply said the first thing that came into her head, terrified that he might walk out on them before the all too short hour, disgusted by their unresponsiveness. In her corner by the window, Sister Tutor, who always had to chaperone the dangerous situation of the nurses being in the same room as a Man, was wagging her head disapprovingly.

'Nurse must know that, in any case?' Steven appealed to her.

'Oh, yes, oh, yes, she should, sir. Indeed she should know.'

'Well, supposing you tell us, Nurse.'

Nurse Lake stood up.

'Sit down!' One of the night nurses woke up and let out a laugh before she had time to clap a hand to her mouth.

Nurse Lake told him, word for word as he had given it them three Thursdays ago.

'All right, all right.' He interrupted her before she had finished. 'I thought you knew it. I'm not such an ass as some of you seem to take me for.' After this, nobody dared to ask any more questions, but it was five to three, and Steven could put his notes into his case, shoot his cuffs and pass a hand over his hair. 'Let's see now. You have your exam after this, don't you? I've set your papers. I gave them to you, didn't I, Sister?' She nodded like a hen pecking for grain.

'What are they like?' asked someone boldly. 'Have we got nice questions, sir?'

'When you see them,' answered Steven, who could not remember now what questions he had set, 'you'll probably wish you were dead.'

A chorus of 'Oh, *sir*!' greeted this. Everyone was quite lively, now that it was time to go.

'And when I can fit it in,' he went on, 'I'll give you each a short *viva*.' Groans, and whispers of: 'My dear, I shall *die*!' or 'What cheek, the last set didn't have it,' 'I wish we'd had old Baxey for our medicine.'

'Don't get alarmed,' said Steven, briskly. 'Just remember that kindliness is my motto, and that I shall not be trying to find out what you *don't* know, but what you do. If anything.' Sister Tutor was making extraordinary movements with her head, and pointing her fountain pen at Steven's back. The time had come, apparently, for the most senior nurse to make the traditional speech of thanks to Dr Sheppard for so kindly earning his twelve guineas.

It was Nurse Lake. She had been rehearsing in bed, in the bath, walking down the street, and in front of mirrors in different lights for days. At last she could legitimately obey her instincts and stand up.

Fumbling with a strand of hair which was escaping from her ribbon, she began: 'May I, on behalf of the class –' but had to start again, because Steven was looking round for some books he had brought in with him and had not heard her.

'May I, on behalf of the class, thank you very much, sir, for your very interesting lectures. I'm sure we have all b-benefited from them very much, and we hope very much that we shall do well in the exam to show how much we have learned from them.' Too late, she realized that she had said 'very much' too often and sat down, breathing heavily.

'Thank you, Nurse,' said Steven courteously. 'It only remains for me to say how much I have enjoyed teaching you. I don't know when I've had such an intelligent class, Sister.' He said this every time, and every time she bridled as if she had brought into the world these stupendous intellects. 'I always start by thinking that I have a batch of cretins before me, and end up by realizing that they err more on the side of hyperthyroidism.' This familiar allusion, which had been appearing in different forms ever since the lecture on the ductless glands, was greeted now with the happy laughter of *ave atque vale*. Steven, feeling as embarrassed as he always did when they all rose together with a rustle of aprons and looked at him, left the room hurriedly.

'The Stinker can be quite decent when he wants to,' someone said.

'I think he's an awful ass,' protested someone else to counteract the disquieting flutters which he aroused in her unawakened breast.

'Just wait till we see our papers tomorrow,' yawned a night nurse. 'He'd better mark decently, that's all.'

'I hope we all do awfully well, don't you?' said Nurse Lake expansively, and hurried away from the cold reception this remark received, so as to be in the clinic before him.

The clinic never opened so smoothly on lecture afternoons. Nurse Phillimore, who had change of preparing it when Nurse Lake was in the lecture-room, had not the faintest idea . . .

Nurse Lake cast a practised eye over the benches outside the green door as she hurried by. It was obvious that Phillimore had not got all the new patients in front. She could see that habituée, Mrs Dollamore, in the front row, and there was a man in a blue blazer right at the back with a brand new folder. She would have to get them sorted out while Dr Sheppard was taking the first history. Inside the clinic, Nurse Phillimore was sitting in Dr Sheppard's chair swivelling it round.

'Nurse!'

The plump girl shot out of the chair grinning from ear to ear. 'Gosh, you gave me a shock. I thought you were the great man himself.'

'He'll be here directly. Oh, Nurse, this clinic is *terrible*. You've laid it up all wrong.' Her distraught eye scoured the room. She pounced on the blotter and moved it an inch to the right, clicking her teeth.

'But surely,' said Nurse Phillimore. 'I went by how it's always done. It looks all right to me.'

'Well, it may do, but it's all these *little* things ...' She opened the door of an examination room and shut it again, making a wind which blew a green X-ray form out of the paper rack.

'Such as?'

Nurse Lake picked up the form and straightened up, looking round vainly for defects. 'Well – the inks, for instance. The blue should be on the right and the red on the left.'

'Oh, gosh, surely he's not going to notice that? He uses a fountain pen, anyway.'

'That's not the point, Nurse. It's just these little things that are so important. If you neglect them, how are you to be trusted in bigger things? Oh, the chair! What have you done to it? Really, Nurse, I shall have to report you to Sister.' Nurse Phillimore had swivelled the chair so far that the seat was at an impossible height, almost off the top of its screw. Nurse Lake gave it a brisk turn the wrong way, and it teetered madly for a moment before falling right off and landing on the floor, looking like a man with both legs amputated.

Steven arrived to find one nurse doubled up with laughter and the other frantic. He enjoyed seeing the seat of the chair on the floor, but he could not make Nurse Lake smile even by propelling himself skilfully round and round in the chair to get it back to its right height. He realized she was shocked with him. She had sent the other nurse out quickly before she could witness too much of this undignified sight.

He caught sight of the clock. 'Well, come on,' he barked at her. 'Let's have some patients; or are you and I going to play musical chairs all afternoon?'

She squeaked at speed to the door and hauled in the man in the blue blazer as being the only new patient of whom she was certain without sorting them out. She left considerable

ill-feeling behind her among the benches, for Nurse Phillimore had, after all, got them in their right order. Mrs Dollamore was in front because she was chaperoning her niece's
clinical début, and the man in the blue blazer was an old
patient whose folder had been lost and replaced by a new
one.

If Mrs Drage, the Lady Almoner, wanted to see Steven,
she usually came in during the clinic. It was the only way to
be sure of catching him, as when he was rushing from clinic
to wards and away to the car he was as difficult to pin down
as a butterfly on the wing. Her method was to nip in between one patient leaving and another going in. Nurse Lake,
if she saw her approaching, would try to foil her by dragging
in a patient while the last was still leaving. She did not approve of Doctor being interrupted. What she really did not
approve of was that Doctor found Mrs Drage, with her pre-
maturely grey hair, delicate skin and slight Canadian accent
extraordinarily attractive.

He looked round, pleased, when she slipped in by the exit
door, which had just released Mr Dakers with a certificate
to prove that he was not the malingerer his firm thought him.
Nurse Lake, entering by the other door with a Colitis, halted.
Mrs Drage was talking to Steven at the desk, tapping the
papers she held with her spectacles. They were laughing
about something. She always had lovely clothes; creaseless
silk blouses and beautifully cut suits, and shoes which she
bought in Canada whenever she went home to visit her
family. People hinted darkly that she must have outside
means, for how could a soldier's widow look so elegant
on a Lady Almoner's salary? She had even been seen going
to the hairdresser as often as twice a week.

'Just a moment, please, Nurse,' Steven said without looking round, and Nurse Lake, with her stockings feeling thicker
and blacker and her shoes more squeaky than usual, took
out the Colitis, who was immediately pounced upon with
pessimistic triumph by its sister, thinking that Dr Sheppard

had fulfilled her prophecy by seeing at a glance that nothing could be done.

'Oh, by the way,' said Mrs Drage when Steven had signed all the forms she wanted, 'I got that little boy into the Cheshire home for you.'

'Little boy? What little boy?'

'Garrard, that woman who was here last week with some story about a drunken husband, behaving as if the Gestapo were after her.' She pronounced it Gestappo and Steven laughed.

'Oh, yes, I remember. Dreadful woman. Gave one claustrophobia. I'm glad you fixed her up. She'd have been sitting on my doorstep otherwise.'

Nurse Lake came in again and stood by the door, creaking impatiently from foot to foot.

'Well, I'll be going,' said Mrs Drage. 'Sorry to interrupt you, but I have to, as you never come to see me.'

'I can't,' said Steven. 'I'm scared of that barrage of typing females in your office.' Nurse Lake put a stop to this foolishness by bringing the Colitis in again, and the clinic went on.

Steven, who was going to be late for dinner, waited fuming for the lights to change at the crossroads of Wigmore Street and Wimpole Street. Looking towards his house, as if he could project himself there by will power, his attention was caught by a thin young woman walking slowly down the pavement on the far side. Where had he seen her before? That smooth, anæmic face framed by the green-scarf turban, the way she clutched her fawn coat round her, and her static, unexpectant expression as if she were not going anywhere were vaguely familiar. A patient, probably.

The lights changed, and he shot round the corner and up to his house halfway up the next block. He would put the car away after dinner, or ring round to the garage. No time now if he were going to change, which Ruth's mother, who always came either in her coffee lace or her bottle-green velvet, would expect.

He shot his case on to the oak chest as if he were playing ducks and drakes, hoop-laed his hat on to a peg, and bounded up the stairs. The drawing-room door opened as he passed, and Ruth called up the second flight after him, 'Steven, you *are* late! Had you forgotten Mother was coming?'

'No!' he called back through his open dressing-room door.

'Well then, I do think – Oh, Steven, you're not going to have a bath now?' The noise of the taps drowned her voice.

No one could have a bath either as quickly or as slowly as Steven. Sometimes, last thing at night, he would lie in it for an hour, adding hot water at intervals, the wireless on the cork top of the linen casket, a whisky and soda and his cigarette case and lighter on the edge of the bath and all the papers he had not had time for during the day growing pulpy in the steam. He would not have let any patient do this, but a doctor was entitled to totter out with his heart pounding and his skin like a washerwoman's.

At other times of day, when he was always in a hurry, Steven could time himself to be in and out of the bath, soaped all over and dried in eight minutes. Drying his back on one of the enormous towels which no one else was allowed to use, he paused suddenly with one arm straight out, and the other bent behind him. Of course! That was who it was he had seen in Wimpole Street. Mrs Whatsis, the woman who had run away from her husband. The woman Mrs Drage had been talking about only this afternoon – Garroulds – Garrard – that was it. What an extraordinary coincidence.

When Welsh brought in the coffee after dinner, Steven noticed something defiant about her back. Ruth had asked her to bring cream for her mother, and the maid had flounced out, banging the door on purpose.

'What's the matter with *her*?' Steven jerked his head towards the door.

'She doesn't care what she does. She's going the day after tomorrow. I *told* you. She only gave me a week's notice.'

'Good God, I hope you've got someone else. Minney'll kick up the devil of a stink if she has to open the door even for half the day like she did when there was a hiatus last time.'

'Of course I've got someone else,' said Ruth proudly, pouring coffee. 'Or rather you have.'

'I –' began Steven incredulously, but as Ruth began to explain, he remembered a telephone call he had to make, and left the room abruptly.

'You shouldn't let him interrupt you like that,' Ruth's mother said, getting her pills out of her bag to take with her coffee when Welsh should consent to return with the cream. 'It's very rude.'

Ruth smiled, 'Mother, he's not a child. And it was something to do with his work, you know. He's very busy .Sometimes I think that we're inclined to forget what an important position he holds in the medical world.'

Her mother, who never failed to impress this position, with exaggerations, on all her acquaintances, sniffed. 'There is such a thing as common politeness, even to one's wife.' After Welsh had been and gone sulkily with the cream, she took one Digoxin and said: 'How's his book going, Ruth?'

'I never ask about it now. He doesn't seem to want to discuss it ... He often works on it in the evenings, though. That's probably what he's doing now, as he hasn't come up.'

'Well, I suppose he'll deign to come up and say goodnight before I go,' said her mother, and swallowed a second Digoxin, her Adam's apple making as much of an obstacle of it as if it had been a pebble.

*

Even then Steven had not realized. He was out to dinner the day that the new maid arrived, and his shock was considerable when the noise of a teacup being put down by his bed at half-past seven next morning made him open his eyes to the enigmatic face, paler than ever at that hour, of Mrs Garrard. He pushed himself up on one elbow, and immediately lay down again, pulling the sheet over his face with a grunt. To him, she was still a patient, and it seemed indecent and undignified for her to see him in bed, especially blue-chinned, with his back hair on end and his front hair in his eyes.

*

She got on Steven's nerves. She wore rubber-soled shoes, and was very neat and quiet at her work, so that you never knew where she was. He imagined that she was following him about. She was always appearing noiselessly in rooms or passages where he was, and whenever he looked at her he caught her watching him with her lizard eyes, although she immediately looked away.

He gathered that she was undyingly grateful to him for what he had done for her, and that she was determined to tell him so at length. He was equally determined not to give her an opportunity to start talking. He had had enough of that in the clinic.

However, she found a willing listener in Ruth. Steven could hear her droning away sometimes when she brought up Ruth's breakfast tray. Snatches would reach him in his dressing-room next door, of what 'He' had said and done, and what little Tom's temperature had soared to when he was ill; no other child in Great Ormond Street had ever reached such heights. Ruth would sit up in bed in her hair-net and her quilted bed-jacket, quite satisfied to listen. She did not get many letters, and, apart from the woman's page, she hardly cared whether she read the papers or not. The story which unfolded itself in instalments throughout the day was based on what Steven had already heard, with many embellishments, and reached far back into Mrs Garrard's courting days, and even her childhood. Ruth was delighted with her. She was a splendid worker, well-trained and thorough, and, above all, so easy to get on with. The deference and humility which to Steven had the jar of sycophancy was to Ruth a welcome change from the veiled insolent contempt which she had imagined in her former maids. She hated ordering meals even from Mrs Hankey, who knew her place like the back of her hand, because she knew that Mrs Hankey knew that she, Ruth, knew very little about cooking. Ruth had never had to do much practical housekeeping. As a girl, her mother had guarded her from it, with the vague idea that Ruth would one day 'do something with her violin playing', and even when this hope fizzled out, Ruth's hands, from habit, still went on being preserved. Her mother could do the work much quicker and better, anyway.

When she married Steven he was already able to afford a living-in servant and a daily woman. Ruth's pregnancy and her subsequent illness had absolved her from doing more than dusting and shopping gently in Ryde as an excuse to have morning coffee and cakes at 'Betty's', in the steep main street, and, by the time they got to Dynsford, Ruth, as the wife of a rapidly-prospering doctor, had neither the need nor inclination to do more.

In the kitchen, Mrs Garrard was accepted as a new cell-mate is accepted by the prisoners on whom he is thrust without choice. Mrs Hankey approved of her being so well-spoken, and Mabel, the housemaid, admired and copied her manner of holding her knife and fork and listened enthralled to the saga of Arthur's vices.

'Tell us again about the last time you saw him – you know, when he struck you,' she would say.

'What a girl!' Mrs Hankey lifted her eyes to Heaven, which was the floor of Mr Nosgood, the dentist's surgery above the kitchen. 'Always was a one for horrors. Sat through *Frankenstein* twice round, she did, because she couldn't tear herself away.'

'Well, so there we were in the bedroom,' said Mrs Garrard, as if continuing a story which had never left off, which was almost what it was. 'I'd tucked Tom down in his little cot and he was asleep at last. The poor little mite was quite worn out after the scene we'd had. I told you, if you can remember, Arthur had been taking on at me for wanting to get him into the country.'

'Yes, yes,' breathed Mabel, like a child who knows *Peter Pan* by heart. 'That was when he called you a –'

'Ssh!' Mrs Hankey was magenta with horror. It was bad enough Ethel Garrard having said That Word, without young Mabel, who hardly knew what it meant, uttering it.

They were sitting round the kitchen fire after supper, Mrs Hankey with her crochet, Mabel with a paper-backed Romance which had dropped to the floor long ago, and Mrs Garrard knitting a green jersey for Tom. 'I'm very fond of green,' she had told them, 'always have been. I'm sure I don't know why, as it's an unlucky colour. I suppose it's because I'm an unlucky person.'

'I caught him looking at me in a queer way,' she continued, her long fingers moving the needles smoothly and rapidly in the German way a former mistress had taught her. 'He'd been drinking, you understand, I knew that, and I'd had plenty of experience of what he was like when he was that way. So I just went on doing my hair. I wore it long; it wasn't till I got home to Dynsford that I had it cut, when I was hiding from him.' One got the titillating impression that she had sacrificed her red tresses for the sake of disguise.

'Well, as I say, he was looking at me; I could see him in the mirror, though he wasn't aware of that, if you get my meaning. He was very red in the face – he always had a high colour, and his eyes were so blue they could look at you sometimes like steel. He comes towards me, slow. I knew what he wanted –' Mrs Hankey glanced uneasily at Mabel, who was drooling slightly, open-mouthed.

Mrs Garrard's steel needles flashed steadily on. She sat back in her chair, her organdie apron smooth on her maroon poplin lap, her blank, madonna face bent over her work, as lifeless as if she were discussing the weather.

'Men are nasty,' she stated. 'I mean, after such a quarrel as we'd had ... I hadn't spoken to him since, all the time I was putting little Tom to bed. Well, when I tried to put him in his place, what did he do but takes hold of my hair where it was hanging down my back, twists it round his wrist like it was so much rope and before I knew what he was at, didn't he catch me a great blow across the side of the face. The bruise has gone now,' she touched her cheek regretfully, 'but it come up at the time all colours of the rainbow. I was afraid to show my face in the street for days for fear of what people would think,' Mabel knew the next bit by heart; her lips were already forming the words silently.

' "All right, my fine lady," he says, in a passion of rage, if you can understand. "All right, if you don't want me, I know someone who does." And with that he snatched up his cap and was gone out of the flat, banging the door fit to wake the dead, let alone Tom, who sobbed his poor little heart out for hours after waking in such a fright.'

'And did you see him again?' breathed Mabel, who knew the answer.

'Never hair nor hide of him. I've no doubt he went back soon enough, but I was gone by the next day, you see, and he'll have found an empty flat with the milk gone off and the fire cold.' She paused on this pleasing picture.

'But I make no doubt he's looking for me, and for Tom, too, for he was downright silly about the child.' Her monotonous voice stopped. It made you want to look over your shoulder, for fear Arthur was even now lurking under the dresser, or about to spring out of the larder, uttering That Word.

Below stairs, Mrs Garrard acquired the glamour of a hunted woman; she was considered rash if she went as far as the haberdashery counter at D. H. Evans'. Above stairs, in both the professional and domestic parts of the house, she insinuated herself more and more into favour with everybody except Steven.

Mr Nosgood, the bald dentist to whom Steven let the ground floor room opposite the waiting-room and a little room behind it where he played with his pestles and mortars, had had a lot of trouble with her predecessor, Welsh. For all her disparaging remarks about Steven, there was no ignoring the fact that he had a lot of springy black hair, a fascinating voice and a pleasing figure, whereas Mr Nosgood's hair grew only in a fringe above his ears, his voice was high and querulous, and he had a pot-belly and shoulders which were rounded from years of bending over gaping mouths. So if telephone messages were to be forgotten and letters mislaid, it was Mr Nosgood who came first. She was never very brisk about answering the bell, as she found it debilitating to come too quickly up the kitchen stairs, but during Steven's consulting hours the door was opened more promptly than when he was out and dentistry alone was being practised at No. 101 Wimpole Street. Above all, Steven was the Master of the house, while Mr Nosgood, although punctilious about his rent, was only an interloper, a Daily, like Mrs Fairchild, who did the Rough downstairs, and looked nothing like her name.

Mrs Marks, Mr Nosgood's middle-aged secretary, who had a small desk in the corner of the back room where the white-coated Miss Minden worked, had always said that Welsh was not worthy of the ménage. The specialist who had owned the house before Steven had kept a Mephistophelian manservant, who was so tall that short patients passed right under his arm as he held the door open for them. He had been very impressive. Steven's secretary, Miss Minden, was as obsessed with appearances as Mrs Marks, but for progressive, rather than old-fashioned reasons. She and Welsh had been enemies ever since the day when Miss Minden, who wore her hair in a bristly Eton crop, had suggested that a nice neat bob might look better on a doctor's parlour-maid than the lank page-boy which Welsh affected. After that she had been 'That Minden', the victim of subtle insults like a cracked cup on her tea-tray, and margarine instead of butter, or the fruit cake which looked all right, but which nobody would eat because Mrs Hankey had overdone the bicarbonate of soda. Welsh also managed very cleverly with the laundry, so that although Miss Minden had three white coats there were days when one was dirty and the other two still at the laundry.

Mrs Garrard, now, was *quite* different, agreed Mrs Marks and Miss Minden, crooking delighted little fingers over the creamy cups of mid-morning coffee which the new maid brought them unasked. She was so quiet and quick at her work, too, and always appeared noiselessly almost before the patients could take their fingers off the bell. One might have thought that she lurked all day behind the front door, but she did not, as Steven could tell you, because whenever he went upstairs, if she were not standing aside effacingly somewhere, there she would be in his dressing-room, dusting, with her eyes on his back while he got out a clean handkerchief.

When he went down to the basement before breakfast to brush Ugly in the tiny back garden, Mrs Garrard always managed to be laying Ruth's breakfast tray in the pantry where the brush and comb were kept. 'I'm very fond of that dog,' she would say. 'I'm funny that way: I've always been fond of dumb animals. I've just given his lordship a cutlet bone.' Steven had given up telling her that Ugly was only allowed big bones, because, as the dog did not like Mrs Garrard, he seldom ate what she gave him. He was too polite not to accept the bone, or the piece of cake, or the left-over toast, but he would simply carry it away and leave it somewhere when she wasn't looking.

One day Mrs Garrard had seen Miss Minden going home with her white canvas shoes in a knitting bag under her arm. 'Surely you don't take those home to clean yourself?' she had said quietly. 'Why don't you leave them here for Mabel to clean? It's her job.'

'Oh no, not really.' Miss Minden shook her cropped head in its smart unbecoming hat. 'She's only supposed to do

Doctor's and Mrs Sheppard's shoes. It's not as if I was resident, you see.'

'Well, you leave them with me.' Mrs Garrard took the bag from her and extracted the shoes in a manner that disregarded protest. 'I'll bring them up for you lovely, and they'll be all ready for you to slip on in the morning.'

Miss Minden's shoes had never been so exquisitely blancoed. They were waiting primly toe by toe under her desk every morning, and when she was summoned into the consulting room by Steven's bell, all the patient could see of her at first was those flashing, snowy feet.

Mrs Hankey, Mrs Garrard and Mabel slept at the top of the house, where small dormer windows were set in the slope of the roof and the cistern announced if Steven were taking a late bath. Next door to Mrs Garrard's bedroom was a slit of a room which had been the kitchen-maid's, when the species existed. It was used now to store cases and any medical books and records for which there was no space in the glass-fronted bookcase in the consulting room. There was also an iron bedstead and a thin mattress leaning against the wall under the sloping roof.

Mrs Garrard had not been with them two weeks when she came into the drawing-room where Ruth was writing letters and said: 'Pardon me. Am I disturbing you, Madam?'

'Of course not.' Ruth turned round in her chair. She was glad of an excuse to stop struggling with a difficult letter to the butcher. For some time his meat had been getting steadily tougher, once or twice he had sent them beef sausages instead of pork, and he had actually told Ruth, over the telephone, that if she wanted the best cuts of meat she ought to come down and choose them herself.

The climax had come when Steven had said one day at dinner: 'How is it that everyone but us seems to be able to get a decent fillet steak? What's the good of Mrs H. being able to make Béarnaise sauce? Guy Phillips asked me to dine at Boulestin's to-night. I wish to God I had.' He was cross; he had refused the invitation because he wanted to write, but the start he had made before dinner had shown him that this was another of those evenings when *The Swift Stream* was going to flow sluggishly.

'I don't know what's happened to Thompson's.' Ruth frowned. 'He used to be such a good little man, but his meat's gone off dreadfully lately.'

'Well, why not switch to someone else? I can't see the use of living in this district, anyway, if you don't take advantage of Selfridge's. I'll have another potato, please, Ethel, sooner than starve.'

'Oh, Steven, I can't. We've been to Thompson's ever since we came here. It would be so awkward. I have to go right past his shop every time I go up to the Marylebone Road.'

'Well, go another way. And the whisky, please, Ethel. I don't know why you don't leave the decanter on the table.' He knew Mrs Garrard disapproved of him having more than one whisky at dinner. When they were eating pancakes, Ruth, who had been turning it over in her mind, repeated: 'It's so *awkward*, Steven. What would I say to him? After all, it's not as if he'd done anything one could lay one's finger on. We must be fair. And I do think one ought to patronize the small shopkeeper, if possible. They're fighting an uphill battle against the chain stores.' She had read this somewhere, and it had stuck. 'But of course, if you really would prefer to deal with Selfridge's ...'

'Oh, Lord,' said Steven, recognizing the implication that it was he who paid the bills, 'I don't care who we go to as long as we can get eatable meat. Your housekeeping money's yours to do as you like with. I don't object to earning it, but I do object to your not knowing how to spend it properly.'

'Perhaps if I were to write to Thompson's and say we're going to change unless his meat gets better ...'

'Good idea.' Steven was bored now.

'It's a difficult letter to write. Steven, you write it. It would carry much more weight from you.'

'Oh, nonsense, Ruth. Don't be so helpless; it's your job.

139

How would you like it if I asked you to make diagnoses for me when I was stuck?'

'Oh, well, of course, dear, I couldn't,' said Ruth, taking this seriously.

She had only got as far as: 'Dear Mr Thompson, I have been thinking that unless –' when Mrs Garrard interrupted her.

She held a letter in her hand, and there was nothing in her expression to indicate whether she had good news to impart or bad. She straightened a sofa cushion and puffed up the vase of roses which Ruth had bought and arranged that morning. It was a great relief to Ruth that Ethel was good at doing flowers. Her own touch was very unsure, and she never could pass a vase which she had arranged without giving them a push or a pull, which never seemed to make them any more satisfactory. Ethel had taken the job unobtrusively from her, and had even put away on the top shelf of the larder the vases she did not like. Ruth did not mind her gradual assumption of proprietary rights over the things in the house. It was a blessing to have someone who took so much interest, and she liked Ethel so much that she wanted her to feel at home.

'I've had a letter from Crosslands,' Mrs Garrard said, picking up some fallen rose petals.

'Oh, yes – ?' said Ruth vaguely.

'That place in Cheshire, you know, Madam, where little Tom is.'

'How is he getting on?'

'Not too well, Madam, I'm afraid, from what I can understand. Would you like to see what they say?' She handed Ruth the letter respectfully, and then proceeded to tell her what was in it, as if she doubted that Ruth could read.

'He's getting much stronger *in himself*, they say, but it seems that he's pining for me, and that's keeping him back. That's the trouble, I suppose, of giving a kiddie too much love and affection. I'm afraid I've never been able to disguise my feelings where little Tom was concerned, and then they miss it, if you can understand, when they have to go away.'

'But of course I understand,' said Ruth, handing her back the letter. 'I ought to ...'

Mrs Garrard was not interested, and went on: 'I'm worrying myself sick about him, Madam, to tell you the truth. When I think of him up there so far away from me, I wish I'd taken a place up there to be near him.'

'Oh, but Ethel,' cried Ruth in great distress, 'I thought you were so happy here!'

'Please don't misunderstand my meaning, Madam. I'm sure this is a very good place and you and Doctor have been so very good to me, I'm sure I couldn't do enough to repay you. It's just that I miss the little chap so much and, especially since I got this letter, I really don't have a minute's peace for worrying about him not getting well through pining.' She kept on in this tenor until she had managed to put her idea into Ruth's head.

'If only you could have –' she mused, biting the end of her pen. 'But Dr Sheppard said he should have country air, didn't he?'

'He did, indeed, Madam, but not at the expense of his pining so, I'm sure. The way I look at it, Madam, is you've got to balance the one thing against the other, if you can understand.' Ruth thought that Mrs Garrard meant that she might have to leave Wimpole Street and go north to Tom. She thought it entirely her own idea, and a very good one, that Tom should leave Cheshire and come south to his mother. It only needed a little prompting from Ethel to make her think of the box-room.

'Being such a little chap, we could leave all the cases and that in there, just so as he had his little corner to sleep in, as there's no space for another bed in my room. I could have all his things in with me. I wouldn't want to put you out, Madam, in the slightest, after all your kindness to me. I'm sure you won't even know he's in the house.'

'Oh, but I shall *like* to see him,' said Ruth. She was not fond of children, but she was even less fond of her own company, of which she had too much.

Meeting Steven on the stairs that evening Mrs Garrard said: 'I'm sure it's very kind of you, sir, to allow little Tom to come here. You don't know what a relief it is to me.'

'Don't thank me,' said Steven hastily. 'I had nothing to do with it. Not that I mind, of course, but Mrs Sheppard arranged it all.'

'Oh, yes, of course, sir,' answered Ethel, fixing him with a look which implied that she knew perfectly well who gave the orders in that house. She had a genius for landing you into roles you had no intention of assuming. 'Dammit,' thought Steven, going on upstairs, 'I will not be her fairy godfather.'

Mrs Garrard, standing in the doorway of the kitchen-maid's room and wondering how many of the trunks she could move into the cupboard under the stairs without any-one noticing, reflected with pleasure what a nice save of money it was going to be. Mrs Drage, the Lady Almoner at St Margaret's, having found out what her wages were, had elicited a contribution towards the country Home. But in Wimpole Street, Tom's small appetite would make no difference to the housekeeping books. She could probably even smudge some of his little things in with her own laundry, which was paid by Mrs Sheppard. She already had her eye on a piece of shantung left over from the new curtains, which would make up into some lovely little shirts.

Chapter 4

—

CONTRARY to Steven's expectations, it was no trouble having Tom in the house. In fact, you would have had to look and listen very carefully to know he was there. He was as quiet as his mother, but without her ubiquitous habits. It had been impressed on him from the start which parts of the house he must avoid. His world consisted of the basement and the top storey, bridged by the narrow back staircase. Mrs Hankey allowed him to put plates into the service lift, and when Mrs Garrard had hauled on it from above, he would stick his head into the shaft and gaze up after its receding bottom. That, and a glimpse through the open door as he passed up the back stairs, was the nearest he got to the dining-room. The drawing-room, the whole of the second floor, where Ruth and Steven slept and dressed and bathed, and the consulting rooms were forbidden him under penalty of being sent back to Cheshire, and consequently assumed the properties of Hell. Obviously something terrible went on there. From the kitchen window he got a foreshortened view of Mr Nosgood arriving and departing, and gathered that he was the chief torturer. Sometimes, when he was in the pantry, a peculiar humming noise vibrated down through the ceiling. It came on and off in spurts, and often inspired the refrigerator to do its periodic gurgle.

The first time he heard this noise, Tom, drying up for Mabel, cocked his red head on one side and asked in his sing-song voice: 'Can you hear something funny?'

'Oh, that's only the dentist's drill, dear,' said Mabel cheerfully. 'You get used to hearing that down here, though I don't suppose them pore patients upstairs ever do.'

So Mr Nosgood had a room full of meek, resigned people, who sat patiently round the wall – Tom imagined them on the floor propped up limply like rag dolls – and waited for Mr Nosgood to torture them with diabolical machines. Whenever the humming started and the refrigerator whirred, Tom would pause in whatever he was doing, look upward and whisper: 'Be patient,' hoping that they would be able to bear it.

He was a detached little boy. He played by himself quite happily for hours on end, and his mother could safely leave him in the kitchen with a book or a lump of plasticine while she was doing her work upstairs.

'I can't see why you don't let him nip up while She's out, and 'E safely in the consulting room,' Mrs Hankey used to say. 'He could help Mabel with the beds or dust a bit. He loves a nice dust, don't you, my pet?'

Mrs Garrard shook her head. 'Better not. Once started, you never know where a thing like that'll stop. Once he's been where he shouldn't, you never know but what he mightn't creep up when Doctor or Mrs Sheppard are in the rooms, and what sort of gratitude would that look like if I allowed him all over the house like a hooligan? Tom, come here, your shirt's outside your trousers again.' She was always pulling and fiddling at him in a proprietary way, as if by constant touching she could make him more hers.

Curiously, he had no wish to explore the forbidden territory. It was Hell, and that was all there was to it. He knew what Hell looked like from his book of Old Testament stories. He had plenty of opportunities to go over the whole house had he wanted to, but the only room that drew him at all was the waiting-room. On his first day in the house he had followed his mother upstairs to answer the bell before she realized what he was doing. His sandals were rubber-soled, like her own neat black shoes, and it was not until she had shut the patient into the waiting-room that she saw Tom crouching between the oak chest and the grandfather clock.

She hustled him downstairs, and as soon as he could get his breath, he said: 'What is that room, Mum?'

'Never you mind, dear. And don't you ever let me see you up there again. Supposing Doctor had seen you.' Doctor, of course, was an ogre more sinister than Mr Nosgood. Tom hoped that he would never meet him, and he had been in the house a week before he did.

The waiting-room, with its hybrid elegance and its un-lived-in air of not wanting you to be there, attracted Tom strongly. He never had been in a room like this before, and sometimes in the evening, when he had seen Doctor go out of the house, and his mother was busy, Tom would creep

144

through the high white door with its glass handle and spend a happy half-hour climbing on the chairs to puzzle out the dark seascapes and admire the rubber-necked ducks on the walls, or sitting on one chair after another to look at the magazines. He felt oddly at home in this most uncosy room. Even the marble fireplace with its electric fire which he had never seen lit and its pinch-waisted copper vases on the mantelpiece was a snug cave to him. You could squeeze in past the fire, which was made to look like coals, and look right up the chimney to a tiny square of sky.

One evening, Steven, returning from a dinner with which he and Guy Phillips had followed a consultation, saw a light in the waiting-room as he came up the front steps. 'My God, these women are careless,' he thought. 'If they had to pay the bills –'

He opened the waiting-room door, clicked out the light and was just going out when a scuffling in the fireplace made him turn on the light again. Not mice, surely, in a room where there never was food.

A very small boy in a green jersey, with light red hair cut square across his forehead, was peering at him between the electric fire and the side of the fireplace. Steven thought for a moment of burglars forcing small boys through narrow apertures to unlock doors for them, remembered that *Oliver Twist* had been written a hundred years ago, and realized that this must be Ethel's brat.

'Come out of there,' he said, and when the boy came, he remembered having seen him in the clinic. 'What on earth are you doing in there?' Steven asked. 'And anyway, you ought to be in bed.'

'I was looking at the stars,' said Tom, as if the answer should have been obvious. 'And I never go to bed till ten.'

'Well, you should,' said Steven. 'I'll have to speak to your mother.' These idiotic women. That was the way they got their children ill, and then expected the doctor to perform miracles on them.

'Come on now,' he said, and, as the boy came to him, he

145

remembered something, and put his hand in his pocket. 'Here,' he said, and gave him a huge red apple which he had taken from the dinner table.

Tom had hitherto only seen Steven's legs going up and down the steps above the kitchen window in the area. 'Mum,' he said when he went downstairs, entering the pantry as if from the kitchen, so that she should not know he had been upstairs, 'd'you know who lives in this house?'

'No, dear, who?' She was laying the early morning tea-tray.

'The man we saw in the hospital at Dynsford when we had to wait for ever and ever and that lady gave me a bun.'

'Well, you know who that is. That's Doctor.'

Oh, no. That couldn't be Doctor. Not the ogre Doctor who would slay you if he caught you, like in Tom Tiddler's ground. That was the man from Dynsford, and he had given him an apple.

*

They did not meet again until the following Sunday, when Steven was brushing Ugly in the garden. Tom strolled out of the back door with a book under his arm and stood watching.

'Like dogs?' asked Steven. The sun was shining and, bar emergencies, he had no work to do today. He was thinking of taking the car out to the country and lunching somewhere, and having a walk; Ruth would not want to come, because she was having a friend to lunch. She and Mrs Hankey were discussing it now in the kitchen.

'Yes, thank you,' said Tom. Steven brushed Ugly's head and Ugly stretched his neck to it sensuously, making slits of his eyes and conscious of admiration.

'What sort of dog is that?' asked Tom politely.

'He's a Cornish Congerhound,' said Steven. George had christened him that. He did look rather like a conger eel, with his white belly and long, flat head and his apparent ability to dissolve his backbone. When Steven brushed his

146

chest, Ugly nearly fell over, because a reflex made him scratch his right ear with his hind leg. Tom laughed at his ecstatic contortions, and it crossed Steven's mind that it was a long time since he had heard a child laugh. The children he saw at the hospitals were usually either too ill or too awed to laugh. Presently he put the comb into the brush and straightened up, leaving Ugly to stretch and shake himself. As he was going into the house, he noticed the book that Tom was holding clutched against his chest.

'Good God!' said Steven. 'Where did you get that?'

'I found it in my room,' said Tom, clutching it tighter, alarmed at Steven's tone

'Goodness gracious me!' said Ruth, turning as Tom came yelling into the kitchen trying to screw out his eyes with his fists. 'Whatever's the matter?' Tom did not know what was the matter. All he knew was that he had got a bad fright when the tall man they called Doctor had suddenly stopped being nice to him, snatched his book quite roughly out of his arms, gone rapidly into the house and up the kitchen stairs, slamming the consulting-room door with a noise like thunder. Perhaps he was the ogre after all.

*

Half an hour later, Steven raised a haggard face from the last illustration of *Holiday House*. He sat for a moment looking unseeingly at the Turner engraving, then he suddenly stood up, picked up *Holiday House* and went into the hall, whistling for Ugly, ignoring Ruth's call and going straight out of the house to get his car.

All the way down to Portsmouth he was remembering. This was how it had always been. An acceptance of the situation that was so natural as to be almost forgetting would occupy him for months at a time until, sometimes for no reason, the emotions which he thought he had conquered would prove that he had only dammed them up at the back of his mind by bursting through and flooding him with the despair of memories too accurately recalled.

Steven was a man who, from the training of his work and from an innate repugnance for lack of control in others, did not show his emotions easily. At the time when Ruth was going from dramatic outbursts and near-hysteria to an equally dramatic burning of toys and clothes, and locking away photographs and stopping short with a name on her lips, Steven had remained outwardly normal. A few lines which had not been there before had appeared in his face, and his mouth had tightened and hardened, but he had given himself away to no one. He had not even talked to Marion.

Probably it was because he had imposed such self-restraint that these extremes of gloom still overtook him after nearly three years. He had determined, in the beginning, that he was not going to betray Carol by shutting her away as if she had never happened, as Ruth finished by doing. He wanted to be able to remember her all the time, sanely, but his thoughts were not so tractable. They would explore the niggling by-ways of sorrow, and manœuvre him through self-condemnation and remorse to the invidious condemnation of others and the quest of a scapegoat.

If only they had gone to Cornwall for the holiday, like the year before. Why hadn't they gone to Cornwall? Because Ruth had not liked it. Why to the Isle of Wight, of all places? Because Ruth had hankered after it. If only they had taken that other house at Bembridge ... if only it had not been so hot that day ... if only that idiot woman had called out before ... There was no end to this fruitless and dangerous and exquisitely painful line of thinking. So, as he apparently could not control his thoughts, he had banished them, and rejected the memories which might have comforted him.

He managed quite well most of the time, until, as now, his pent-up emotions got their own back and overwhelmed him.

Driving through the switchback heath country of East

Hampshire, Steven was remembering vividly that last time he had driven down to Portsmouth. He had a Rover then, a dark red saloon, on whose back seat Ugly used to stand swaying and gazing enigmatically through the back window at the traffic behind. The Sheppards had taken a furnished house for two months. Ruth and Carol had settled in there, and Steven had come and gone from Dynsford, spending as much time on the island as his growing practice would allow. Failing to get the Bembridge house, they had taken a white cottage on the slope of the valley at the mouth of Wooton Creek. Steven thought, now, that he had never wanted that house, forgetting how charmed he had been with the miniature oak-lined inlet, where the gentle brown stream of Blackbridge Brook slipped modestly into the Solent. The house had blue doors and shutters, and a terrace cut out of the hillside where they used to have all their meals when it was hot. Steven remembered the flies and wasps. Ruth made a great fuss about them, and Steven could see her now at tea-time, swatting with a rolled-up newspaper at the jam-crazy wasps, and hear Carol saying: 'I've told you, Mummy, they won't sting you if you leave them alone.' She was always telling her mother things. Even at seven she knew a lot more about many things than Ruth did. Instead of taking the paddle steamer to Ryde, Steven used to cross on the ferry which came straight to Fishbourne Creek, although he left his car in Portsmouth Harbour, as it was not worth the expense of bringing it over every time.

It was the middle of August. Ruth and Carol had walked down to the slipway to meet him, and Carol's long, straight legs were as brown as an Italian child's under her faded cotton frock. When she grew up, Steven thought she was going to be the sort of girl who could look really attractive in old clothes, although at the same time she would have a flair for dress, and people would envy him when she took him out in London as a relief from importunate young men.

They had been at Fishbourne long enough for it to seem like coming home. The short view across the valley from the window of his room was getting familiar. He planned to take the house again next year. He changed at once into the old clothes he kept there, and after lunch he and Carol went down to their favourite sunbathing spot, an outcrop of rock in a clearing among the trees. Ruth would come down later with the tea basket and her sunshade. She did not stand the sun well and, as she was four months pregnant, she usually rested on her bed in the afternoon.

Carol had swum since she was five. At seven, she could swim out quite far in the calm water of the creek at high tide, her thin arms and legs working like a frog, her long, dark hair streaming out behind her like seaweed. Steven slept, and woke to see her through half-closed eyes at the water's edge below him, trying to make Ugly go into the sea. It was the only place where he would not follow her, and while she was swimming he would run anxiously over the muddy sand, putting a paw into the water at different points, moaning at himself for not daring to take the plunge.

Carol looked back at Steven, and saw that he was awake. 'Daddy!' she called. 'There's a car ferry coming in. Can I swim out to it?'

'No. It's too far, anyway.'

'But it's coming nearer,' she said logically.

That was the unforgivable, unforgettable thing: his dropping off to sleep again. But he had not thought she would go into the water then, and if he had, she had often been in without him.

It was that woman's scream that woke him. It came even before Ugly's barking, or the shout of the sailor at the wheel of the flat-bottomed ferry with its drawbridge bows. That terrible woman in the pink-flowered dress and the yellow straw hat, whose voice, of all the voices which clamoured at him afterwards, he could remember telling him what had happened.

'On the slipway I was. I saw it all. Oh, my God, I saw it all. The little girl was swimming out towards the boat. I said to myself, that's dangerous, I said. They shouldn't let her do that. But she'd have been all right if the boat hadn't altered its course – slightly off it he was – to come square on to the slipway. I saw it hit her head ...' Her voice had trailed after him as he walked quickly away up the gravel road with Carol's body in his arms.

*

Steven got off the steamer at Ryde and walked down the pier and up the hill past the house where they had lived, and where Carol was born. The doctor who had bought the practice from him when he went to Dynsford had put him up whenever he could spare the time to come and see Ruth in the nursing home where she had had her miscarriage. She had been too ill to come home for some time. He remembered how odd it felt to be in a house where you once lived, and which was yours no longer. You kept noticing the furniture as you never had your own. Dr. Dakers had been so kind and so humble, looking dumb agony at Steven because he could not find the words of sympathy which Steven did not want. Steven had slept in the spare room which he had always hated, and the Dakers used to have cold suppers at half-past six with every conceivable sauce and pickle on the table. Steven, very busy at Dynsford, although his senior physician at St Margaret's had offered to take as much of his work off him as possible, used to arrive on the last evening boat, sleep the night, see Ruth the next morning and go straight back to Portsmouth. He must have been very rude.

Ugly had been terrible. He had never been in the Ryde house with Carol, but he was always seeing things, and pricking his ears at sounds that were not there. He had continued to do this afterwards at Dynsford. That was what had made Ruth want to get rid of him.

When, after four hours' travelling, Steven came to the small grave in the high churchyard that looked over the tiered roofs of Ryde and across the water to Hampshire, it meant nothing to him. The child who had been so agonizingly with him when he had held *Holiday House* in his hands,

151

and seen the familiar pictures, was not with him any longer. She was not here, anyway.

He got back to London at seven o'clock. He felt very tired.

'Any calls for me?' he asked Mrs Garrard, who materialized as usual in the hall.

'Not that I know of, sir. But Madam has answered the phone once or twice.'

Ruth was in her room changing. 'Steven, where on earth have you been? Disappearing like that. If you hadn't told me you meant to go out I'd have been worried sick.'

'Well, I did tell you.'

'Yes, but you never said good-bye, or where you were going, or when you'd be back. Henty Davies has rung up twice. He wants you to have another look at some man at Hampstead with an empyema or something. I expect you know what he's talking about.'

'I'd better go round before dinner,' said Steven wearily. 'But I must have a drink first.'

'Your day in the country doesn't seem to have done you much good. Where have you been, anyway?'

Steven paused in the doorway, looking at her expressionlessly. 'To Ryde,' he said. 'They're keeping up the grave very well.'

'I know. I went there the other week.'

'Good God, why didn't you tell me?'

'I don't know. Why didn't you?'

'I don't know,' said Steven miserably, and went to see his pneumonia patient at Hampstead.

Chapter 5

—

EVER since Easter Ruth had been asking: 'Where are we going for our holiday this year?' It was now the first week in July and Steven was still answering: 'God knows. It doesn't look as though I'll get away at all with all this work about.' Ruth always wanted to plan months ahead, to book rooms and confirm them two or three times by letter, to look up trains and wonder if the A B C were out of date, to worry about whether the car would forget to meet them at the other end. Steven's idea of a real holiday would have been to see the sun shining one morning and say: 'Let's chuck some stuff in the car and get out of here for a bit – go across to France and just drive about, staying where we like for as long as we like.' He saw people like Mark Stainer disappearing to Scotland for two or three weeks to finish a book, or another patient, Clifford Halliday the actor, flying to the South of France between plays to get himself a new tan, and it annoyed him that he would never be able to do anything like this until he retired, when he would probably be too old to enjoy it.

Once, he and Ruth had taken advantage of an unexpectedly slack week-end to fly over to Le Touquet, where, as a great favour, they were given a cramped room looking on to a back-yard where argumentative men emptied dustbins at five o'clock in the morning. Ruth spent most of the time bewailing the fact that she had packed in such a hurry she had brought all the wrong clothes; not that a month's planning would ever have made her look right in a sun-soaked, beachcombing atmosphere. She had spent most of the day sitting under a striped umbrella reading, or buying anti-midge lotion at the chemist's or having grenadine and pâtisseries at the shadiest tables in cafes. In the evening she had hung on Steven's arm at the Casino, not wanting to gamble herself, and begging him to stop playing before he lost any more.

Lying in bed one night, she announced: 'Steven, I think it would be nice to go to Italy this year. I lunched with Betty today, and she was telling me about a place they went to at Whitsun – on Lake Como. They had fresh peaches at every meal, and at night the fishermen go out in boats and sing under your window. Doesn't it sound *romantic*?'

Steven, who was reading an interesting book, grunted, and turned over a page, Ruth hummed a snatch of *Ciri, biri, bin*, slightly off key. 'Of course, if we *are* going, we ought to make arrangements soon. Why don't you go to Cook's and ask about it?'

'Why don't you?' asked Steven.

'Oh, darling, you know I'm hopeless about that sort of thing. I could never go abroad by myself in a million years. Those customs. I might go and get some booklets, though. Betty said at this place they used to take little steamers across the lake and have tea at a place on the other side. She said the Italians were charming to them. Lots of them don't like Mussolini a bit, though they have to have his picture painted on the walls of their houses. Did you know that? Steven, you're not listening.'

'No.'

'Well, I think it's very silly of you to let the summer go by like this. You said yourself you needed a holiday, and you do look tired, you know. You ought to give yourself a real break before the winter. Think, you could take your typewriter and really get on with your book. Betty said they had a balcony that kept the sun all day. You could sit there like Somerset Maugham and nobody need come near you. You could have your meals on a tray.' She glanced at him to see how he was reacting, and sighed. 'Perhaps you'd like to go to Wales again then, and fish. I'm sure I wouldn't mind a bit, although there wasn't much for me to do. I should take some knitting with me this year, I think. It always helps to have something to do with your hands in an hotel ... What are you reading, darling? Oh, *How Green was my Valley*. I started that, but I couldn't get on with it. It's very queer, isn't it? So *Welsh*. But then, you like the Welsh, don't you? I suppose it makes a difference if you've lived among them. Do they really talk like that? No one at Glyncastle did. All the waiters seemed to be Cockney, d'you remember? And that awful Scotch chambermaid who ruined my hot-water bottle. I still think the hotel ought to have taken something off our bill for that.'

'Look, Ruth,' suggested Steven quite kindly, 'why don't you read, or go to sleep?'

'I don't feel a bit sleepy. And I've finished my library book.'

'There's a bookcase full in the drawing-room. Why not read something decent for a change?'

'Oh, Steven, I often do. I read a Dickens the other day. It was awfully funny. People kept looking at me in the train because I laughed out loud.'

'There's plenty of stuff there besides Dickens.' Years of practice had made Steven quite good at concentrating on a book and throwing out enough remarks to keep her satisfied.

'Well, there's Shakespeare, of course, but we did him at school. I often think I ought to have another try at Jane Austen, but somehow I've never able to get *in* to her. Would you like to go to Bath, Steven, for a holiday? They say it's very beautiful. If we do go to Italy, I think I shall read *Gone with the Wind* again. It's always better to take something you know you like when you go abroad, then you can't get stranded with nothing to read.'

Steven finished a chapter, put the book on his bedside table and switched off the lamp. He lay on his back in the darkness with his hands behind his head. 'It's silly to talk about going abroad now, Ruth,' he said, 'when we might be at war at any moment. Nice fools we should look stuck in the middle of Europe unable to get home. How would you like to spend the war in an internment camp?'

'Oh, darling, there can't possibly be a war yet. I'm sure they'd give us warning. I can't think why you're always saying there's going to be one. You said it last year, and you see, you were quite wrong and I was right all the time.'

'I wish to God you were right this time,' said Steven.

'Wouldn't it be *awful*? D'you think it would affect your work much? That would be terrible, just when you're getting on so well. We might even have to give up this house as it's so expensive to run.'

'We shall,' said Steven, 'if I manage to get into the Navy.'

Ruth laughed. 'Oh, darling, you're not still thinking about that, surely? I'd thought you'd given up all idea of it after Munich? I mean, even if you are right, and there is going to be a war, you're much more useful doing the work you are. I know it's awfully patriotic of you and all that, but really I don't see why you should give up all you've worked for for so long.'

'As a matter of fact,' said Steven, 'I saw a man today who's going to try and pull strings for me.' He heard Ruth draw in her breath and, with a sudden twinge of compunction, put out his hand to her across the space between their beds. 'Ruthie.' He didn't often call her that. 'You wouldn't mind, would you? We shouldn't be so well off, I know, but money's never meant all that much to you, has it? We could take a small place in the country perhaps, and I could come there on leave. Or you could go and live with your mother in Wimbledon, if you liked.'

'I wouldn't mind if you wouldn't mind,' answered Ruth, squeezing his hand and hurting him with her ring. 'But you'd hate to give all this up – your position, and all the people you meet –'

'I should love it,' said Steven fervently.

'But you don't have to join up in anything,' said Ruth nervously. 'I don't expect they'll take you, anyway. You're too old.'

Steven took his hand away. 'I'm not too old.'

There was a lot of rustling and creaking and blowing of nose and drinking of water as Ruth settled down for the night. 'Steven,' came her muffled voice just when he was dropping into sleep, 'd'you honestly think there'll be a war?'

'I've told you,' mumbled Steven, 'yes.'

'Well, if there is, I shall be a V.A.D. I don't see why I should be left out of it any more than you. I might even start going to Red Cross classes now. I saw an appeal only the other day. It might be rather interesting. Shall I, Steven?'

'Jolly good idea.'

'Yes ... yes.' Ruth contemplated with pleasure the idea of having something to do with her day. She pictured herself in the uniform. Would she ever be able to keep that cap on her thick hair? She thought about nursing for five minutes and felt a vocation creeping over her. She began to feel noble. 'D'you think I should make a good nurse?' she asked.

'Wonderful.'

'Steven ... Steven ...'

'Oh, Ruth, what? Do let's go to sleep. I've a heavy day tomorrow.'

'You haven't kissed me good night.'

*

For nights before Dr Sheppard's examination, Nurse Lake sat up with burning eyes and throbbing head studying her Medicine. Often she dozed over it and woke in a panic at so much precious time wasted. Sometimes, after midnight, to fend off the black curtains that kept coming down in front of her eyes, she would get up and make herself a cup of tea in the little pantry at the end of the corridor.

Night Sister, doing a round to trap anyone who had gone to the Saturday night dance at the 'Stag and Hounds', had once caught her there in the act of pouring water from the kettle to the pot.

'Nurse!' she hissed in the voice which years of night duty had made incapable of articulating properly. Nurse Lake's heart dropped like a plummet into her quilted black slippers. She put down the pot and kettle quickly and clutched at her cotton kimono which, thinking herself the only person about, she had left immodestly hanging open.

'Whatever are you doing, Nurse?' whispered Night Sister, automatically switching on her torch, although the light was on in the pantry.

'Making tea, please, Sister.'

'You've been out, Nurse.' It was a statement rather than a question. Not having been long at St Margaret's, she was unaware that Nurse Lake and the rowdy dances at the 'Stag' were poles apart.

'Oh no, truly I haven't, Sister,' gulped Nurse Lake, feeling as guilty as if she had.

'Well, what are you doing out of bed, then? You know lights are supposed to be out by half-past ten.'

'I – I couldn't sleep, Sister.'

'Well, I've never heard that tea was particularly good for insomnia.' Night Sister had a habit of raising her head and snuffing the surrounding air when she felt she had made a good remark. As she was always making good remarks, her nostrils had become permanently dilated, like a rocking horse. 'I shall have to report this to Matron,' she said. 'Let's see, you're a staff nurse, aren't you?'

'*Acting* staff nurse,' murmured Nurse Lake humbly.

'And here you are taking advantage of your position before you even get it.' She sniffed the air again, and put her hand on the light switch. 'Empty that teapot and get straight into bed. I can't have you people gadding about at all hours of the night. No wonder the day sisters are always complaining that you're all so slow at your work.' As she had scarcely any truck with the day sisters, she had made this up on the spur of the moment. Anyway, it kept her in the pantry just long enough to miss seeing Nurse Bracken creep into her room at the other end of the corridor with her lipstick all over her face and her dancing shoes in her hand.

Not content with torturing her brain at night, Nurse Lake always took a book on duty and snatched odd moments, while she was cleaning instruments, or when Sister was at dinner, to cram another fact or two into her head. She became vague and forgetful in her work, and made stupid mistakes. The abuse she received she bore proudly, martyring herself for Steven, her sole aim in life to be top in his exam.

And it seemed that she would be. She had liked the paper, and had found herself scratching away with her thin-pointed nib long after most people had blotted their papers, underlined everything possible in red and were staring about them, knowing that they ought to re-read what they had written, but not wanting to for fear of depressing themselves with the inadequacy of their answers. Afterwards, during the frantic post-mortem which broke out as soon as Sister Tutor had collected the papers and gone out, Nurse Lake divined that they had not liked the paper as well as she had. She knew she had answered that diabetes question perfectly. Could it be that Dr Sheppard, remembering how she had reeled off the difference between hyper- and hypo-glycæmia at that last lecture, had set it as a special gift to her? She kept silent, revelling in the anguished: 'My dear, I was paralysed! I couldn't even think of the names of all the glands, let alone what they do to you.' 'What *did* he mean by that blood-pressure question? Which is systolic and which diastolic, anyway?' 'He is a stinker. Fancy giving us Disseminated! I remembered about the pill-rolling symptom, anyway.' 'But, you idiot, that's Parkinson's disease. It's intention tremor in Disseminated.' 'Oh, *no*! Oh, well, I've failed anyway, I'm sure, so it's no use worrying, but the thought of having to sit through all those lectures again ...'

Nurse Lake pretended, with the others, that she thought she had done badly, but secretly she believed she would be top. Would he say anything to her about it when he discovered the identity of the numbered candidates? Would he perhaps say to Matron, as Dr Munroe had once done about Nurse Blacker, that if her practical work was as good as her written, she was one of the best nurses the hospital had ever had?

But then, of course, he knew her practical work from the clinic. She could not wait for the results to come out. Each week she plucked up courage to ask him diffidently: 'Have you marked our papers yet, sir?' and when at last, instead of 'Sorry, haven't had a moment, yet,' he said: 'Yes. I did them last night, as a matter of fact,' she waited, holding her breath, for him to say something more. The clinic was over, and he was washing his hands, scrubbing meticulously round his nails, as he always did, no matter how clean they were already. He knew that she wanted him to tell her which number he had put first, and felt ashamed that he could not remember. The examination obviously meant so much to her that he could not reveal such lack of interest. He said nothing, and rinsed his hands, feeling her eyes piercing his back.

Waiting behind him with the towel, she moistened her lips, cleared her throat, squeaked from one shoe to the other and stammered: 'I sup-p-pose you couldn't tell me who was top, sir?'

'Ah,' he took refuge in archness. 'That would be telling. You'll have to wait till Sister gives you the results. Anyway, there's the oral yet. We're having that today as soon as I've been round the wards. Those marks get added on.' He held out his hand for the towel.

'But if, sir,' she lunged forward, 'you could just say whether we've all passed the written?'

'Yes. Most of them were very good papers indeed. You can't all have been asleep all the time, after all.' He cut short her over-effusive laughter with: 'No, wait a minute, I had to fail one, though.'

That would be Nicholson, the admitted fool of the class, who never passed any exam until she had sat it three times. 'Oh, what a pity, sir,' said Nurse Lake smugly.

'Yes, I like to pass you all if I can, because it only holds up your training, doesn't it? But this girl made such a damn-fool, criminal mistake that I couldn't let it go. I mean, if she put into practice what she's written she'd be a public menace.'

Whatever could Nicholson have put? She was always

doing the wrong thing, like that time on night duty when she gave breakfast to a man who was going to have a gastroscopy, and the nearly disastrous occasion when she was allowed to count swabs in theatre.

'What did she ...? May I ask what it ...? Nurse Lake hovered behind him as he crossed to the desk to get his case.

'The wretched creature went and muddled up an insulin and a diabetic coma. Went and gave a hundred grammes of glucose to a man who was already stinking of it, and shot fifty units of insulin into a man who'd apparently just had a whole phial. Either way she'd probably kill him.'

Nurse Lake's heart did its plummet act into her squeaking shoes, and left the whole of her body cold. A ghastly doubt began to creep over her.

'It was probably only a slip,' Steven went on, taking off his white coat and wondering why she was not proffering her usual help, 'but I couldn't possibly let it go. She had all her facts right, but a girl with a mind woolly enough to mix up the two things might do anything, so I couldn't give her any marks for that question, and of course it pulled her total right down.' He wanted to justify himself. He had felt guilty last night at failing someone for a careless mistake, but he felt very strongly about nurses who made careless mistakes. They had killed patients for him before now, and had once landed him in the High Court.

He tossed his white coat on to the chair, whence it fell to the floor. Nurse Lake picked it up without thinking, feverish questions milling around in her head. Hyper, hypo; she had always had to think several times to remember which was which. Could she have mixed them up? How could she? But already as she straightened up again, clutching the coat, she was convinced that she had. She could see the sentence in her handwriting, running across the top of the page – she had remembered so carefully to start each question on a new page – 'Hyperglycæmia is an insulin coma.' But she had done that question so well! Yes, but he had said she got all the facts right. That counted for nothing if she had made that hideous, damning mistake.

'I say, Nurse, where's my? –' Steven turned round and saw her staring eyes and quivering mouth. He had never seen her face ashen like this. Her head had no blood left in it to blush with. No wonder she felt faint. She nearly toppled over as she said huskily, fixing him with those horror-stricken eyes: 'What was the number of the one who failed?'

'Good Lord, you don't think it was you, do you? Here, hold on a minute–sit down, Nurse, you don't look a bit well.' He swivelled the chair round towards her and pushed her into it, then taking her by the back of the neck, pushed her head down to her knees as far as her rigidity would allow. 'Put your head right down. It's the heat, I expect.'

From her crouching position, looking extremely ridiculous, like some animal coming out of its burrow, she forced her head back to look up at him. 'I think it was me,' she whispered. 'What was the number?'

'Oh, I say.' This was terrible. He felt like a hangman. 'It can't have been you. Just a minute, I'll have a look. I've got the list here ... Let's see ... No. Six was top. That you, perhaps?' She shook her long chin at him dumbly. 'Number one was the one I failed,' he said uncomfortably. Nurse Lake's head dropped forward. The returning blood sang in her ears like a humming-top. The thought that she might be sick at his feet did not even worry her.

'I'm terribly sorry, Nurse, but I'm sure you understand. Let me get you a glass of water.' Futile suggestion. There was no glass about, anyway. Nurse Lake suddenly threw back her head and stood up. Her face was still greyish-white, but the colour was beginning to creep up her neck.

'I do beg your pardon, sir,' she said, jabbing at her crooked cap. 'I don't know what you must think of me. But I did so want to –' She nearly said 'be top', but substituted 'pass'.

'Well, of course, of course.' He nearly patted her shoulders in his relief that she had pulled herself together. 'Who doesn't want to pass every exam? But you can always take it again, next year. You'll have Dr Baxter then, and he'll be much easier game than me. In any case, you've still got a chance to pull up on the oral. You answer everything I ask you and I'll smudge you through, eh?' His heartiness was painful. Anxious to be gone, he picked up his case and made for the door. She stood quite still, shaking her head hopelessly, more to herself than him. How could she hope to answer anything in half an hour's time? This was what shock must be, that you were always learning how to treat. Idiotic thoughts came into her mind. Perhaps she should cover herself with blankets and give herself strong, sweet tea. That reminded her of Night Sister catching her in the pantry, and the memory of all she had gone through in vain flooded through her in a tidal wave that pressed behind her eyes so forcibly that she could hardly wait until he had shut the door behind him before she sank into his chair, put her head on the desk and howled into his white coat that smelled of him.

*

Upstairs, Steven met Dr Baxter just coming out of the women's medical ward with his house-physician, a vivacious young woman with hair like black silk, who treated the old man as if she were his daughter. Old Dr Baxter, with his slipping spectacles and his thin fluff of string-coloured hair, had been an institution at St Margaret's long before Steven came to Dynsford, and had steered him through the dilemmas of this his first honorary appointment. His own ambition had never looked beyond Dynsford, and he had always laughed at Steven's restlessness for London. He laughed at him now for his reluctance to sever connections with St Margaret's.

'Hullo, young Steven!' he called, smiling with spontaneous pleasure before he remembered to draw his mouth down and be a character. 'Doing a bit of slumming?'

'What are you doing here on a Thursday afternoon, sir?'

asked Steven, while young Potter, like a dog on a leash, stopped a few paces behind him and yearned at Miss Natalie Thorne in her brief white coat and disturbing stockings.

'That's what Sister wanted to know,' said the old man, looking balefully at the swing doors of the ward, 'though why in thunder a man can't do his round in the afternoon instead of the morning only God and the nursing profession know. Anyone would think this place was run for the benefit of the nursing staff. And blast you, I couldn't get any attention, because they're all as busy preparing for your coming as if you were the Messiah.'

'I told you you wouldn't be popular doing a round at this time, sir,' said his house-physician.

'I'd forgotten it was Thursday. What is it about him, Natalie? I can't see it.'

'Nor can I,' she said, and young Potter sucked in his breath at her irreverence. 'Never mind, sir, when you were his age, two nurses and an assistant matron drank lysol for love of you, you told me so yourself.'

'Did I? That sounds like a good story. You must tell me about it sometime.' He laid a hand on Steven's arm. 'Come round for tea when you've finished here. I'll go home now and tell Agnes. She'll be so pleased. It's a long time since you came to see us.'

'I'd love to –' began Steven, thinking with pleasure of the warm old house behind the church where he and Ruth, but more often he alone, had had so many meals when he lived at Dynsford.

And then he remembered. Damn. 'Oh no, I can't, sir. I've got to give the nurses a *viva*. I shall be late back in town as it is.'

'*Viva!* What are you talking about? I've been teaching these nurses for thirty years and I've never heard of such a thing.'

'Oh, I usually do,' said Steven. 'You can't tell from their papers whether they've got any common sense, and I have got some kind of conscience about what I pass on to the suffering public.'

'Well, you've got more courage than I have. Some of these young women scare me stiff. And they've got a beautiful way of twisting your orders as if they knew you were an old fool who didn't know what he was talking about.' Dr Baxter often looked like an impersonation of himself by Lionel Barrymore. 'And this woman's no better.' He poked at Miss Thorne with a knotted forefinger. 'She listens to what I tell her and then goes and does just what she likes, and usually the patients do better. It's most disheartening.' Natalie looked demure. Young Potter shifted his feet and cleared his throat. He was enjoying this snatch of badinage between great men, but uneasy lest they should start discussing him.

Steven would have loved to go to tea with the Baxters. They lived in the old vicarage, one of the few really graceful houses in Dynsford, with a Queen Anne exterior and an interior that smelt of wood fires and Mrs Baxter's lavender water. Their daughter was a widow who had been living there with her small boy when Steven was in practice at Dynsford. He and she had been on the verge of getting involved when that last Isle of Wight holiday had shut Steven up inside himself like a monk in a cell. He had not seen the Baxters' daughter since Carol died.

'How's Janet?' he asked.

'Fine, fine. Heard from her only two days ago. She's with her second husband in Burma now, you know. They've got a little girl.'

'I know.' She would never have married that gingery engineer if she had gone on seeing Steven.

'Well, I suppose I ought to get on, sir. Do remember me to your wife. Perhaps I could look in another week when I've got more time.' There was always seed cake on the Baxters' tea-table, and crusty new bread with the holes full of butter. Blast these nurses.

One thing about the *viva*. It would be a good excuse not

to stay for tea with Sister Grainger. As he went through the swing doors, an untidy young nurse who was rushing screens from one side of the ward to the other flung him a panic-stricken glance and another who was trying to coil the blood-pressure armlet inside its box let the whole thing spring out again and ran to fetch Sister, who was sorting out old Baxter's scattered X-rays at the other end of the ward. She came skimming towards him, rolling down her sleeves and looking right and left for her cuffs, annoyed, because she liked to have the ward just so for Dr Sheppard. He never knew that on Thursdays the awesome words 'Dr Sheppard's afternoon' were on everyone's lips since they came back from dinner, and that his patients had their beds tidied six times between two and four o'clock and were not allowed to have their tea in case he came early.

Sister was also annoyed because his oral examination would take two of her nurses off the ward during Washings, that major campaign which began every evening at five o'clock and involved much scooting about with bowls and tooth mugs, and hauling nightdresses off protesting women and agonized cries from nurse to nurse as they passed in flight of 'We'll never get done!'

Halfway down the ward on the left, a minute figure was propped up in bed like a doll, with its hair screwed back into a thin plait tied with a piece of bandage.

'Good Lord,' muttered Steven to young Potter, 'isn't that old Mother Munn?'

'Yes, sir. I meant to tell you. She was brought in two days ago in a coma – simply loaded with sugar.'

'How many units did you give her?'

'Fifty, sir, and another thirty that evening.'

'Hm.' Young Potter tried to guess from his face whether he approved. Steven had stopped at the foot of Mrs Munn's bed and was gazing at her severely. 'You haven't been sticking to your diet, have you, Mrs Munn?'

'I have been coming up to the Casualty twice a day,' she said happily, ignoring his question. 'Never miss, rain or fine.

You ask any of the nurses.' Steven sighed. He knew that nothing could uproot her conviction that as long as she had her pricks morning and evening, nothing else mattered. 'I get these turns, you know, Doctor,' she added soothingly. 'On the 'Igh Street it was this time. Come ever so sudden, you wouldn't believe. One minute I was looking in Bennett's window at the potted plants and the next I was waking up in this very bed.' She smoothed the sheet admiringly.

'Yes, well, one of these days you'll have a turn that you won't wake up from.'

Mrs Munn cackled. Dr Sheppard was a great one for a joke. He gazed at her thoughtfully for a minute, stroking up the side of his hair, and then turned to his house-surgeon. 'I wonder if we could get her into some kind of an institution,' he murmured. 'Somewhere where she'd have to stick to her diet. She'd be much better off. You might speak to the Lady Almoner about it.' Young Potter made a note in a small brown diary. He always made notes now on his rounds with Steven, ever since that dreadful time when he had forgotten to have a blood count done, and Steven had pulverized him in front of the nurses.

Sister Grainger was officiously arranging charts on the counterpane. Behind her, the nurses were drawn up in order of seniority, one with a pile of notes, another with the big envelopes of X-rays, and the untidy little probationer, who had only been there two weeks, wondering if it was better to stand with her hands behind her as taught, or in front of her to cover the stain on her apron.

'These are her sugar charts, sir,' put in Sister, tracing the descending graph with a scrubbed finger, as if Steven was a kindergarten child.

'Yes, yes.' He had already taken them in at a glance. 'Where's her blood-sugar report? That's what I want to see.'

'Nurse!' Sister turned accusingly to her staff nurse, who scrabbled vainly through Miss Munn's notes and looked up in agony.

'No, no, Nurse. On my *desk*,' hissed Sister. 'It only came

up half an hour ago. And find my cuffs!' she added, her face changing from storm to sunshine as she turned back to Dr Sheppard. She was always leaving her cuffs in unlikely places – behind the sterilizer, on a patient's locker, in the mending basket – and the nurses were supposed to smell them out by instinct. 'Sister's cuffs!' whispered the staff nurse to the first nurse, as she hurried to the desk, and 'Sister's cuffs!' grunted the first nurse to the new probationer, and they all scattered like casting foxhounds, so that when Steven wanted screens round the next case there was nobody to bring them.

The other patients were always sorry when screens went round a bed and they could not see what was going on. The visits of doctors, especially doctors like Dr Sheppard, enlivened the monotony of the routine existence. However, Miss Hannaboy would tell them all about it afterwards.

Steven got through his round quickly, and made for the Matron's office, where the oral was to be held. He was followed by the unspoken disappointment of Sister Grainger, who had bought chocolate biscuits and could hear the electric kettle simmering in her sitting-room as she stood outside it and watched him go down the passage, absently pulling on the cuffs which had been sitting all the time on the little shelf which held the Christmas Fund box.

*

Steven got his chocolate biscuits anyway, because he had tea with the Matron while the candidates waited in the corridor outside and tweaked at each other's aprons and polished one shoe against the stocking of the other leg. Steven would have preferred to have got on with the examination while he was drinking tea, but the Matron, who was a kindly old soul, in a cap like a muslin sugar-bag, could not have been seen drinking tea by her nurses, so he had to wait. At last she had finished, and she rang for the maid to remove the tray, and indicated to Sister Tutor, who was perching on the edge of a chair trying to get sand cake out of her teeth with her tongue, that the first nurse might come in.

'Perhaps you would like to sit at my desk, Doctor,' she suggested magnanimously, and he went to the other end of the room and sat at the big, tidy desk, where Sister Tutor had left a beautifully-ruled chart for him to put down his marks. This was the end of the room used for official business and tellings off. The other end, where Matron sat in an arm-chair, was used for cosy chats with troubled nurses, and had seen much weeping.

The first nurse came in and darted a scared glance and an 'Excuse me, please' at Matron before daring to look at Steven.

'Ah, good afternoon, Nurse,' he said pleasantly. 'Come and sit down.' He indicated a chair at the side of the desk. The nurse, who looked like a flaxen fieldmouse, darted another involuntary glance at Matron. One had never sat down at this end of the room before. But Matron was sitting comfortably back with her hands folded in her lap and her face benign, so the nurse sat down, carefully folding up the sides of her apron on to her lap, so as not to crease it. This was not going to be so bad. She had been sick twice since breakfast, and had eaten neither dinner nor tea. She began to feel quite hungry with relief when Steven asked her her number, told her she had written a very good paper, and invited her to tell him anything she liked about acute nephritis.

Steven enjoyed being able to thaw out nervous girls. He also enjoyed deflating the bumptious ones, like Nurse Hooley, who flounced in with her bosom straining at her apron and answered his questions in a scornful manner as if, as she had repeatedly assured the nurses outside, she thought the whole thing ridiculous. He let her have a few easy questions, which she answered pityingly, as if surprised that he did not know, flinging triumphant glances toward Matron to see if she was noting her cleverness. Matron sat still looking benign and swaying slightly back and forth and planning how next week she was going to put Nurse Hooley on night duty in the Maternity ward, where the eternally yelling babies and the eternally nagging midwife had between them pricked tougher balloons than this.

Steven, having discovered from her paper the gaps in her knowledge, then proceeded to hammer away at these, watching her with sadistic pleasure go through blustering and hedging to stammering and finally sulky silence.

'Well, go on,' he prompted, smiling. 'Answer my question.' Her fine eyes lowered at him. Her bosom heaved.

'Say something. Anything.'

'I don't know, sir.'

'Ah!' he leaned back. 'That's better. Never be ashamed to say "I don't know". Better people than you have said it.' He was apt to get slightly pompous on these occasions. 'Anyway, it's you who's here to learn, not me, so just listen while I tell you.' But she would not listen properly. She kept looking about her with a half-smile and saying: 'Oh, I know,' until Steven, who could cheerfully have beaten her with a nailed stick, said: 'Since you know so much, my dear, I won't waste any more time on you.' His sarcastic sweetness glissaded off her, and she left the room with the same bounce that had made the floor spring when she came in, not waiting for the door to shut behind her before she announced: 'Of all the stinking asses –'

Steven was pleased to see Nurse Bracken. She was pretty and lively and intelligent, and he could picture her at home. He had the feeling that she was laughing at him, but he rather liked it. She probably laughed at her father, and he would like it, too. Carol would have been like this when she was grown up, but he would never have let her be a nurse. What was Mr Bracken about to let his daughter go when he should have been enjoying every minute of her at home? Chap didn't know his luck.

'How old are you, Nurse?' he asked suddenly, interrupting her eager dissertation on the thyroid gland.

'Twenty, sir,' she said, surprised, giving him one of her

bright, candid looks. He felt very old. He saw himself with her eyes as an immaculate, rather sententiously cynical Personage in whom success had supplanted *joie de vivre*. Come to think of it, that was probably how most people thought of him. If Matron had not been there, he would have said something ridiculous and frivolous, just to show her. Instead, he said: 'Thanks, Nurse. You've done very well,' and decided to put her top, liking the smallness of her waist in her stiff belt as she left the room.

Nurse Lake did not think he was old, anyway. At least, she thought he was God, which made him ageless. She crept into the room, looking battered and moist-eyed, with the blush rushing up and down her face like waves on the shore. She sat down and fixed him with the red-hawed look of a beseeching dog. He had no choice but to ask her things he knew she knew. Her utter dependence on him sapped his resolution to fail on principle whoever had made that idiotic mistake about diabetes. And she had that soluble look about her as if she might burst into tears at the slightest setback. Weakly, he asked her to talk about anything she liked, and she gave him, almost word for word, his own remarks on anæmia. The Matron smiled and nodded the muslin sugar-bag. Nurse Lake's practical work was excellent and conscientious, and she was pleased to see her doing well in her theory. She was going to make a useful, governable staff nurse, one of the ones whom Matron would consider making a Sister later on. Of course, the girl did not look happy – she never had. There was something behind her – a man, perhaps – the Matron would get it out of her one day over a cosy chat.

Steven had the uncomfortable feeling that Nurse Lake thought he and she were in some kind of conspiracy. She wore the memory of that scene in the clinic like a secret badge identifying them as collaborators. When she got up to go, she gave him a long look of sickening gratitude. It was almost as if she had touched him with a fawning, clammy hand. He turned with relief to the pert little Cockney who followed her in with tight sausage curls and bulging calves, and probably a healthy liking for being cuddled in the back of cars.

When they had all gone he added up the marks, made Nurse Bracken top, and found that, with the marks she had gained for her oral, Nurse Lake had passed. Sister Tutor came in to be congratulated on her brilliant class, and flustered out to pin up the notice on the green baize board in the hall.

Matron wanted to have more tea brewed, but Steven, who had a private call to make in Wimbledon, was anxious to get away. He had had enough of women for one afternoon. He went into the Honorary's room to get his hat and bag, and while he was straightening his tie in the mirror which hung in the worst possible light, the door opened and someone came in, cleared her throat on a high note and said: 'Oh – excuse me, sir,' feigning surprise to see him there.

He did not have to see her in the mirror to know who it was. He turned round with a discouraging 'What now?' expression on his face, and Nurse Lake, twisting her hands just inside the door, said her piece in a rush.

'I've just seen the results, sir. I just wanted to say thank you ever so much. It was ever so kind of you to do it, and I'll never forget it, not till the day I die.'

'Good God! What on earth are you talking about?'

'For passing me, sir. I know I didn't deserve it. You don't know how much it meant to me. I'd have died if I'd failed. I hope you didn't mind my coming in here, but I just had to thank you.' Her long face had all gone to pieces; radiant, three-cornered smiles, earnest frowns and haggard emotion flashed about on it like the lights on a pin-table. Steven looked round him, like a trapped animal at the high dirty windows, the buff-coloured walls where the leather chairs stood against the brown dado, but the only way of escape was the door against which she stood. He picked up his case and strode up to her and mercifully she stepped back so that he did not have to touch her to get at the door.

'Nonsense, Nurse,' he said firmly. 'You're being hysterical. I wouldn't pass anybody who was not up to standard. I don't do that sort of a favour.'

She put out a hand and touched his coat. 'Ah, but I know,' she said softly, 'and I'll never forget it. If there's ever anything I can do for you ...' Her whisper pursued him as he fled down the corridor. He could feel her standing looking after him, and to slow down and walk normally as he approached the populated area of the front hall required every effort of will he possessed.

He left the building so rapidly that young Potter, who had been hanging about to catch him, had to run after him across the gravel car park, his progress impeded by a small fibre suitcase and a tennis racket in a press.

Steven was already in the driving seat as he galloped up. 'Thought I'd missed you, sir,' he panted.

'Got to rush off,' grunted Steven, jerking his head away from Ugly's caresses. 'Lot of work to do.'

'Oh, well, I just wanted to tell you, sir.' Young Potter raised his voice as Steven started the engine and revved up, 'I thought you'd like to know that I've heard from Sir George Levinson. He's willing to give me a trial. Isn't it grand, sir?' His plasticine face was joyous.

'Oh, grand,' said Steven, letting in the clutch. 'It's up to you to make good with him now.'

'Oh, I will, sir, I hope. I don't want to let you down. I know I'd never have got the chance if it hadn't been for you. I'm so very grateful, sir.' He hung on to the side of the window as Steven engaged the gear and moved slowly forward. 'Thank you most awfully, sir.' Good God! Was there to be no end to this stifling gratitude? Steven had an impulse to let the car leap forward and leave young Potter sprawling on his back on the gravel with his suitcase and racket flying. Instead, noticing these for the first time, and that the boy was in a brown suit instead of his usual flannels and sports jacket, he said: 'Going somewhere? Want a lift to the station?'

'Oh, thanks most awfully, sir, if it's not out of your way. I'm going home, as a matter of a fact. Got a long week-end.'

'Hop in, then.' Steven pushed Ugly into the back again and young Potter cantered round the front of the car which, as it was still moving, nearly knocked him down, and scrambled awkwardly into the seat next to Steven with his suitcase balancing on end between his knees and chin.

'Where is your home?' asked Steven, as they went down the hill.

'Wimbledon,' said young Potter with bright innocence, and Steven sighed to himself.

'That's where I'm going,' he said resignedly. 'Take you all the way if you like.'

Steven drove in silence, and faster and more jerkily than usual. Young Potter, finding his tentative conversational openings discouraged, concentrated on holding on to his hat and swallowing down his heart each time it leaped into his mouth at what seemed an inevitable collision. He was also busy making plans for what was going to happen when they reached his home. In the Potter household Steven's name was legendary. He had assumed for Mr and Mrs Potter the same God-like aspect that he had for their son, who talked of little else when he was at home. He was always hinting at the exciting intimacy between himself and his chief, and his: 'Doctor Sheppard told me' and 'As I said to Doctor Sheppard' might have been on a gramophone record. He knew that his mother boasted about it over the Wimbledon tea-tables, as his father did at the office and at the club house of the South London Bowling and Billiards Society. It was essential that they should witness this proof, this being driven right to the door in an expensive open car.

But supposing his mother were not looking out of the window, or did not come to the door before Dr Sheppard had driven off? There would be nothing to show that he had ever been there except their son's early arrival and the carefully preserved ashes in his pipe of the fragrant tobacco which Steven had handed over in the oilskin pouch striped with his old school colours. Could he possibly ask Dr Sheppard in for a glass of the sherry which his father kept locked in the left-hand compartment of the dining-room sideboard? It would be awful nerve. Would he come? Not if he was on his way to a case. He was already late for his consultation; that was why he was driving like this. But if, schemed young Potter's fond brain, it could be arranged that he saw the case first, he would have relaxed slightly by the time he got to 95 Blenheim Gardens. Of course, Dr Sheppard might change his mind about taking him all the way home; it would be out of his way if he were going back to town by Parkside and Putney Bridge.

What should he say? 'I suppose you wouldn't care to come in for a drink, sir?' No, better take it for granted that he would. 'You'll come in for a drink, won't you, sir?' 'You'll come in for a quick one.' '... One for the road ...' He tried to imagine his house through Dr Sheppard's eyes. It was small, of course, but it always looked comfortable and clean. His mother made the linoleum in the hall shine like a mirror, and there was that nice brass urn thing that usually had flowers or leaves in it, and that lacquer tray where they kept the circulars and catalogues. His parents? Nothing to be ashamed of as there was in some people's. He would never forget the time he had gone home with Jackie Grenfell and Jackie's father had been drunk and shouted him out of the house. Please God, let Mother be wearing that brown dress with the lace collar and not that blue silk thing that makes her look too fat; and don't let Dad have run out of sherry, and let Marjory be upstairs doing her homework, or out at her music lesson. Oh, good, it's Thursday; she will be.

Steven's voice broke into his thoughts: 'We're getting into Wimbledon, aren't we? You'd better direct me. I'm not very well up on this jungle country.'

'Well, actually, sir,' said young Potter. 'it's more Raynes Park where I live, only we like to call it Wimbledon.' He laughed apologetically.

'Oh?' said Steven, who was ignorant of these subleties. The boy cleared his throat. 'Er – where is your case, sir? I don't want to take you out of your way.'

'Wimbledon Park. Somewhere near the tennis courts they tell me. House called 'Treetops' – damfool name. Know it?' Know it? Know 'Treetops'? Why, the things that went on there were one of his mother's pet subjects.

'I should think I do, sir. That's the Crawleys' place, the chocolate people. They're supposed to be rolling in money.'

'Think I'd be going there if they weren't?' muttered Steven, and young Potter glanced nervously at him to make sure he was joking. Dr Sheppard wasn't like that. Although he had such a high position and famous people galore as patients, he would work himself to death for a sick tramp. Everyone knew that.

'As I know the way,' he said craftily, 'wouldn't it be better to go there first, then you could drop me afterwards on your way home?' Raynes Park was well off the route between Wimbledon and London, but perhaps, as Dr Sheppard did not know the district very well, he might not realize this. Anyway, it would be something to tell at home that he had been inside the grounds of 'Treetops'. He might even see the great Mr Eustace Crawley himself, pacing the drive in anxiety for his wife's condition. It would be she who was ill. She was always being ill, and having famous doctors to see her. Funny, really, that Dr Sheppard had never been called in before.

When Steven suggested that he should come inside and hear the consultation for the good of his education, he was overjoyed. 'But d'you think I really could, sir?' He dithered half in and half out of the car, while Steven was already halfway up the steps which led to the studded front door of the imitation *château*. 'I mean, the Crawleys might not like it.'

'Nothing to do with them. Lawson won't mind; I know

him quite well. I don't say you can go into the old girl's bedroom,' he added, as young Potter joined him on the top step, pulling at the jacket of his suit and shooting out his arms in an endeavour to make the cuffs of his shrunken shirt appear below the sleeves.

Hollywood's idea of an English butler opened one side of the door and took their hats, and young Potter followed Steven up the wide, noiseless staircase, trying to flatten down his springing blond hair. What a house this was! Every bit as wonderful as they said. He tried to take in as much as he could for future recounting. The hall was a vast square well, round which the staircase climbed, and on the first floor you were level with a chandelier like a young power station. Young Potter glanced nervously up along its chain to the massive hook which secured it to the ceiling. There were tapestries on the walls of the corridor along which they walked, glossy tables holding vases and ornaments, and slender-legged chairs so delicately wrought that you would never have dared to sit in them. One arm-chair, with a high tapestry back and lions' claws for feet, had a rope stretched across the seat to discourage even the idea.

'Ghastly place,' muttered Steven over his shoulder. 'Might as well live in a museum.' Although he did not agree, young Potter was glad Steven thought it ghastly; Blenheim Gardens might stand a better chance by comparison.

Dr Lawson was waiting for them in a deeply-carpeted sitting-room. Flowers were everywhere, the chintzes were glazed like porcelain and there were shelves full of unthumbed books. Beyond the windows could be seen an expanse of lawn surrounded by box hedges clipped into animal shapes and ending in a clump of trees. You would never have thought you were in Wimbledon. The only sounds were the whirr of a lawn mower, a solo from an evening bird and the faint throb of a wireless in the next room.

Dr Lawson was thin and ashen-faced, with a troubled look in his eye and lines drawing down the corners of his mouth; what young Potter had come to recognize as the perfect picture of a duodenal ulcer. He would suggest this to Dr Sheppard afterwards.

'Sorry I'm late, Lawson,' Steven was saying as they shook hands. 'Had a clinic this afternoon, and you know what a devil that is for getting away on time.'

'Pity the poor Honorary,' said Dr Lawson in a dry, flat voice, and looked enquiringly towards young Potter.

'Oh – this is my house-man, Potter,' said Steven. 'Hope you don't mind my bringing him in, but he was in the car with me and I thought he'd be interested to hear about the case.'

'Oh, by all means. Glad to see a little youthful enthusiasm,' said Dr Lawson despondently. 'Do sit down, won't you, Mr – er, and Sheppard, I've got the notes of the case here on the table, so we can get right on with it if you're ready.'

Young Potter admired the way Steven stood by the table with his hands in his pockets and just nodded his head or grunted, without interrupting while Dr Lawson was expounding the case. Afterwards, he began to ask questions, pertinent ones, with long stretches of thought between, while young Potter sat on the edge of the sofa, straining to maintain his intelligent expression.

'Yes,' said Steven at last. 'I think you're right. Everything points to a metabolic disorder. I think we can discount that unexplained recurrent pain as a neurosis, in view of the lady's character.'

'Glad to have my opinion confirmed,' said Dr Lawson joylessly.

'I can't quite see why you called me in, though,' said Steven. 'I should have thought, under the circumstances, a gland man – someone like Rayner Jordan –'

One side of Dr Lawson's mouth twisted upwards in what was presumably a smile. 'She would have you, old boy,' he said. 'She'd heard about you from her friends. Ready to go in now?' He jerked his long head towards the door of the room where the wireless was.

Young Potter, rising when he did, was excited to see Dr Lawson slip some kind of a tablet from his waistcoat pocket to his mouth. He was so intrigued by this possible confirmation of his ulcer diagnosis that he jumped, and stammered when Dr Lawson suddenly turned on him with: 'Well, young man, let's hear from you. What do you think of the case, eh?'

'Oh, I – er, well sir, on the face of it – that's to say – I should definitely suspect some – er, metabolic disturbance. Of course, one can't be sure without seeing the patient.'

One side of Dr Lawson's mouth went up again. 'That I'm afraid I can't let you do,' he said. 'The lady's a bit doctor-conscious. More than one new physician at a time might quite unbalance her.'

'Oh, but of course, I wouldn't dream –' Young Potter knew he was being laughed at. Steven came to his rescue with a friendly: 'You stay here, old chap, and smell the flowers. I shan't be long.'

As they opened the bedroom door the dance music swelled for a moment and then was swiftly cut off. Young Potter caught a whiff of some heavy perfume and a glimpse of a mound of lace-edged pillows, from out of which a white Tennysonian arm rose languidly, before the door shut behind Dr Lawson's drooping back.

Young Potter sat down again on the edge of the sofa and bit his nails. He had never seen Steven in action on a private patient. Although he knew that he would be paralysed if he ever had to go into a chamber like the one from which he could hear deep-throated murmurs and once a high affected laugh, he would have loved to be in there studying the technique. Did one sit by the bed, or stand by it, chin on chest, rocking slightly on the heels as was effective in the ward? Or did one walk up and down, barking out questions and pretending to be more interested in the books on the shelves or the view from the window than in the patient? And did one call the patient Mrs Crawley or Dear Lady or Madam or what? And what did one do about making an examination when there was no chaperoning nurse?

The door opened and Steven's head looked out and said: 'Get my neurological set out of the car, there's a good chap.'

After some delay, caused by his shutting the front door on his way out to the car and having to ring for the Hollywood butler to open it again, young Potter knocked at the bedroom door and was told to come in. Dr Sheppard was sitting by the bed with the Tennysonian arm extended palm upwards on his knee, taking Mrs Crawley's blood pressure. The gauge of the baumanometer stood on the bedside table among a bowl of fruit, bottles of scent, a frosted jug of orange juice and the silver-framed portraits of a youth with a narrow head and shifty eyes and a beautiful girl with a cloud of black hair, the edge of the picture cutting off her naked shoulders only just in time. Dr Lawson stood by the window, blocking the light like a darkling cloud, hands behind his back, neck poked forward and chin hanging. Mrs Crawley was a petulant-looking woman in a chiffon boudoir cap, lying with closed eyes, her free hand impatiently plucking the sheet as if the whole thing were more than she could bear. All this young Potter had time to take in before he tripped over a footstool, heard an irritated: 'Who –?' from the bed, and hurried out, the thick carpet clogging his feet.

Back in the sitting-room, he closed the door with infinite care and passed a large hot hand over his face. Because to be like Steven was his life's ambition; he intended, eventually, to be a West End consultant. But would he ever achieve that ease, that blending of nonchalance and good manners with which Steven made himself at home in the most intimidating surroundings? Sitting there by that fabulous bed, he had looked just as if he were sitting by a high black iron bed on wheels in the ward. His pulse was undoubtedly no faster than if it were Mrs Munn's hand he had on his knee. Young Potter knew that his own would be racing at contact with such expensive flesh. He remembered that emergency appendix, that exquisite girl who had been admitted by mistake to the general ward and had had to stay there for a while before she could be moved to a private room. Every time he approached her bed something had happened to his throat so that he could not speak without clearing it between each embarrassed sentence. He had examined her sketchily in the middle of the night before she went to theatre, and even in her extremis of pain, her huge eyes, their lashes sticky with sweat, had seemed to be disparaging him, mocking him. He had dared to suggest to Sister next day that screens should be kept round the bed, and Sister, whose opinion of young Potter was no higher than his own, had replied that if the Queen of England were in her ward she would get the same treatment as everyone else, and that if he were going to put that fractured femur up in extension would he kindly get on with it, because her nurses were busy and dinners would be round in half an hour.

He often wondered what Steven had been like as a house-man, and could never imagine him as anything less than a younger edition of his present self. He had probably, even then, had everybody in his pocket, like Arthur Davies, the R.S.O. at St Margaret's, who had a Lagonda and two suits of tails, and who worked from choice, not necessity. Of course, to have been born and bred in private patient circles was very different to having been brought into the world by the district midwife of Penarth. He knew very little about Steven's background, but he was not a man you would associate with struggle and hardship. The gods had always loved him, just as young Potter loved him, with a devoted admiration untainted by the gall of jealousy.

The outer door opened and a tall man with untidy grey hair and thick-rimmed spectacles came in. His mouth had spoken so many millions of words in its day that it was as flexible as old machinery belting.

He stepped briskly forward, rubbing his hands. 'Ah, good evening, good evening, good evening!' he cried, unwilling to let the phrase go without making the most of it. 'Allow me to introduce myself. Crawley's my name – Eustace Crawley. This' – with a sweep of his hand – 'is my house, and you, I suppose, are the doctor. Am I right?'

'Well, actually,' stammered young Potter, who had risen and was standing uncomfortably with bent knees, because Mr Crawley was pressing him back to the sofa, 'I only came with Doctor Sheppard. He's –'

'Quite, quite, quite,' said Mr Crawley, stepping suddenly sideways and sitting down on the sofa with a slap of both hands on his knees. 'Will you have a cigarette?' A silver case flew open under young Potter's nose.

'Thanks very much, sir, I –' He jumped as a huge flame sprang up dangerously close to his eyebrows.

'Let me make myself quite clear from the start, young man,' said Mr Crawley as he lit both their cigarettes, and extinguished the lighter with a noise like a pistol shot, 'I don't believe in doctors, never have and never will. No, no! I know what you're going to say.' He held up a hand, although young Potter had only opened his mouth to cough, for the cigarette was very strong. 'You're going to tell me that without a doctor I should never have come into the world, but that's where I can prove you wrong, because my mother gave birth to me on the floor of a native hut in central Tanganyika, where she and my father, who were trekking from the Cape to Nigeria, paused just long enough for this event to take place.'

'Really?' muttered young Potter, exquisitely embarrassed. 'Nigeria, sir?'

'Finest country in the world,' said his host, hypnotizing him with the horn-rimmed spectacles. 'Fortune to be had for the taking for an enterprising young man, which was what I became, having no education to cramp the development of my native intelligence.'

'Oh yes, of course,' murmured Potter, remembering the well-known advertisements of a podgy infant crawling toward a huge steaming mug: *Crawley's cocoa every day keeps big and little ills away*. 'Coconuts.'

'The bean, my boy, the bean!' cried Mr Crawley, slapping the other's knee in mistake for his own. 'The magic little cocoa bean, worth a million of your pills. Ah, but I'm forgetting, you're not the doctor, are you?'

'Well, not exactly, sir, but I am a –'

'Quite, quite, quite. Well now, look at me. I always say – Ha, ha, ha – I always say I don't need a publicity agent – though I've got one, mark you, the finest in the country – I'm a walking advertisement for my own chocolate. I'm a strict vegetarian. Nuts and fruit and vegetables, of course, but principally chocolate in all its forms. Look at me! Now can you honestly say you'd find a fitter man in a day's march? I'm fifty-two. I was up at six this morning. I've done a day's work in the City that would kill most people, and I've just had a round of golf, a cold bath and dictated a dozen letters. Feel my pulse, young man. Any fault to find with that?' He pushed back his sleeve, and young Potter, mesmerized, put two fingers on the other's wrist, disliking the cold, reptilian feel of his skin.

'Never a day's illness in my life!' cried Mr Crawley triumphantly. 'Just look at me, now. Did you ever see a fitter man? Now tell me quite honestly. I'm always interested in other people's opinions.' He sprang up, indicating with the palm of his hand his flat stomach and throwing back his flopping grey hair with a proud jerk of his head. Young Potter, feeling like someone asked to give an opinion on a painting, stared without knowing what to say. Mr Crawley certainly did look healthy. Apart from a dark mole on the bridge of his nose and two on his left temple, he appeared to be a body unblemished by the passage of fifty years. The body took a turn to the window and back, the thick carpet springing under his jaunty step. Suddenly he sat down again, bouncing young Potter's end of the sofa up as if it were a see-saw.

'Brought my family up the same way,' he announced, 'and what's the result? Boy's already making a name for himself in the City and the girl's married the heir to a baronetcy and a thousand-acre estate. Loveliest bride of the year, they called her, and, by God, that was an understatement. And let me tell you this, they've never ceased to thank me for it.' His eye ran swiftly over young Potter. 'Wish you were my son,' he said. 'I'd have that fat off you in a couple of weeks.' The boy shifted his plump behind and glanced in agony at the closed bedroom door. Would Steven never come to his rescue?

'Tell you what,' said Mr Crawley. 'You want a job? Of course you do; all young men do. Look, I'll make you an offer.'

'Thanks very much, sir, but I've already got a very good job in hospital –'

'Now look here,' said Mr Crawley, rounding on him severely, 'you've been trying to lead me up the garden. You told me you weren't a doctor.'

'But I never –'

'I suppose you thought that I wouldn't talk to you if you were, knowing how I feel about the profession. You needn't have worried, young man, I don't care who I talk to, duke or dustman, they're all one to me. I could give you a job to-morrow that would put you right at the top in five years' time. I could make a success of you, you know. I've never put my hand to anything yet without making a success of it. That may sound like boasting to you, but, believe me, it's not. It's just a simple statement of fact.

'No,' he said, and suddenly his face fell and he pounded the palm of one hand with the fist of the other. 'I'm a liar.' All his energy now switched over to gloom. 'I'm a liar,' he repeated.

'There's just one thing I've never made a success of, more shame to me, and it doesn't seem that I ever will.'

'Really?' murmured young Potter, with reviving hope.

'Yes.' Mr Crawley gave a violent nod towards the bedroom door. 'My wife. She will be ill. I can't stop her. I've worked myself to death over that woman, but she's made up her mind to be ill and have doctors. I've failed with her. It's a bitter thing, you know, my boy, failure.'

'Well, sir, but if she's really ill, I don't see that it's your fault.'

Mr Crawley sat up again with a shout. 'But you don't understand! She's not ill! There's nothing wrong with the woman at all. She's simply got into the hands of the doctors, and damn her, she loves it. Look at to-day now. She's got this Harley Street quack down to try and cure this pain that I could cure with diet in a couple of days – not that she'd have had it at all if she'd stuck to my regime. He and Lawson, that's the local robber, are in league, of course, to exploit cases like this. They're all in league, the whole boiling of 'em, and she won't see it.'

'Oh, but I say, look here,' began young Potter, going red.

'Stubborn?' interrupted Mr Crawley. 'Let me tell you, my boy, if you're ever thinking of getting married – but better advice still – don't get married. Women can play the very devil with a man, even a man like me. I could tell you some things about my wife that would surprise you. Let me see now,' he leaned back, stretched out his legs and opened his mouth. 'Where shall I start?'

Don't start at all, screamed Potter's unspoken thought. This was terrible. Would the consultation in there never finish?

'It was when we first came back to England,' Mr Crawley was saying. 'I was madly in love with her, of course – young fool that I was – and she with me, or so I thought. I was a splendid physical specimen in those days, even better than I am now, if you can imagine that. You see, the galling part of the whole business was that the other chap was nothing but a *weed*. That was what I couldn't understand. Perhaps I'm being modest when I say that I could understand her falling slightly out of love with me; after all, these things do happen. Familiarity – you know what it breeds.

'But what I could not understand, and never shall to

this day, was that a woman like her, a splendid woman – she'd been brought up on the Asher-Bloomfield system before I switched her to my own – should exhibit suddenly such lack of pride in body.' Once started, it was impossible to arrest his juggernaut speech. Young Potter sat there with glazing eyes fixed on the bedroom door, praying for release.

'That was when it all started,' Mr Crawley was saying. 'This being ill, I mean. It was almost as though this young reptile had infected her body with his own rottenness, but as I keep telling you, it was purely of the imagination. There was nothing wrong with her. I examined her myself time and again –'

The unappetizing picture which this conjured up was mercifully wiped from young Potter's vision by the opening of the bedroom door and the appearance of the two doctors, returning the nightmare air of the sitting-room blessedly to normal.

Young Potter sprang up and Steven threw him a 'Sorry to have been so long.' Dr Lawson, who had just taken another pill, swallowed and said: 'Ah, good evening, Mr Crawley. May I introduce Dr Sheppard? He's very kindly been giving me a second opinion on your wife's illness.'

'How do you do, sir?' said Steven. 'A very interesting case,' nodding towards the bedroom, 'but I think you needn't worry. In my opinion, Dr Lawson is on the right lines, though, of course, it's only fair to tell you that it may be a long business.'

Young Potter was hovering miserably in the background, longing to warn Steven what Mr Crawley was like, but powerless to do more than make a few ineffectual gestures which nobody noticed. If only Dr Sheppard would come away quickly, but, of course, it was part of his job to deal courteously with the husband, the man who paid the bill.

Mr Crawley was pumping Steven's hand brutally, his features distorted by a horrid grin. 'If I had my way, Doctor,' he said, quite pleasantly, 'I'd run you out of here with one hand on the back of your neck and the toe of my boot in the seat of your trousers.' Dr Lawson, who was used to this kind of thing, smiled wearily. Steven raised his eyebrows, extricated his hand, looked at it, and said: 'I'm so sorry you feel like that, Mr Crawley. I understand you don't approve of doctors.'

'Scum of the earth!' cried Mr Crawley in vibrant tones. 'Never called in one yet and never shall. And look at me. Should I be the man I am to-day if I'd let you tinker with me? Never a day's illness. Never missed a day's work.'

'Oh, I quite admit,' said Steven soothingly, 'that we are often quite superfluous. All the same, in the case of someone like your wife, who is really ill, I'm afraid the finest will power in the world couldn't take the place of medicine. She really needs treatment, Mr Crawley, and it's up to the professional conscience of Dr Lawson and myself, if nothing else, to see that she gets it.'

'Oh, go ahead, go ahead!' He laughed loudly, but without humour. 'Treat her till you're blue in the face for all I care. I threw my hand in long ago so far as she was concerned. But,' his eyes contracted to pebbles behind the thick lenses of his spectacles, 'don't expect me to pay the bills, that's all. I'm too old a hand to be fleeced.'

'But of course,' murmured Steven politely, 'I wouldn't dream ...'

'And you needn't be afraid you won't get your money,' shouted Mr Crawley commonly, 'because she's got lots of her own.'

A voice floated through the bedroom door. 'Laddie,' it called. 'Laddie!'

'Excuse me,' said Mr Crawley, briskly, 'my wife is calling me. So I'll wish you good evening.' Young Potter, whom only five minutes before he had been using as a father confessor, he ignored completely; he did not shake hands with Dr Lawson, who did not expect it, but he held out his hand to Steven, who said as he shook it and withdrew his own quickly: 'I'm so sorry you feel like this about us,

Mr Crawley. But if ever you should change your mind and need any medical help, I should be only too glad to do anything for you.'

'Laddie!' wailed the voice again, and Mr Crawley made a noise like 'puh!' and marched into the bedroom.

In the car, Steven said: 'A most extraordinary man. A little psychological treatment needed there; I'd love to have the chance to do it.'

'Not much hope,' grinned young Potter. 'Didn't he glare when you said that about if he ever needed medical help?'

'Yes, it's sad, isn't it? Because he will, and sooner than he thinks.'

'How d'you mean, sir? I mean, I thought he seemed remarkably fit, for all his cranky ideas.'

'See those moles on his face?'

'Good Lord, sir, you don't think –?'

'Mm. Malignant. I'd bet my bottom dollar.'

Steven was quite aware that the roads through which young Potter was directing him were not on the way for London. He was also aware that the boy thought that he did not know this. He kept stressing brightly: 'Then you'll be able to go back by Wimbledon High Street, sir, come out by the Common and get right on to Parkside.' It made you feel very old when young people started trying to bamboozle you. *Lazy young devil, trying to wangle a lift all the way home. I ought by rights to chuck him out and make him walk*, thought Steven, but he was so late already, and tired, that he could not be bothered to do anything else but drive meekly where he was told.

'It's the next turning on the right, sir; just by that pillar box.' They turned up an avenue of semi-detached little Victorian houses, many with agents' boards leaning out of their square of front garden.

'Just here, on the left, sir. Ninety-five.' *Chez* Potter differed only from the rest in that it had a flagpole sticking out of one of the top windows, from which Mrs Potter was wont to hang the Union Jack whenever the Royal family got married or crowned or buried. As Steven drew up at the kerb, young Potter, who had been swallowing nervously ever since they turned into Blenheim Avenue, now tried to give a final swallow and clear his throat at the same time, which nearly choked him, but managed to come out with: 'Do come in, won't you – for a drink, sir?'

'I won't, old boy, thanks all the same. I must get back.'

'Oh, but sir, do. Just for a glass of sh-sh-sherry. My people would so love to meet you.' He spoke gruffly, diving in the back of the car for his case.

'No, really I –' began Steven, but as the boy lugged the case over the top of the front seat he caught the naked disappointment in his face, sighed and said: 'All right, then. Thanks. But I mustn't stay more than a minute.' Young Potter glowed. He hurled his things on to the pavement and himself after them and dashed round to open the door on Steven's side.

'W-what about Ugly? Would you like to bring him in?'

'He'll be all right in the car. Stay there, Ugly.' He held up a forefinger, but Ugly, who only obeyed this order when it suited him, hopped over the side when they had gone up the garden path, mingled with their legs and pushed in at the opening door, causing Mrs Potter to scream sharply and step back against the wall with one hand to her mouth.

Steven made a grab and caught him by the tail, which made him turn round so that he could hold his collar. 'I'm awfully sorry,' he said, straightening up so that his top waistcoat button was on a level with Mrs Potter's eyes.

She looked at her son. 'Well, Boy, this is a surprise! We didn't expect you so early.' This nickname, which had been used ever since he could remember, had never struck him as unfortunate until now.

'Dr Sheppard very kindly gave me a lift. Er – this is my mother, sir. Mother, this is Dr Sheppard.'

'Oh, *how* do you do? This is a treat. We've heard so much about you, Doctor.' She held out a fat little hand, genuine delight dimpling her muffin face. Thank goodness she was wearing her blue silk. And to think that she had taken off her overall only five minutes ago. What a bit of luck!

'Very glad to meet you, Mrs Potter,' said Steven. 'I can't stay more than a minute, I'm afraid.'

'You must come in and have some sherry, sir,' said Boy, making shepherding movements with his hands. They could not all stay in the hall for ever. 'Let me take your hat, sir.'

'I'll just sling this dog outside,' said Steven. 'I must apologize for his pushing in like that. His manners are rather erratic, I'm afraid.' He laughed, and Mrs Potter laughed too, glad of the excuse to do so. She laughed a lot, often for nothing at all.

'No, no. Let him stay, the dear. Isn't he a big chap?' She chirped at Ugly as if he were a canary, at the same time drawing back out of his range.

'Where's Dad?' asked her son.

'In the sitting-room, dear. Come along in, Dr Sheppard. What a wonderful stroke of luck that we're both at home when you call,' she exclaimed, although she and her husband seldom went out in the evening.

The sitting-room was a small but pleasant room, opening through french windows on to a sloping bank of garden, carefully jigsawed into lawn, flower beds, crazy paving and tiny vegetable plot. There was too much furniture and too many pictures on the walls and Mrs Potter said the amount of ornaments made it a terror to dust.

Dad, having heard the voices in the hall, had knocked out his pipe and buttoned up his jacket and waistcoat and was now standing in a host-like attitude before the embroidered firescreen in the grate. Mrs Potter was thankful that he was always so good with men. He talked to Dr Sheppard just as if he had been one of his cronies from the South London Bowls and Billiards Club. He was very fond of dogs so Ugly made a good conversational focus.

'Shall I get the sherry, Dad?' hinted his son, although

no one but Mr Potter ever handled the key of the left-hand door of the sideboard.

'No, no, I'll get it,' said Mr Potter. 'You'll have a glass with us, won't you, Dr Sheppard? It's quite a decent wine, though I say it myself. I get it from a man who comes to the office. It's a sideline of his, and he never touches the inferior stuff. You've got to be careful with wine these days; there's a lot of poison floating around.'

'Thanks very much,' said Steven, dreading what it might be like. 'I'll just have one, and then I must go.'

Surprisingly, the sherry was very good. Steven looked at Mr Potter with new eyes, wondering what it must be like to live in a cramped house like this in a place that took hours to get to from anywhere; to lead the sort of deadly humdrum existence of work, sleep, monotonous Sundays, negligible holidays and worrying over accounts; to have a son like young Potter, to be married to a glorified house-keeper like old Mother P., perching on the edge of the most uncomfortable chair, sipping sherry as if she did not like it, and smoking a cigarette right in the middle of her mouth.

Boy also sat on the edge of his chair, following every word and every move, like a stage manager uncertain of his performers. Whenever he spoke, he kept saying 'we', bracketing himself and Dr Sheppard together, colleagues in work, friends off duty, as it seemed now, from the pleasant, natural way in which Dr Sheppard was behaving. There he sat, in the chair in which his mother usually did her mending, well back, with his legs crossed. He had asked permission to light his pipe. What did he think of them? He seemed almost to be enjoying himself. It did not even matter after all that his mother was wearing that ugly blue silk thing. She had already made one of her inane remarks at which the family always laughed, but which an outsider might not understand, and Dr Sheppard had actually laughed too, and not seemed to think her silly. Even Ugly lay quite at home on the woolly hearthrug, flat on his side. He was apt to do this in the Underground, or in shops, or even sometimes in the middle of the street while he was waiting for Steven.

'By the way, we went to the Crawleys' this evening, Mother,' said young Potter casually, flinging ash on to the carpet.

'Use an ashtray, dear.' She hurried over to him with a brass bowl that had been made in Japan and bought in Dawlish. 'Well, fancy that. How exciting. On a – on a case?'

'Yes. Dr Sheppard was called in for a second opinion on Mrs Crawley.'

'O-oh.' Her mouth and eyes were round. She was longing to ask what was the matter with this notorious Wimbledon character, but of course it would not be the thing. Boy was always talking about professional etiquette. So she laughed instead.

Steven laughed too. 'Yes, you're quite right, Mrs Potter. It is a comic household. Ever been inside the house?' She shook her head. As well ask if she had been to the moon.

'I hear Mr Crawley's a bit of an eccentric in his way,' put in Mr Potter. 'Very shrewd business man and all that. Must be worth millions, and they say he started from nothing. I met a man the other day who'd come into contact with him in a business capacity and, from what he said, I gathered that the man wasn't – well, quite like you and me. Another glass of sherry, Doctor? I mean, *a* glass of sherry, as they say in the Navy. Boy, you're the butler.'

'No, really, I won't. I must be going.' He half rose, but he had to sit back and hold out his glass to prevent young Potter pouring it on to the carpet.

'This is certainly very good stuff,' he said, holding it up to the light. 'What did you say the brand was? I wouldn't mind getting hold of some.'

Young Potter was in heaven. Dr Sheppard asking *his* father's advice about sherry! This certainly vindicated all Dad's fussing about the sideboard key and keeping this sherry for special occasions, and boring everybody about how good it was. Perhaps he did know something about wines after all. He looked at his father with a new respect.

Steven found that he was sipping his sherry slowly, instead of tossing it down and going. Curiously, he was quite enjoying himself. There was nothing about young Potter or his family or the conversation that was at all inspiring, yet there was something about this innocent atmosphere that was ridiculously soothing, and made him realize how tired he was, and how loth to pit himself against the traffic on the way to London. It was a relief not to have to make an effort, not to be witty, or diplomatic, or wise or patient, nor to wonder what people thought of him. He had nothing to gain from these people, nor they from him, perhaps that was it.

'Mr Crawley's trouble,' he told them, 'is that he doesn't like doctors. We were flung out on our ear, practically.'

'Never!' Uncertain whether or not this was a joke, Mrs Potter decided to laugh, anyway. 'What a terrible thing! I'd like to go and tell them some home truths. Where should we all be without doctors, anyway? That's what I'd like to know.'

'Darn sight better off, probably,' murmured Steven. 'I'm quite sure that —' He was just going to say something brilliant, young Potter knew, when that brat of a sister of his came charging into the room in the most disgusting green gym tunic, much too short, with ink on the collar of her blouse and on her fingernails and her black stockings spiralling round her skinny legs.

She stopped short, pushing back her spectacles and pulling up one stocking with a writhing movement. 'Oh – company,' she said disparagingly, and turned to go.

'No, no, Margie,' chided her mother. 'Come in properly, dear, and be introduced. This is Dr Sheppard, that Boy works under at the hospital. Doctor, this is my youngest, Marjory. She's still at school.'

Marjory goggled and pulled up the other stocking before coming slowly forward, shaking Steven's hand and dropping it as if it were a frog. 'Fancy you coming here,' she said, indecently voicing everybody's thoughts.

The charms of puberty, thought Steven, and wondered whether Carol could ever possibly have become like this. No.

'I thought you had a music lesson to-night,' said her brother. She made an unbecoming face at him. 'Old Robbie's sprained her wrist. So sucks.'

'You haven't done your homework, have you, Margie?' asked her father hopefully.

'Sure.' She got a footstool and sat by his feet, leaning her sharp spine against his legs and gazing intently across the hearth at Steven.

'Boy's going to be a doctor, you know,' she announced. 'That's Boy over there,' nodding at her brother.

'I know.' Steven laughed. 'Going to be a very good one, too, I think. I hope. He'll hear about it from me anyway, if he lets me down.'

'Oh, I don't think he'll ever be much good,' she said, eliciting a 'Margie!' on an indrawn breath from her mother. 'I mean, he's all right now, p'raps, but can you see him having a practice of his own? I can't.'

Neither could Steven, if it came to that, but he said: 'I don't see why not. He's got as good a chance as anybody else. He's got more sense than I ever had at that age – and more knowledge probably – but I muddled through all right, bluffed people along until I found my feet.'

Boy murmured deprecatingly, treasuring these words, but almost had to leave the room in his terror that they might go on talking about him. To avert this danger, he asked boldly: 'You've never told me anything about your first jobs, sir. I mean, I can never imagine you as anything but having *arrived*. Dynsford wasn't your first practice, was it? No, of course, you were in the Isle of Wight before that, you told me.'

'Oh, I had a long way to go before I got to Ryde,' Steven said. 'I was in Chester for a while, and in Wales, besides going back to my London hospital as first assistant while I got my M.R.C.P. Chester!' He laughed. 'My God, I'd almost forgotten that place. That was a pretty queer set-up for a young man's introduction to general practice, if you like.'

It was just like that picture of 'The Boyhood of Raleigh'. They were all sitting round, hanging on his reminiscences, even Margie, who had discovered Ugly's passion for having his ears mauled about.

'Er – in what way, "queer", sir?' prompted young Potter.

Steven laughed again, remembering the shock of arriving at that horrid little flint sentry-box of a house, jammed between two others exactly similar in a terrace outside the city walls. It had not even that merit, it was not even in the beautiful part of Chester. He could hear now the shuffling footsteps which answered his ring. He had nearly run away when that old witch put her face round the door.

'Everything was so *old*,' he said. 'House, furniture, servants, patients, equipment, even the dog – and the food, of course; you had to hack your way through the buns at tea with a pick and shovel. And the doctor – I was to be his assistant, because the practice was getting too much for him – he was the oldest thing of all. He was crumbling to bits before my eyes. I always expected that one day he wouldn't come down to breakfast, and I'd go up to his room and find him – you know, like the man in that Poe story, what was it? – a loathsome, nearly liquid mass of indescribable putrescence.'

'No,' interrupted Marjory. 'A nearly liquid mass of loathsome – of detestable putrescence.'

'That's it,' said Steven surprised. 'Have you read it?'

'Course,' she said scornfully. 'We did it at school.'

'Margie goes to quite a progressive school,' explained her father.

'Oh, I see. Well, anyway, there was something rather Poe-like about the whole establishment. It was always in half-darkness, because the lights kept fusing, and we had to use a couple of oil lamps, which were never trimmed, and were always at their last gutter of oil. Everyone crept about in carpet slippers, and there was a ghastly old clock with no minute hand, in the hall, like a coffin, which used to whirr for about five minutes, and then go "bong!" in the middle of the night, like the noises in the vaults of the House of Usher. But that housekeeper – she was the worst. She never spoke to me all the six months I was there, and she had only one tooth and a withered hand. Ugh!' He shuddered. It was a long time since he had talked about any of this. Ruth had never cared to hear about it. It was all going in *The Swift Stream* of course, slightly embellished. Rather a good thing to talk about it now; he was remembering things this way that he thought he had forgotten. When he got home he would make some notes, perhaps leave the hospital part, and get his hero on to this, while it was still in his mind.

'But why did you ever go to a place like that, sir?' asked young Potter. 'I mean, surely –' Implying that the world must have been Steven's oyster from the very start.

'Oh, I don't know. I suppose I thought it would be experience. I wanted a job in a hurry, too. I'd had a row at the hospital, and wanted to get out. Some silly affair – I can't even remember now what it was about. I'd been there too long, I suppose. You know what it is living in an institution; you can bear it for just so long.'

His house-physician nodded. Didn't he know? Had he not recently almost come to blows with Jackie Grenfell for no better reason than that they had faced one another across the breakfast table for nine months?

'Of course,' went on Steven, 'coming like that straight from a London hospital that was so well equipped and so clean, and so up-to-date in everything, this Chester place was even more of a shock. If you could have seen the old man's dispensary! I wonder he didn't kill off all his patients. But then, most of them were dying, anyway, so it didn't make much odds. You've never met such a collection of old crocks and chronics as he had on his books. It was a fine experience of the symptoms of gout, arthritis, sclerosis, bronchitis, varicose ulcers – every phase that the body goes through in its last stages of dissolution. Of course there was no diagnosing, that had all been done years ago, and treatment – they were mostly beyond that. Pretty disheartening, really. I wonder I didn't cut my throat. I nearly had it done for me, anyway, in the end.'

'You're joking, Dr Sheppard,' said Mrs Potter, getting ready to laugh.

'Oh, well, let's say that she happened to have the carving knife in her hand, and that she just happened to stumble forward against the bed when I was in it, though what she was doing in my bedroom in the half-light with a carving knife, history doesn't relate. Anyway, I nipped out of the other side pretty quick, and was packing my bags the next day. That was when the old doctor did almost dissolve into your nearly liquid mass, Marjory. He broke down and cried, said he'd got fond of me – like a son. I suppose he thought he'd never get another assistant if I went. But it was ghastly. My spine crawled all the way to London in the train. I had to go and have a Turkish bath.'

Mrs Potter laughed. 'You make it sound like a novel, Dr Sheppard. Do go on. It's tremendously exciting.'

'Oh, I don't know. Things always sound better in retrospect. At the time it was just depressing.' He sat thinking for a moment, watching the dusk gathering up to the french windows. Silently, young Potter refilled his glass. His mother warned him by gestures not to do the same for the rest of the family. There would be little enough left, as it was, for Dad's birthday party next week, but it was not every day that the great Dr Sheppard arrived from Olympus to sit among them and talk just as naturally as if he had been in his own home among his own family. To her shepherd's pie drying in the oven she never gave a thought.

'Then of course,' resumed Steven, not realizing that last time he had picked up his sherry glass it had been almost empty, 'I went to Wales. That was a very different cup of tea.'

'Was that where you were in partnership, sir?' asked Boy. 'I remember you saying once that you'd never go into partnership in practice again.'

'I wouldn't. And don't you, either, if you can help it. It's all right in theory, but human nature and theory aren't compatible. Two men – I don't know – they don't seem to be able to live together without rows any more than two women can. There's no partnership that lasts, except marriage, and that doesn't often.'

'Present company excepted,' put in Mr Potter, smiling at his wife.

'Oh, rather.' Steven raised his glass to them. How Marion would laugh if she could see him fitting so well into this Home Chat atmosphere. But he liked it. It answered some need in him at the moment.

That house in Llandovery had been rather like this one. Clean and comfortable and unexacting, and infinitely tasteless. 'We had a maid in Wales called Betty,' he said. 'She was a marvel. Cooked like an angel and kept the house spotless, but never wanted to clean round you – you know.' He nodded at Mr Potter, and everybody laughed. They knew. Mrs Potter was always cleaning round people, begging them not to disturb themselves, but making life unbearable until they did.

'She married the man who brought the coals. He was a patient of ours, a hyperthyroid, that was what got her – the way his eyes glistened. I always thought that it was her going that really started to break up the partnership. We were never so comfortable again, and little Willie Pugh – that was the other chap's name – got restless and started to listen to his Nonconformist conscience.'

'Ah,' said Mrs Potter. 'Chapel. All the Welsh are Chapel folk, aren't they? We used to be, when we were in Cornwall, but somehow, since we've been here, and with the church so handy and the vicar such a gifted man – he broadcasts sometimes, you know – we drifted away from it.'

'It was one of those stark kind of creeds,' said Steven.

'Brethren, or Hot Gospellers, or Holy Rollers or something. Being a Christian, he called it. I'd always thought that anyone baptized in the church was a Christian, but apparently not. You have to have seen the Light. He was always trying to convert me to his rather depressing faith, and I'd lead him on and let him think he really was getting somewhere and then when he'd talked himself dry for about two hours and was panting for a drink, which, according to his lights, poor chap, of course he couldn't have, I'd make some frightful blasphemous remark – vile of me, I suppose, but he drove me to it – and he'd have to start with me right again from the beginning.'

'Did he try and convert his patients?' asked Mr Potter.

'Well, lots of them had got the bug already. But the others? No, he didn't. He was too shrewd a business man to risk losing them that way. He'd worked up a jolly nice little practice for himself. It was one of those long, thin towns, with more people in it than you'd think, and our only competition was a drunken old scoundrel at the slum end who used to spend his more sober hours acting midwife to the local cows. I was a year and a half there. I got a lot of experience out of it, wouldn't have missed it for anything. We had a couple of outbreaks of poliomyelitis –'

'Infantile paralysis, Mother,' explained Boy in an undertone.

'– and this chap Pugh and I worked out a new system of remedial exercises to try and combat the paralysis. The same sort of thing that they're now doing so much good with in America, only far in advance, of course, of anything we ever tried. But we did get some good results. I used it as the subject for my thesis for my M.D.'

'Oh, you got that, did you, sir, while you were in Wales?'

'Yes. I'd been putting it off and putting it off. Awful fag, you know, writing a thing that length; wait till you have to do it.' The thought of this ordeal had ceased to appal young Potter. He simply knew he would never be able to do it.

'It was soon after that that Willie Pugh's conscience began to make trouble. It had been telling him all along, apparently, that he ought to go and be a missionary in Central Nyasaland, or some such deserving place, but the practice going so well damped it down a bit. That was his idea in advertising for a partner, actually. He intended to palm off his half on the other man, and clear out to carry on the good work among the blacks. I couldn't have bought him out if I'd wanted to, of course, but he didn't know that, because I arrived with some quite decent London clothes, and a car and one thing and another. Well, as I say, he used periodically to go all mystic, particularly after Betty left, and he used to get "guided" to do things. That was all right so long as he confined it to letting God choose his tie for him in the mornings and having bread and dripping for supper, but when it came to sitting around the house waiting so long for guidance to go and deliver Mrs Williams, at Bryndydwy, that I had to go myself, in the middle of my surgery, I got a bit fed up. We had a row, and then we made it up, and he prayed over me for a bit, and finally said that he couldn't reconcile his conscience any longer, and he was going to London in the morning to see about getting drafted out to "The Field".'

'Hunting?' asked Mrs Potter, puzzled.

Steven laughed. 'The Mission Field, he meant. Well, I didn't think it was worth arguing that he was much more certain use to the people of North Wales than problematical use to the natives of Central Africa, who'd got along very well for centuries with their own medicine men, so I told him he'd better start finding me another partner.'

'Then, I suppose, he tried to persuade you to buy his half of the practice?' asked Mr Potter.

'Yes. And the joke was that he couldn't understand that for me this Wales business was only a stepping stone to something higher. He couldn't see why I wasn't prepared to live and die in Llandovery, making a comfortable little income, working damn' hard and never being heard of again. Of course, at that age the idea made me laugh. Now, I sometimes wonder. It wouldn't have been a bad life ... uncomplicated, you know.'

Mrs Potter laughed. Obviously now he was joking.

'I wonder where little Willie is now,' said Marjory. 'Been eaten alive, should you think?'

'I wouldn't be surprised. Hope not, though. He wasn't a bad little chap, really. He was rather pathetic at the end, going round buying all his equipment. They have to take everything with them, you know: pie dishes, washing basins, spoons, besides all their medical stuff. You couldn't move a foot in the house by the time he'd got everything together. I had to help him pack it into crates. That was when I smashed this thumb.' He wiggled his left thumb at them, with its knot on the joint where the fracture had been.

'I've often wondered how you did that, sir,' said young Potter, who had watched Steven's hands at work so often that he knew them like his own.

'I say!' said Steven suddenly. 'Is that the right time? Good Lord, I must go. I'm most terribly sorry, I've been sitting here gassing about myself for hours. Why on earth didn't you shut me up before?' He got up. Outside the french windows, blue shadows hid the garden. It was twenty to eight. Ruth would be furious.

'We've loved it,' said Mrs Potter. 'It was so good of you to come.'

'It's been tremendously interesting,' said her husband, getting up. He had been interested, and he did like Steven very much, but he did want his dinner.

'Oh, don't go, sir,' said young Potter. 'Have – have another sherry,' he said desperately. 'One for the road. Anyway,' he added, trailing Steven and his mother to the hall, 'you haven't finished the story. You're still in Wales, knocking nails into crates. What happened afterwards?'

'What happened was that I made the only shrewd business deal I've ever made in my life. I discovered a man who was willing to buy the practice for quite a decent sum, so I bought little Willie out, half with what I'd earned while I'd been with him and half promised of what I *would* earn after he'd gone, and when he had gone I sold the practice, cleared out and paid little Willie or the hot gospelling society who'd inherited all his wealth. See?'

'Oh yes, sir, fine, fine,' said young Potter, who had not quite followed all this. Really, it made him smile to think that he hoped one day to emulate Dr Sheppard. There was so much more to doctoring than just the mere practice of medicine. How was he ever going to be able to cope with all the business side of it: the deals and partnerships, money invested in a practice, money which you had not even earned mortgaged in advance against the possibility of earning it? He could not even master his weekly accounts, which rarely amounted to much more than his fares to Wimbledon, stamps, laundry and an occasional supper at the Dynsford Dive. He sighed. Steven, putting on his hat in the hall and murmuring polite things to his mother, was already a being from another world, although in the sitting-room there he had been on their level. But as soon as he had gone there would be nothing except the fast-vanishing dent in the arm-chair and the nebulous fragrance of his pipe to show that he had ever been there.

He would forget them as soon as the front door was shut, and the opportunity of a second visit would probably never arise. Only a miracle had brought him there this time. Already young Potter could hardly believe that it had happened.

The shepherd's pie smelt very strong in the hall. Mrs Potter was always lavish with the onions when Boy was coming home.

'I say,' said Steven, 'have I been keeping you from your supper? Why on earth didn't you turn me out?'

'Oh no, *no*, Dr Sheppard,' lied Mrs Potter. 'We never have our meal till eight.' Her son stepped heavily backwards as he heard Marjory behind him draw breath to speak, and turned her: 'But, Mum, you know we –' into a yelp and a hiss as she drew back her own foot to hack her brother on the shin.

*

Ruth made no bones about the time she was accustomed to have her dinner. She was already halfway through when Steven got home. 'You're very late,' she said with her mouth full. 'Where have you been?'

'Telling the story of my life in a semi-detached house in Wimbledon,' said Steven wearily, helping himself to whisky.

'Don't be silly, dear,' she chided. 'And hurry up with your dinner, because I promised Ethel she could go to the cinema.'

'What is this?' he asked, poking his fork into the food Mrs Garrard had put before him with one of her neat gliding gestures.

'Mushroom soufflé. That's why I didn't wait for you; otherwise it would have spoiled.'

It had spoiled. Steven ate it without tasting it, shared his cheese with Ugly, and took his coffee down to the consulting room to get on with *The Swift Stream* while his memories were still fresh in his brain.

Chapter 6

—

ON August 4th, 1939, Ruth had a profound thought. She voiced it from her bed to Steven, shaving in his dressing-room next door. He was using his electric razor, and did not hear her.

'Steven, you might answer when I talk to you.' She raised her voice. 'I said ...'

'What's all that?' He switched off the current and waited patiently, with the razor poised against his cheek.

'I said the Great War started twenty-five years ago to-day, and here we are heading for another war.' This fact was by now apparent even to people like Ruth.

As if he didn't know it. He was going to the Admiralty again to-day. Only way with these people was to go on pestering them, make such a nuisance of yourself that eventually they gave you what you wanted to keep you quiet. 'What?' he said.

'I said the Great War started twenty-five years –'

'All right, all right, I heard you.'

'Why did you say "what?" then? You're always doing that.'

'Sorry. Habit, I suppose.' The razor hummed again.

'Well, it's most annoying. Darling, I'm terribly worried about to-day.'

'Why?' he mumbled out of a distorted jaw.

'You know perfectly well. I told you, it's my V.A.D. exams. I'm sure I'll never pass; there's such a terrible lot you have to know.'

'Oh, you'll do fine.' He walked through to her, wiping his face on the towel. 'What is it – First Aid? All you need know about that is how to treat shock, and how to stop hæmorrhage, which I've drummed into you till I'm blue in the face, and not to move the patient before you get expert diagnosis.'

'But you don't understand, darling. There's much more to it than that. We're supposed to *do* the expert diagnosis.' He made an exclamation of ridicule, and she looked hurt. 'It's quite different to what it was in your day. V.A.D.s are to be trained so that they could manage all on their own.'

'All in twelve lectures.'

'Oh, we've learned all about it. How to tell the difference between a fractured skull and a fractured spine, how to set a collar-bone – clavicle, I mean. How to tell whether it's opium or belladonna or alcoholic poisoning, only I've forgotten that one; it's something to do with the pupils of the eyes. Or is that cerebral hæmorrhage?'

'You get unequal pupils there, and –'

'Oh, I know *that*,' she said. 'But, Steven, there's such an awful lot they might ask, and then there's all the Home Nursing on top of that, and the practical work as well. I'm sure I shan't pass; I've never been any good at exams. I couldn't bear to fail. You have to take all the lectures again if you do, and I couldn't face those treks down to Chelsea again after dinner. They wore me out.'

'Considering you always went in a taxi –'

'Oh, I *didn't*, quite often I went by bus. I think we ought to save all we can these days,' she added, pursing her mouth. 'We never know what may be in store for us. Steven, are you in a hurry this morning?'

'Not particularly. I've got a clinic about ten-thirty, nothing before that. I thought of taking Ugly in the Park.'

'Do be a dear, then, and ask me some questions while you're dressing. Here,' she patted the eiderdown. 'Come and sit by me on the bed. Oh, mind the tray! Look out, you nearly spilled the coffee. That's a lovely shirt, darling.' She fingered his sleeve, then put her hand inside the cuff opening and stroked his arm. 'I might get you some more for your birthday, if you like. Where did I get them?'

'You didn't. I got them myself at Justin's.'

'Did you? Would you like me to get you some more, or is there anything else you'd like better? You're so difficult with presents, you know; you always like to choose your things yourself, and then it isn't a surprise. I know you've never used that ashtray I gave you last Christmas, although you said you liked it, because I found it at the back of a drawer the other day. And it was terribly expensive – real alabaster.'

'Look, Ruth,' he changed the subject, 'if you want me to hear your First Aid let's get on with it, because I want to get out before it gets too hot.'

'I'll give you the book then.' She scrabbled among the untidiness on her bedside table, and Steven helped himself to a piece of toast from her tray and buttered it.

'I don't want the book,' he said. 'Who's examining you, a doctor? I'll ask you what it's useful to a doctor for you to know.'

'But it has to be what's – Oh, well,' she gave up, realizing that he would do it his own way or not at all, 'go on then.'

He sat on the edge of her bed, with his braces hanging and his collar undone, eating the toast, and she leaned back against the pillows with her eyes shut, preparing to use her intellect.

'Tell me then,' he said, 'how you would recognize a simple fracture.'

'Oh, that's easy. It goes by the vowels, a, e, i, o, u. A is – oh no, that's something else. No, I know, it goes by the initials of a sentence. What is it? Please Put Sixpence In Uncle's Cap. P is pain, of course –'

'Is that the way they teach you to learn things?'

'Yes, of course, it's the modern method. Don't interrupt me. P is pain; now another P –'

'You mean you have to stand in the middle of the road on a rainy night, with traffic bearing down on all sides, reciting poetry before you can decide whether a man's broken his neck. It's a sweet picture.'

'Be quiet, Steven; you're not being very helpful. I can't think of the other P. What would it be?'

'Palpitations?' he suggested, taking another piece of toast.

'Oh no. I know what it is. It's Please *Drop* Sixpence, not Put. D is deformity.'

'Sounds feasible.'

'S for swelling, I for immobility. In Uncle's – U for unnatural mobility; that means when you've broken your arm and it goes all flobby – it would, wouldn't it?'

'Oh, certainly.' He spread marmalade on the toast, taking all the rind.

'Cap C for crepitus. You move the bones and you can hear them grinding against each other. Ugh! I should hate to do that.'

'Please God you'll never have to,' said Steven. 'If you're going to pick up fractured legs and yank them up and down to see if you can hear crepitus, you're going to be a menace to society, Ruth.'

'I'm only telling you what they teach us, and they ought to know.' She opened her eyes and stretched out a hand to her breakfast tray. 'Steven! You've eaten all my toast! I do think that's beastly of you; you're going to have your own breakfast downstairs in a minute.'

'Sorry, I thought you'd finished.'

'Of course I hadn't. I've got a trying morning in front of me.'

'Ring for some more, then. There's no bread shortage yet, is there?'

'I don't like to keep asking Ethel to come up all those stairs.'

'Good God!' He got up from the bed. 'Anyone would think that woman was paying us wages the way you treat her.'

'Well, go to the top of the back stairs and call down. I don't want to take advantage of her when she's so willing. You don't seem to realize how lucky we are.'

'I wouldn't dream of bawling down three flights as if this were a tenement,' he said, ringing the bell at the head of Ruth's bed. 'Personally, I can't stand the woman. I wouldn't care if she left to-morrow. And that brat. He's lost all those tennis balls I gave him, and now I suppose I'm expected to find him some more.'

'Now you're just being silly,' said Ruth calmly. 'Ask me some more questions. You haven't been much help to me so far.'

Steven went into his dressing-room. He had got up this morning in a good temper, which was rapidly wearing off. 'All right,' he said sulkily, choosing a tie. 'Tell me about a Colles' fracture.'

'Oh, that's easy. Tablespoon deformity.'

'What the devil are you talking about? Is that another modern idea?'

'You know what I mean – dinner fork.'

'Could you draw it?'

'Oh, we don't have to do any diagrams. It's only a written exam.'

'Well, how would you immobilize it?'

'Let's see. You put it in a Carr's splint and put a sling on.'

'And where are you going to find a Carr's splint in the middle of a bombed and burning house, in the name of God?'

'You needn't blaspheme. Oh, Ethel – I wonder if you'd mind very much asking Mrs Hankey to do me a little more toast? Don't think I'm greedy; Doctor's helped himself to most of my breakfast.'

'If I hadn't got the right splint handy,' went on Ruth, after Mrs Garrard had gone out without a word, 'I should give the patient something like a pencil or a cork to hold and splint the arm with an umbrella.'

'An umbrella and a cork, I see,' said Steven kindly.

'Now let's do some nursing,' said Ruth. 'Oh, but you wouldn't know anything about that, would you?'

'My dear Ruth,' said Steven, coming to the communicating door, circling his shoulders to settle his jacket comfortably, 'I haven't worked in hospitals for nearly twenty years without learning something about the noble profession. Tell me how you'd prevent bedsores.'

'They're always asking about bedsores,' said Ruth petulantly. 'I'm quite sick of it.'

'You'll probably get that in your exam.'

'Well, I know it anyway, so we needn't bother with that. I say, Steven, have you asked the Matron yet about my doing my fifty hours at the East Central?'

'I did mention it, but she hasn't got a vacancy just yet. She said she'd take you as soon as she could.'

'Goodness knows when that'll be, and the war may come, and I shan't get a job anywhere until I've finished my training.' Now that she had accepted the idea of war, Ruth, who had not the slightest idea what it implied, was quite looking forward to it.

'I do think, considering the position you hold there, darling, she might have got me in straight away. Do ask her again.'

'Oh, I will if I get the chance,' he said irritably, 'but good Lord, I hardly ever see the woman. I've got plenty of work to do there, you know, without tracking her down all over the hospital.'

'Well – Oh, thank you so much, Ethel. I'm so sorry to bother you. Do you think, when I'm dressed, little Tom could come up a bit and let me practise bandaging him again? He didn't mind last time, did he? He seemed to quite enjoy it.'

'Certainly, Madam. He'll be only too pleased, I'm sure. If you ring when you're ready, I'll send him straight up. He's not doing anything; he's always at a loose end when I'm working.'

'Oh, dear. He ought to be going to school, really, oughtn't he?'

'The Inspector called again yesterday, Madam, but it's all so difficult. I don't want him to go to the council school, as you know, and get in with all that rough crowd of children. I had wanted something better for my boy – that was one of the reasons I took him away from his dad, if you can understand – but at the moment, what with helping my mother to pay off the instalments on the bedroom suite, I don't see my way clear to paying fees for him anywhere.'

'Now I've told you, Ethel, you don't need to worry about it,' Steven heard Ruth say, and groaned to himself. 'You know I want little Tom to have every chance, just the same as you do. I'm very fond of him – both the doctor and myself are.'

When Mrs Garrard had gone, Steven, who was ready to go down, came to the communicating door and Ruth, opening her mouth to say something, saw that it was the wrong time to reopen the subject of Tom's school fees, and said brightly instead: 'Well, good-bye, dear. Have a nice walk. You're in to lunch, aren't you?' She would tackle him about it again at a more favourable time. But there seemed to be so few favourable times with him these days. He needed a holiday, that was probably what it was, and of course he was worried about the war.

'You know I'm not in to-day, Ruth,' he said. 'I told you yesterday.'

'I'm sure you didn't. Oh, dear, and we were going to have veal-and-ham pie. Mrs Hankey will have made it already.'

'Well, it'll keep, won't it?' Steven kissed her good-bye two inches off the top of her head. 'Save me some for to-night – with a cos lettuce. Only we never seem to get cos lettuce these days.'

'The trouble is,' said Ruth, looking worried, 'that with Mrs Fairchild staying to lunch, *and* little Tom's appetite so good, they always finish up everything downstairs. And I don't like asking them to leave things. It looks as if I grudged them the food.'

Mrs Garrard, bringing him his breakfast, seemed to have 'school fees' carved accusingly in each stone-like eye. He knew he would have to do something about it eventually, and he was quite willing to start young Tom on the flinty road to 'bettering himself'. The child was bright enough to make it worthwhile, but he was not going to be forced into it by this conspiracy of taking it for granted.

He fidgeted while Mrs Garrard moved about the room, shifting coffee pots unnecessarily and lifting up the toast rack as if she could not tell without doing so whether there was enough toast in it.

'That's all right, Ethel, thank you,' he said. 'I don't need anything else.' The woman never seemed to realize that breakfast was a meal that should be taken unattended. When he retired and had his house in the country – Shropshire, it was going to be; somewhere on the smooth swell of the Long Mynd – he had it all planned about breakfast. He would get up early and go for a ride, or do some writing, and breakfast would be waiting whenever he wanted it in a room where the morning sun fell across the table and made the marma-lade transparent.

There would be bacon and eggs or kidneys or sausages on one hot plate and coffee and hot milk on another, a cold ham on the table, with a long flexible knife, halves of grape-fruit all ready sectioned, with a candied cherry in the middle, huge blue-and-white coffee cups like bowls, all the morning papers, balls and rolls of pale, dewy butter, the kind of marmalade that was all chunky dark brown rind, and black cherry jam when you got tired of that. When he had guests, the women would all breakfast in bed, and the men would straggle in at any time they liked, without rubbing their hands and making plans for the day or expecting to be passed things.

And there would be porridge in some kind of special heater, with thick yellow cream and damp brown sugar. Or golden syrup, perhaps? When he was a boy, he used to spend so long making patterns with the syrup running from the spoon, that his porridge used to get cold before he started it. So his mother had bought him one of those plates with a compartment underneath for hot water and a picture of bears skating, which revealed itself to you as you finished the porridge. He had taken this plate everywhere with him after he was grown up. It had been useful for keeping meals hot when he was out late on a case. Then Carol had used it, but after she died Ruth had hidden it away. Steven had found it at the bottom of a packing-case when they moved into Wimpole Street, and had insisted on using it again, but Phyllis had managed to break it quite soon.

*

In Regent's Park the cloudless sky was pale blue and the early haze over the sun toned everything down to water colours. He walked beside the lake, passing the people hurrying towards work as if they were drawn there on strings, crossed the bridge by the boating pond and came out on to the open space of faded grass. In the hazy light the houses and trees in Prince Albert Road looked farther away than they were, and people walking on the criss-cross paths looked small. A girl was coming towards him from a long way off; he watched her all the way. Her long, straight legs and feet moved parallel, instead of bulging out, or waddling or wambling or turning over at the ankles, as most women's did. As she came nearer, he saw that she was wearing a linen dress the colour of blackberry juice mixed with cream, with a square neck and buttons all down the front. Her legs were bare, and she carried a pile of books. She passed him, and then they both stopped, turned and looked at each other again, smiling uncertainly.

'Surely –' he began.

'It is Dr Sheppard, isn't it?' she asked. He had not the slightest idea of her name, but he remembered, now, that he had met her at Mark Stainer's sherry party last spring. She had been wearing a black dress, then, with a cameo brooch and her hair piled on the top of her head instead of swinging round her shoulders in a shining brown curtain as it was now. She had been handing round drinks and cigarettes, not exactly a hostess, yet obviously more than a guest in Mark Stainer's flat. His girl-friend probably.

They did not shake hands, because her arms were full.

'How's the book going?' she asked, and he remembered having unburdened himself to her, over the fifth sherry, of his hopes and plans for *The Swift Stream* on which he was then just starting.

'It isn't, I'm afraid. Good Lord, fancy you remembering.'

'Oh, I've heard about it since, off and on, from M.S. I'm his secretary, you know. I wish you'd send him as much as you've written. He'd like to publish it, if it's any good at all. People are awfully interested at the moment in books about doctors, but you want to get yours in before the entire medical profession publishes its memoirs.' She had a charming smile, enhanced by the fact that her normal expression was serious. When she smiled, her lower lip came down squarely and her eyes did not crease up or twinkle, but went on looking at you, large and full and candid. It was a real honest smile, not just a social pleasantry.

'What was it called?' she asked. 'I've forgotten.'

'*The Swift Stream.*' It sounded silly, and he wondered whether he ought to change it. Or did all titles spoken out loud sound silly to their authors? 'It's rotten, though – not going a bit as I meant it to. I've been afraid to send any of it to Stainer in case he should damp it. If he did, I know I'd never have the heart to start again, or probably to write anything else ever.' She had been walking quickly before she stopped, and was standing now on one leg, as if she were in a hurry to get on.

So he said: 'You going to the office? I'll walk along with you, if I may. I'm only out giving my dog a run.' Ugly was a long way ahead, annoying a red chow, who kept snapping at him, and running a few yards with her tail between her legs, before stopping to make sure he was still following her. Steven whistled him, but as he paid no attention, he said: 'Oh, well, he'll come in his own time,' and turned and walked along the path beside Mark Stainer's secretary. He wished he could remember her name.

'I expect it's awfully good, really,' she said kindly. 'Have you shown it to anyone at all? Your' – she did not know whether he was married, so she said – 'your family?'

'No. I told you, it's rotten,' he said.

'Of course, M.S. can be awfully brutal in his criticisms. He doesn't mince his words just to give struggling authors encouragement ... I wrote a story once.' She laughed. 'I thought it was pretty good, and had visions of myself being an author, and not being a secretary any more. Then I showed it to him and – well, I'm still a secretary.'

'Probably he didn't want to lose you,' Steven said.

Her hair swung as she looked at him. She would be as tall as most men, but she had to tilt her head a little to look at Steven. 'That's kind of you,' she said, 'but – no. It was terrible, really. I read it through the other day and blushed. I'm glad I got an honest opinion on it, though, because I might have gone on kidding myself that I could write. As it is, I'm quite happily resigned to the fact that I never shall. It's like going on the stage. Most girls are convinced that they could act if only they had the chance, and they fret about it and feel ill-used until they're allowed to have a try and find out they can't. But do send him your stuff. If he thinks it's any good he might give you some tips that would help it along a bit.'

'It's such a mess. I'd have to get it straightened out and then decently typed. Trouble is, I don't get long enough at it at a time. If I could spend some solid, consecutive hours on it I might be able to get it into some sort of shape.'

'I expect you're very busy,' she said. She didn't say it must be so interesting being a doctor, or I always think I would have liked to be a doctor.

'No busier than most people, I suppose,' he said. 'But it takes me such hours to get down to it. I fiddle about with my head full of other things, and only begin really to write when it's time to stop. If I could be one of those chaps who can shut himself up for weeks on an island off the coast of Scotland – but I probably wouldn't do any work there, either. I'd fish, or something.' He turned, and seeing that Ugly's attentions to the chow were becoming half-hearted, he whistled him again. Glad of an excuse to get out of the situation with dignity, for the chow had bitten him on the nose, Ugly came bounding over the grass at once with his tail circling.

'Oh, is that your dog?' said the girl. 'Isn't he lovely? He's got foxhound blood, hasn't he?'

'Yes,' said Steven surprised. 'Most people don't see that because it only shows in his markings.'

'We used to walk hound puppies when I lived in the country,' she said. They had reached the left-hand bridge over the lake. 'I go over here,' she said, 'and go out by Albany Street and through to Bloomsbury Square. Don't let me take you out of your way. I'm late, though, this morning. I believe I shall have to get a taxi when I come out of the Park.'

'I'll walk down and get you one, then,' said Steven, 'if I may. It's on my way home.'

When they were standing on the pavement at the corner of Albany Street and Euston Road, and every passing taxi seemed to have its flag down, making Steven feel inefficient, the girl said: 'It's probably awful cheek asking you, but I suppose you wouldn't let *me* have a look at your book? Not that I'm such a judge, of course – "I know what I like", as they say – but I haven't been a publisher's secretary for two years without knowing a bit about what sells and what doesn't.'

'I say, would you really?' Steven forgot about looking for taxis. 'But, you wouldn't want to. It's terribly bad. I couldn't inflict it on you.'

'Honestly, I'd like to, if you wouldn't mind. I've got the usual morbid interest in anything to do with medicine, any-way. No – I didn't mean that.' She smiled at him. 'But I would like to read it, unless, of course, you'd rather not.'

'I'd simply love to get an intelligent person's opinion on it, only you would give me an honest opinion, wouldn't you? Don't tell me it's good just to be kind.'

'Of course not. Will you send it me? You could send it to the office, because I open all the letters and manuscripts first, anyway.' You fool, she was telling herself. Here you are planning this all across the Park, and then you go telling him to send it. But he gave her a second chance.

'I'd rather not send it,' he said, 'because I've only got one copy. Tell you what, why not meet me for a drink somewhere after work, and I'll bring it?'

'All right,' she said. 'When?'

'Any time. To-day, if you like. I don't believe I've got much on this evening. Let's see, Bloomsbury Square ... What about the Bodega, you know, near the B.B.C.? That all right for you?'

'Yes, lovely. I could be there about half-past six.'

He would have to find out her name sometime. It would have been better to have asked her right at the beginning of the walk instead of leaving it until now.

'I'm sure you don't know my name, do you?' she asked. 'One never hears names at parties, does one? It's Stephanie Baird.'

'Of course I know your name,' he said. 'It struck me at

the time, because it's the feminine of my own – mine's Steven.'

'Oh, how funny – oh, look, there's a taxi. Do yell for him. Taxi!' It stopped for her before he had a chance to hail it, and she got in neatly and leaned forward with her long legs tucked to one side. '88 Bloomsbury Square. Could you tell him?'

'See you to-night,' he said, through the window. 'Don't forget.'

He walked home, scoffing at himself for feeling young and buoyant and favourably disposed to the most irritating-looking people he met in the streets. You silly old fool, he told himself. You must be nearly twice her age. You'll probably never see her again after to-night. She's only doing this because she's kind and you reminded her of her Uncle Joe, or something. She'll send you the book back by special messenger long before she could possibly have had time to read it properly, with a polite little letter to say she thought it tremendously interesting, and she's so looking forward to reading it when it's finished. She's not for you. She's for some callow young bastard with broad shoulders and a tapering waist who's at the beginning of his life – which is what I feel like at the moment – and she'll marry him, and he'll be killed in this war that's coming and she'll be a widow with a child to support and get skinny and come to you in ten years' time to have her varicose veins injected. Because even if they do take you in the Navy now and you don't get sunk by a German submarine, they'll kick you out of it after the war, and you won't be able to retire, because you'll never make a living for yourself and Ruth by writing, but someone else will have pinched the West End trade while you're away, so you'll be in general practice in Raynes Park or somewhere with fees that she can afford.

Quite unchastened by this vision, he went jauntily round to get his car, slapped the bent back of old Jarvis, white-washing the tyres which a street cleaner had sprayed while the cab was working the night clubs, and drove to the East

Central to get his clinic done before it was time to go to the Admiralty.

*

Ruth was normally a heavy sleeper, but if Steven had been out, she always woke up when he came to bed. He undressed quietly in his dressing-room, ran the bathroom taps with caution, and crept into the bedroom in the dark, feeling like the guilty husband on a comic postcard.

Ruth switched on the light and sat up, her hair-net coming down over her eyebrows and her face glistening with the cold cream which she used either too lavishly or not at all. 'Steven,' she said, and looked at the clock. 'You *are* late. Where on earth have you been? Ringing up like that at the last minute to say you wouldn't be home to dinner. And then just leaving a message with Ethel ... I wanted to speak to you. They rang up from the hospital at seven o'clock to say one of your private patients had perforated – Mrs Rowntree, I think they said – and they were going to operate.'

'Oh, God,' said Steven. 'Well, I couldn't have done anything, I suppose. It's Ringtree anyway, not Rowntree. Who was going to do it?'

'*I* don't know. That was just the message they gave. I told them I'd give you the message as soon as you came in, but then of course you didn't come. Where *have* you been? Not with George I know, because Marion rang up to ask if you'd done *The Times* crossword puzzle, and if so, what was twenty down.'

'Oh, I met a friend I hadn't seen for ages,' said Steven wearily. 'We had some dinner.'

'I'd kept you some cold veal-and-ham pie – *and* a cos lettuce. I shan't bother to get you things you like again.' Ruth slumped down in bed and hauled the sheets up over her shoulder. 'Hurry up and turn the light out,' she said crossly. 'I'll tell you to-morrow about my Red Cross exam, since you're so obviously dying to know.'

He sat on the edge of his bed and dialled the number

of the East Central Hospital. Night Sister told him that Mrs Ringtree had died half an hour after coming back from theatre, that Mr Ringtree had said some nasty things about Steven not being there, and was asking for a post-mortem.

Chapter 7

—

IT was Nurse Lake's day off. She woke at eight o'clock, looked at her watch and began in a panic to get out of bed and reach for her uniform, before she remembered and lay back again on the pillow with her hands behind her head. She stretched her thin body luxuriously, until her toes touched the iron rail at the foot of the bed, and contemplated her boudoir.

Besides the high black bed on wheels in which she lay, it held a wardrobe, tilting slightly forward so that suitcases put on the top of it crept imperceptibly towards the edge and about once a week fell with a crash in the middle of the night. Next to the wardrobe was a wooden chair with her uniform dress draped over the back, an armoury of pins like Miss Murdstone's keys hanging from the pocket. Behind the door hung Nurse Lake's uniform coat and cape, half covering the notice of Bedroom Rules, scrawled over rudely by a former occupant. Nurse Lake had tried to rub out the scribbling in case anyone should think she had done it, but the rude nurse, who had run away one night to marry a marine, had done it in indelible pencil before she left, as her *in memoriam*.

She had also bequeathed the large ink stain on the green rug in front of the dressing table, which stood where neither electric nor natural light could reach its mirror. You were not allowed to move the furniture in your room. If you did juggle it laboriously around in the middle of the night, you found it all moved back again the next time you came in. Nurse Lake had covered the dressing-table with an embroidered runner from home. On one side was a photograph of her father and mother, taken on holiday three years ago and looking hot. On the other was her younger sister, scowling in a gym tunic, with her black hair in a fuzz round her face. A china tray with the Eastbourne coat of arms held the large black pins which anchored Nurse Lake's uniform cap to her head. On the window sill was a school edition of the *Golden Treasury*, a novel from the twopenny library called *Romany Wildcat*, a bible, a dictionary, several nursing text-books and the precious note-books which held the records of Steven's utterances. Most people found that the window sill was not an ideal bookcase, because if you left the window open at the bottom, your books might get ruined by a sudden shower, but Nurse Lake never opened her window at the bottom. She was always cold, even in summer.

Eight o'clock. They would be cleaning the clinics now, polishing up the desk and brass taps, opening the windows to let out the smell of the cats which used Outpatients as a night club. It was Monday. There was Dr Baxter in No. 1, the Gynæ clinic in No. 2, Dentals, of course, and Ear, Nose and Throat in No. 4. Would Nurse Phillimore ever get those ear mops made right? She had shown her dozens of times how to shred the wool and twist it on the sticks, but some of the nurses never seemed to realize how much care you had to give to these little things. Dr Bellenger had sworn to go to Matron if they were not right this week, and of course it would be Nurse Lake's fault, even though she were not there.

It was hardly worth having a day off, or any off duty during the week, because when you got back something had always gone wrong and you were responsible. And then there was the question of the blood pressures in the Gynæ clinic. Miss Knatchbull always liked the new patients to have theirs taken before she arrived. If only Sister would do it – but she always took tea with Theatre Sister after lunch, and only appeared five minutes before the clinic was due to start. Even Nurse Lake had got into trouble last week for making an anæmic patient register two hundred, which Miss Knatchbull had queried and insisted on taking again herself, grumbling at the waste of time and making a sarcastic remark in front of the patient, when she found it was only a hundred and eighty. Which was unfair, because everyone knew that the blood pressure of a nervous patient could vary by at least ten millimetres in half an hour. Nurse Lake had said this to Sister afterwards, but she had only snorted and said: 'Don't get so worked up, Nurse. These doctors must have their little grumble – keeps them happy – but you don't have to pay any attention.' That was all very well. She hadn't been made to feel a fool in front of the patients and triumphant juniors.

This week, Staff Nurse Anderson, who was relieving Nurse Lake's day off, would be taking the blood pressures, and although she was State-registered, everyone knew how slapdash she was. And did she know about keeping the specimen tubes of saline in warm water? Nurse Lake could not remember having told her. She had tackled her last night after supper about some of these things, but Anderson had been so silly, only half-listening, and waving her away with an: 'All right, all right, Lakey. I was in Outpatients before you were born. Stop behaving as if you were the only one who knew anything about it. We shall get on just ducky without you – much better probably.' That was what you got for being conscientious.

She heard the maids come into the corridor and start banging about in the other rooms. Nurse Lake put on her cotton kimono and black quilted slippers, and went into the room next door, where Amy, with her hospital cap like a fluted pudding basin hanging from the back of her head by one hairpin, was examining the photographs while she flicked at the dressing-table with a duster.

'Any chance of tea, Amy?' suggested Nurse Lake diffidently.

'Sorry, love,' said Amy carelessly. 'Sister's on duty and got the caddy locked up, even if there was any milk, which there isn't.'

'It doesn't matter at all,' said Nurse Lake. 'I just thought

I'd ask.' She went back to her room to get her towel and sponge-bag for the bath. Some of the nurses always seemed to be able to get tea out of the maids, even when Home Sister was about. It was funny, because Nurse Lake was always careful to be very polite to the maids and often called them 'dear', and never left her room untidy. Yet they would do anything for someone like Parker, who had once called Amy 'You fat, thieving cow', and whose room was disgusting, with spilt powder, and shoes kicked under the bed, and her dirty aprons lying all over the floor.

Nurse Lake's people lived near Eastbourne, which was too far to go on her days off. Sometimes she went to an aunt in London, but mostly she stayed at the hospital, going to all the meals in the dining-room just the same, because it seemed a waste of money to eat out when you could get your food for nothing here. The other nurses who did not go home were allowed to have breakfast in bed if they could get a friend to bring it them at the nine o'clock break, but since Audrey Lake's special friend had left to do her midwifery, there was no one she could ask to bring her a tray.

So when she had had her bath and dressed in her brown-and-yellow patterned silk dress, she went across the yard and up to the dining-room, where the nurses on duty were having tea and bread and cheese. If you wrote your name in a book the night before, you could have cooked breakfast saved for you, but Nurse Lake had been so busy telling Anderson about the Gynæ clinic that she had forgotten to do this.

One of the dining-room maids was stacking clean cups round the tea urn on the side table. 'D'you think I could have some breakfast, Mabel?' Nurse Lake asked her, looking more like a horse wanting hay than a nurse wanting bacon.

'You didn't put your name down, did you?' said Mabel warily.

'No, I forgot, but I just thought, if there was any to spare –'

'Sorry, Nurse,' Mabel picked up her tray. 'I daren't. Not with Cook in the mood she's in this morning.'

Nurse Lake had tea and several thick slices of bread and cheese. The other nurses were in a hurry, bolting theirs, because they had to get over to the Home and make their beds and change their aprons. It was pleasant to be able to sit and enjoy a second cup of tea, for which you never had time on the other days of the week.

'Got the day off, Lakey?' asked Nurse Bracken, as she got up. 'Doing anything nice?'

'I thought of going up to London to look at the shops, and go to the cinema perhaps.' She could afford this at the beginning of the month; could even, perhaps, have some lunch at Lyons.

'Oh, what fun,' said Nurse Bracken kindly, thinking how bleak it must be not to go home to a doting family and your own bed, and a mother who planned all week what she was going to give you to eat. 'Got to fly now. We've got three cases for theatre and I haven't even done the first prep. That partial gastrectomy man decided to vomit, and I had to pass a stomach tube – all in the middle of making beds. Have a good time!'

Nurse Lake wondered how she could keep so cheerful about it all. If she were as busy as that she would be in a panic, and would spend the whole day in yesterday's apron, because there was no time to change it, much less time to go up to the dining-room for a cup of tea, although you were supposed to go away for your meals whatever happened. She had once been made to go to dinner in the middle of laying out a corpse, and had to come back and finish it with treacle pudding sitting on her chest as heavily as the sandbag which she had left propping up the body's chin.

*

In London, she migrated, without thinking about it, towards Oxford Street. She would not admit to herself that her real purpose in coming to town was not so much to look at the shops as to hang about in the neighbourhood of Wimpole Street on the chance of seeing Dr Sheppard. She had been doing this every week for some time. There was nothing she would rather do, because all her waking hours and many of her sleeping ones as well were filled with thoughts of him. He was becoming more and more of an obsession with her, an obsession which was no longer satisfied by the magic hours in the clinic on Thursday afternoons.

She would not speak to him if she saw him; she just had to see him. The week before last she had been lurking before the window of the Times Book Club, whose display she knew by heart, when his car had turned into Wigmore Street from Wimpole Street and made straight for her. She had bolted into the Book Club and upstairs, becoming absorbed in a shelf of books from where she could see the NUT-SO desk, in case he were coming to change his book. She knew he belonged to the library, because she had seen its label on a book when his case was lying open on the desk in the clinic.

Even if she did not see him, at least she was near him, nearer than if she stayed in Dynsford, which only existed for him on Thursdays. She went into all the stores along Oxford Street, browsing over the haberdashery counters, buying a packet of pins here, a shoelace there, choosing a birthday card to send to her mother next week, putting off the peak moment of her day, when, with throbbing heart, she would walk up one side of Wimpole Street and down the other. She rationed herself to passing his house only twice. If she were not strict, she might have hung about under the opposite lamp-post all day, until she was arrested for loitering with intent. If he should look out and see her passing once, or even twice, he could put it down to chance, but if he saw her going up and down like a sentry, he might suspect something.

Either just before or just after lunch was the best time, because he might then be either going in or coming out. Not having had a proper breakfast this morning, she decided to have an early snack at Lyons and come back to Wimpole Street about two o'clock. As she walked along the crowded street, people jostled and bumped into her, perambulators took chips off her ankles and dogs wound their leads round her rod-like legs, but she kept on her course like a sleep-walker, living in the serial dream into which she relapsed at all moments of the day when it was not imperative to think of anything else.

It was a dream of endless variations, but the theme was always the same: Steven was in some situation where Nurse Lake was necessary to him, where he had to be aware of her. An awareness that blossomed gradually to a beautiful inti-macy, usually on quite a spiritual plane, but venturing some-times, according to the state of Nurse Lake's glands, into realms where her imagination had to be eked out by books and films. No one had ever kissed Nurse Lake, but Steven had kissed her, in her dream, in a way that would have sur-prised him considerably.

Although she was spinning fantasies, her practical mind was at infinite pains to make the sequence of events logical. In one dream she and Steven were on a desert island to-gether, but they never arrived there haphazard; the dream began long before that with a minute scheme of her having to accompany one of his patients over to America to benefit by some new treatment. Steven was going, too, to study the process. Everything was worked out, even the position of their cabins and what they had for meals. This was part of the delight, spinning out the preliminaries so as to postpone the exciting moment when they at last met under the palm trees, or when she pulled him on to her raft, or supported his body in mid-ocean (having of course learned to swim in the early part of the dream story). Sometimes his wife was taken ill just before sailing, sometimes she came with them and was drowned in the shipwreck.

Another dream was that Nurse Lake was staying alone at a remote cottage on a moor. Out walking one day, she came upon a car which had run into a telegraph pole when its driver fell asleep, worn out with working for others. She pulled Steven out of the wreckage just before it burst into flames, and with the help of a friendly peasant, who was in-debted to her for delivering his wife of a son, she took Steven on a hurdle to her cottage, where, because he had broken a leg, he had to stay and be nursed by her. Had it not been for the brilliance and devotion of her nursing he would never have walked again. This was one of the dreams that sometimes became glandular. She had read *A Farewell to Arms*, and knew what a man with one leg could do. There were dreams where his wife died or divorced him and he married Nurse Lake. This called for a lot of imagination.

Sometimes he was attacked by bandits and left for dead, sometimes he contracted a fatal disease through his devotion to medical science. There was one where he actually died of malaria in an African jungle, and Nurse Lake died with him in a pair of linen trousers and a white shirt open at the neck.

One of the best, the one in which she was indulging on this Monday morning as she ambled along Oxford Street with her head in the air and a strand of slippery black hair escaping under a green felt beret, was that Steven had been shanghaied by gangsters to tend their leader, wounded in a gun duel with the police. Nurse Lake, walking through the streets of London, just as she was now, paused on the edge of the pavement to let the traffic go by before she could cross the road. Happening to glance into a sinister black saloon car driven by a scarred man in a pulled-down felt hat, she saw, protruding from a rug at the back, on which another scarred man was sitting, a hand wearing the signet ring which she, from her acute observation in the clinic, knew to be Steven's. With a cry of 'Follow that car!' she leaped into a passing taxi, and after a hectic chase, during which her ingenuity alone prevented the black saloon shaking them off, she arrived at dead of night among warehouses, with the sound of lapping water close by.

'Wait here for me,' she ordered the taxi driver. (She, who, on the rare occasions when she took a taxi, overtipped the driver from fear of him.)

'No fear, Miss,' he said. 'Unhealthy quarter this is. Wouldn't catch me hanging around here at this time of night. Better hop in and let me drive you back.'

'No,' she said, throwing back her head and clutching tighter the little black bag she carried. She was usually a district nurse on these occasions, so that she could have the instruments handy for sewing up Steven when she found him gashed and battered. 'No, cabby, I'm staying. I have work to do.'

'Well, you're a plucky one and no mistake,' he said admiringly, and drove off, leaving her alone among the looming shapes of the warehouses. Finding a door, she went up a staircase, at the top of which there was a light and the murmur of men's voices. Boldly, she went through the door, and the jaws of all the men in the room dropped to see a woman standing there. Steven, who was bending over a cot in the corner in his shirt sleeves, looked up, and she saw his face light with joy, but he instantly made a sign warning her to play his game.

'A nurse! by all that's holy!' cried one of the scarred men. 'She can help us.' She was seized, and dragged roughly over to the cot – there was quite a lot of masochistic pleasure in this part – and then she and Steven pretended not to know each other, whispering out of the sides of their mouths while they gave the leader of the gang a blood transfusion. Walking through the doors of Lyons, she saw, not the crowds of people, nor the counters of buns and bread and sweets, nor the peaches and the flowers and the theatre-ticket bureau, but Steven's bare forearm under the rolled-up shirt, tautly muscled and brown against her own white arm working so close. He had a cut on his head. 'It's nothing,' he whispered to her.

She went downstairs and sat alone at a small table against the wall, dimly aware that the band was playing a selection of Viennese waltzes. The best part of the dream was now approaching. The gangsters revealed that, far from letting Steven go free when he had finished his work, they were going to shoot him before they cleared out, to stop him squealing.

'Shoot de goil!' suggested someone.

'Yus,' cried another, 'do 'em bofe in.' Sometimes the gangsters were American, sometimes Cockney; Nurse Lake was not very familiar with either tongue.

Steven, who was getting rather weak by this time from loss of blood from his head wound, although Nurse Lake had staunched it with her handkerchief, cried from the floor:

'What's yours, Miss?' A harassed Nippy slapped a menu on to the table and leaned sideways away from it as if she were projecting her body in thought towards the kitchens.

'Oh!' Nurse Lake jumped and looked at the menu with unfocused eyes. 'Coffee, please, and a – and a –' She couldn't think of anything she wanted, so she said 'two Bath buns,' although she did not particularly like them.

'Coffee and two Bath!' The waitress threw the cry into the air, scribbled on a bit of paper, tore it off and dashed it on to the table, whisked up the menu and was gone, leaving Steven to say:

'No, no. Spare the girl. She's done nothing to you, she'll not tell on you. I'll put her on oath to forget this whole business.' Bless him, he was trying to save her but her honour and the sacred cause of British justice would not allow it.

'No,' she said, and sank on her knees beside him on the floor – they often held hands at this point –'if you let me go I shall go straight to the police. If one of us must die, we die together!' This part was very tragic. She did not allow herself to look forward to possible escape, but really imagined her life was coming to an end and Steven's with it. It was appalling to think of. Her face was red, and she gazed with moist, unseeing eyes at the leader of the band who, wearing green satin trousers and a ruffled shirt, was stretching his accordion almost to breaking point before plunging into the impassioned opening chords of *Vienna, City of my Dreams*.

The wounded gangster chief, who had the decency to say to Steven: 'Thanks, pal, you saved my life,' was carried out to the car, and the most scarred man of all took aim at Steven and Nurse Lake from the other end of the warehouse. There were now two turnings which this dream could take. One was that Nurse Lake, having been almost killed by the first shot, threw her body across Steven's for the second, thereby saving his life, unknown to the gangster who had fled, having no more bullets. The other was that she was only slightly wounded, but feigned dead so as to be able to leap up and staunch Steven's wound as soon as the scarred man had gone. The first ending was the best when time was short, as, for instance, at dinner-time, when Matron was rolling her napkin preparatory to putting it in her ring and standing up for Grace. The second ending was full of the most interesting possibilities, and could be dragged out almost indefinitely.

'Tea and Welsh, dear?' asked the Nippy breathlessly.

'Well, actually, I did say coffee and –'

'That's right.' The waitress whisked away the plate, whirled round and caught the agonized distress signals of the man who had ordered Welsh Rarebit.

'Coffee and two Bath, dear.' The coffee was very hot. Nurse Lake began to eat one of the buns. It was only one o'clock; she would do the second ending.

The first shot grazed her leg, or her hand. It was not allowed to do more, because she must not be incapacitated. She had work to do. She fell back with closed eyes and heard the hum of the second bullet and the thud as it buried itself in the wooden wall behind. There was a low moan from Steven, and he fell on top of her. She opened her eyes. The scarred man was gone. Steven was shot through the neck, bleeding to death from the right carotid artery. Breaking bits off the bun and putting them into her mouth with rapid, automatic movements, Nurse Lake now knelt behind Steven and put into practice the first-aid lessons to which she had attended so carefully. This was the most difficult place of all to stop hæmorrhage. The pressure point was against the back of the clavicle. You had to put your thumb into the hollow below the shoulder and press the artery forward against the bone until the bleeding ceased. How long she knelt there she did not know. It seemed ages before the blood clotted enough for her to be able to release her pressure, fold her handkerchief over the actual wound and bandage it with the belt of her uniform coat. Steven, of course, was unconscious by this time, so she treated him for shock by covering him with her own coat and some sacking, and administered some morphia from the case which he had brought to treat the gangster chief. The Dangerous Drugs Act stated that morphine, cocaine, ecgonine and diamorphine, and their respective salts, etc., etc., must never be given unless checked by a State-registered nurse, so to quiet her conscience she always made herself State-registered in the dream.

Luckily, there was some bottled blood left over from the gangster, so she now gave Steven a blood transfusion with the same apparatus. It would have been better still if she could have run some blood straight in from one of her own veins, but she was not quite sure how this was done, nor whether it would be possible without assistance, and she never cheated in her stories.

The rest of the dream was that she nursed Steven for long days and nights in the deserted warehouse, stealing out at dusk to get milk and food for them. There had to be some reason why she could not get help. It would spoil everything if the police came and had him taken to hospital, even if it was to St Margaret's, because obviously no one but the Sisters would get a look in at nursing him there.

Drinking her coffee with little finger stiffly raised, she wondered whether it would be awful cheek to make one of the gangsters Steven's uncle, or his cousin, so that although he had been ready to kill Steven to save his own skin, family ties and honour obliged Steven not to raise the alarm until this despicable relative was safely out of the country. It would have to be something like that. Nurse Lake was not going to forfeit those cosy nights among the sacking.

It was a quarter to two. She wandered out among the tables and past the cash desk, was hauled back by the doorman to pay her bill, came blinking out into the sunlight of Marble Arch and turned left among the preoccupied crowds, making for Wimpole Street with the rapt expression of a girl going to meet her lover.

*

Steven and Stephanie Baird were lunching in the upper room of a small and expensive Soho restaurant. There were only three other tables on this floor, occupied by foreigners too busy eating to take any more notice of the couple in the window than Steven and Stephanie took of them. In an age when most girls were elongating their heads with upward swoops and rolls, Stephanie was wearing her hair flat across the top, caught at one side with a childish slide and brushed smoothly down following the shape of her head at the back until it turned outwards into the trough of soft curls that swung round her neck like a bell. She was a very clean-looking girl. Her clothes were always spotless and pressed, her nails dead white at the tips, and her face and neck looked as though she lived anywhere but in London. She looked like the Ideal of the women's magazines; the girl who never shirked her nightly beauty routine, nor neglected to rinse out her stockings, nor hang her dress away on a hanger with a lavender bag on it however tired she was. She obviously wore clean underclothes every day, and sent her shoes to be mended before it was too late. She was the sort of girl whom you could never imagine looking anything but trim under any circumstances. If she went down a coal mine and came up with smudges on her face, she would still look no dirtier than a film star whose coal dust has been carefully put on in the make-up room. Stephanie was like this because she was innately fastidious, and because she had always been poor and lived in tiny houses or flats where her bedroom was so small that life in it became impossible unless you were scrupulously tidy. When she was doing her secretarial training, she had taken it very seriously, and seldom gone out in the evenings for fear of being tired at work, so she always had plenty of time for washing and mending and doing her hair and nails. When she became Mark Stainer's secretary she went out even less for fear of not being able to cope with the job next day, and was even more careful about her appearance to compensate for any faults in her performance. So that by the time she had got on top of life and could manage Mark Stainer and his affairs as easily as she managed the men with whom she went out as often as she liked, her scrupulous ways had become second nature, and she would as soon have come out without her skirt as with a button missing from her cuff.

She still lived with her father and mother, in the slightly larger flat which the contributions from her wages had made possible, and although they had a daily maid, she still made her bed and tidied her room before she went to work, and never left open pots of make-up and dirty bits of cotton wool scattered on her dressing-table when she dressed in a hurry to go out in the evening. When she cooked, she always washed up as she went along, and always sieved the potatoes before mashing them, and cut salads up into neat shreds and shapes, with the tomatoes and radishes looking like red water lilies. Afterwards, she always put the silver into one jug to soak, and the knives into another, with the handles out of water, and always wiped the plates after draining them on the rack and kept a special cloth for the glass.

Her mother said she would make a perfect wife for some man, but her father said she would drive any man mad in a week.

She was twenty-five, and she had never been in love. She had often tried to be, and nearly succeeded, until morning catarrh, or spots on the waistcoat or blackheads on the back of the neck had put her off. She had been attracted to many men, and was very much attracted now to Steven.

Which made it all the more difficult to say what she thought about his book. Knowing how unsure of it he was himself, she would have loved to be able to praise it, and to tell him to go right ahead without altering anything, but she had promised to give him an honest opinion, which she probably would have given him whether she had promised or not.

He was sunk in gloom by the time they got to *mousse aux marrons*, which was a speciality of the restaurant.

'Don't tell me any more,' he groaned, pushing the smooth, lavender-grey cream about with a fork. 'I know it all already. Everything you've said so far about that wretched book is true. You have a most remarkable critical faculty, Miss Baird.'

'I'm so sorry,' she said. 'I didn't want to be unkind about it, and if I didn't think there was a lot in it that was awfully good I wouldn't bother pulling it to pieces. I can't think how I dare, anyway, because it's ten times better than anything I could write. You will go on with it, won't you? It only wants rewriting in the bits where it's too scrappy, and pulling into shape – you know, given more continuity between the different episodes, so that the reader doesn't get so flabbergasted by the sudden jumps.'

'Oh, I shall give the whole thing up,' he said quickly. 'I simply haven't the time.' He was a little irritated with her. Now that she had pulled *The Swift Stream* to pieces so ruthlessly – and for all her kindness and tact, she had been pretty damning – he began to think it wasn't so bad after all. It was just as good as a lot of novels that got published nowadays by people who had nothing else to do all day than sit at a typewriter. He'd like to see anyone do better with only the stolen scraps and snatches, which were all the writing times he had.

'You're annoyed with me, aren't you?' she said. 'But it isn't *my* fault. It's the fault of your being such a successful doctor. You want to write, and you could write, but the greatest genius couldn't write without time to do it in.' She leaned back, pleased to see that she had said what he wanted to hear.

'You're absolutely right,' he said eagerly. 'That's been my trouble all along. That's why this damn' thing lacks continuity as you so truthfully put it, because I've always had to work at it in jerks and snatches, and that's the way the story's come out – jerky and snatchy.' They seemed to have been talking about him for a long time, but she did not appear to mind.

'I think it's an awfully interesting story, you know,' she said. 'Is it the story of your life?'

'More or less.' He grinned. 'With embellishments.'

'I do hope you go on with it. But look – don't send it to M.S. without touching it up a bit. He's awfully downright and prejudiced, and if he doesn't like a thing once he usually won't look at it again, whatever the author does to it. Sometimes they alter the title and pretend it's a different book and catch him that way.'

'If you knew the agony I've been through over writing even what's there,' Steven nodded towards the manuscript lying on a chair between them, 'you wouldn't talk so airily about touching it up. It would be ten times the agony having to go over it again. I'd rather throw the whole thing on the fire and start a book on bees. Shall we have coffee? I'll have to fly in a minute, because I've got an appointment at the hospital at half-past two, and I expect you want to get back to the office.'

She did not tell him that Mark Stainer had given her two tickets for the open-air theatre and told her to take the afternoon off and take a boy friend, as he was going out of town and would not need her.

She took a mirror out of her handbag and was gratified to see that her face and hair were intact. It was a lovely handbag of pigskin, which she tended regularly with saddle soap, cleaning her initials with methylated spirit and turning the inside out to brush it.

'I was thinking,' she said leaning forward to stir her coffee so that her hair swung over her cheek, 'as your talent seems to run to short, disconnected episodes rather than a continuous narrative – and some of the episodes are awfully vivid, you know, in themselves – why don't you make it a book of short stories or sketches? All connected with hospital and medicine, of course – you don't want to lose all that gorgeous material – even, perhaps, all about the same doctor and the same hospital. But each story could be complete in itself. Some of them might be so short you could even write them at a sitting. It would suit you much better really, wouldn't it?'

'I don't know. I'm not keen on short stories myself. They're awfully unsatisfying. It would be a lot easier to do, though. If you knew the hours I've spent trying to get this objectionable young man from a school to hospital and from being a raw young house-man to being R.S.O. with the whole place at his finger-tips ...'

'I know,' she said sympathetically. 'That's why I suggested it.'

'Kindergarten exercises for the kiddies?' So she thought he couldn't write a novel?

'Don't laugh at me,' she said. 'I'm trying to help you.'

'God knows why. It's not because you think I have a literary future, I know that. It's because you like me – and that's not as conceited as it sounds, because I like you, an awful lot, so it might as well be mutual.'

She began to gather herself together, pulling down the jacket of her linen suit, pushing back her chair. 'I ought to be going,' she said, 'and you must, if you've really got to be at the hospital at half-past two.'

'I wish we could go out somewhere this afternoon,' he said, studying her. She was intensely pleasing to look at. 'I'd like to put you in the car and take you into the country somewhere – on the river, perhaps – and give you tea in an orchard and stay there till the midges started biting. Then on the way home we'd have dinner in one of those dear little unspoilt country pubs that don't exist, and then we might come back to town and dance.' What was that song? '*I'm quite insane, and young again.*' He did feel quite absurdly young, and wondered whether his knees would crack if he danced.

'That would be fun.' She did not tell him about the afternoon off and the two tickets for the open-air theatre.

As they went through the downstairs restaurant, Marion

got up from one of the tables and put a hand on Steven's arm. 'If it isn't the great Dr Jekyll himself! I thought you were always too busy to have any lunch. Who's the popsie?' Stephanie had walked on, not seeing that Steven had stopped.

'Oh, cut it out, Marry,' said Steven uncomfortably, conscious that her lunch party of three over-hatted women were watching him and listening.

'It's all right, darling,' she said. 'I shan't tell Ruth. I'm on your side.'

'Don't be so absurd. It's not a question of –'

'Oh, don't worry. I know how careful you famous doctors have to be. Er –' She cocked her head and an eyebrow upwards. 'Hence the upper room, I take it.'

'Oh, damn the upper room, and damn being a doctor – and damn you, Marion,' muttered Steven, and turned away, followed by little trills of laughter from Marion and her over-hatted friends.

*

It was a wonder, thought Nurse Lake, that everyone who walked up Wimpole Street did not notice how No. 101 stood out from the rest like a jewel in a row of pebbles. Yet they passed without a glance at its glossy green front door, flanked by the two domed ground-floor windows with their stiff muslin curtains, its black-and-white chequerboard steps and its green area railings, each topped by a golden spearhead. Walking up from the south end of the street, she could see it all the way. It called to her with an ever-increasing clamour that reached its crescendo as she drew level, paused for a second on the opposite side and walked on with the call of the house pursuing her all down her spine.

She walked up as far as the pillar box, posted an imaginary letter and turned back. The house's presence struck her full in the face, like the dazzle of a setting sun. Slowly she walked towards it, prolonging this last encounter, for she would not allow herself to pass it for a third time, but would

235

walk straight on into Oxford Street and take a bus to Piccadilly Circus, where she would go into any cinema and sit in
the dark and go on with her dream.

One of her stories was that his car would be standing outside the house, and that, as she passed, he would come out
and offer her a lift. That was a promising start to all kinds of
developments. Sometimes he was going to Dynsford and
drove her all the way down, and she was seen by some of the
nurses or even the Matron perhaps, riding by in her glory.
Sometimes he was rushing to an urgent case, and asked her
to go with him to help, sometimes they were in a road acci-
dent together and she pulled him out from under the burning car and then went back to save his dog.

She drew level with No. 101, paused and looked across the
street. She did not know the house's internal geography, but
she was as sure that the window on the right of the front
door was his consulting room as if it had had his name written across it in gold letters. And yes – as she looked, a figure
moved in front of the light, bending over in blurred silhou-
ette behind the muslin curtains, in just the way that Steven
bent when he was talking to a shorter person or to someone
sitting down. If he were to straighten up while he was standing near the window he would look over the top of the curtain directly at her. Alarmed, she moved on, looking over
her shoulder, but, with the window now at an angle to her
sight, she could see nothing. Still, she had seen him; she
could exist now until Thursday.

'Open a little wider, please,' said Mr Nosgood, bending
still lower over his patient in the right-hand front room. 'Ah!
Tha-a-at's better. I shall just have to use the drill on this
one – it won't hurt you at all.'

Chapter 8

—

BECAUSE Steven never spoke to her now about his negotiations with the Admiralty, which were somewhat hanging fire, Ruth thought that he had abandoned that mad idea of going into the Navy.

'He's realized at last what I've said all along,' she told her mother over a salad lunch in Oxford Street. 'He'd be much more useful where he is, even if there was a war.'

'Which there won't be,' said her mother, taking it out of a stick of celery. 'It said so last Sunday. The stars are all wrong for it.'

'All the same, Mother, I do think you ought to go and get a gas mask. After all, they are free.'

'Indeed, I shall not. They needn't think they can force me to do anything I don't want. We all have our rights as citizens. And how do they think I could possibly breathe in one of those things? It's all I can do to get my breath as it is, sometimes.' Her bosom rose and fell at the thought.

'What shall we have to follow?' Ruth picked up the menu. 'Do you want the trifle? Or there's fruit flan, or caramel custard, or blackberry tart.' She screwed up her mouth. 'That'll be too sour, probably. They have lovely ices here, with nuts and fudge sauce.'

'Oh no, dear,' said her mother with a sad smile. 'Not with my neuralgia. You have one, though. I'll call the girl. Goodness, look at her! Deliberately not looking. Really, they get more Bolshie every day.'

'Perhaps I'd better just have a water ice,' said Ruth regretfully. 'I've been putting on weight recently.'

'Nonsense, you're just right as you are.'

'Steven says –'

'Oh, Steven says, Steven says. Don't always echo that man to me. He hasn't bought you body and soul. You give in to him much too much, you know. If you'd behaved a bit more sensibly with him we shouldn't have had all this nonsense about going into the Navy.'

Ruth's colour rose at once in defence of him. 'He's entitled to do what he thinks is right, Mother. I never criticize him, though I have told him that I think it's folly to have worked so hard and have got such a good position only to throw it all away.'

'On a misguided patriotic impulse. Anyway, he's much too extravagant in his tastes ever to adapt himself to the pay of a naval doctor. I don't suppose he's thought about that. And what about you? He hasn't thought about that either, I suppose. What does he think you're going to live on?' They would chew over Steven like this for hours, like dogs with an old bone. Ruth's mother snapped her fingers at the damp waitress and said: 'We *would* like to order our sweet, Miss, if you can spare the time.'

'I'm quite prepared to sacrifice myself, if it were ever really necessary,' Ruth said with the intense expression which brought her eyes even closer together. Her mother ordered, stabbing the menu with a bluish nail. 'His idea was that we should take a small place in the country, where he could come when he was on leave. Or I could go and live with you, he said, if I liked.'

'Thank you very much,' said her mother. 'I had thought of having your Aunt Margot wintering in the spare room as a P.G. – much as I should like to have you, of course.' A plate arrived in front of her and she picked at it with a dissatisfied fork. 'If this is their idea of trifle, I wish I'd had the flan.'

'In any case,' said Ruth, delving into the cream that surmounted her ice, 'as I said, he seems to have given up the idea. He's got interested in his book again, too. He'd not been working on it recently.'

'About time that masterpiece was finished, if you ask me,' said her mother. 'I'm sure it doesn't take real authors so long to write a book.'

Ruth also discussed Steven with Mrs Garrard. She discussed everything with her, pleased to have a confidante. Mrs Garrard never disagreed or argued; she simply absorbed everything you told her, as if she were storing it away, like a policeman taking down a statement to be used in evidence. They also talked endlessly about Ruth's activities as a V.A.D., which were even more engrossing than Steven's foibles.

The East Central Hospital had a waiting list of at least thirty V.A.D.s wanting to do their fifty hours of practical training. They could not make an exception, apparently, even for the wife of one of their foremost Honorary Physicians. Ruth was sure that Steven had not really pressed them about it.

'Why don't you go and see Matron yourself, then?' he said. 'See if you have better luck with her than I did.'

'Oh, Steven, I couldn't, I wouldn't dare do it on my own,' said Ruth, which was what she had also said to his suggestion that she should try one of the other London hospitals. So he had tackled the Matron of St Margaret's for her, and Ruth now drove down with him every Thursday and spent three hours in the Maternity ward, while he did his clinic and his rounds. It would take her a long time to get in her fifty hours at this rate, but she did not mind. She was quite happy.

The despot of the Maternity ward, one Sister Archer, who had a high Roman nose and hips that looked as if she were wearing panniers under her apron, treated Ruth like Royalty. Most of the V.A.D.s spent their time cutting bread and butter, washing up on the maid's day off, folding the dirty laundry and sluicing out the 'sundries'. But Sister Archer would as soon have asked Ruth to rinse out a dirty nappy as she would have thought of asking Steven. Apart from Ruth's reflected glory as Dr Sheppard's wife, Sister Archer was a woman who prided herself on knowing What was What and Who was Who, and here was an opportunity to prove it.

She always arranged to be on duty on Thursday afternoons, and Ruth's first task, after hanging up her dark blue coat and cap, which she wore well down on her head like a Canadian trapper, and donning the white cap and apron laundered at great expense by the Wigmore Hand Laundry, was to take a cup of tea in Sister's sitting-room. Sister Archer had been at St Margaret's for ten years, so no one would listen any more to her stories of her father's spacious house outside Huddersfield, where he kept two cars and a library full of classics, all of which Sister Archer had read before she was grown up. But Ruth would listen. The other Sisters were tired of never being able to mention a play or a film or a book without Sister Archer having already seen or heard it, and found some inner meaning which more superficial minds had missed, but Ruth was not tired, and told Steven what an intelligent woman Sister Archer was, and would he lend her his school prize copy of the poems of Alfred Tennyson, as Ruth had promised he would?

After the tea, Ruth was allowed to give a blanket bath to one of the safely convalescent mothers, who, realizing from Sister Archer's frequent social appearances round the screens that this was no ordinary V.A.D., did not dare to suggest that she might rinse off the soap before drying her.

Then: 'Mrs Sheppard can feed Baby Thompson,' Sister would tell the staff nurse, who foresaw hours of back-patting to rid Baby Thompson afterwards of his wind. If he needed changing, Ruth would change him, with pursed lips and a worried frown. She had never been any good at this with Carol, and had always hated doing it, but as she had told Sister Archer, she wanted to do *exactly* what the other nurses did, and did not shirk anything.

'For a married woman,' said the staff nurse, tidying up in the bathroom after Ruth, 'she's the most ham-handed female I ever saw. Hasn't she got any children of her own?'

'They did have one, I believe,' said Nurse Hooley, 'but it died or something. And no wonder, with her looking after it. Poor old Stinking Steven, fancy being tied to a drip like that.'

'No wonder he's got an eye for the girls,' said the staff

nurse, who liked to hint darkly at what had gone on between her and Steven when she was in Outpatients.

At half-past three Ruth would come heavily into the ward pushing the tea trolley, and give all the mothers their wrong diets. A probationer would follow her round putting things right, and remain to pour out the second cups when Ruth was summoned to Sister's sitting-room. The other V.A.D.s had their tea in the nurses' dining-room, but Sister Archer thought it neither right nor nice for Mrs Sheppard to do that. The nurse who was off duty on Thursday mornings always had to buy home-made cakes at the 'Dynsford Pantry', Sister's own painted tray would be laid with the lace cloth and electroplated tea service which she had brought from home, and Sister would brew and dispense tea with much ceremony and high-level conversation which lasted until the nurses had got safely through the scramble of Washings and Ruth could make a few beds with the staff nurse. This was a laboured business involving much discomfort to the patient and wear and tear on the nerves of the staff nurse, who had to slow down her tempo by half and stand silently fuming at the thought of all the dressings yet to do, while Ruth made and remade a corner, determined to get it like the pictures in the book.

She would then bath a resentful baby and, Sister having gone off duty, be given one or two unnecessary odd jobs to keep her out of the way until the message came through on the house phone that Dr Sheppard was ready to go home.

By this time Ruth always looked as much of a wreck as if she had done a day's hard labour. Her soft thick hair would be escaping in every direction from under the cap which had miraculously shed all the Wigmore Hand Laundry's starch, her shoes would be covered with talcum powder and her apron soaking wet right through to her dress. The staff nurse would stop doing a dressing to sign Ruth's Red Cross book, which meant she had to scrub her hands all over again, and Ruth would put on her coat and the Canadian trapper's cap, lose her way going out of the building and finally arrive at the car, where Steven waited for her, as he did not want to be seen in the hall with her looking like that.

All the way home she would regale Steven with stories of her prowess, and slightly distorted medical titbits which did not seem to interest him as much as they should. On the first Thursday she was so tired that she had supper in bed. Steven counted on her doing the same the following week, and arranged to take Stephanie out to dinner.

In the car, Ruth said: 'I'm not nearly as tired as I was last week. Of course, I'm getting into the work now, that's what it is. Sister said she'd never known anyone pick it up so quickly. Shall we go out to dinner, darling? It's only cold at home, so Mrs Hankey wouldn't mind. We might go to that new film at the Empire. Sister saw it on her day off: she says it's wonderfully good.'

'Oh, Ruth,' said Steven, 'I'm sorry. Any other night I'd have loved to, but I've got a dinner on to-night. I did tell you this morning, only you were so busy telling Ethel what it was like to be a nurse that you probably didn't hear.'

'She's very interested in my nursing,' said Ruth defensively. 'She would have liked to be a nurse herself, you know, if she'd been strong enough.'

'Not her,' Steven laughed shortly. 'Catch her doing anything that meant looking after anyone else's interests but her own.'

'What an unkind thing to say.' Ruth turned a grieved face to him, and pushed some hair back under her cap. 'And you know it's not true. You just talk like that to be clever. I hate it when you're in one of those moods.'

'You don't have to be very clever to see that our Mrs G. is the world's champion grabber,' said Steven. 'Oh, I grant you, she doesn't always ask for things right out; she simply absorbs them in a kind of passive way – like a sponge that's entitled to soak up as much water as it can hold.'

'I don't know what you're talking about,' said Ruth in the cold voice she used when she thought Steven was being silly. She hummed a little, tunelessly, and pretended to be very interested in the factories along the Great West Road. 'Who are you going out with to-night?' she asked presently.

'Oh – a man I know. Someone connected with Mark Stainer, as a matter of fact. We're going to talk about the book.' Feeling guilty, he tried to ease his conscience by keeping as close as possible to the truth.

He and Stephanie did talk about the book quite a lot when they were together. Each one, unsure of the other, clung to it as a good excuse for keeping in touch. She maintained her interest in it, and he made himself work at it so as to justify that interest, and so as to be able to ring her up and say: 'I've finished another chapter. Would you like to be a dear and vet it for me? ... No, I don't like to post it. Where could I meet you? You doing anything to-morrow night?'

Although he had at first been unwilling to redraft it on the lines she suggested, he had, on thinking it over, liked her idea of disintegrating it into separate stories. As he considered the idea and developed it, he began gradually to fancy it was his own, and to congratulate himself on having found a new impetus for *The Swift Stream*'s sluggish progress.

It was not called *The Swift Stream* any more: it was going to be called *Three o'Clock in the Morning Courage*. They had gone to the public library together and plodded through a dictionary of quotations to find this. He had already written three stories – two about the young doctor, and one very poignant one about a theatre porter in love with a female house-surgeon who hardly knew he existed, and he had many more embryos in his head, only waiting for time to be matured on paper. When he was in the Navy he would have time. There would be evenings and evenings when he could be alone to develop himself as an author. How many books might he not have written by the time the war was over? He might even retire from the medical profession, take that house on the Long Mynd and simply be an author.

He said this to Stephanie that evening, encouraged by her faith in him. She had liked the last story: she genuinely seemed to believe that he was capable of writing the sort of stuff that the public wanted to read. She was wearing a black dress with a square white collar which broadened her shoulders and made her waist nothing.

'But,' she said, 'you surely wouldn't want to give up being a doctor? You told me yourself how much it means to you – what a thrill it is when someone gets better entirely through your doing.'

'Oh, well, you kid yourself it's your doing,' said Steven easily. 'But it isn't really, you know. All you can do is to give a little fillip to nature's powers of resistance. In any case, probably why I like doctoring is because it flatters my ego, and I can sublimate my creative instinct in it. If I was writing, I should be sublimating it that way, and perhaps I shouldn't have any urge to be a doctor. My ego would be quite happy, too.'

'Does everybody have to sublimate their creative instinct?' she asked.

'Mm-hm.'

'I'm not sublimating mine. There's nothing creative about pounding a typewriter and getting M.S. out of engagements he's made and doesn't intend to keep.'

'Oh, well, you're a woman. A very attractive one, and probably very highly sexed. I wouldn't know – unfortunately.' He tried out remarks like this sometimes, as much to titillate himself as her.

'Stick to the point,' she said. 'Go on.'

'Your body is preparing itself for the inevitable time when you marry and have children. Your glands are all working together with that end in view, and they're not going to be sidetracked into giving you urges to go and make plaster busts or to reform the housing laws or to write a three hundred thousand word best-seller about life in ancient Rome.'

'So *that's* why I've never wanted to do any of those things!' she said, and laughed happily. 'But what about the women who do write and paint and go into Parliament? Why do their glands make them want to do it?'

'Law of compensation, my good girl,' he said. 'They're usually as ugly as sin, so their glands know it's no good preparing them to lead a full sexual life, because they'll never find the man to give it to them.' Marion would have enjoyed this conversation, he thought. It was just the sort of pseudo-scientific boloney she loved. He did not know why he was using it on Stephanie, except that it didn't seem to matter what they talked about, they always had a good time doing it. He looked up to see that the restaurant had been emptying round them unnoticed.

'What next?' he asked. 'Want to go somewhere and dance? It's a bit late for the cinema. And anyway –' And anyway, Ruth might decide to take herself to the cinema, although she seldom went out alone at night. He could not remember which film she had wanted to see, and the thought of running into her made him feel like the husband on the comic postcard again.

'I ought to go home,' said Stephanie. 'I've got a heavy day to-morrow; it's the board meeting. I really should get to bed early.' She had never been dancing with Steven, and she did not think she wanted to. She was afraid of finding that he did not dance very well, that there were things that younger men could do better than he. She did not want to get to Quaglino's and catch herself wishing, even for a moment, that she were there with Peter.

Steven drove her home, to the slab-faced block of flats behind Kensington High Street. He had kissed her for the first time the night they went to Great Fosters, and having broken the ice, they now kissed in an understanding, restrained and civilized way whenever they said good night. She seemed quite satisfied with this for the time being, and Steven was not risking a rebuff by going any farther. Anyway, she was not the sort of girl whom one messed about in cars. And years of nurturing his professional reputation had got him out of the habit of things like that a long time ago. He had not had even the mildest affair with anybody since that unsatisfying business with Margot Ainsthorpe, after which he had felt so bad that he had been painstakingly nice to Ruth for weeks.

Driving home through the Park, he had a very odd feeling. He felt that he was not real. He knew he was flesh and blood because he could see his hands on the steering wheel, with the tendons sliding under the skin as he turned them, and could see his legs moving up and down as he pressed the accelerator, or went from the clutch to the brake and back again, but he suddenly felt like a lay figure, an effigy, a dilettante dressed-up doll, playing a sophisticated game that got him nowhere. It was all very well acting the part for the benefit of rich patients, but when his working day was finished he should have had a real self to slide back into, like a pair of slippers. But where was his real self, his honest-to-God masculinity? Had he lost it through all these years of dissembling and being what people expected him to be? Even with Stephanie, he felt that he was acting up to her conception of him, unable to be completely natural because he was always on the watch for the first sign that she thought him a bore. He felt empty. His head felt empty, and he could not believe that seven pints of warm blood were chasing themselves round his body and in and out of his heart and lungs.

When he got home he went down and found Ugly in his box bed under the kitchen stairs. It was rather a smelly bed, but Steven wanted an animal smell like this. He picked up handfuls of skin on the dog's neck and buried his face in the warm, electric hair, which shone under the passage light with the gloss of its own vitality.

'What I need, Ug,' he mumbled, 'is more male company. I'm becoming a tame cat.' Ugly rolled his eyes back until the whites showed, and panted slightly in his passion of joy at this midnight visit. 'I'll ring up Guy or someone,' Steven told him, 'and we'll have some golf this week-end. Yes, and you can come, too. You're getting fat and sissy yourself.'

Guy Phillips was a bone specialist, whose chief claim to fame was his invention of a particularly sadistic pin to drive through people's heels for the extension of a fractured leg.

He was so short that when he operated he had to stand on a little wooden box. When he performed at nursing homes and hospitals where he was not known, confusion sometimes arose because he put on the gloves laid out for the sister or nurse. He was very ugly, with triangular eyes and a long upper lip like a monkey, but this was offset by the charm in his broad, curling smile, quick, light movements and rapid, breathy, amused voice. He and Steven had been at medical school together, had lost touch when each went his separate way into the provinces, but had come together again as naturally as two balls of mercury when they both came to London.

While he was still a student, Guy had married a stately girl who had gone to the altar in flat heels and still been taller than her bridegroom. She had given him a son called Terence, who was measured anxiously on the nursery door every week to no avail, and who now, a sub-lieutenant of twenty-two, was only slightly taller than his father. Guy also had two adolescent daughters, who had chosen to take after their mother, and were still sprouting. Maimie, at fourteen, could already cover her father's hand with her own and hide it. 'Upon my word,' Guy told Steven, with more awe than distress, 'I think the girl's got acromegaly.'

Steven asked Miss Minden to ring up Guy and suggest golf on Sunday. He sent a patient into the examination room to undress and waited, drumming his fingers on the desk and wondering why he could not work up more interest in Lady Norton's chronic asthma. Miss Minden came in with some notes, cleared her throat, as she always did before speaking, and said in a low voice: 'I have Mr Phillips on the phone now, Doctor. He's afraid he can't manage Sunday, but could you do Saturday instead?'

'Saturday?' Steven pulled the morocco-bound engagement pad towards him. 'Lord, no. I've got a clinic in the morning, and a couple of consultations in the afternoon – and that woman out at Pinner. Is he on the telephone now? I'd like to talk to him.'

'I'll put him through,' said Miss Minden, going out with a warning glance towards the examination-room door to remind him not to talk too loud. She did not approve of Steven discussing his recreation during business hours.

'Guy?' said Steven. 'Look here, why can't you do Sunday? Golf or tennis, I don't care which. I shall go mad if I don't get a bit of honest exercise.'

'I'd have loved to, Steve, but Terence's ship is in dry dock at Chatham, and I've promised to go and lunch on board. They picked up some quite superior sherry in Spain on the way home, apparently, and – look here, why don't you come along, too? You're rather keen on ships, aren't you? Terence's captain is a great chap – like you to meet him.'

'Oh, but I say,' said Steven, ready to jump at the idea, 'I can't possibly butt in like that. I mean, after all, one doesn't just walk into a ship as if it was a restaurant and say: Lay another place for my friend.'

'Don't you worry, old boy. I'll ring up Terry and fix it. He'll be awfully keen to have you. After all, you are the boy's godfather.'

'Oh, my God,' said Steven. 'So I am, and I've forgotten his birthday again.'

'I know,' said Guy. 'That's why I've just reminded you.' Steven heard a click as Miss Minden lifted her receiver to see whether they were still talking.

'I must go,' he said. 'I'm supposed to be working. Where shall I meet you on Sunday, if you're sure it's all right?'

'Pick me up here. We'll take your car. I can't face that drive along the tramlines. I'll let you know the time when I've spoken to Terence.'

'That's grand. Good-bye.' Steven put down the receiver hastily as Miss Minden came in and stood by the door looking at him.

'See if the patient's ready, will you?' he said, jerking his head towards the door of the little side-room. Miss Minden crossed the carpet in her large white canvas boats, knocked at the door, opened it just wide enough to put her head

248

in and then stood holding it open for Steven to enter where Lady Norton lay overlapping the couch in a flowered silk wrap with her stockings hanging down over her shoes.

On Sunday morning, Steven was just going to get his car, when the Matron of his pet nursing home round the corner rang up to inform him that Mr Fletcher said he was dying and would Dr Sheppard kindly come round and do something about it?

Steven walked round to the nursing home on the way to the garage. Curse Mr Fletcher. This would make him late at Guy's. What an unholy profession this was which put you at the mercy of the very dregs of humanity, even on a Sunday. For Mr Fletcher was, if not the very dregs, pretty near the bottom of the bottle. He lay flat in bed looking as scared as if he had indeed seen the angel of death, and begged Steven, in a choked whisper, to give him something to finish him off.

'You're supposed to be sitting up, you know,' said Steven, 'with that chest of yours.' He did not have to bother to be suave with Mr Fletcher, who worshipped him blindly, and thrived on mild abuse.

'I know, I know,' moaned the patient, turning his little head from side to side on the pillow, 'but it's my back. I get such a dreadful backache.'

'Trouble with you,' said Steven, 'is you've been too long in bed. You're perfectly well enough to get up now. In fact, as you know, I've ordered as part of your treatment that you should, but Matron tells me that when the nurses come to get you out of bed you refuse.'

'Indeed I do, dear Dr Sheppard, indeed I do. I'm not well enough for it yet; believe me, I'm not able. Don't forget, Doctor, I've been a very sick man. It's left its mark on me, it's taken its toll. I shall never be the same man again.' Mr Fletcher had come into the nursing home with pneumonia a long, long time ago. Although he had been cured of it for

249

weeks, he clung to it desperately, refusing to be dislodged either from his bed or from his twelve-guinea room. All he asked was to be allowed to lie there surrounded by tins and packets of patent foods, waited on hand and foot by nurses who had been trained for higher things, and swallowing, at regular hours, sugar pills or peppermint water or something equally harmless, which he referred to in an awed whisper as 'my draught'.

'Well,' asked Steven briskly, 'is there any special reason why you sent for me to-day?' He was longing to get out and away to Chatham.

'I hoped you might be able to give me something for my head, Doctor,' whimpered Mr Fletcher, pressing the backs of his hands against his temples. 'I've had such a dreadful night – not a wink of sleep, and I thought if only I could just see you ... You do me so much good.'

'Couldn't sleep, eh? Why was that? Traffic keep you awake?'

'Oh no, you know I always say this is one of the quietest corners of London, as far as *that* goes. It's just that – but no, I wouldn't want to get the nurses into trouble – but that new night nurse is so very noisy. Kitchen sounds, and doors opening and shutting. Oh, dear! nobody knows what I suffered. And then on top of everything, just as I might have dropped off to sleep, they started the lift up – in the middle of the night!' He gazed tragically at Steven, his eyes swimming with self-pity.

'I expect they had an emergency in,' said Steven shortly. 'You don't expect them to carry patients up the stairs just because you don't like the noise of the lift, do you?'

'Oh, ha, ha, you're joking, Doctor, of course, but ... If you could perhaps just speak to the nurse. She'd take it from you. They all think very highly of you here, you know.'

'Is that so?' murmured Steven. 'Thanks very much. But I don't know how you think I can speak to the night nurse when she's probably been in bed and asleep for a couple of hours. They don't work all night *and* all day, you know.'

Mr Fletcher produced his sycophantic little laugh again, which brought on his absurd little cough, which he tried desperately to make worse by whoops and heavings.

'I say, I say,' said Steven, 'that chest really is bad, isn't it? But no wonder you can't get your breath lying in that position. Come on, you really must sit up.'

'I can't do it without help, Doctor. I'm much too weak.'

Steven was loth to lay a finger on the little man himself, so he rang for the nurse, who hurried in, crackling and buxom, with a 'What *now*?' expression, which softened when she saw Steven.

'Oh, I beg your pardon, sir. I didn't know you were here,' she said. 'Did you want something?'

'Mr Fletcher wants to be helped up, that's all, Nurse,' said Steven, waving a hand towards the bed. 'I want him to sit up, and to *stay* sitting up, even if you have to strap him to the top of the bed.'

'Yes, *sir*!' said the nurse with relish. 'Come on, Mr Fletcher, upsadaisy!' She put both arms round him and lifted him into the air as if he were a doll, planting him down on his little behind, and thumping up the pillows behind him as if she wished they were him.

'You're so strong, Nurse,' he moaned. 'Oh, dear, you do shake me up.' He rolled his eyes at Steven, as if to say: See how she treats me.

Sleeves rolled up and hands on hips, the nurse stood regarding him menacingly, daring him to slip down the bed again. Steven picked up his hat. 'Well, you'll be all right now, won't you, Mr Fletcher,' he stated rather than asked. 'I'll look in in a few days' time to see how you're getting on. Oh, Nurse, you can give him a tablet now – for his head.' He winked at her out of the side of his face which Mr Fletcher could not see, and hurried out.

The Matron of the nursing home caught him in the hall. She was a corseted woman, with a steely eye and iron-grey hair dragged into a knot high up the back of her head that pushed her cap forward like a helmet. She and Steven were old friends.

'Ah, Dr Sheppard,' she said, 'I wanted to see you before you left. It's about Mr Fletcher.'

'Listen, Matron,' said Steven, trying to edge past her, 'if I hear another word about Mr Fletcher I'll go raving mad. And it's Sunday. I'm going out to enjoy myself.'

'I'm sure you are,' she said soothingly. 'But before you do I just want a promise from you that you'll get rid of Mr Fletcher soon. My nursing home isn't an hotel, you know. He's not ill any longer, he's driving my nurses insane by ringing his bell all day and all night; the cook has threatened to give notice if he asks her to make any more nut cutlets – and I want his room.'

'As far as I'm concerned, he can go as soon as you like,' said Steven airily. 'Soon as you like. I'll leave you to tell him. Excuse me, Matron, I really must go; I'm late, as it is.'

She still stood between him and the door, stepping adroitly to one side as he tried to get past her. 'You know perfectly well,' she said, 'that he won't take it from me. Don't you think I haven't tried already, dozens of times? You're the only one who can persuade him, and I'd like you to do it to-day, please, while you're here. I know you too well. You'll not come back for days, since you haven't any other patients in at the moment.'

'Look, Matron,' pleaded Steven. 'Not now. I'm in an awful hurry. I'll come back, honestly. To-morrow, if you like.'

'Dr Sheppard.' She fixed him with her cold grey eye, tapping her foot. 'You'll go back into that room now, or you'll not leave this building.' She folded her arms.

'I've told you, Matron – I haven't time.'

'Are you going upstairs?'

'I can't. I – Oh Hell !' He threw his hat furiously on to the hall table, turned and ran up the stairs, bursting into Mr Fletcher's room without knocking, to find the little man drawing happily on a cigarette, with the *News of the World* propped against his knees. He at once lowered his knees and the paper with them, dropped the cigarette into the glass of water by his bed and flopped back his head, closing his eyes.

'Ah!' said Steven viciously. 'Glad to see you looking better, Mr Fletcher. I've just come back to tell you I've been thinking it over, and I've come to the conclusion that you'll never get really well until you get out of here and get home. Get some fresh air – a change of scene – get among your own people and your own things.'

'But I've told you Doctor. I'm not able –'

'Yes, you are, you're quite well enough. There's nothing more we can do for you. There comes a time, you know, when you don't make any further progress until you get out of the sick-room atmosphere. Besides, think what a lot of money you're wasting.'

'As to that, that doesn't worry me at all. I can quite well afford it.' Wait till you've seen my bill, thought Steven.

'But you see,' continued Mr Fletcher piteously, 'who's to look after me at home? Servants are all very well, but you can't expect them to be nurses, too. My children are out all day, and my wife – well, I really couldn't land all that extra trouble on her.' Mr Fletcher knew quite well that no one at home would be willing to run about after him.

'Well, you'll have to come to some sort of arrangement,' said Steven. 'I can't be responsible for your case if you stay on here. Why don't you get a private nurse in, if you really feel you need it? Though I can assure you that your only hope is to do a bit more for yourself.'

'I don't know how my wife would feel, I'm sure, about having a nurse in the house. You know they often make a lot of trouble –'

'Think it over,' said Steven, with one hand on the doorknob. 'But take my advice: go home, and get well.'

Mr Fletcher turned his head sideways on the pillow. 'I'm a nuisance to you, aren't I?' he said plaintively. 'I've tried not to make any trouble, but you want to get rid of me, I can see that. Oh dear!' he laid a hand on his chest. 'Why does my heart flutter so when I'm upset?'

'Wind, I expect,' said Steven. 'And you're quite wrong. We don't want to get rid of you at all. I'm simply advising you to go home for your own good.' He ground out the words in slow exasperation.

'You're ever so kind, Doctor,' said Mr Fletcher. 'Good-bye for now,' and snuggled into the pillows as if he intended to stay there for life.

The buxom nurse was writing at the desk in the passage. She stood up as Steven came out and smiled at him.

'That man!' he said, and mopped his forehead.

'He is a little treasure, isn't he? We all just love him.'

'I'm sure you do. By the way, Nurse, how would you like a nice cushy little bit of private nursing, if Matron would let you go?'

'I wouldn't mind, sir. I've been thinking about taking a private job for a change. What's the case?'

'Mr Fletcher,' he said, and ran down the stairs, skidded along the hall and escaped into the street.

*

Guy was ready and waiting for him in his Chelsea house. He was in the drawing-room, with his watch out. Through the french windows, Steven could see his tall wife, gardening gently.

'You're late, Steve,' said Guy. 'Why can you never be on time? I'm not too sure of the way down to the docks, and I wanted to give us plenty of scope to get lost in.'

'Sorry,' said Steven. 'Had to see a patient.'

'Had to see a patient, had to see a patient,' said Guy testily. 'On a Sunday. You physicians have got your lives shockingly badly arranged. You're still as ridden by your work as if you were a country G.P. I was going to give you a drink, but there isn't time now.'

'Can't help it,' said Steven. 'It just happens. And I'll have that drink, if you don't mind. I need it. I've just been attacked by a Matron.'

'Oh, poor old boy. Well, in that case you do need it.'

Guy rang a bell by the fireplace. 'Bring us a couple of gimlets, quick as you can, will you, Annie?' he said to the maid.

'I'll just go and say hullo to Elizabeth while she's getting them,' said Steven, moving towards the garden.

Guy groaned. 'In that case, we'll never get away. And Terence will be furious. He told me not to be late, because his captain's dead nuts on sitting down to meals at the right time.'

'If I had a son,' said Steven, 'I wouldn't be as scared of him as you are of that boy.' In the garden, Elizabeth looked up, pleased to see him. She had the ravaged face that very thin women get at middle-age, but a delightful smile and kind, good-tempered eyes. She gave him a rose for his buttonhole, patted his coat and stood back, admiring him.

'You get handsomer every day, Steve,' she said. 'I don't wonder half the women in London are in love with you. Have you got a young woman? I hope so: you deserve it.' She and Guy had once been on holiday with Steven and Ruth. Every night in their bedroom she had said to Guy: 'Much as I love Steve, I'll never take a holiday with that woman again.'

*

After a maddening drive to Chatham, and a nightmare journey through the dockyard, during which they once nearly hit a train, twice pulled up short with their front wheels teetering over the edge of a basin, and once had to drive right into a shed to avoid a lorry on a narrow track, they rumbled over a bridge which looked as if it might rise into the air at any moment, and Guy called: 'There she is!'

Terence's ship had been in the Mediterranean for four years and she was painted a pale grey, patchy now and daubed here and there with pink and darker blotches as if an artist had been trying out his colours on her. She was a small destroyer, and in the dry dock which could accommodate the *Hood*, looked like a baby in its parents' bath.

Guy's son was waving from the deck, and Steven and Guy, the latter quivering like an excited terrier, went down the gangway to a pert salute from Terence and a solemn one from a ginger-haired young man patterned with freckles and pimples. Steven barked his shin on a bit of iron.

'Excuse the mess, sir,' said Terence. 'It's always like this when we're refitting. You won't know us in a few weeks.' He had only joined the ship two months ago, and used the first person plural whenever possible. The ship was in chaos. There were sailors slung about all over her with caps on the backs of their heads, paint pots, grease guns and oily rags. Dockyard mateys, incongruous in their civilian clothes, were camped out all over the place, determinedly insolent in contrast to the sailors' politeness. One old man, in a cloth cap and a dirty white scarf, who was sitting on a hatch with a dog-racing sheet and a can of tea, did not even pull in his legs as they went by. They all stepped carefully over the corduroys tied round with string, and a yard farther on Terence slayed a sailor for leaving a minute oil can in their path. Steven wondered whether he had over-abused the man for their benefit, but realized that he saw nothing odd in it – nor did the sailor. It was part of the game that had to be played if the ship was going to be any use.

In the wardroom, which was stuffy and hot, with fans whirring and a wireless blaring, they found three other young men and a rugged figure with a narrow blue stripe on his arm, who was called Chiefie. They had several glasses of the superior sherry, and then the Captain, stocky, and jowled like an American, clattered down the companion-way, hung up his cap and slipped among them quite diffidently. He treated the other officers and they him almost as equals. There was just that tendency to see that he had everything he wanted before helping yourself, and to laugh at all his jokes, which were not very good – that showed that he was the Captain.

'Turn that blasted wireless off, can't you?' he said to the red-haired boy. 'How anyone's expected to digest their lunch with that row going on ... No wonder you young chaps all get gastric ulcers. Isn't that so, Dr Sheppard?'

'Oh yes, yes, rather,' said Steven, and joined in the general laughter which greeted what was evidently a familiar joke.

The Captain and Guy had met before. They talked for a while, watched by Terence, who was pleased to see that the two old men were hitting it off. Then the Captain turned to Steven and threw out a few gruff conversational feelers. When he saw how interested Steven was in the Navy, he visibly relaxed and expanded. At ease in and master of his own world, he was nervous of people from other worlds outside his cloistered range.

The lunch was excellent. With the dessert, although it was a hot day, came port in large glasses. Afterwards, the older men fell into deep arm-chairs, while the boys perched on the fender and the settee that ran under the portholes. The atmosphere was mellow. Steven felt happy, and remembered his queer feeling driving through the Park last night. He felt real now, and wondered why. Was it because he had had more to drink then he was accustomed to at lunch-time? Perhaps. Was it because this was the Navy, for which, ever since his short experience in the last war, he had always felt he had an affinity? Yes. Was it because there were no women about? Quite likely. Was it because it was not only unnecessary but impossible here to put on his social act? Watching the young men departing to work, he envied them deeply, even the spots and callowness of the ginger-haired sub-lieutenant. He envied them their easy acceptance of this masculine, responsible, uninhibited world.

He began to talk to the Captain of his hopes of getting into the naval medical service. The Captain was appalled. He knew Steven's reputation and position. Naval surgeons were quite a different breed. One might become a Dr Sheppard after having been a naval doctor, although that was unlikely, but one did not become a naval doctor after having been a Dr Sheppard.

'You'll stagnate,' he said, 'you'll positively stagnate.'

'Not if there's a war,' grinned Steven.

'Oh, war.' That was inevitable. They had all been training for it, anyway, since Dartmouth.

'But what about your practice? You don't want to lose that, surely?'

Steven kissed his fingers into the air. 'I'd love to. I've had enough of private patients to last me a lifetime.'

'Now you're talking rot, old boy,' said Guy puckering his monkey face.

'No, honestly. I wouldn't miss it, if I could make enough to live on. After all, I haven't got children like you.' He nodded at Terence sitting on the settee with one leg tucked under him. 'They're what keeps a man chained to the treadmill.'

'But if you go to sea, sir,' said his godson, 'you'll go mad with boredom. I mean, in between actions there'd be nothing to do but pare off the bos'n's corns, and sit around in the wardroom waiting for someone to stand you a drink. You should see our doctors. I heard of one who took out a chap's kidney, just to keep his hand in, and didn't discover till afterwards that he'd already had the other one out. Fact.'

'Of course, you could always have a shore job in a base hospital,' said the Captain. 'I imagine there'd be plenty to do there in war-time. Or you could be on one of those panels of consultants that the Services share. I believe those chaps still manage to keep a small private practice going.'

'That's not what I want.' Steven shook his head. 'I want to go to sea – get away from the land and all the people on it for a bit.'

'I repeat,' said Terence, 'you'd go mad with boredom. What'll you bet?'

'What have you got?' asked Steven. 'Bet you all those birthday presents you've never had, if you like. Anyway, I might get sent to a hospital ship. There'd be plenty to do there, I imagine, except on the trips out. But in any case, I'd find lots to do. I'd be able to read all the things I've always

258

wanted to and never had time for. And I –' he tossed it out casually, 'I'd do a bit of writing.'

'I wrote a story once,' mused the Captain, his gaze focused in the region of the Dogger Bank, and then looked round the wardroom hastily, to see if anyone had noticed. It struck Steven that, although he had been deferring to his host, the Captain must be nearly ten years younger than he. But his face was lined and marked and matured, and there was already more grey in his curly hair than in Steven's. He must have seen a lot of life in his short time, real honest-to-God elemental stuff in a turtle-necked sweater and sea boots; the satisfaction of physical effort and achievement ...

'You must see a lot of damned interesting stuff,' the Captain was saying, as if he were stealing Steven's lines.

'Too many people,' said Steven. 'Too many women.' He sank deeper into the leather arm-chair and stretched out his legs until he could put his feet on the fender.

Terence had sat up at the magic word. 'Yes, but I say, sir. The opportunities, I mean.' He giggled. 'After all, a doctor ... A girl friend of mine told me that she found all doctors attractive because she felt they knew so much about her.'

'You don't have to tell poor Steve that,' chuckled Guy, whose cigar was now burned down in better proportion to his face. 'Tell 'em that story about the Duchess in the bath – no names, of course.'

Steven told it coarsely, amusingly. That kind of thing seemed very remote now, that side of him, that person who moved with such polished assurance about the bedrooms of the rich and spoiled.

Presently, the Captain heaved himself out of his chair with a grunt and excused himself on the grounds of work. Terence offered to show his father and Steven over the ship. He insisted on taking them everywhere, and Steven, following him in landsman's fashion backwards down the iron ladder to the boiler-room, wished he were more suitably clad than in the soft dark grey flannel with a faint chalk stripe.

He was very fond of this suit, and always hung it away with extra care, and sent it regularly to be sponged and pressed by the 'Fetch and Deliver Valet Service', but it did not seem to matter now about the grease mark on the trousers and the oil stain on the cuff, although he knew he would regret these later.

In the cluttered purgatory of the boiler-room, a middle-aged sailor called Fat was mending a hand lamp. How he had ever got in through the small round opening in the deck above the iron ladder was a mystery. Either the ship had been built round him, or he had come down here as a lad and never gone up since. If the sweat was running now in the gutters of all his chins, what must he be like when they had steam up?

He was evidently a friend of Terence's. 'My father and Dr Sheppard want to hear all about the boilers,' he said, although neither Steven nor Guy had shown the slightest curiosity about the mammoth slagged cylinders.

'If the gentlemen will come this way ...' Fat prowled about the boiler-room like the custodian at Wookey Hole, laying affectionate hands on sinister bits of machinery, and stroking one of the boilers as if it were his favourite elephant, making them look inside to see the openings of the myriad pipes, as surprisingly numerous as the cells in a fly's eye.

He was master of his own little world, as the Captain had been in the wardroom. If the Captain had come to Wimpole Street, he would have cleared his throat, fingered his tie, fiddled about with his wallet, uncertain if one really paid cash and, if so, to whom and when, telling Steven things that, being English, he had never even told his wife. So, too, with Fat. If he had been just a fat man in Steven's clinic, he would have been a jelly of nervousness, cap on knee, bunch-of-banana hand continually passing over his face as if there were reassurance in the familiar feel of his own features, laying his life, loves, habits, idiosyncrasies and personal crises humbly before Steven, but down here he was the oracle, dignified by his knowledge and experience, making the other three men feel inferior.

They went all over the ship, even into the Captain's day cabin, where, surrounded by model yachts and photographs of a nice English lady and even nicer small sons, the Captain was reading a novel in an arm-chair.

'He never can stand sociability for too long,' Terence said, by way of explanation rather than apology.

They went ashore by the gangway, and plunged down a hole in the quay to get to the bottom of the dry dock. The stone staircase was green and slippery, and Steven descended like an old man unsure of his legs. It seemed like taking advantage of the ship to be thus prowling round her indecently exposed bottom, which only the fishes were supposed to see.

A cook slung a bucketful of dirty water out of a hole in her side without looking, and had to stick his head out of the hole as if pilloried to be told off for the double crime of nearly hitting them and of littering the dock.

'Kind of chap who slings ash all over the carpet,' said Terence. 'We may have to be here weeks. Very jolly to be surrounded with refuse all that time.' Steven tried to imagine the other boys of twenty-two being concerned about refuse or ash on the carpet, or in showing visitors kitchen gadgets as Terence had done in the galley. But in an all-male world, men were interested in womanly things.

Dodging trams and Sunday bicycles on the way home, Steven reflected that women were almost completely redundant. Things got done just the same but without so much talk. Steven could have been domesticated if he had had the time and the encouragement. In his younger days, at Llandovery, after Betty left, and at Ryde, he had sometimes penetrated into the kitchen to make an omelette, but it always upset the current cook, as Steven's idea of omelette making was to cook it, eat it and forget to wash the pan. In Wimpole Street, of course, he was considered far too august to do anything except mend fuses, and even that Mrs Hankey thought not quite the thing, and was relieved when Mrs

Garrard quietly took over the job which had always been Steven's. The last time he had gone through his ritual of sending someone out for fuse wire, taking off his jacket, getting the step-ladder and someone to hold it while he was on the top, removing every connection to find the one which Ruth had fused by dropping the iron, Mrs Garrard had emerged from the kitchen on her rubber soles and said: 'I have already done that, Dr Sheppard.'

Guy, who had been sleeping lightly, woke up. 'You ought to get young Terence to take you to sea some time,' he said. 'He took me up the East Coast once. I was sick as a dog. It was grand. I say, what a mistake to drink all that port in the middle of the day.' He nodded off again.

Every other Sunday, Mrs Garrard had the whole day off, besides her half-days on Wednesdays when Miss Minden had to answer the front door bell, because Mabel had been deaf since a bungled mastoid in childhood.

Mrs Hankey, sitting comfortably in the knowledge that she need not stir until it was time to start cooking dinner, would tell her: 'There's the bell, dear.'

'Get on,' Mabel would say. 'That's only a bicycle.'

'I'm not in the habit of telling lies.'

'Well, I never heard it.'

'I think you should go up, dear. Doctor's patients don't like to be kept waiting.'

By the time they had argued it out, the bell would have rung again, and Miss Minden would have opened the door. So Miss Minden was one of the people who missed Mrs Garrard on her afternoon off. Also, she did not get the kind of tea tray to which Ethel had accustomed her. Mabel had a heavy hand with the bread knife, so on Wednesdays Miss Minden usually brought in cakes from the A.B.C. for herself and Mr Nosgood's secretary.

Mr Nosgood missed Ethel, too. She always contrived tactfully to bring him his tea between patients, but Mabel always managed to dump it in the little dispensary when he was just starting on a case. This left him the choice of letting it get cold or of abandoning the patient with propped-open mouth on the pretext of mixing a stopping. If he did this, and had his tea hurriedly in mid-case, there was the danger of taking in air with it, which might cause an embarrassing moment when he was bending over the patient afterwards. Also, when it was fish-paste sandwiches, one had to suck a pepper-mint afterwards, and this all took time.

Ruth missed Mrs Garrard, too, and told her so when she got back, a compliment which Ethel absorbed, as she did everything, as her due.

'Oh, well, Madam, we can't all be perfect,' she would an-swer Ruth's wail about Mabel's method of serving dinner. 'It's not everyone can wait at table, but then, I've been trained for it, you see. Sir Manton Noakes would have every-thing just so. And before that, when I was with her lady-ship, the butler there used to put us through our paces you wouldn't believe.'

Ruth had never given the whole of Sunday before; her parlour-maid used to go off after lunch. But Mrs Garrard's mother's legs had been playing her up again, which necessi-tated her being visited at least once a fortnight, and all the afternoon trains were conveniently inconvenient – so slow, and, what with having to get back by little Tom's bedtime, it was hardly worth going unless Mrs Garrard could take the 10.30 from Waterloo.

Sunday breakfast, therefore, was the only one of the week which Steven enjoyed. There was no chance of Mrs Garrard hanging about watching him, and bringing him more toast which he did not want. As soon as she had put everything in the dining-room, she would go upstairs, taking off her cap as she went, and change into the green marocain dress and fawn jacket which was the summer equivalent of her long fawn coat and green trousers. She then wound the inevitable scarf round her flat red hair, changed her black, rubber-soled shoes for imitation ice-calf with straps and pointed toes, took out her gloves and the black glacé handbag which Ruth had given her on her birthday and went downstairs to pick Tom off the kitchen chair, where he had been planted to keep clean since being dressed in the blue linen knickers and silk shirt which Ruth had given him when it got too hot for jerseys.

On the Sunday when Steven went to Chatham, Mrs Garrard and Tom took the train for Dynsford. It was a close, moody, sunless but stifling day, and Tom showed signs that he would be in a temper before they got home. The weather never affected Mrs Garrard, and she never got into a temper. When a heavy woman with sharp heels trod on her foot getting into the carriage, Mrs Garrard simply swallowed and looked at her without acknowledging her apology. The heavy woman sat down, unbuttoned her coat, counted her parcels, checked her ticket, opened her paper, and looked up as the train started to see Mrs Garrard's gaze still fixed enigmatically on her. This made her feel uncomfortable. She read a paragraph or two without taking anything in, and risked another look. Perhaps there was something wrong with her hair or her hat. She put up a questing hand, but everything seemed all right. Perhaps there was a smut on her face; she would get out her mirror presently when that cold-looking woman was not watching her. She looked like the sort of person who, if she did not like you, would bide her time and stick pins in a wax effigy when she got home.

Mrs Garrard looked at the heavy woman's feet for a while, then at all the feet on the opposite side of the carriage. Everyone else had a Sunday paper of some sort, but Mrs Garrard seldom read the papers. She was much too interested in her own affairs to bother herself about what the world was doing. When people talked about a war coming, she thought: Oh yes, well, let them get on with it. It was no business of mine.

Tom read a comic paper, swinging his legs restlessly, and occasionally asking a question with the accent on the '*Why?*' which gave his voice its sing-song quality.

At Dynsford, they had half an hour to wait for the bus

which would take them to Reddage, the village where Mrs Garrard's mother lived. Tom wanted to go into the Station Café for a lemonade and a bun, but Mrs Garrard did not see the sense in paying for something which would spoil his appetite for a free lunch.

When the bus came, it was a double decker, to Tom's joy, and he insisted on going upstairs and clattering right to the front. They were the only passengers on top, and the conductor, who was a happy man, with a round red face and a perfect liver, made a joke about having to come all the way up the stairs just for them.

'Well, you see,' said Mrs Garrard seriously, 'it means so much to my little boy to ride on top, and I suppose I'm silly, but I just can't deny him.'

'I know what it is,' said the conductor, turning the handle of his rural ticket machine. 'Got three of me own, and they do what they like with me. *What* they like! Why only last Saturday –' But Mrs Garrard did not want to talk about his children. 'So I always say,' she went on, 'we don't know what's in store for them in the future, so we should let them have all the fun they can, poor little mites.'

This made the conductor laugh. He pulled off the long paper tickets and gave them to Tom. 'There you are, young Horace,' he said. 'Yes, so, as I was saying last Saturday, what did those young devils of mine do but –'

'Don't kick your shoes like that, Tom,' said Mrs Garrard. 'You'll ruin them. And look at your tie! Whatever do you do to get it screwed round like that?' She started pulling and picking at his clothes, and the conductor said: 'You ought to see my three – regular scarecrows! Where they pick up the dirt from beats me.'

'I always try to keep little Tom looking as nice as possible,' said Mrs Garrard, licking her handkerchief and wiping round her son's mouth, 'even if it means denying myself. I think it's only right.' The conductor went away whistling to ring the bell, and felt glad that he was on early turn, and would be going home in an hour's time to that house of noise and disorder, where his fat wife, whose face was a contrasting shade of red to his own, mauve-hued from having worked a degenerate heart too hard, would place before him cold meat pie and potatoes and lettuce from his own garden.

Mrs Anderson, Tom's grandmother, lived in half a flint cottage which was the last house at the eastern end of Reddage. It was not really a village, being separated from the nearest factory estate only by half a mile of arable land and cabbage fields. There was nothing rural about it except the benightedness of its shops and the dullness of its inhabitants. Even its one farm was slab-faced and sooty, with corrugated iron roofs on its outbuildings and messy cows that looked as unlike a pastured herd as street arabs look like country children. The fields were flat, and fenced with barbed wire instead of hedges, and the liveliest thing about the neighbourhood was a commercial aerodrome which discharged its planes day and night directly over the roofs of Reddage. Its three public-houses were austere establishments, where the reception was colder than the beer. There was a chapel with a tin roof and warning posters about the wrath to come, and a church with a slate steeple and tinny bells, a vicar with a potato in one cheek and a plum in the other, and a verger with a mild form of paralysis agitans. There was no reason for anyone to live there except habit or lack of initiative. The more mobile inhabitants escaped by bus and bicycle, whenever possible, to the wild delights of Dynsford, and the others stayed at home and struggled with grudging gardens and listened unselectively to the wireless, and read the *Dynsford Courier* from cover to cover.

It was a drab place to live in, and the Andersons were drab people. He worked sourly for a firm of plumbers in Dynsford, and brought gloom into whatever houses he visited with his carpet bag, while his wife had one particular meal for every day of the week, and such time as she was not preparing it and battling with the dirt which blew over from the factory estate she spent resting her legs.

She had her feet up when her daughter and grandson

arrived, and would not take them down to answer the front door, so they went down the side path and came into the kitchen through the lean-to scullery. Mrs Anderson was in the front room, her body, in a black overall patterned with puce and emerald flowers, in one chair and the lisle-clad bolsters which were her legs bridging the gap to another. She had to be kissed, and then Tom went and stood by the bow window, holding the lace curtain aside to see the next bus go by.

'Well, Ethel,' said Mrs Anderson, and 'Well, Mother,' said her daughter. 'So here we are again you see.' She did not ask after the legs. She was tired of them; they had been going on for too long. Her mother would have to develop a new symptom if she wanted any interest, which was Ethel's nearest approach to sympathy.

But Mrs Anderson had something even more important to talk about. She had been chewing it over ever since it happened, and her heavy, hippopotamus face was working now as she sought how best to give it dramatic expression. Ethel began to talk about the weather: wasn't it close, and the train journey had been so trying and really the bus service got worse, but her mother interrupted her, leaning forward, and even taking down the legs to mark the importance of her announcement.

'I've got something to tell you, Ethel,' she said hoarsely. ' *'E's* been here.' Having launched her bomb, she leaned back to study its effect on her daughter. If Ethel had not been so pale already, she would have blanched. As it was, her usually calm eyelids fluttered and she sucked in her lower lip, holding it with her teeth to keep it from trembling. There was no need to ask who 'E was. Her husband, Arthur, had been called that ever since he had shown his true colours as a brute and a monster.

'What did he want?' she asked, closing her eyes for a moment.

'You,' said her mother. 'And little Tom. Your Dad was here. Last Saturday 'E come. I thought of writing to you, but then I thought better to wait and tell you direct. 'E came on the three-thirty bus. We tried to deny him entry, but of course 'E come round the back, and busting right in here as cool as you like. Terrible 'E looked. There was violence in that man's eye if ever I saw it.'

'Oh my God,' said Ethel. 'You didn't tell him where I was?'

'Not I.' Mrs Anderson put up her feet again. It didn't do to let the blood into them for too long. 'Your Dad looked like giving it away – you know what a fool he can be – but I told him we didn't know where you were. Said you'd gone abroad. Not that 'E believed it. You could tell that.'

Ethel licked her lips. 'So what did he do?'

'Oh, 'E stormed and shouted and threatened – you know the way 'E carries on – and 'E'd had a good few already as like as not, but 'E didn't get nothing out of me, though it made me feel bad for days afterwards. My legs came up alarming.' She looked at them proudly. 'They're nothing now to what they were. 'E's been living with this creature from the flats, it seems, since you left him, but 'E's broken with her now, and it's you 'E wants, and it's my belief 'E'll not rest till 'E finds you.' The bus had passed, and Tom had come back from the window, to lean against his mother, bored.

'Run along and play somewhere, dear,' said Mrs Anderson. 'He mustn't H-E-A-R,' she mouthed. 'What mustn't I hear?' asked Tom, interested, and Mrs Garrard said: 'Oh, it doesn't matter about him. He's heard so much already, it's a wonder it hasn't turned his little brain. Where's Dad?'

'The usual place.' Mr Anderson had a pint of bitter every Sunday morning in the saloon bar of the 'Earl Grey', speaking to no one and downing his beer in small, wry sips without visible enjoyment.

He came home at dinner-time. Ethel, who was pulling out the flaps of the table in the window and laying the cloth, saw him stumping with slightly bent knees up the path in his bowler hat, high Sunday collar and spotted bow-tie. He wore very large, stiff boots with solid, round toes turning slightly upwards. They never looked like part of him, but walked on their own, carrying Mr Anderson with them. He had another pair, equally large and stiff, but they did not creak like these Sunday ones. Ethel could hear him coming through the closed window. She agitated a corner of the curtain and he gave her a nod, pulling down his nostrils and the corner of his mouth afterwards in the sniff with which he righted his face after all displays of emotion.

He came in by the back door, wiping his boots first on the scraper and then on the mat. Ethel, going through to get the potatoes, met him in the kitchen and kissed him without enthusiasm. She had inherited from him her impassiveness of expression as well as her red hair and freckles. Mr Anderson had freckles all over the backs of his hands and up his skinny white arms too, although no one had ever seen them. His grey hair was still streaked here and there with its former gingery-yellow, so that it matched the tea and tobacco stains of his moustache.

'Well, Ethel.'

'Well, Dad.'

'Where's the boy?' He was fond of his grandchild in an undemonstrative way, and had once made him a miniature bath with a real waste-pipe and taps that could be connected to the water supply and turned on and off. It had taken him nearly a year to make, and when it was finished he did not want to part with it, so it was kept at Reddage as a treat for Tom to play with when he visited his grandparents. As far as Tom was concerned, it was the only thing that made the visits worth while, because the food was nothing special. He came running in from the back garden now, and clamoured round his grandfather: 'The bath, Granddad, the bath!'

'After dinner,' said Mrs Garrard. 'Have you washed your hands?'

But since their last visit her father had completed the geyser, which was heated from underneath by a spirit lamp, and he took Tom off at once to the tool-shed which was his workshop.

With a shrug, Ethel carried the potatoes through to the front room and started doling them out with cold meat and beetroot and a heartless, dark green lettuce on to four plates. You never helped yourself in that house. Someone served you, and you ate what you got, with neither appreciation nor dislike. If you wanted more, you said : 'I'll have another portion of that, since there was no soup', or 'If there's no sweet to follow'. Never 'since it's so good'.

Mrs Anderson let down her legs with a sigh, and hitched her chair up to the table, and presently Mr Anderson's boots carried him in and deposited him with his back to the window where he hooded his light-lashed eyes for a moment and suggested, without pressing the point, that God's holy name be praised for these and all His gifts.

Tom sat on a chair with two cushions, and became absorbed in trying to hide under a lettuce leaf the meat which his mother had cut up for him.

'Well, Ethel,' said Mr Anderson, his moustache going rhythmically up and down, and occasionally from side to side as he met a bit of gristle, 'your mother told you, then, that 'E's been here.' Ethel nodded, searching delicately in the pickle bottle for a cauliflower piece.

'Well, what are you going to do about it?'

'What can I do, Dad? I'm not going to let him find me. I'm not going back to him – not ever. I wouldn't lower myself. And I'd rather die than let little Tom go back to that sort of life, especially now that he's getting such a good start. Mrs Sheppard's going to help with his fees you know, at the St Leonard's House Day School, up Baker Street way. She's ever so fond of him. "He mustn't go to a council school, Ethel," she said. "He's too good to mix with that class of child." '

'Well, so she should pay something,' said her mother. 'Dear knows *you* can't afford to on the wages you get, though, of course, it's *He* that really pays, isn't it? She not having a penny to bless herself with.' *He*, heavily aspirated, was Steven, as opposed to the *'E*, which was Arthur Garrard.

'Better tell 'em about Arthur coming,' said Mr Anderson. 'See if they can do anything about it. It's not right that your mother and I should be troubled this way – scaring the old lady half out of her wits, not to mention upsetting me for the rest of the day. They ought to do something about it. After all, they did beg you to go and work for them; it's only right they should take the responsibility.' This distortion of the circumstances of Ethel's engagement in Wimpole Street had gradually evolved, until it was now an accepted theory that the Sheppards were under an obligation to Mrs Garrard, rather than she to them.

'That's right,' said Mrs Anderson. 'They ought to do something about it. I'll have a little more potato, Ethel, since you gave me such a small helping the first time.'

'All the same,' said her daughter, 'I don't quite see what they could do. Eat up your meat, Tom. You won't get no pudding else.' With one ruthless sweep of her fork, she removed the lettuce leaf and disclosed the carefully-concealed food, some of it chewed and spat out again.

'There's always the police,' said her father in a rumbling voice.

'On what grounds? *'E's* committed no crime, when all's said and done. You can't take a man into custody for seeking after his own wife and child, if you get my meaning. And whatever happens, Arthur mustn't get to know where I am. I should be afraid to show my nose in the street for a moment if I thought there was any chance of that. I shall be scared to leave here to-night as it is, for fear 'E's watching for me. Oh dear, I wish we hadn't have come. Why didn't you write?'

'Not safe,' said her mother, who had had no intention of forgoing the drama of breaking the news personally.

'Well,' said Mr Anderson, with an attempt at Sabbath wit, 'what's for afters, as they say?'

'Bread-and-butter pudding,' said his wife. 'You like that.'

'*I* don't,' stated Tom.

'Hush, dear,' said his mother, 'that's rude. And you're not

to pick out all the currants, as you did last time, and leave all the bread.' Which was what Tom proceeded to do and, as the pudding was sparsely populated as far as currants were concerned, this did not take him long. He then sat kicking his heels against the chair leg and his toes against the table legs, waiting for the others to finish disentangling their false teeth from the sodden bread. He was not worrying. He knew his mother inside out, and realized that she was much too preoccupied with the subject of the monster "E', whom he pictured in a blue shirt like his father, but with the head of some undefined beast with slavering jaws, to make him finish his pudding. She had her days when she would have made him stay there until he ate it, or would have served it up again at tea, but to-day she had removed his plate of masticated meat without comment, and now when Mrs Anderson said: 'There's a wicked waste for you! He should be made to eat that up, every mouthful, Ethel,' his mother simply said: 'He's got a delicate stomach. He's been faddy ever since his illness, poor little mite. But I think you're right, Dad, I'd ought to tell Doctor about it. He must do what he thinks fit, for go on in this state, like a hunted fox, I cannot.'

*

The train was full coming back from Dynsford. Ethel and Tom got into a carriage which already held the right number of bodies on each side, many of them amplified by large bunches of flowers, vegetables in paper carriers and other spoils of a day in the country. They looked at the newcomers hostilely, and the men shook out newspapers and hid behind them to affirm their resolution not to give up their seats. However, a thin woman had unwisely left a triangle of seat showing between herself and the window, and on to this Ethel insinuated herself so determinedly that everyone on that side was forced to move uncomfortably close together, and a small man in a cloth cap at the far end was squeezed right forward like a cherry stone between a thumb and forefinger, and had to balance on the edge of the seat for the rest of the journey.

Mrs Garrard took Tom on her knee, where he sat with his legs dangling like limp little Bologna sausages, his socks coming down over his shoes. Once or twice he made a square mouth as if he were going to cry, but presently he went to sleep instead, and his mother sat and stared out over his hot, dishevelled red head and planned what she was going to say. It would make a good story in the kitchen, and would revive her aura of a fugitive in hiding, which had rather waned now that she had lived in Wimpole Street so many weeks unmolested. Then she would tell Mrs Sheppard, who could be relied on for interest, if not for any practical help. Mrs Sheppard would then tell Doctor, who would not at first be interested, but would absorb the story gradually through repetition and constant allusion, until he realized his own part in it, as he had with the school fees. Mrs Garrard herself would make constant sideway references, such as asking him the legal position of a hypothetical case, or enquiring wistfully whether he thought the Home in Cheshire would take Tom back, for his own safety, 'though how I shall bear to part with the little chap I *don't* know.' The more she thought about it, the more she was convinced that Doctor must do something about it. After all, as her employer, he was responsible for her. She was not prepared to worry over what he could do; that was his affair. But he must do something.

It was disappointing that when she got back there was no one to tell. Dr and Mrs Sheppard were out, so Mrs Hankey had gone to the pictures, and Mabel, who had been told to sit in Miss Minden's room and strain her ears for the door and telephone, was in bed. Mrs Garrard put Tom to bed and gave herself some supper, picking at it as delicately as if she had been in company, dark phrases of disappointment running through her mind. 'I could be murdered in a ditch and no one care.' 'Not even so much as leave a kettle boiling for a person.' 'It's not safe for me to be alone in a great house like this with only a kiddy and a wanting girl.' She decided to wait up for Ruth like a well-brought-up lady's maid, and tell her the story when she got back.

Steven had taken Ruth on the river. He had got back mellow from Chatham and done two hours' work on the story of a night nurse and a dying patient, which, on re-reading, had moved him quite gratifyingly. This and a drink made him mellower still. Towards evening the clouds, which had been pinning London down, had broken up, and cleared away, to sail flat-bottomed and gold-crested along the horizon. With them had gone the oppressive, sticky heat of the day, and the sky, pale blue above and greening towards the west, was as clean and clear as though being covered up all day had preserved it for just this hour.

There was birdsong in Cavendish Square, and all the front rooms of the house were pooled with the last light of the sun before it disappeared behind the opposite roofs. It would have been a good evening to take Stephanie out, to drive in the car with her sitting there so clean and miraculously undishevelled by the wind. Her lips never cracked and the lipstick never coated on them as on most women's when they drove in an open car. Her skirt never bagged at the back from prolonged sitting, and when she wore dark glasses they never left a red ridge across her nose. But he had rung Stephanie from a call-box on the way back from Chatham, and her mother had told him that she was spending the week-end with her friend Ida, and would not be back until Monday morning. So he was able to appease his conscience towards Ruth by suggesting supper in a punt, which had once been one of their routine pleasures, in abeyance since the time when they had driven all the way to Staines only to find that because Steven had had to visit a case on the way, it was too late to get a boat. Ruth had been martyred, and refused to eat their picnic supper on the way home instead. Steven had found a delightful spot, down a side lane away from the main road, where they could take the rug into a field and imagine they were in the country. But Ruth had said she was not hungry, and refused to get out of the car, and Steven had sat stubbornly on the other side of the gate with Ugly and eaten cold salmon and strawberries without enjoyment, until a courting couple who passed staring on the field path had made him feel too ridiculous to stay there any longer. When they got home, Ruth had refused his suggestion of coffee and sandwiches, but when she thought he was asleep he heard her get up and creep down to the kitchen.

However, that was a long time ago, and she jumped at the suggestion to-day. It was sweet of Steven to think of it. She knew that recently she had been annoying him more than usual, but the harder she tried, the more irritating he seemed to find her. She had worried a lot, and prayed about it, and even told her hairdresser, but here he was suggesting something that was just like old times, and in a flash all was rosy again.

'Oh, darling, how lovely!' She glowed like a girl and went over to kiss him.

'Look out, Ruth! Damn it, you've spilt my drink.'

'Oh, dear. Never mind, I'll move this chair over, then Ethel won't see the mark.'

'It wasn't the carpet I was worrying about –'

'I'll go down and get the supper together while you go and get the car,' she said eagerly, feeling domesticity coursing through her veins, seeing herself with the loaf on end and the knife in a jug of hot water, cutting sandwiches swiftly and deftly.

'Rustle up something nice then,' said Steven. 'Not sandwiches, for God's sake. Isn't there some of that chicken left we had last night? A cold wing and some lettuce, and some of those pears Marion sent? I'll get a bottle of hock out and we can take ice in a thermos.'

Praying that they would not have finished up the chicken in the kitchen, Ruth hurried downstairs and tiptoed to the larder to find out, but Mrs Hankey heard her and came down the passage saying: 'Was there something you were wanting, 'M?' She did not like Ruth poking about her basement. It was not right, either. If a lady wanted something, she should ring for it.

'Well ... the Doctor and I thought we'd have supper on the river as it's such a lovely evening, so I thought I'd just come and see what we could take. I didn't want to bother you.' It was awkward to mention the chicken without first finding out if it was there. She edged on towards the larder, humming.

'Why didn't you tell me before, 'M?' asked Mrs Hankey, following her. 'I could have made you something nice. A veal-and-ham pie perhaps, or some sausage patties.'

'We've only just decided. What were we going to have for supper?'

'Well, I was going to give you the cold chicken, with a salad ...'

'Oh, that's lovely!' Ruth laughed in her relief. 'We'll take that, then.' She opened the larder door and found the half-eaten bird in the meat safe. 'Perhaps you wouldn't mind just jointing it for me, and we could wrap it in lettuce leaves.'

'Oh, but not just to eat like that, 'M, in the fingers,' said Mrs Hankey, stepping in front of her to take out the chicken. 'Let me make it into some nice sandwiches for you. Doctor likes sandwiches.'

'Doctor doesn't *want* sandwiches,' said Ruth triumphantly. 'He's just said so. He wants a wing of chicken and some lettuce. Oh – and we'll take this bit of cheese. It looks rather nice. What is it?'

'Groo – er, they call it, 'M. It only came yesterday. I wasn't going to send it up because it smelt so strong.'

'Oh no, I think it looks nice. We've got some of those water biscuits that Doctor likes, haven't we? Gracious! I never knew we had those tins of green figs. We must have them some time.' She began to move things about on the shelves. She did not often come into the larder. 'What happened to those plums in brandy that that patient sent?'

'You had those, if you remember, when Sir Herbert and

Lady Harriman came to dinner. That's tinned salmon, 'M,'
she said as Ruth picked up a tin with a torn label. 'That's
only cheap stuff; you wouldn't fancy that. I get that now
and again for little Tom. He just dotes on it, and he's got
such a fly-away appetite, I try and give him what he fancies.
And we fall back on it sometimes when there's nothing
else.'

'But I love tinned salmon!' exclaimed Ruth, hugging the
tin fondly to her. 'I'd love to have it sometimes. It reminds
me of my youth.' she giggled. 'Tinned salmon and bread and
butter for tea – what a long time ago that seems.' She waited
for Mrs Hankey to say: 'Not so long, surely, 'M,' but she
was too busy trying to manœuvre Ruth out of the larder to
pick up her cue. 'If you'll just come along and show me
which pieces you'd like,' she hustled.

Ruth dropped a tin of loganberries, replaced it so that
Mrs Hankey should not see the dent, and followed her back
to the kitchen, leaving the larder door open. Ugly, who had
never known this to happen before, left his dinner, which he
was pushing about in a tin basin at the bottom of the stairs,
slipped in, and with eyes and ears straining guiltily backwards, bolted down the wedge of Gruyère which Ruth had
left lying on the lowest shelf.

Steven, coming down to the wine cellar, found him in the
passage, gulping and heaving, like a snake trying to swallow
a rabbit. Seeing the larder door open, he shut it quickly,
hoping that Ugly would manage to swallow whatever it was
he had taken before he brought it up. When he went into the
kitchen to get the ice out of the refrigerator, Ruth was packing the picnic case while Mrs Hankey made coffee. He
leaned over his wife's shoulder.

'Look, darling, if you'd put that tin in *that* way round, and
then the cups longways, it would all fit in and there'd be
room for both the thermoses. Or is it thermi?'

'Don't ask me,' said Ruth happily, 'you know I don't
know anything about things like that. Oh, I haven't put the
cheese in. I found a lovely bit of strong Gruyère, darling.

277

I thought we'd have that with some water biscuits – and there's some celery.'

'Good.' He struggled with the ice tray, nearly fell over backwards when it came out suddenly, and went out saying: 'I'll go and get the car. Be ready in about ten minutes.'

'Oh, Steven, I can't! I must change.'

'What on earth for? Wear that thing you've got on,' he called back, having no idea what she was wearing. 'It looks grand.' So he liked her green linen. She herself had liked it in the shop, but had been regretting it ever since she got it home. She had shown it to Steven when she first wore it, but he had been reading, and only looked up for a moment and mumbled. But he liked it, in spite of her mother's insistence that green killed her. How funny men were though, never saying what they thought. It just showed you only had to know them to live happily with them. This evening she felt she knew Steven, and that they were happy. She would wear the green linen dress on the river and they would have a happy evening.

'It's the most extraordinary thing,' she said, coming back from the larder with wrinkled brows. 'I can't find that cheese anywhere. I didn't bring it in with me, did I?' They searched the kitchen. They both searched the larder again. 'I daresay you left the door open,' said Mrs Hankey, ' and his lordship found his way in. He's very fond of cheese is that dog.'

'But the door was shut when I went along. I don't see how he could have.'

'Well, it's a mystery to me, 'M.' Ruth had the uncomfortable feeling that Mrs Hankey thought that she had taken the cheese for some reason, so that when Mrs Hankey offered her instead a piece of Dutch, which was obviously the kitchen's property, she felt bound to refuse, although Steven might be disappointed. She would take some Gentlemen's Relish; that would do to spread on the biscuits.

She and Mrs Hankey locked up the picnic case, opened it again to put in salt, shut and opened it once more to put in the table napkins on which Mrs Hankey insisted. 'What with eating the chicken in the hand ...' She would really have been happier if they had taken finger bowls.

'By the way,' asked Ruth with a pang, 'what did you have for your supper last night, then, if you didn't have the chicken? I never like you to leave things, you know, that we send down.'

'Oh, that's quite all right, 'M,' said Mrs Hankey, her Victoria-plum face drawn down in a martyred expression. 'We foraged quite sufficient.' She thought it unnecessary to mention that their foraging had gleaned in the kippers which the fishmonger had sent extra Saturday afternoon. They paid for being eaten fresh, anyway.

'Where's Mabel?' asked Ruth as she was going out.

'Up in her room reading. Some love tale. I don't know what that girl doesn't fill her head with. No wonder she's not quite the thing.'

'Well, she can come down and sit somewhere where she can hear the bells. Why don't you go out for a bit? I know it's not your day, but you'd like to go out, surely, in this lovely weather?'

'Well, thank you very much, 'M, I would rather like to go and see the picture at the Regal as it happens,' said Mrs Hankey, who had been considering slipping out since she heard that Ruth and Steven would not be dining in. 'But of course, if you'd rather I didn't go ... I shouldn't like any of the Doctor's patients to phone or call and not get proper treatment.'

'Nonsense. Mabel has managed before. She'll be perfectly all right.' Ruth was going to have a lovely evening. She was going to enjoy herself. She wanted other people to enjoy themselves, too. She wanted to be a generous, well-loved mistress, of whom her servants said: 'I'd do anything for her.'

*

They drove to Staines, where the bow-legged boatman remembered, or pretended to remember, them from many years ago. Steven could punt well. It was one of his accomplishments, learned at Cambridge, and, even out of practice, he could still do it elegantly without getting himself wet. Ruth lay facing him on cushions, with one arm behind her head and the other hand trailing in the water, her legs stretched and looking rather large. Ugly sat in the bow and barked arrogantly at passing boats, or stood rockily peering into the river as if about to plunge, although wild horses would not have dragged him into the water. Steven got himself into the rhythm of punting. The drop of the pole, the unheard thud and the crunch of gravel under the hook, a long, straight push, neither pulling the stern of the boat under the pole nor driving it away, a push to the farthest limits of the arms, then the hand-over-hand swing down the ascending pole while the boat glided forward, delicate movements, with the wrist curved to keep the water from running down your sleeve. Then, at the psychological moment, when the top of the pole is so high it must topple over, away with the right hand and the pole drops smoothly through the slack left hand at just the right angle, until at the thud and crunch your body swings to the push again. He resurrected an old dream, one of the things they had often talked about doing but had never done because of his work.

'We always said we'd take a house on the river one summer, Ruth, remember?'

'It would have been lovely, only it might have rained and we might have been flooded out if we'd been in a bungalow.'

'It wouldn't have been a bungalow.'

'They mostly are.'

'And you always said that you'd be afraid Carol would fall in the river.' He would have liked to talk about Carol now, but Ruth had stiffened and pursed her lips, and looked away from him at the bungalows passing on the opposite bank, so he thought about Carol instead. He had been teaching her to punt during the last year of her life. When they lived at Dynsford he used to drive her to the river on hot summer evenings. She wore a bathing dress under her cotton

280

frock and had to take the frock off before punting because she got so wet. When Ruth came too, the punting never went so well, because she would shout advice and raise alarms about other boats and swans. He often told himself that he and Ruth might have got on better if Carol had lived, or if they had had another child, but thinking back there had been just as many disagreements and discordances when Carol was there. More, in fact, because the child had often been a bone of contention between them, whereas now they owned nothing jointly that mattered enough to either of them to quarrel seriously about.

They never had proper quarrels, because Ruth was too dependent on him ever to set herself up for long against his opinions or decisions. Hoping to please him, she would abandon her tenets, and even contradict herself flatly, unable to see why she only aggravated him the more.

After he had been punting for a while in silence he called out: 'Say when you want to eat and I'll find somewhere nice to tie up.'

'Whenever you like, darling. I'm not hungry – at least, we'll have supper when you want it. You choose a nice spot.' She hoped he was not looking forward to the cheese. She shaded her eyes with her hand to watch him punting. No wonder other women on the river looked across the water at him. He was as handsome as he had ever been, like this in his white shirt and white flannel trousers, with the sun behind him, his strong forearms brown and dripping below the rolled-up sleeves. He never seemed to lose his sunburn, even after nearly a year without a holiday from London. His face was always slightly brown, too, an even colour, not flushed, with hectic veins like some men, and never grey or pasty even when he was tired. When he was tired his eyes looked darker and deeper set, and his cheek bones seemed more prominent, and his lips closed in a tighter line than usual, as if he were making an effort to keep himself going. At such times, she would say: 'You're driving yourself, darling. You shouldn't do it. Ring up that patient and tell her you'll come in the morning,' or 'Don't do any writing to-night,' or 'Why not cry off your clinic just this once? Other people do. The house-man can take it.'

And Steven would say: 'Oh, Ruth, for God's sake. Work doesn't get done like that. And how could I relax with all this stuff hanging over me? Telling me not to do things isn't any help.' The only helpful thing would have been some-thing practical, like getting out one's car, or writing a letter or making a telephone call for which he had no time; or for a soothing-looking woman silently to hand him a drink and not talk until he felt like it. That was what Stephanie had done last time they met for dinner, when he had arrived an hour late and so tired that he had seriously thought of put-ting her off. But once he got there, he was thankful he had not. Having soothed him she began to be stimulating and, magically, he was equal to the stimulus, and fancied that he was no longer the drawn, middle-aged man whom he had seen in the mirror of the gents' cloak-room, so used-looking that he had hardly dared go in and sit next to her spick-and-span youth.

He punted upstream until they were clear of bungalows and boat-houses for a spell, and on the left bank there were willows, if they could find a place where somebody else was not already making love or drinking stout or playing the gramophone. There was plenty of traffic on the river on an August Sunday evening. Collarless men in double-scullers were catching deliberate crabs for the amusement of the shrieking girls who sat opposite them pulling the wrong rud-der strings. Fathers, see-sawed almost out of the water by the weight of their family in the stern, rowed manfully, with oars going very deep into the water and high into the air, like fishermen in a choppy sea. Lean men in vests, with faces as sharply concentrated as the bows of their racing skiffs, slid backwards and forwards on seats little bigger than a roller skate. Men who could punt did it conscientiously, like Steven, with a touch of hauteur; men who could not essayed it just the same and drove their boats round in circles which their womenfolk, all paddling frantically against each other, tried to correct before the blaring, singing steamer bore down on them. When it had gone, and everyone it had passed had said: 'I should hate to be on one of *those*,' in spite of the obvious enjoyment of those on board, its backwash caused shrieks of delighted alarm, and spread to the moored boats, rocking the lovers pleasantly and making gramophone needles hiccough and jump a couple of grooves.

There were beautiful girls in canoes and bathing dresses, there were less beautiful girls, who yet managed to feel like Helen of Troy because they had got a man and he was rowing them while they reclined in a becomingly feminine attitude. Cycling was fun, but really it wasn't a patch on the river for making a man aware of you. Especially tandem cycling; he couldn't even see you then, which perhaps was just as well, but all you got of him, instead of this openshirted figure smiling at you as he swung his body rhythmically, was the smell of his black alpaca cycling jacket when he got hot.

Steven turned into a backwater and made for a secluded spot in a little bay of the bank. 'Keep low,' he shouted, but of course Ruth sat up and turned round to see where they were going and was fortunate not to have her eyes put out by the willow branch which struck her sharply on the head. After she had held her hand over her eyes for a bit and said: 'I'm all right, I'm all *right*,' while Steven, knowing that one is better left alone under these circumstances, got on with tying up the boat; she was indeed all right, and asked to have the place kissed by Steven. But as he was on the bank and the boat was swinging out into the river, he blew her one instead. Ugly had leaped ashore and disappeared.

'Where shall we eat?' asked Steven. 'On the bank or in the boat?'

'Oh, in the boat, shall we? It might be damp, and we haven't got a rug. Hand me over the case and I'll unpack the supper.'

'Let's have a drink first.' He opened the bottle of wine on

shore, and then got back into the boat and sat on the cushions opposite her, his feet next to her green linen dress, her brown-and-white buckskin shoes touching his thigh. Ruth opened the case, saw the one thermos of coffee and was appalled. Had she spoilt the evening after all? It was bad enough about the cheese, but – 'Steven, I forgot to put the ice in!' she moaned, raising an agonized face to him.

He grinned. 'I know you did. That's why I brought it.' He produced the thermos from the bag that had held the wine, and Ruth's face came untied again. She even consented to have a drink. 'It's not that I really *like* it, you know,' she exclaimed. 'Alcohol always tastes so bitter to me; I don't know how people can talk about it like they do. Still, wine's different really, isn't it? I know people always think I'm queer when I refuse cocktails, but I honestly hate the taste. It's not that I want to be a spoil-sport. Sherry now, that's not so bad. I quite enjoyed that sherry they gave us before dinner at the Watsons'.'

'I should think you might,' said Steven, filling her glass. 'It was Bristol Cream.'

'Oh, well, I don't know all the names, of course. Well, here's to us, Steven!' She raised her glass.

'Us,' he said. 'And everybody in England. And the war. And may we come out of it all right, whatever it's like.'

'Oh, darling.' Ruth pouted. 'Don't spoil such a lovely evening by talking about the *war*. I'd quite forgotten about it. Perhaps it'll never come. Something'll happen, like last year.' She snuggled comfortably back on to the cushions.

'Never come!' said Steven. 'It's here. Don't you read the papers?'

'Oh, you mean about the Russians and Germans signing that pact? I know you thought that was significant, but I've been thinking it over, and after all surely every peaceful gesture counts in the world to-day, no matter who it's between. Shall we start the supper? I've got a lovely cold wing for you. I was afraid they might have finished the chicken downstairs, but luckily they hadn't. Poor things, I don't know what they live on; they really are good. We're awfully lucky, you know, darling, to have such easy servants. Some people have their lives simply *ruled*. Marjorie Watson was telling me that night we dined there –'

'Look,' said Steven. 'This is our evening out. Let's not talk about servants, shall we?'

'Oh, all right,' said Rúth stiffly. 'I'm sorry, I didn't know I was boring you.' She handed him his bit of chicken wrapped in a lettuce leaf, and he took it and began to chew on it thoughtfully, thinking about the war, unaware that he had done more than momentarily offend her.

'Any bread? Oh, thanks.' She gave him a roll, and then sat looking at him, not starting her own bit of chicken held ready in one hand. She must say something to get them going.

'Well!' she began brightly. 'You haven't told me anything yet about lunching in the ship. Did you enjoy it?'

'What? Oh yes, rather. Yes, it was great fun. That's a nice lad of Guy's.'

'Terence. Well, he used not to be. Don't you remember when he was running round with that awful Ledbury girl when he was only twenty?'

'He started young, like his father. Guy was married before he was out of medical school. All the know-alls said it would be the ruin of him, that he'd never pass his exams with a wife to take his mind off work, but actually he did better.'

This was the kind of idea which appealed to Ruth. She took a bite of chicken and leaned forward, stressing her words. 'Elizabeth has been a help to him, then, in his career.'

'I suppose so. Yes, I suppose she has. She's given him confidence, and she's awfully good at saying the right things to the people who matter.'

Ruth sighed. 'I wish I was.' She waited, in case he might say: 'But you *are*!' and went on: 'Steven, I want you to tell me honestly. Have I been a help or a hindrance to

285

you in your career?' She had her earnest face on – eyes very close together, teeth biting at her lower lip. 'I know I'm no good at all the social things and knowing what to say to people, but I have taken an interest in your work. But do you sometimes think you would have been better as a bachelor? Is it in spite of me that you've got on?' Twilight was rising from the water all round them, enclosing them in a quiet that was enhanced rather than broken by the occasional lap of water under the punt's flat bow. Already the trees and bushes on the bank held darkness tangled in their branches. It was a perfect hour for confidences, Ruth thought. The hush of evening simply begged to have intimate, serious things spoken about in slow, deep voices. She threw away her chicken bone, and it fell with a little splash into the water and sailed away.

'Ruth, what utter bilge you talk,' said Steven. 'The only thing that's been a hindrance to me in my career is – my career.'

'I'm afraid that's too deep for me.' She smiled towards the glimmer of his white shirt. 'What do you mean?'

'I mean that I'm not sure whether I chose the right one. I don't believe I was ever cut out for that sort of life. I don't like people enough.'

'Oh, darling! Now it's you that's talking utter bilge.' She loved to echo his expressions. 'You know you love being a doctor – curing people. You couldn't be so good at it if you didn't.'

'Oh, being a doctor, yes, that's all right. But you know me – I've got to be successful at anything I do – do it better than the next man – and apparently you can't be a successful doctor without being at the beck and call of half the bores in creation.'

Although his tone was light, Ruth knew that he was talking seriously. It was not often that he talked seriously to her. She sought for an intelligent question, to draw him out still further, and not finding one rustled in the picnic case and said, quickly, so as to gloss it over: 'I'm afraid

I didn't bring the cheese after all, darling, but there're some biscuits with Gentleman's Relish on. Will you have one of those?'

*

The boatman had said to them: 'Mind and be back by ten. I like all my boats in at ten.' So at about half-past nine, when Steven was dozing, Ruth began to fuss. 'It's lovely here, darling,' she said, slapping at the midges which were biting her legs through her stockings, 'but we'd better go soon, hadn't we, or we shan't be back by ten. The man'll be furious if we're late.' She had an innate fear of everyone to whom she paid money – servants, taxi-drivers, shopkeepers, hairdressers – she strove to placate them all.

'He won't mind,' mumbled Steven lazily. 'He'll simply charge us a bit extra.'

'Where's Ugly? Ugly! Ugly! Ugly!' she called, in a high, unresonant voice, although he never came for her. Life in the punt became uncomfortable as she wallowed about packing up the picnic case, trying to make Steven eat the last water biscuit, putting on her cardigan, looking for her handbag, so Steven gathered himself up with a sigh and stepped on shore to untie the boat and whistle for Ugly. The dog embarked with a plunge which nearly sent Ruth, who was kneeling up, toppling into the water. Frightened, she took out her fright on Ugly in abuse. Steven was always surprised by Ruth's occasional flashes of virulence. She never abused or shouted at him. It might have been better if she had. He would have shouted back, and perhaps thrown something at her, and she would have had a good cry and it would have done them both a lot of good.

Punting her back effortlessly with the darkling stream, Steven thought about Stephanie, and wondered for the hundredth time what Ruth would say if she knew about her. She would either become martyred and tell him that *of course* he must do whatever he wanted; she was not going to stand in his way, or she would take the whole thing in the grand tragedy manner and say that her life was finished and Steven had murdered her heart. Either way, she would enlarge the affair to monstrous dimensions. Steven knew perfectly well that this was not an affair to move mountains and start revolutions or break up marriages. It was a delightful friendship bordering on a love affair that was neither hectic nor complicated. Stephanie gave him great happiness and comradeship. She radiated some chemical affinity to his own personality that he had never found in any of the women who had hankered after him. She made him happy, and gave him something to look forward to. But how explain this to Ruth, who was the kind of woman who would create a divorce where there was no question or desirability of one, so that in the end no one was happy?

*

Before Steven could turn his key in the lock, the front door was opened from the inside.

'Oh, Ethel,' said Ruth, 'you shouldn't have waited up. How nice you look in your mufti.'

'It's only my old green, Madam,' said Mrs Garrard, taking the picnic case from Steven. 'If you'll pardon it, might I have a word with you, Madam? There's something you ought to know, and I felt I shouldn't sleep a wink without I told you to-night.'

'Oh, dear,' said Ruth, into whose mind always flashed the dire word, Notice, whenever Mrs Garrard had anything on her mind, even if it was only the need for new teacloths. She looked at Steven, who had gone through the hall to hang up his hat. 'What are you going to do, darling?'

'I'm going to do a spot of work on a case. Don't wait for me if you want to go to bed.'

'I'll go up then. You can come and talk to me while I do my hair if you like, Ethel.'

'Very good, Madam.' She tailed Ruth upstairs.

*

Ruth, lying in bed worrying, heard Steven come into his dressing-room and opened her mouth to tell him about Arthur Garrard. Then she remembered what he had said on the river about not talking about the servants, and closed it again. If she told him now, he would not listen properly, and it would be difficult to reopen the subject later. She would wait and tell him at a favourable moment. He would know what to do. Something must be done. Poor Ethel could not go on in this state of uncertainty. Moreover, supposing her husband did find her and take her away. Life at 101 Wimpole Street would be unthinkable.

She was glad she had not broached the subject when Steven called out: 'Nurse Sheppard!' which was a joke he knew she liked.

'Yes, Doctor?' She played up brightly.

'Here's a test for your medical knowledge. Woman aged forty-five. Secondary anæmia plus high blood pressure –'

'That doesn't sound right,' interrupted Ruth triumphantly. 'If you had too little blood you'd have a low blood pressure.'

'Well, it is right. It is possible if the arteries are sclerosed. Anyway, I haven't finished. Deafness, slight mental confusion, vomiting after food, pains in limbs, progressive loss of weight and general debility. You'd say aplastic anæmia, wouldn't you, Nurse?'

'It does sound like it, yes,' said Ruth, who had never heard of aplastic anæmia. She loved being talked to like this.

'Well, you'd be wrong,' grunted Steven. 'Sternal puncture – N.A.D. Think again.'

'I don't really know what to say.' Ruth knitted her brows and racked her brains. How wonderful if she were to hit on the right answer.

'Neither do I,' said Steven. 'Fat lot of use you are to me.' He began to sing quite cheerfully. That was all right then; he wasn't annoyed with her for not knowing.

Chapter 9

—

IT was a comfortable enough office, solid, old-fashioned, and sensible, but not inappropriately luxurious. There were no soft carpets or exotic inkstands or streamlined furniture, or water colours on pastel walls. The windows were high and not particularly clean, and bookcases full of bound ledgers and reference books formed three sides of a square round the heavy old desk, which was more like an outcrop of rock than a piece of furniture. A room in which hours of good hard work could be done, and sensible decisions made.

The decision which the bald, pippin-faced surgeon-captain behind the desk was making at the moment seemed to Steven the most sensible that had ever been made in that office.

'That's settled, then, Dr Sheppard,' he was saying. 'You'll be called up at the outbreak of war. Of course, we don't know just when that'll be –' They grinned at each other, like two men who knew a thing or two. 'But anyway, this should leave you time to – what's the expression – put your house in order. Of course, there's no need to tell you how much the Admiralty appreciates your readiness to give up your very considerable position.' Steven muttered something. 'We'll be calling up a good many doctors before we're done,' went on the naval officer happily; he was quite looking forward to the war. 'And I don't suppose they'll all come as quietly as you.'

He rose and held out his hand, as Steven had done so often when it was time to get rid of people.

'It's definite, isn't it,' said Steven, picking up his hat and stick, 'that I shall go to sea? I mean, that's what I want most particularly. That's why I've been making such a nuisance of myself all these weeks.'

'That's not for me to say, of course,' said the other, going to the door with him, 'but I'll do my best for you.'

'Thanks.' Steven paused. 'You see, I –' He realized that what he might be going to say would sound as if he was joining up from selfish rather than patriotic motives, and changed it to: 'I certainly hope you'll be able to wangle it for me.' They shook hands. 'Well, thanks again, Captain Ramsay, for all you've done.'

'Not at all, my dear chap, not at all. And don't you worry.' He became rather bluff. 'I'll do my best for you, I'll do my best.'

When Steven had gone, Captain Ramsay chugged across the corridor into the opposite office.

'Busy, Scottie?'

'Not extra.' The hook-nosed man with the untidy grey hair looked up.

Captain Ramsay perched a spreading thigh on the corner of the desk and reached over to help himself to a cigarette from the silver box which was engraved 'J. H. C. McDermott from his friends and patients in H.M.S. *Polyphemus*'.

'Got a match?' Captain McDermott clicked a lighter for him in silence and raised his triangular eyebrows questioningly. Ramsay was always coming across the corridor at odd moments. The best thing was to let him get rid of whatever was on his chest right away and then he would go and you could get on with your work.

'Just had that Sheppard chap in to see me again,' he said, swinging his leg, toppling off the desk and going to look out of the open window at the shimmering Horse Guards Parade.

'The Harley Street consultant who wants to run away to sea?'

'That's the boy. Decent chap; I took to him a lot. He's going to be very useful to us too – a man with his experience.'

'Have you fixed him up?'

'More or less. He's as thrilled as a kid going to Dartmouth. Funny thing, isn't it? He's got to the top, and here he is mad keen to take a jump off. I thought of recommending him for that base hospital in Somerset. They'll be wanting a good man there.'

'You'll not be trying to get him sent to sea, then?'

'Good God, no. Can't afford to waste these top flight chaps like that. That's what happened in the last war. They let all the best chaps get picked off doing front-line jobs that lesser useful people could have done. Things are going to be different this time. Organization of manpower, it's called. People are going to be put to jobs as near as possible to what they made a success of in civil life.'

'H'm. Aye, that's sound. Take your finger out of that hole in the curtain, there's a good chap. You'll only make it bigger.'

'There he goes,' said Captain Ramsay. 'Spry as a young bird. Just getting into a most decent-looking car. I bet he makes a packet out of these rich old dames. Silly ass. I wouldn't chuck up such a good thing ... That's a fine lock he's got there for a long car. I say, you ought to see the way he whistled out of that car park – very pretty.'

Captain McDermott had started to write again during this running commentary. He had a lot of work to get through before lunch.

'Well, I'll be getting along.' Captain Ramsay trundled himself across the office. 'Cheerho. See you later.'

*

Stephanie reacted to the news in just the right way. Ruth had said 'Oh,' and let her face fall before she remembered to pick it up and ask interested questions. But Stephanie was instantaneously pleased, and said: 'Everything seems to be going right for you all at once, doesn't it? I had a word with M.S. to-day about your stories. He seems to like them. He wants to have a talk with you some time.'

'Probably wants to slip in a free consultation. He still

owes me some money, by the way. What kind of a secretary are you that you can't get these bills paid?'

'I don't have anything to do with his money matters. The accountant does all that.'

'So it won't be you who pays me the vast royalties earned by *Three o'Clock in the Morning Courage*?'

'No.' She held her hand out across the table. 'Steven, I do hope it does tremendously well.'

He took the hand and studied it. Its smoothness and shapeliness always gave him great pleasure. Her nails were perfect; glossy coral, with half moons the same shape as the white tips. The wrist that emerged from the starched cuff of her blouse was small and delicate, but too supple to be the kind of brittle little joint that goes with chicken-boned legs and spiky knees. 'It'll be all due to you if it does,' he said. 'I really believe this short kind of stuff is my *métier*. I've got ideas already for several more stories. I'm going to get on with them as soon as I've got my affairs straight.'

'It must be an awful job. What's going to happen to your practice?'

'Well, being a consultant isn't like being a G.P., you know. It's not exactly a practice. You haven't got so many regular private patients. All my hospital cases are being taken over by the other honoraries. The agents think they'll be able to let off Wimpole Street as soon as I want to go. There's a radiologist after it already.'

'What about your wife?'

'She'll go to her mother, and take her beloved Ethel with her, plus brat.'

'Where will you go when you're on leave, then?'

'Oh, I shall go there, I suppose.' Steven made a face. 'But I mean to look around for a cottage in the country – Shropshire. Ruth can go there or not as she likes, but I shall have it always to come home to. I rather thought –' he threw it out lightly '– you might come there sometimes.'

Stephanie laughed. 'With Ruth?'

'Without Ruth.'

'Oh, I see.' Her hair swung over her cheeks as she looked down. 'Well, I might.' Steven was not worrying about the future. He was too happy in the present. The future, anyway, seemed quite clear and uncomplicated, although it appeared to have both Stephanie and Ruth in it.

'I'm glad for you to be getting what you want,' she said when they were sitting in the car just round the corner from her home, 'but I'm going to miss you dreadfully.'

'You won't,' he said. 'What about all your boy friends?'

'I don't really like any of them much, you know,' she said speculatively. 'Will you mind if I write to you an awful lot?'

'I hope you will. I shall live for your letters.'

They both began to feel sentimental and pleasantly melancholy. He was very much the hero going off to the wars, while she, the little woman, waited for him at home, Keeping herself Nice for him. Like any lusty young sub-lieutenant, he would come on leave to her with boyish eagerness. Poor old Ruth was rather crowded out of the picture. He would spend a lot of his leave with her, of course, and they would get on much better for having been parted. But she would be with her mother. She would be all right. She was already planning to get into the hospital in Guildford as a V.A.D.

The next day, Stephanie lunched with her friend Ida. They had salads and brown bread and butter and coffee at a low table in a clean little feminine place near Blooms-bury Square. The waitresses wore cretonne overalls and the tables had green glass tops and green-and-white spotted china and china spoons to eat your fruit salad with. It was not odd nor indiscreet that she told Ida everything about Steven. She had always done it with all her men, and Ida with hers, in a tone of wondering interest at the eternal oddities of the male. Even when Ida married she had rung Stephanie up the next morning, and when Stephanie married she would probably do the same. It did not make them any less nice girls; this was just one of the things that they did.

'So it's to be love in a cottage,' mused Ida. She was wearing her hair piled on top, with a hat made of four flowers among the ash-blonde curls.

'Apparently,' said Stephanie. Being a working woman, she was more plainly dressed than Ida, but with no less care.

'And will you?' asked Ida with interest.

Stephanie shrugged her shoulders. 'It's ages off. You never know what may happen. He's sweet, though. He *is* a darling, and I'm awfully fond of him. I don't know when I've been as fond of anybody, really.'

'Of course,' said Ida judicially, 'he's a bit old. In a few years' time he'll be a dirty old man.'

'Oh, darling, that's a horrid thing to say. He never will be. But of course, he is a bit old. I do wish I'd met him sooner – I mean, if I was the same age.'

'He must have been a knock-out as a young man,' said Ida.

'He still is,' said Stephanie defensively. 'And he's so clean. I do like that in a man.'

*

It was very embarrassing about Miss Minden. She came in one morning with Steven's letters, and he dictated answers to them as he always did, without looking at her, swivelling about in his chair, glancing through a medical magazine, leaning back with his eyes on the ceiling, moving about the room, or standing by the window and lifting a corner of the curtain to look out at the close huddle of back walls and roofs, or turning his waist in a miniature practice golf swing. She always sat in the patients' chair by his desk, pad on knees, white cotton legs neatly together and canvas shoes inanimately side by side, as if they were put out for cleaning. But this morning she twice asked him to repeat himself, which was unusual for her, and when he said, in the middle of a letter: 'By the way, have you seen that confounded bag of mine? I've lost it again,' the poignancy of the familiar allusion made her voice falter and weaken.

He looked at her then. 'You're not very well, are you, Miss Minden?' he said kindly. 'Anything I can do to help?' Her long, bony nose was red and unusually shiny, and her eyes were like an angora rabbit's, as though she had not slept all night, which she was fully persuaded she had not.

'You must excuse me, Doctor,' she said, looking down at her pad and scribbling nonsensical shorthand furiously. 'Please pay no attention to me. I shall get over it directly. It's just the first shock of the news. Changes are always upsetting to me.'

'Good Lord, I didn't know you were upset about your change of job. I thought we had all that out the other day. You seemed quite happy about going to Mr Walter Curd when I leave. But in any case, I may not go just yet. I don't know – we none of us know when the balloon's going up. But if you don't want to go to Mr Curd, for Heaven's sake say so. I wouldn't have fixed it up for you if I hadn't thought you'd like the work.'

'Oh, it's not that, Doctor, it isn't that.' She raised the pink eyes to him again. 'I'm sure the work with Mr Curd will be all I could wish for; I hear he's an extra pleasant gentleman. We do hear these things, you know, about the other members of the profession.'

'Well, then. Now, where was I with Mrs Madden? Oh yes, about the Calcium Gluconate.' He was in a hurry to get his letters done. He had a lot of work to clear up.

She was still looking at him, exquisitely sharpened pencil motionless. 'It's just the thought of leaving you, Dr Sheppard,' she said, 'that's cut me up for the moment. After all this time together ... you've been so good to me ...' Her trembling expression was so like Nurse Lake's that Steven was reminded of that hideous scene in the clinic. Surely Miss Minden was not going to cry? She had never cried. But a great pear-shaped tear was standing on her right cheek, as big as if it had been forming during the two years of her employment with him, and, fascinated, he watched it fall and blur the pencilled shorthand on her pad.

'Oh now, Miss Minden, that's just silly,' he said, falsely hale. 'I know it's always hard to make a break when one's so well into the work, but you've got your career to think about, don't forget. Mr Curd's a very important man in his line, more important than I'll ever be. You're doing yourself a lot of good by going to him, you know.'

She shook her head lugubriously. 'I don't want to leave you, Doctor, and that's a fact.'

'And I don't want you to go. I'm most unwilling to part with you, believe me. I've already told you, haven't I, how much I appreciate all you've done for me? You've been invaluable, Miss Minden, quite invaluable.' He sat down briskly and began to arrange papers on his desk in an effort to break the spell of her sentimentality. Perhaps this would have been the time to give her the cheque he had in mind for her. No, perhaps not. Perhaps, in any case, it should have been some more personal present instead of a cheque, although he knew she needed the money. But he could not face giving her a bottle of scent, or a bracelet, or some such unsuitable bit of flattery if she were going to melt all over him like this. Scarcely a word unconnected with work had passed between them before; that was what made this so indecent.

Bravely, she swallowed, ran the nail of her third finger under her eye and said meekly: 'Dear Mrs Madden, re the injections that you have been having twice weekly now since – I'll look that up for you, Doctor.' She sniffed.

'I wish you would. Oh, by the way, before I forget, where *is* that bag of mine? You always seem to know.'

But this was too much for her. 'It's on the half-landing, Doctor, where you always leave it when you come down in a hurry in the morning and have to go back for your breast-pocket handkerchief,' she gasped and fled from the room.

*

Mark Stainer met him for lunch, bringing with him the typescript of Steven's book. He put it on top of the radiator behind him, and although Steven's eyes kept straying to the bulky envelope, he did not like to allude to it before Mark did. During lunch Mark talked of anything and everything but *Three o'Clock in the Morning Courage*.

Steven had cold game pie and salad, followed by cheese and biscuits, but Mark, who had refused a cocktail and then told the waiter 'My usual,' picked his way slowly through steamed fish and sieved spinach, and then messed about with a nasty-looking plateful of ground rice.

Steven, who hated talking symptoms out of consultation hours, let the fish go unremarked, but at the ground rice he raised his eyebrows and said: 'I thought I'd cured you. Last time I saw you I told you you could have small amounts of anything you liked within reason. Don't tell me you're eating that stuff for fun.'

Mark looked at the spoonful which was halfway to his mouth, and put it back on the plate again with a grimace. 'It's just about all I can manage these days.'

'Same old pain?' He nodded.

'Well,' said Steven, 'you'd better let me examine you again some time. But make it soon, because I may be shutting up shop any of these days, as I told you. I'd like you to see a surgeon, really, you know.'

Mark raised his delicate little hands with their manicured nails. 'Heaven preserve me from that,' he said plaintively. 'You did the trick once before for me with your nostrums, whatever they were. I've been hoping you'll be able to settle my recalcitrant vitals again. Apart from the fact that I have a positively morbid fear of the knife, I simply couldn't spare the time to go into hospital for an operation.'

Steven saw his chance. 'I suppose you haven't had time to read my stuff, then,' he said diffidently.

'Most certainly I have,' said Mark, and began to talk about the ballet. It was not until the table was cleared for coffee, which Steven took alone, that he reached backwards and brought the envelope on to the cloth between them. 'Well now,' he said, gazing intently at Steven from under the shadow of his great domed brow, 'touching the question of the masterpiece –'

'D'you like it?'

'But of course I like it. Enormously. I realize, naturally, that you've a lot of work to do on it yet. Some of the stories want trimming and titivating, and the last one, of course, is only a sketch of what you have in mind. You'll be elaborating that.'

'Oh, of course,' said Steven, not admitting that the last story was meant to be a delicate little vignette, complete as it stood. 'I'll have plenty of time for that, I imagine, when I get into my new job, much more than I have now.'

'Quite, quite.' Mark mused, caressing the envelope. 'I would like to publish it; it would give me enormous pleasure, but I'm thinking primarily of yourself. If you're going to be a writer, it's essential that you should get off to a good start. Your first book must be one that the public will take to its heart. Untold damage can be done by an inopportune or too-hastily-considered first book. However good the next are, their chances are jeopardized before they even appear, perhaps irretrievably. The memory of the public, my dear Sheppard, is as of the elephant, and their prejudices are legion. The truth of it is they won't take short, bitty stuff, except from an established favourite. What they hunger for is novels.'

'But Stephanie told me –'

'What a sweet child that is,' said Mark. 'I can't tell you how devoted I am to her.' Steven looked at him sharply, but no, he was pretty sure Stephanie had told him the truth; the little man's affection was unfounded on sex.

'I mean,' he said, 'she didn't tell me that the public wanted to read short stories, but it was she who advised me to write the book in that form, rather than as a continuous novel. It started as that, you know, but it wasn't coming off. I'm much better at this kind of thing.'

'Oh, indubitably,' said Mark. 'Indubitably. Waiter, you won't forget that glass of hot water, will you?' He looked at his watch, a lady-like little affair with an oval face on a fragile gold-link band. 'Talking to you,' he said, 'I'd no idea it was so late. I shall really have to tear myself away. Be good enough to bring my bill, will you?' he asked the waiter who brought his hot water.

'No,' said Steven firmly. 'This is my lunch.'

'No, please.' Mark looked at him reproachfully. 'I couldn't dream of it. Surely you'll allow me the pleasure of giving one of *my* authors lunch?'

'Well, that wasn't the idea,' said Steven, 'but thanks very much. And now, what do you want me to do? I'll take this stuff back, shall I, and work on it, and then let you have it again?'

'Please,' said Mark, brushing off his lapels, although he had eaten nothing that could have left crumbs. 'Do that. And by the way, I'm not very taken with the title. I don't know why, it doesn't mean anything to me.'

'It's a quotation,' said Steven. 'Er-Thoreau. I thought it rather conveyed the spirit of a hospital.'

'Oh quite, quite,' said Mark. 'But somehow it just doesn't seem to strike a chord. You might choose another, will you?' he said, as if titles grew on every bush.

'And when I get time,' said Steven, who, having thought himself nearly finished with *Three o'Clock in the Morning*, did not relish the idea of struggling with it any more. 'What do you suggest I make a start on next? You'd like me to try a novel, would you?'

'I would indeed. *Very* much. I'm confident you can do it. I shall look forward with most exceptional interest to reading any further work you do.'

'I needn't tell you how much I appreciate the chance you're giving me,' said Steven as they got up. 'It makes such a difference if you're writing something specially *for* a publisher and not just on spec, with the prospect of touting it round hopelessly from firm to firm, not even being sure that they're reading it.'

'You need never be afraid of that,' said Mark, with his gentle smile. 'I'll get Stephanie, then, to make an appointment with your secretary for a consultation. I must get you to fix me up before you go away. I have no faith in anyone else at all.' He threaded his way out of the restaurant, hailing innumerable people, and Steven followed him, nursing his envelope, far more interested in the vague ideas that were drifting through his mind, waiting to be materialized under his fingers on the typewriter, than on Mark Stainer's gastric ulcer.

Several days later, Mark Stainer's assistant manager, a bright, bizarre young man called Ambrose Braine, perched on the corner of his desk, and said: 'By the way, M.S., what about that Doctor chap whose stuff was lying about here. D'you mean to do anything with it?"

'Not at the moment, Amby, no. I've given it back to him to "polish".' Mark was very good at speaking in quotation marks. 'It's not really our line, you know. The material's all right, but the execution's pretty amateurish. I doubt whether we should ever do any good with him. Pity he doesn't stick to his own job. However, I've told him to get on and write a novel ; that'll keep him happy for a bit."

'What's the point of stringing him along, though, if you don't mean business? There's enough junk in this place as it is without cluttering it up with the manuscripts of all the lame dogs you take a fancy to.'

'My dear Amby,' Mark studied his nails, frowned at one of them, took a pair of nail scissors shaped like a stork from his inside pocket and snipped off a minute shred of skin. 'He is the only doctor to whom my stomach bows the knee. Besides, I owe him money.'

*

There were four public-houses in Reddage, besides the two uncomfortable, grudging hotels – 'The Mitre', where you could get a drink but not a decent meal, and Richardson's Temperance Hotel, where you could not even get a drink. The other haunts of vice were 'The Merry Monarch', which was modern Tudor and sold cocktails ready mixed in bottles, 'The Nag's Head', which sold good beer and huge, jaw-breaking biscuits in glass jars on the counter and was the darts centre for the neighbourhood, 'The King's Parlour', which was cosy and stuffy, with tiny windows and a big fire in winter, much haunted by old men with gnarled hands, and 'The Earl Grey', a square granite building, which stood at the windiest corner of the village and was the same colour inside and out as its name. It was typical of Mrs Garrard's father that he never went anywhere but the 'Earl'. Besides his Sunday morning visits, his boots sometimes carried him down there in the evenings after tea. He would push open the door which had 'SALOON BAR' frosted into the glass of its upper half and stand looking glumly round the silent company before stumping up to the bar and ordering his pint of bitter from Miss Parkinson, who would go on knitting or reading a paper-backed novel or adding up accounts without a sign that she had heard. Presently, however, she would put down with a sigh whatever she was doing, rise and reach for a glass, displaying the stained armpit of her black dress, pull down a beer handle, dump the glass among the wet rings on the counter and level off the top with a wooden spatula, giving you a look as she sank on to her stool that charged you with having taxed her to the limits of her strength.

One evening in the last week of August, Mr Anderson was down at 'The Earl', hunched on the green leather settee in a corner, with his glass of beer on a cardboard mat on the cigarette-scarred table before him. He was reading the evening paper, folded very small, showing by an occasional sniff and a still further drawing down of his sagging face how much he disliked what he found therein.

Custom was not brisk. Miss Parkinson was on her stool crocheting a beige silk scarf which never seemed to get any longer, a man with a bowler hat on the back of his head was staring hopelessly into space over a small stout, two middle-aged women were pickling themselves sourly in gin on the wooden perforated bench which looked as though it had come from a continental third class railway carriage, and a small, humble man in a check cap worn quite straight, with the snap fastener undone so that the crown bulged up like a sponge bag, was standing by the bar, because he was happier here than at home, where his wife and sister-in-law talked at but never to him.

He was longing to chat to someone, but saw no hope of response, until the frosted door opened and a stranger came in, a burly, violent man with low-growing black hair and a red face, who appraised the company with a glower, strode up to the bar, downed the pint of beer which Miss Parkinson, startled by his virility, unusual in this moribund place, drew for him quite quickly, and turned round, wiping his mouth with the back of his huge hand.

'A little cooler out to-night, I think,' ventured the man in the check cap. Without answering or even looking at him, Arthur Garrard pushed himself off from the bar and went straight over to where Mr Anderson was still brooding unawares over his six square inches of folded newspaper.

'Well, Dad,' said Arthur, making an insult of the name, and Mr Anderson looked up to find the other towering over him like a tree. He made a defensive movement to rise, but Arthur sat down opposite to him and put his arms in their too short jacket sleeves and frayed blue shirt cuffs on the table. 'I just been up to your place,' he said, jerking his head. 'Couldn't get a word of sense out of the old woman, but I thought I'd find you here.' He had a hoarse, nicotiny voice, the kind of careless Cockney accent that pronounces no consonants, and a slight impediment, an occasional thickening of his sibilants, as if his tongue were too big for his mouth.

'Don't know what you want to come bothering us again for,' grumbled Mr Anderson. 'If it's Ethel you're after, I told you last time you come, I don't know where she is no more nor you do. Got some job somewhere – Might be John o'Groats, might be Land's End for all I know.'

'Come off it,' said Arthur rudely. 'You're a dirty old liar, and as rotten a one as your old woman. She's just been telling me a pack of whoppers. Now I suppose you'll start, but don't expect me to believe you, that's all.'

Mr Anderson wished he knew what his wife had told Arthur. They should have arranged some story between them for such a contingency as this. He sniffed. 'Why don't you keep away?' he said. 'I should have thought you'd made enough trouble already without keep on pestering. Ethel don't want you, anyway.'

'Ah, but I want her,' said Arthur. 'And I want young Tom. They're mine, both of 'em by legal right, and anyone who tries to do me out of me rights – well, he'd better look out, that's all.' There were black hairs on the backs of the hands which he clenched and unclenched on the table top.

Mr Anderson shifted on the settee and took a pull at his beer to give himself courage. 'You make me sick,' he said sourly.

'*I* make you sick!' It did not matter that Arthur raised his voice, because the other occupants of the saloon bar were listening, anyway. '*I* make you sick! And what d'you think you make me, you lousy little bastard plumber's mate?'

Mr Anderson was incensed. He took all epithets literally. That the accusation of being verminous, illegitimate and not even a plumber in his own right should have been heard by Miss Parkinson, the man in the bowler hat, the two gin-drinking women and the man in the check cap was too much.

'Don't you dare talk to me like that, Arthur Garrard,' he began in a rumble that started somewhere in the caverns of his enormous boots.

'Don't even know where your own daughter and grandson are!' jeered Arthur. 'Oh, very funny; tell us another.' He turned round and pointed Mr Anderson out to the rest of the company. 'What d'you think of this poor old bleeder?' he roared at them. He turned back to his father-in-law, with his hands on the edge of the table, forearms braced and elbows sticking out. 'For two pins I'd knock some sense into your silly old head with my bare fist, but I don't think you're worth grazing me knuckles on. You don't know nothing. "I don't know where me daughter is." ' He made a poor attempt at mimicry. 'I suppose that's about all I could expect from a poor old sod like you.'

Goaded to the limits of discretion, Mr Anderson said: 'I know more than you think. I know more than you do, Arthur Garrard, about where our Ethel is, and I'm not telling, so put that in your pipe and smoke it. I'm going home.' He finished his beer and tried to stand up. He wanted to walk out on Arthur with dignity, but Arthur's bulk had pushed the table so close to the settee that he could not get out.

'Trying to be smart, eh?' said Arthur. 'That's a good one. You don't know any more where Ethel is than my foot.' Mr Anderson felt very silly standing crushed with bent knees between the table and the settee. He thrust his long face forward, like a horse yawing at its bridle. 'Yes I do then,' he said childishly. 'So there. I know exactly where she is. Get out of the way and let me get out, or I'll have the law on you for obstruction.'

Arthur still sat there, leaning back now with his arms folded and his feet braced against the table legs. 'You dirty old liar,' he said. 'Don't try and play games with me. All right, where is she then? Tell me, tell me, if you know so much. Or are you too scared?'

'Scared of you!' Mr Anderson sniffed. He tried pushing against the table with his stomach, but it would not yield. 'I'll tell you this much,' he said from his pillory. 'She's where you'll never find her, nor get her back even if you did. She's with a better man than you'll ever be in a million years, a well-to-do man 'oo knows how to look after her in the way that's fitting.' He looked round the bar to see if the others were listening. 'And 'oo knows how to look after little Tom too. St Leonard's House Day School, Baker Street, West One, that's where he goes, as befits his breeding – on his mother's side only, mind you, God help him if he'd stayed with you to be dragged down to the gutter.' He sniffed to right his face, which had become quite animated during this speech.

'Oh, they are, are they?' Arthur let down the front legs of his chair with a crash. 'And 'oo is this God Almighty – *if* he exists. Some twopenny-halfpenny pimp –'

'He's a very famous doctor,' said Mr Anderson. 'Everybody knows him. You ask anybody round Dynsford way if they don't know Dr Sheppard, up at the hospital.' There was a small murmur from the onlookers. Everybody knew Dr Sheppard.

'You're a lying old bastard,' said Arthur grimly. 'I've had enough of fooling around with you.' He got up so suddenly that the table rocked and Mr Anderson, who had been leaning against it, staggered forward. Arthur strode over to the door with his arms swinging, looking like a gorilla dressed up in a shabby workman's suit.

'That will be eightpence,' announced Miss Parkinson in her voice which creaked from rare use.

'The old boy can pay,' Arthur flung over his shoulder.

'I will,' said Mr Anderson, coming round the table. 'Just to get rid of you. And let me tell you this, Arthur Garrard, if you dare show your face round here again I'll set the police after you.'

'Oh, go and — yourself,' grunted Arthur, and banged out through the door so violently that the frosted glass quivered in its putty.

Mr Anderson took out a little leather purse, and as he put some money on the bar the man in the check cap saw his chance of conversation at last.

'Quite a nasty customer,' he said. 'May I congratulate you, sir, on the way you handled the situation?'

'Mind your own business,' said Mr Anderson very disagreeably, and was carried by his boots over the linoleum and out into the violet evening.

Chapter 10

—

STEVEN had told as few people as possible at St Margaret's that they might soon be losing him. He did not feel like facing the good-byes and regrets of the female staff. But when he arrived with Ruth on Thursday afternoon for what might be his last clinic, he found that everybody knew. He had forgotten the speed with which gossip spreads in hospital. Old Baxter, who was taking over his cases, had told Theatre Sister, which was as good as shouting it from the roof with a megaphone.

First it was the front porter, a medalled last war veteran, who left his loose box to catch Steven crossing the hall.

'I hear you're leaving us, sir,' he said. 'May I say how much we shall miss you?'

'Oh – thanks very much, Roberts,' said Steven, querying mentally how much he ought to give him. 'And thanks for everything you've done for me. I shall miss this place, too, but I must say I'm not sorry to be getting into the Navy.'

The porter's face kindled like an old war-horse. 'Wish I was coming with you, sir,' he said. 'I'd give my right arm to get into this scrap.' Which would not have helped much, as he had already lost the left one.

Ruth, in her stove-like dark blue coat and trapper's hat, pressed close to Steven as they walked down the corridor. Now that she had got used to the idea of Steven's abandoning her, she was beginning to be proud of him. 'He's a splendid man, isn't he?' she said. 'Those sort of people are the backbone of England, aren't they?'

As they passed his office, the secretary of the hospital came

307

out. 'So we're losing you, Dr Sheppard,' he said. 'There's a lot of people will miss you in this place, not least myself.' He held out his hand. 'In case I don't get a chance to see you again, may I wish you the very best of luck, and thank you for all your valuable work for this hospital, and hope that we shall see you back with us again soon?'

'They think a lot of you here,' said Ruth with satisfaction as they walked on. At the stairs they parted, Ruth to go up to the Maternity ward, where she was to break the devastating news to Sister Archer that she might not be coming any more, and Steven to go below to Outpatients. 'I'll give you a ring when I'm ready,' he said. 'I'll try and skip Miss Grainger's tea. I want to get away as early as I can so that I can give Ugly a bit of a run on the way home. The poor old boy's had rather a thin time these last few days. I've been so busy.' He was not happy in his mind yet about Ugly's future. Ruth had offered to take him to her mother, but Steven thought he would try to find a home for him in the country somewhere – at a small kennels, perhaps, or with a farmer. Later on, when he got his cottage, he would be able to leave him there, with the imaginary retainer type of ideal gardener-handyman whom he was quite sure he would find. If only one could explain to dogs about leaving them, and spare them the shock of discovering themselves abandoned. He could visualize the way Ugly's ears would be glued as flat to his head as his tail was to his white, conger-eel stomach. He would go about for a time showing a lot of the whites of his eyes. Steven minded leaving him very much.

There was a clatter on the stairs, and young Potter skidded down, nearly colliding with Ruth going up.

'Awfully sorry, sir,' he panted. 'Had to cut down for an intravenous. I'd got into the vein first shot with a French's, but the nurse pulled the needle out putting on the strapping, so I had to cut down, otherwise I'd have been there to meet you.'

'That's all right,' said Steven. 'I don't need you yet. I'll do my rounds after the clinic.'

'M-m-m-may I say, sir,' asked young Potter, hanging on to the banister post and swinging his leg, 'how glad I am for your sake that you've got what I know you wanted. It'll be terrible here without – I mean, I'm awfully sorry that – I mean we shall all miss you. My people asked to be remembered to you, sir,' he gabbled, afraid that Steven might be offended by the intrusion of Wimbledon into working hours, 'and to say that they wish you all the best – the best of luck, that is –'

'That's extraordinarily kind of them,' said Steven. 'Please remember me to them next time you go home.' He turned to go downstairs. 'Oh, by the way,' he said, pausing, 'I knew there was something. How's that patient of mine in Private Wards – that carcinoma of œsophagus?'

'I'm afraid she's not too good, sir. They're doing the gastrostomy to-morrow, but –' He shrugged his shoulders. 'The growth appears to be pressing on the trachea now. Mr Munroe doesn't give her very long, I think, though he means to operate.'

'Lord,' said Steven. 'Poor woman. Tell you what, I think I'll just pop up and see her now and get that off my chest.'

'I shan't be here much longer myself now, sir,' said young Potter as they went up the stairs together. 'I'm supposed to be starting at the London General next month, though I still can't believe my luck to get with Sir George Levinson. I'm sure something will happen to stop me going there; I'm such dead nuts on it.'

'Why should it?' said Steven.

'Well, they might call me up, you know, sir.'

'Yes, I suppose they might.' Steven had been so obsessed with his own future that he had not had time to think about other people going into the Services, too.

'If they do,' said young Potter gallantly, 'I shall be only too glad to go, of course. But I shall be awfully sorry to miss this chance, especially after all the trouble you've taken for me. I can't tell you, sir, how grateful –'

'Forget it,' said Steven, cutting short the recital that he had already heard *ad nauseam*.

'Yes, but not only that, sir,' young Potter breathed below his right shoulder, hurrying up the stairs a step or two behind him. 'All the time I've been here. It's meant so much ...'

Steven pretended he had not heard. 'Don't bother to come up with me,' he said. 'I don't need you, and I'm sure you're busy.' He shook him off on the third floor, and went through the swing doors into the soft-footed, flower-scented atmosphere of the private corridor. Sister came out of her office. 'Oh, Dr Sheppard,' she cried in the society voice which she kept for the doctors she liked and the best quality patients, 'I was so afraid we weren't going to see you any more before you left. Dr Baxter told me he'd be taking over from you.'

'You don't think I'd go without saying good-bye to my old friends, Sister?' asked Steven, in the manner she loved. 'May I see Mrs Pagett? How is she?'

'I'm not a bit pleased with her, sir.' Sister bustled beside him with metallic noises from her apron, which never did enough work to get soiled or unstarched.

'It's just a question of whether she starves to death or chokes to death first, isn't it?' said Steven.

'Oh, I know it's inevitable, sir, but I never give up hope. I never give up a patient, you know, until the last breath is out of their body.' She put a hand on Mrs Pagett's door knob. 'Do you want me to come in with you, sir?'

'No, don't bother, Sister. I'll go in alone,' said Steven. 'I shan't be long. I'll see you when I come out.'

She opened the door for him with a flourish. 'Here's Dr Sheppard to see you, Mrs Pagett,' she said with her gummy smile, and stepped back to let him go in, shutting the door behind him as carefully as if the room were a pack of cards.

It was a pity that whoever had washed Mrs Pagett that morning had tied a blue ribbon round her lank grey hair. It would have been better just to have brushed it back from her gaunt cheekbones, the shiny white knobs of her temples. She might have had periwinkle eyes once, which a blue ribbon would have enhanced. She might have been a pretty woman once. You could not tell now. The weeks of painful, difficult swallowing had brought into prominence the bones of her skull; her paling, sunken eyes were agonized by the anxiety of each breath. She wore oxygen spectacles, a frame supporting a tiny tube in each nostril, connected with the cylinder by the bed.

The nurse who was sitting by her with a work-basket and a pile of mending stood up as Steven came in. It was Nurse Bracken.

'Afternoon, Nurse,' he said, thinking how incongruous her exuberant charm was in this room which already smelled of death. 'How's the patient?' He smiled at Mrs Pagett and she smiled at him, her narrow chest labouring. 'Getting some relief from those specs I expect, aren't you? What's she on, Nurse?' He glanced at the dial on top of the cylinder. 'Continuous oxygen?'

'Five minutes every quarter of an hour, sir.' Nurse Bracken looked at her watch. 'It's due off now.' She turned a screw and the faint hissing ceased. She hovered, uncertain whether Steven wanted her in or out of the room.

'That's all right, Nurse,' he said. 'Don't bother to stay. I'll keep Mrs Pagett company while you get on with one of your odd jobs.'

Mrs Pagett's hands had been lying patiently outside the counterpane, as inanimate as if they were cut out of paper. As Nurse Bracken went out, she moved them and picked up a pad with a pencil on a string from her bed-table. They had given her this when her voice began to fail. While she was writing on it, Steven saw the torn-off sheets covered with a large wavering scrawl. Odd sentences caught his eye.

'*You look tired, Nurse*', he read, and '*Could you open the window?*' and '*My feet are cold*'.

She showed him what she had written: '*Mr Munroe is going to operate to-morrow*'.

'I know,' he said, his answer sounding to him unnaturally loud because she had not spoken. 'Good thing to get it over, isn't it? You'll have a local anæsthetic, you know, so you needn't worry about the breathing.'

'*Will I be better afterwards?*' she wrote.

'Of course,' said Steven. 'We'll be able to get some nourishment into you then, get you a bit stronger.'

She smiled at him again. Her smile was still very sweet. She wrote: '*I feel sleepy. Too many injections.*' Her eyes closed for a moment and then she opened them again and wrote: '*Afraid to sleep in case I stop breathing*'.

'Oh, nonsense,' said Steven. 'You breathe all the better when you're asleep. Your body'll go on doing it for you, more steadily and rhythmically than when you're making a conscious effort.'

Presently she closed her eyes again and her lower jaw dropped. In the long interval between each breath she looked quite lifeless. Steven, with a faintly guilty feeling that he was prying, looked again at the sheets of paper scattered on the bed-table. '*My hair was your colour when I was young,*' he saw. '*Don't pretend, dear. You know I won't.*' '*I wish I could go home.*' He suddenly had an idea.

Ever since his lunch with Mark Stainer he had been struggling to think of a plot for a novel, trying, considering, rejecting. How did people think of plots, anyway? Did they grind out something in hours of patient thought, or did it come to them in a flash, as he believed his plot had come to him in this room? He would built it round the scraps of paper written by a woman who could not talk. He would have to make the medical details different, of course – a throat operation, perhaps, a tracheotomy for diphtheria. No, that was a bit too unusual in a grown-up person. Supposing he made it a woman who had tried to commit suicide by drinking something like lysol? The corrosive burns could easily set up such an inflammation in the larynx that a tracheotomy would have to be done. The attempted suicide would be the culmination of a life whose phases could be introduced by the scribblings prompted by her wandering memory.

As he stood with folded arms looking down at Mrs Pagett, his brain excitingly busy, he was studying her detachedly, already more of an author than a physician, more interested in her as a subject than as a patient. He was in the future, seeing himself at work on this novel, juggling out the design of it, seeing its possibilities.

He came back to the present with a start as the opening door woke her and, his sympathies heightened by a guilty feeling that he was exploiting her, looked at her neither as a patient nor a subject, but as a human being.

'Excuse me, sir,' said Nurse Bracken. 'It's time for the oxygen.' She crossed to the cylinder and turned the screw, regulating the flow carefully by the dial. Mrs Pagett smiled at her and wrote on her pad: '*Isn't she pretty?*' showing it only to Steven.

He laughed. 'You're right there,' he said, and Nurse Bracken, sensing that they were talking about her, pretended still to be absorbed with the dial, although it was now correct.

When Steven said good-bye to Mrs Pagett he did not tell her that he might not see her again. It would sound like desertion. In any case, even if he came to the hospital next week, he did not think she would be there.

He had seen many people die, and he had seen many people dying, and he had learned, for his own sake, to be able to wash death from his memory as easily as a surgeon washes blood from his hands. But as he hurried along the corridor so as not to be caught by Sister, and quickly down the stairs, he was haunted by the contrast between the life flickering so painfully out up there and his own life stretching before him now with the promise of so much. What would it feel like to know, as Mrs Pagett undoubtedly knew? Would one fret to finish all the things that one had

313

yet to do? Would one pine for the chance to make a last-minute attempt to justify one's existence, or would one, as patients seemed to do, give up the world as being supremely unimportant in face of what was ahead? But the world *was* important, while you were in it.

When people died, they just went away from their bodies. You could see it. One moment there was a person lying on the bed; the next, that person had gone right away and left behind a meaningless shell. That was why, after the apprehension of seeing your first death had proved to be groundless, there was nothing horrifying nor even pathetic about a corpse. There was nobody there to pity. Pity was what you felt for people before they died, people like Mrs Pagett.

*

Since last Thursday's clinic, Nurse Lake had heard that she had passed the examination which entitled her to wear a bow under her chin and change the ticket on her bedroom door to A/Staff Nurse Lake. By next year, if she passed her State Finals, she would be wearing a dark blue belt and her ticket would say: 'Staff Nurse Lake'. But Steven might not be there.

That was the thought that haunted her dreams and drummed through her waking brain, obsessing her study hours so that she did not see how she was ever going to pass the State examination. It had once been the goal of her life, but now it did not seem to matter so much in face of the appalling rumours that Steven was leaving. She meant to ask him this Thursday if it were true.

If it were, he probably would not mind her asking, and if it were not, the relief would be so great that she could bear him to be cross about the spreading of false gossip. They said he was going into the Navy. Well then, when she was State-registered she would become a naval nurse. Their paths would cross, and she would work for him again. They would work together, a superb team, saving the lives of gallant seamen. This promising dream story, which was as yet only in the first stages of its development, was the only thing which brightened the gloom which had cloaked her since she had heard that he would probably not be coming to the hospital much longer.

Anyway, there was still this Thursday, which was a particularly exciting one, because he had not yet seen her in her bows. She would burst on him with the full glory of an exotic flower opened overnight.

Instead of going to dinner that morning, she spent the half-hour in her room arranging herself. First she put on a clean apron, a new one, enamelled with starch and rather too long, because it had not yet been washed enough to shrink it to a less archaic length. Now she clamped a clean white belt round her waist, whose slimness went unremarked because there were no curves above or below it. She changed her shabby, night-duty shoes, which had been good enough for the orthopædic clinic that morning, for her best pair which she had spent fifteen minutes on the floor burnishing last night. She had spent even longer making up a clean cap, washing her hands twice during the process, and arranging the pleats as she drew up the strings with mathematical precision. It sat now on top of her nightdress case like a crown on a velvet cushion in Westminster Abbey awaiting the ceremony.

She took out her black pins and pulled off the old cap and the rolled stocking round which her hair had been turned up. One of the nurses had given her this tip about using a stocking instead of a ribbon, and it certainly did make a neater, firmer roll, even with her unwieldy hair. She wondered if Steven had noticed that for some weeks now she had had no sticking-out ends.

She brushed out her black, greasy hair and combed it until the comb ran through it like water. After three attempts she got it properly rolled round the stocking, spreading it out on top so that glimpses of fawn lisle did not show at the parting. Her bows were sewn on a piece

315

of tape which was put round her head behind the ears and tied on top. It looked very odd without a cap, but Nurse Lake stood for a little in front of the mirror, gloating over the effect which she had coveted ever since, in her first month as a terrified Junior Probationer, she had seen one of the staff nurses daringly remove her cap in a ward bathroom to do her hair in the patients' mirror.

Bows certainly did make a difference. They gave you an air of authority. The juniors would have more respect for her now, she told herself, although none, except the very newest, who had not yet got wise to 'Old Lakey', had shown the slightest signs of it. True, Nurse Phillimore addressed her with emphasis, on every possible occasion, as *Staff* Nurse Lake, but this was only her tedious idea of a joke.

She picked up the clean cap and, like the Archbishop of Canterbury, raised it high and lowered it into position behind the roll of hair. Now the black iron clips went on, squeezing the cap to its accustomed narrowness. The bows under her chin made her face look longer than ever. People with round faces, like Nurse Bracken, who had also just won her bows, looked like nice little dressed-up cats in theirs. Nurse Lake's bows, which always worked loose and hung an inch below her chin, looked more like a medallion on a horse.

The door opened and Home Sister's grey head looked in, followed after a wider opening of the door by her body. 'Why aren't you at dinner, Nurse?' she asked.

Nurse Lake had whirled round from the dressing-table and instinctively put her hands behind her back. 'I, er – I – oh, I didn't want any, please, Sister. I had a pain.'

'Then you should have reported sick at nine o'clock.'

'But I didn't have the pain then.'

Home Sister disregarded this as irrelevant. 'Well, you'll have to go to Matron in the morning. You know perfectly well you're not allowed to miss meals.'

'Yes, Sister. I'm sorry, Sister.'

'I should think so. You a staff nurse. How can you possibly hope to train the juniors if you don't set a proper example? It's not good enough, Nurse.' Her face was so troubled that Nurse Lake began really to think she had committed some crime. Indeed, after nearly three years in hospital, she knew it was a crime. As Home Sister went out, she dashed obsequiously forward to hold the door for her.

One last look in the mirror, then she put on her clean cuffs and went out into the corridor, through the door and across the courtyard to the main hospital building and down the back stone stairs to Outpatients. She wished she had not got to go to Matron to-morrow. Still, she jerked up her chin, it was all for Dr Sheppard.

She heard his familiar, quick footstep coming along the Outpatients' hall and jumped up from his revolving chair, putting a hand up to her bows to make sure they were straight before he came into the room.

She knew just what he looked like, she knew just how his voice sounded, she knew the thrilling, sinking feeling that seized her just below the breastbone whenever she saw him, but each time she was unprepared for the full éclat of his appearance. The very air seemed to be galvanized when Steven came into a room. Everything had more meaning. Even the furniture and the long brass handles on the taps took on a reflected glow. She had read about people having auras, different-coloured radiances visible to the psychic. The aura of Steven's own personality within which he moved was dazzlingly visible to her. She could not take her eyes off him.

He whisked his case on to the desk and plunged into the white coat which she was holding out for him. 'Afternoon, Nurse. Many for me?' He seemed in more of a hurry than ever to-day. Perhaps he had not had time to notice her bows. She went and stood in front of the desk so that he could see them, while she answered: 'Thirty-four, sir, besides the weekly injections. Ten new cases.' He had pulled a piece of paper out of the letter rack and was scribbling on it. 'Right,' he said, without looking up. 'Injections and repeat medicines first, then the new ones – *you* know. Quick as you like.' He was jotting down a few notes for his novel while they were still fresh in his mind.

Nurse Lake had planned that he would say: 'Congratulations, Nurse,' or 'There's something different about you. What is it? Oh, yes, you've got your bows. Well done!' or even: 'How nice you look in your bows,' but he went on scribbling, so she squeaked over to the door and called in the first patient. He had all afternoon in which to notice. He must see them soon.

He gave the injections. He always gave intramuscular injections himself, as he said that no nurse could be trusted to avoid the sciatic nerve. Nurse Lake did not take this as a personal affront. It was simply an indication of what a conscientious doctor he was. However, she did think that now she had got her bows he might let her do them. But then, he didn't know she had got her bows yet. If he had not said anything by the end of the afternoon, she would find some way of mentioning it casually, in that precious moment alone with him when the last patient had gone. That was when she was going to say: 'If you'll excuse a personal question, sir, is it true you may be leaving us soon?'

The fifth new patient was a tough old charwoman, in a hat like an earthenware basin and men's boots. She had a slight beard, a hoarse bass voice and eyes like little black boot buttons. She called Steven: 'Doctor, my darling,' and she and he cracked a lot of jokes, none of which Nurse Lake thought funny. Steven insisted that she should rest her badly thrombosed leg and knock off work for a time, and she hobbled out, chuckling and making promises, but when she had gone, he said to Nurse Lake: 'The old devil. She doesn't mean to do what I say. She'll go on working till she kills herself. I know that type. Can't think why they come to a doctor at all. Still, I'm glad they do. I like these lively old birds.' He laughed and Nurse Lake laughed with him obediently. He looked at her back view as she crossed to the door to call in the next patient. She looked a bit different to-day. What had she done to herself? Oh well, women were always looking different, but then, this one was not that kind of a woman. She was just one of his crosses, of whom he would soon be quit. He was not going to say good-bye to her, if possible. Heaven preserve him from a scene.

The scene which happened now was over so quickly that Nurse Lake could never give a coherent account of it afterwards, although she was questioned over and over again. The sixth patient was a hulking great ape of a man with a red face and low-growing black hair. He came just inside the door and then stopped, lowering. She shut the door and touched his arm. 'Go and sit by the desk, please.' He shook her off as if she was an insect, and she realized that he was very drunk. She had not noticed this when he was outside. He had just sat hunched up on the front bench with his feet stuck out, apparently half-asleep. He stood now with one hand in his dirty jacket pocket and the other crumpling his green folder, swaying backwards and forwards. Oh dear, he should never have been let in. She must get him out. Perhaps Steven would manage it. He had put both hands on the desk as if ready to raise himself out of his chair.

'You Dr Sheppard?' the patient threw at him.

'Yes.'

'Dr Steven Sheppard?' The man spoke the sibilants thickly.

'Yes, will you come and sit –'

'Then you're the bleeder who's pinched my wife and kid, you lousy, rotten, tricking swine – I'll –' The rest was drowned in the shattering crash of the pistol which he fired as he pulled it out of his pocket. The puzzled expression on Steven's face was still there as his arms crumpled and he leaned slowly forward against the desk.

It was exactly like the story which Nurse Lake had made

up about the gangsters shooting Steven in the carotid artery. Only this time she did not rush forward and find the place to stop the hæmorrhage against the collar bone. She did not try to stop the man as he threw the gun at her and staggered out of the door into the commotion outside. She did not do anything except stand there wringing her hands and whimpering like an animal, while Steven's life pumped out of the great shattered hole in his neck.

THE END